The Redneck Run II—Shine—Shay Lawless
Copyright © 2019 by Shay Lawless

ISBN-13: 978-1-940087-34-4
ISBN-10: 1-940087-34-1

## Chapter 1—Another No Show

It's Friday night. I'm sitting on a torn vinyl stool at the Crazy Kettle Bar in New Alliance, West Virginia waging worthless bets with the bartender, Billy Winkle. It's the same bar stool I sat on a year ago waiting for my maybe-dead-ex-husband to appear. He never showed. I guess just like the birth-daddy I never met, everybody who leaves this Podunk town never returns.

New Alliance is what most folks would call a ghost town. It would probably be just like most other old coal and railroad towns in our neck of the woods after the mines closed down—nothing but run-down houses and dilapidated mobile homes along dead-end roads. It isn't dead at all. It got a spark of life not so long ago.

If you don't know, it is the home of two recognized elements that have kept us alive and thriving—the Boar Mountain Resort and Country Club and the National Fire Mountain Redneck Run. The owner of the resort hires a lot of locals in housecleaning and maintenance which helps pay the bills of almost everyone in the little town of New Alliance settled in its shadow in the valley below. Although the Redneck Run used to be just a fun way for us locals to race ATVs in the mud and compete for beers, now it brings in a hundred-thousand tourists a year with a multisport quadrathlon.

"Can I get you another Shirley Temple, Brandy?" Billy swipes a raggedy, used-to-be-blue cloth on the counter in front of me, then leans in on his elbows, arms crossed. "I got a guy down there says he'll pay for whatever *that dark-haired beauty with the tangerine colored eyes is drowning her sorrows in tonight.* I'll bet ten bucks he doesn't know it's ginger ale."

"Naw." I hold him off with a hand over the last of six smudged shot glasses, glad he didn't attach *that scrawny little thing* which most people adjoin to my description like a P.S. to a Dear John letter further explaining in sordid detail the reasons for the breakup. "He'd be disappointed. Besides, I've already had enough. I'm driving." He chuckles. Billy follows my eyes when I turn to see who is coming in the door to the bar. It's not who I'm waiting on.

"He's late again, huh?" Billy's tapping his fingers to the muffled beat of 1980s music screaming out of an old jukebox and banging off the dark, beer-stained walls. I turn back, sniff the air. Nobody's smoked in here for a couple of years, but it still carries the deep scent of cigarettes from the smokers standing outside the front doors. Every time someone lugs back the handle and opens the door wide, the smoke wafts into the bar in a burst of warm air and the diluted scent of cheap tobacco.

"Yeah, he's late again." I'm talking about Bear Vega—my beautiful brown-eyed, tall, and mid-size buff soon-to-be-ex-fiancé-if-he-stands-me-up-again. Along with his mama, Amelia, he runs the big Boar Mountain Resort. "Five bucks says he doesn't show," I mutter. "*Again.*"

In my defense, it isn't just the no-shows. Evan, the security attendant at the Boar Mountain Resort parking lot, attached an addendum to my private theory he's seeing someone else which causes his long list of tardiness. Evan usually has the boom gate bar lifted when I get to the entrance of the resort so I can enter—I am one of the runners training for the event. He waves my truck past. We've got a thing—I always bring him a coffee in the morning—six sugars and two teaspoons half and half. As I pass, I hold it out the window without stopping. Evan grabs it up like we're passing a baton at a race and gives me a thankful thumbs-up. A month ago, however, his usual lazy wiggle of fingers and grin changed to a flat-palm demanding me to stop. While we fumbled with this change of venue and I almost dropped the coffee between the car and the gazebo-booth, he leaned his elbows on the window between us. *Brandy, I'm not telling you this. But I am, if you know what I mean. Bear and that bitch, Meghan, have been coming in a couple of hours earlier than everybody else. My cousin is on the cleaning staff, and she says it's closed doors up there in his office until folks start arriving.*

*That bitch, Meghan* is one of the bleach-blonde twins who is also training for the event *and* she sings in the Holy Trinity Church choir that Bear directs. She may sing like an angel and appear like eye candy to all the fifty-and-ups settled in the pews on Sunday morning, but she is my nemesis. As soon as backs are turned, Meghan is always bullying me. She outwardly flirts with Bear even in my presence. I had confronted Bear about it. What did he say? *Oh, don't listen to those dumbass locals. They say all sorts of stuff because they're jealous.* Well, those dumbass locals are my cousins and aunts, uncles and friends I grew up with on the mountain. He might not run downtown and grab lunch for them because they only get a half-hour break and can't afford the too-expensive stuff on the resort menu, but I do. He may not pass them at the grocery and gas station and stop to chat, go to their kids' birthday parties, or give them a jump when their rundown cars don't start up after their shifts on cold January evenings. I do. I'm a local. Was he calling me a dumbass too?

"Again," Billy repeats. He rips me from my thoughts that were partially swaying toward Bear flicking on his desk lamp right before he bends pouty-lipped, long-legged Meghan over his desk and rips off her dress. Billy stands up straight. "It's his loss, you know?" He looks around the room. It's pretty dead tonight. "What's the story I heard about Vega getting run off the road a couple of months back?" He turns back, gives me a sly grin. "I hear you tell it pretty well."

"I shouldn't."

"Oh, you *should*." Billy slaps the mungy cloth on the counter. It adds a musty scent to the already stale air. "My cousin, who works the resort pool, says it's hilarious."

"Alright," I fake-grumble, feign he has to pull my leg. He doesn't. I love telling this story. "Here's how it goes. Bear was on his back on a weight bench and lifting one of the standard Olympic barbells they've got in the training room at the resort," I tell him. "He's supposed to get someone to spot him so he doesn't accidentally drop the bar on his neck. He never does." I don't add it's because he used to be chubby. He's still self-conscious about his body, so he works out when the training room is closed.

"Yeah. So?"

"Just as Bear lifted the weights off the bar and started to bring them down to his chest, something startled him. He jumped. One leg kicked up, and the weights shifted along with the bench, and he keeled in slow motion to the right. Then BAM! He hit the floor flat on his face with the barbells pinning him on the ground for about forty agonizing seconds." I pause for effect, drawing it out like a comedian readying to reveal the punchline of a joke. "Unbearably hilarious, that is, for those of us who heard him whining about the sore neck he got when an alleged *dumbass local* in a crappy truck jammed on his brakes in front of him, and he slid off the side of the road."

For God's sakes, I rubbed his neck for five days feeling sorry for him. "As the security video clearly shows, Bear had been startled by the tiniest shadow of a plump mouse scampering across the hardwood floor which also came in early to avoid the crowds. Bear had yelped like my five-year-old sister squealed when she stepped on a mouse trap in my Pops' shed, jumped, and well, you know the rest of the story." Unfortunately for him, so did half the security staff and me because they know I like a good joke on Bear. "My belly was sore for a week laughing at the video," I tell Billy. "And by the way, he's still sticking to his story—he's sore from getting *rear-ended*." I use the fingers of both hands to give air quotes. "And for me getting ahold of that security video."

Billy laughs and watches me pat my bare head before he leaves to wait on another customer. It's a habit I can't break. Back a year ago, I wore an old ballcap all the time. Now and then, I'd touch the bill, rub it with my fingers in the same way my 5-year-old sister still lugs around this raggedy blue comfort-blanket and scrubs it across her lips until she gets a blissful smile. Whatever burdens that a kindergartener shoulders fade away. I still reach for my ballcap for my own consolation. The blanket was the only gift our mama ever gave my sister, just like that ballcap was the only present my ex-husband, Josh, had given me. But Mama sold all her welfare checks for beer and pot. Josh had too many other secret wives to spend money on me. Stuff like that makes people weird. I'm weird like that. I suppose my little sister is too.

Last year, I was also dressed in a black-lace, spaghetti-string cami top, stiletto heels, and a cheap black miniskirt I'd gotten at The Goodwill. I went home with a scratch on my bare thigh from the tears on the shabby vinyl bar stool. Now, I'm wearing a four-hundred-dollar Elaine Clary cocktail dress and more modest one-inch pumps. My thigh is still going home with a crease from the stool.

I'm tapping my fingers gently to the music. I'm trying not to peer to the left at a guy who pulled in on a huge Harley with paint stripped off to a gray and rust-pocked chrome. He reminds me of a mixture between a WWE wrestler (the ones they call the high flyers because of all the acrobats and aerial attacks) and the image of an over-muscled, wild-haired Hercules on the cover of a kid's book on Roman mythology. It is the same book my cousin, Kenny, fastidiously places in front of his stash of soft porn Backwoods Babes magazines when his mama comes to visit. That stack, by the way, is now eight inches over his mama's direct line of vision in the top of his closet. Recently, while nosing around, she found his whole squirreled lot under his mattress and made him start going to Wednesday church.

High Flyer Hercules keeps trying to catch my attention with a nod that I avoid by snapping my gaze away. He's been leaning with his elbows on the counter downright staring a hole through me. I end up observing the same fifty-something lady in a miniskirt and dyed-orange-brown hair who is slow-dancing herself around the tables almost the same as she was doing last year. But this year, she isn't chain-smoking cigarettes, dead-drunk, and working rum and Cokes for blowjobs. She's now slightly tipsy, donning two nicotine patches on her right arm, juggling a tray of beers, and working for minimum wage—and the occasional beer. She dances over toward me and does a little wiggle—ah, I catch the waft of stale cigarettes on her clothes. I guess she's still smoking too.

"Hey, baby girl, what you doin' alone and gussied up?"

"I'm meeting Bear, Mama," I tell her blandly.

"If I had my druthers, I'd like to meet him with my fist," she hisses hotly. Mama holds up her hand, clenching bony fingers tightly. I eye the chipped pink nail polish that faithfully matches the toeless dollar store glitter pumps on her feet. "I heard what he done to you.

Everybody know'd it. He got himself a girl on the side. That's Meghan Reynolds. He got himself a little something-something, and he dumped you."

A little *something-something*. I hate that saying. Mama uses it way too much when she makes excuses for her married boyfriends who don't stick around—*they want a little something-something,* she always declares, *no harm in that.* "No, Mama. It's a small town. People talk. It's not true," I lie. I think my mama's crazy. I don't tell anybody that, especially her. "Don't talk like that. We just never got along." Sadly, I'm not sure if *never* is the truth or not. Bear hasn't been around enough to assess our compatibility rank. "Please don't add to the gossip." I shift uncomfortably. I know that even though she was a shitty mama, she can still see through my deception. I hope not too deep. What is my greatest fear? Turning out like my mama with a long line of bad, married boyfriends, trust issues, and being alone. "Be nice."

"Oh, I'll be nice." She furrows her brow, bobs her head up and down. Still, it sounds like a threat. Mama double-pats one of the nicotine patches with the palm of her free hand like it's a button used to activate a morphine pain relief pump. "These keep me sane. They won't let nobody smoke inside. They make me a little high, too, when I sneak a smoke." She looks me up and down. "You're getting too big for your britches, ain't you? That dress is expensive, baby girl, I know that. You *look* expensive like one of them pretty designer dress-up dolls I seen in the commercials on TV, Holiday Barbie or something. By the way, that guy over there wants to talk to you."

I follow her finger, cringe. She is pointing across the oozy darkness of the bar counter and about eight seats down. I blink at the same gargantuan man who has been staring at me. He seems to size me up. I size him up in return. He looks like he stepped out of a 1960s biker movie. He's big and hairy with beefy, bare arms covered by a tight t-shirt. His skin is covered with tattoos of lizards, snakes, and a chubby, naked woman with super-human boobies and one stiletto-heeled toe stuck in the air. I'm not usually into the High Flyer Hercules type. Yeah, I know Bear's a bigger man, but he was chubby when I met him. The buff grew on me later.

"You're kidding me, right?" I snap my eyes back. "I'm not talking to that man. He looks like every one-night-stand killer on the cliffhanger commercials for crime TV." She stares at me with the accusing eyes of someone who might be so desperate to quit lugging around beers until two in the morning that she'd open her trailer door every Tuesday and Thursday for this guy if he'd pay her rent.

"Don't look at me like that." She gives my chair a snippy bump. "I know where you was this time last year."

I scowl. I limit the line of focus to the counter and not my mama or High Flyer Hercules. This time last year, I was working my fingers to the bone waitressing at Beverly's Hometown Diner and working at Mister Smiley's Super Grocery Store. I was frantically trying to finish my culinary arts degree and pay my last semester with the tips I'd earned, and she stole it all out of an old metal coffee can I'd hid on a shelf. And the ex-husband never showed. I'd nearly hit rock bottom. This year was looking up. I got my degree. I had a fiancé and an engagement ring with a diamond the size of Texas. Well, until everything started going to hell again. I can't find a job being a chef. The diamond ring is settled on a damp napkin next to my empty ginger ale shot glasses. And it is noticeable to everybody in this bar that I've been waiting far too long again for a man who won't be coming through those doors. I'll shame myself no farther. I guess I'll add Bear's name to the list of men in my life who never show up, just another no show. I push myself off the seat, sick with heartache, ready to openly sob. "Billy," I choke back a lump in my throat, wave the bartender back over. "If he comes, can you give Bear the ring?"

# Chapter 2— Living the Dream . . . Team

Boar Mountain Resort and Country Club is settled on top of the mountain bearing its name. The property overlooks the town of New Alliance like a high castle hovers over its kingdom. At this very spot, the five-person team of runners I call Amelia's Dream Team, representing Boar Mountain and called the Fire Mountain Shadows, pause to catch our breaths after a six-mile run.

Well, four of them need to catch their breath. I don't. I don't divulge that fact because Bear told me it would be to my advantage to stop with them instead of running ahead. It makes them a bit saucy that this isn't even a warmup for me. I stop because they do. I don't fit in anyway. The four slowpokes were a team long before I started running with them this year for the Second Annual National Fire Mountain Redneck Run. I am the outsider, the poster child for the resort. It isn't a secret among these girls the only reason I was chosen as one of the runners is that I was going to be married to Bear, secondary only to the fact I was the only person on the team who is a redneck and *from* Fire Mountain.

We are the resort's chosen few for the Fire Mountain Redneck Run who have begun training for the event in September. Well, four of them are specially culled from the surrounding region to represent the resort by Mila Boucher who sits at the helm of Amelia Vega's consulting and marketing team. They are what her team considered as *athletic and beautiful, well-spoken model representatives of the moral core values of the community*. Me, I was tossed into the mix so the local tourism agency didn't get all fired up for not using somebody home-grown. My now ex-fiancé got a little hot under the collar when they tried to get the second-place winning runner as the fifth because I was called *too mouthy*. That *my* ragtag team won the event last year was of no significance in the selection. They still believe it was only by luck, I cheated, and a pack of dogs chased the lead runner off the trail.

Where we are standing now is directly across from the mountain where I was born and raised—Fire Mountain. Mama had me at the Fire Mountain View Trailer Park and Campground. I was born during a weird snowstorm right in the middle of hunting season, and she could barely get down the mountain on time to get to the hospital. I lived with her for three and a half years. Then one day, she dropped me off with one of her boyfriends, and she didn't return until she had to reapply for her food stamps.

That old boyfriend of Mama's, his name is Lee McAllister, and everybody calls me Lee McAllister's daughter even though the only thing we have in common are the freckles on our face. He's camo pants, beat-up trucks, and torn Yankee flags flying off the porch. He's a bit tetchy at times and tall with buzz-cut ginger-red hair he hides under a ballcap. I call him Pops. Even though he wasn't my real daddy, he loves me, won't say anything bad about my mama, took care of me, and tucked me gently in at night. His family became my family. Since last year, he's started taking care of my little sister, Kaylee, too.

He's the one who cooked with me when I was little, so I have to give him credit for me becoming a chef even though he tells me all the time it was a waste of four years for me to go to college to get my degree in culinary arts. He says I cooked just fine before I dumped all my good-earned money down the higher education toilet. Of course, I've seen Pops spoon ground coffee right out of the can into a cup of tepid water instead of running it through the coffee maker while still donning the same blissful look to his eyes as if he'd brewed it while he sips and sifts the grounds through his teeth.

I almost always ease away from the four other women (pretending I'm trying to get better service on my cell phone) and to the far end of the resort parking lot. Here, it dips down along the outside of the 4-lane running track. I can peer through the stainless-steel security fencing erected around the perimeter of the resort and see just a bit of the graveled Locust Ridge Road everybody calls Fire Mountain Road. It leads to my Pops' house and where I live.

Yeah, I still live there. It was probably one of the leading factors Bear and I would fight. It isn't that he doesn't like Pops; I think he looks at Pops as a father figure. I watch Bear eyeing him all the time, mimicking the way he wiggles his hat on his head when he's got a mystery to solve like how to get his truck unstuck in the mud after piling the cargo bed too full of cut wood. He's even shown up at the house wearing a flannel shirt and a ballcap that I swear he must have driven over six times with his pickup truck to make it look worn in like Pops' hat. He snatches on to the sides of his jeans like Pops does too, wiggling them up when he thinks nobody's looking. Bear thinks I'm too old to live at home. I am. But it's not easy finding a chef job after college in a small town in West Virginia that doesn't even have a restaurant.

"You *sound* hillbilly. You *look* like a caged feral cat waiting to jump free every time we stop here." That's bleach-blonde, six-inches-of makeup and red lipsticked-lips Michelle Reynolds's voice I hear behind me. She's a little bit surly toward me. Her daddy, Big Don, was the town chief of police and had it out for all of us over on Fire Mountain. He was forced to quit for police misconduct. He banged up my car and pushed me down one day, and it was caught on video. Once everybody saw what happened, a lot of others stepped up with the same struggles with Big Don. He almost went to jail. Strangely, Michelle and her twin sister, Meghan, blame me for his troubles. Even odder, his brother who everybody calls Dee, was second in charge of the police and he took over when Big Don *retired*. He's, by far, worse than Big Don ever was bullying everybody over on Fire Mountain.

I'm not thinking of all that. I want to run today. Yes, Michelle is right. I do feel like a caged animal. I don't like to be fenced-in and staring through the bars of the security barrier while my feet pump the hard, asphalt-scented surface. I want to torture my muscles, feel the pain of the workout. Sweat. Bleed. Heave deep breaths to the pound of my heart. I like the dirt paths and the non-dirt paths, jumping the old oak tree roots and tripping once in a while so that I go skidding on my belly in the dirt and leaves. I want to feel the twigs snap at my arms, the thorns from the blackberry brush catch on my legs once in a while. I want to make my path and not know exactly where I'm heading. I hate circling, circling, circling on a man-made level track like a vulture flapping over its dead next meal. I detest mellowing out my Fire Mountain twang and watching every word that comes out of my mouth so I don't sound like what Michelle calls *hillbilly*.

I take in a breath of summer air—grass freshly cut by the resort lawncare service, the fusty scent of old autumn leaves, and the hint of rain in the air. I'm staring out over the deep green pines and the maples and the oaks with their jade-colored immature leaves, trying to catch a bit of gravel-dirt road. I hear the grunt-grunt-grunt of a motorcycle. It is deep-throated and pauses almost directly across from me. Until then, I'd been listening to the other runners drone and chatter on about this or that. Now, the motorcycle catches my attention. I can't make out more than an ant-size dot.

"Are you even listening?" Michelle's voice is squeaky and finger walks spiderlike up my back. It ends like one of the annoying jabs of my cousin Kenny's fingers wet-willy poking in my ear. God, that annoys me.

"Yes, I heard you." I've heard her gossip about Preacher Murphy's 16-year-old daughter, Benji, who keeps sneaking out to meet with her 21-year-old boyfriend. She's ranted on about Chloe Stephens who dyed her hair blue and made fun of the way Trina Pierson, with the cleaning staff, walks with a sway.

"Then what's your problem?" Michelle spats, catlike. "You *really* should try to fit in with us instead of the poor white trash working at the resort. You're stuck with us, and you know that, right? One of us is going to be a backup. If you don't act as part of the team, then I'm betting you'll get the boot." They are all squeezed together, lanky and too-hairy arms banging off each other like Sasquatch skeletons.

"The problem is, Michelle," I grunt back dully. "I don't *want* to hear you." There are five of us total, all women—Me, dark-haired Janie Mills and Carrie Edwards with sandy hair and mousy face. Then there are the model-perfect twins—Meghan and Michelle Reynolds. She's right. They will only need four runners for our part of the event. "If I had my choice, I'd be a part of my team from last year and not you four brainless twits."

"God! You are such a bitch!" That's Janie. She and Carrie are attached to the twins like remoras cling to a shark. Similar to their sharksucker equivalents, the two women are more annoying than dangerous. They don't initiate the attacks on me; they hitch a ride on the twins' backs, hang on tightly, and enjoy the little bits of scraps the two drop after a feeding frenzy on me.

"That's why we call her *Dolly*," Carrie pipes in with a screechy whine. That's what the four call me when Bear isn't around. It stands for Dollar Store Dolly. They say that's what I look like— one of the thrift store knock-off dolls with cheap, plastic bodies and too-big heads sitting on a shelf that nobody wants until Christmas Eve and there isn't anything else to buy for a cheap gift. They think I'm poor white trash trying to hide beneath the expensive clothes I'm expected to wear representing the resort for the Run—

"You're standing on the largest state-of-the-art fitness center and athletic facilities, Brandy," Carrie gripes at me. "But your eyes are begging to be released back into the wilds of hillbilly heaven. God, what is wrong with you? Do you like the thorns and yucky mud?"

I do. I don't say that, though. It would just be more fodder for Carrie to make fun of me. They are so different from me. These women are subdivision born and bred with mamas and daddies who went to every football game to watch them cheer, walked hand-in-hand with them to church every Sunday, and probably read to them every night until they were eighteen. Pops helped me set up a deer blind for hunting (I could never shoot one) and my big-as-a-bear Uncle Pete taught me how to ride an ATV. Nope, we are not the same.

I hear light laughter. I turn to take in Carrie sharing an eye roll with Janie. Neither has mentioned that Bear hasn't been down to meet me for our customary sharing of cool bottled water at my break. They less-than-discreetly overheard our conversation this morning in the parking lot that was as simple as this:

"—no, I don't remember anything about a text to meet you last night at the Crazy Kettle." That was Bear.

"I find that hard to believe. Last week, you replied with: *Babe, be there at eight. Happy early anniversary.*" That was me.

"Anniversary? I've got no clue about what you're talking about. What anniversary?"

"Our first *kind-of* date. We met at the Crazy Kettle."

"I already knew you. Is there such a thing as a *kind-of date*?"

"Not anymore." I had folded my arms across my chest. "It's right up there with my birthday you missed when you were out of town."

"I sent you flowers."

"Your *assistant* sent me mums. They smelled like a rotting corpse. You know how I know she sent them?" I asked his deadpan face staring at me. "The dipshit forgot to tell the florist they were from you. They had *her* name on them. So that you know, you sent me daisies for the last two times you didn't get home for important events in my life like when you forgot to show up for my last day at my internship and when I graduated with honors. I hate daisies. They mean death—you know, like *pushing up daisies*. What was your assistant thinking?" He started to answer. I held up my hands to stop him. "Listen, I'm not stupid. I know you've been traveling to marketing events without me. I'm done. You can pick up the engagement ring at the bar. I left it on the counter."

Meghan had stood five feet away not at all

embarrassed she was standing next to Bear and in a private conversation. She's Bear's mom's right-hand girl. The Chosen One. She's also been enlisted to represent the Redneck Run in the media and was shoved to the forefront as Bear's assistant. I know if Amelia Vega had a choice, Meghan would also be Bear's girl. Maybe she's got her wish. I'm sure the girls training with me knew before me IT was coming. IT. The breakup. I don't even want to say it. My little heart hurts so bad today I can't even outrun the pain. He didn't even bother to text me or call me. Instead, he sent more mums. I sent them back.

# Chapter 3—Getting Stalked by High Flyer Hercules

All four women blow out long sighs and make a big deal of it before they take off at a leisurely jog without me. They are most definitely as useless as tits on a bull. I watch them leave, turn my attention back to where the motorcycle was and is not anymore. I wait until the other runners are far out of sight. I press my forehead to the fence hard enough it hurts a little. It takes the focus off the mean girls and losing Bear. I don't cry much, but sometimes that big ball of hurt settles in my throat so hard, I feel like if I don't let my pain out in tears, it'll never go away.

The self-imparted pain helped. I pull away and take in a breath. I slyly look to the left and right, make sure nobody sees me. I take twelve steps forward and to a small section of the parking lot edge that collapsed above a rusted pipe during never-ending rains last spring. There's a two-foot gap between the fence and asphalt. I kneel, swoop beneath the fence, and slide on my butt down the hill.

I rise. A smile creeps on my face while I steal into the deep forest of the mountain below the resort. The coolness of the canopy touches my cheeks. I find an old deer trail and add my footprints to the dirt by the random mark of hooves. For thirty-three minutes I am free from the prying eyes of those at the resort who feel they must make sure I don't wiggy-out and do something hillbilly and mar their spotless reputation. It is the time that it takes for the other runners to make their way around the track that completely circles the building and before they realize the little chick flew her coop. Three minutes after they pass the place I snuck out, I slip back through the hole in the fence. I come up behind them as if I'd been there the entire time.

I've only got one place where anyone can see me. It is the rear entrance to the resort called Pineback Way. Only the staff, garbage pickup service, and food deliveries enter here—and the occasional visitor who missed the entrance and sees the EMPLOYEES AND DELIVERY ONLY signs out on the main road and are looking for a place to turn around.

As I slip through the trail that pops out and listen carefully for cars, I catch a bit of Pineback Way and ready myself to burst through the brush to whizz through. It is quiet barring the sound of one of the resort tractors mowing in the distance and an occasional car swishing past far off on the highway. Safe. I'm good to go. One toe brushes the mowed grass along the edge. I smile softly to myself. The next thing I know—BOOM! I didn't see his shadow. I saw nothing in my path until I belly-smashed into him with a soft thump like I've run headfirst into a wall that's getting ready to be sided and it's got the foam board insulation tacked on to it. Still, my body isn't absorbed into his hard abs just like it would bounce off the insulation. Instead, it careens backward.

I make dainty tipsy pat-pat-pat steps in reverse before falling straight back on my butt with arms waving in the air. I feel the bits of gravel against my thighs burning as I skid slightly. Sweat immediately bursts out on my temples when I make a wild swing of my head back and forth to figure out what wall I'd hit.

I blink. *Holy hell.* It's High Flyer Hercules who was watching me at the Crazy Kettle. He's huge and hovering above me, that scary-as-hell biker from the bar. I spiderwalk backward, heels digging into the grassy road edge. I'm in the middle of nowhere. This guy's going to do bad things to my skinny little body, murder me, and leave me naked on the side of the road for some garbage worker to discover me.

I make a hacking cat-spitting-up-a-hairball cough. That's my scream settled like a thick wad in my throat. My Pops says I've *got a mouth on me* and that means I can be a bit sassy. However, I've never been a fighter. I'm more prone to holding up my arms in defense which is what I do now—hunker up to a squat and wiggle up one elbow that waves awkwardly between us. He snatches me up by my wrist with one huge paw covered in black tattoos of wolves and panthers when he takes a step forward and stretches one arm out and tows me upward

"What the hell are you doing?" he growls at me. I rise, snap my arm away, and step back. I wait for a blow to my face. It doesn't come.

"I'm—running." I'm taking three steps backward, blinking once at him, then over his shoulder where I'm going to make my escape. That, I'm good at—fleeing scared-dog style with my tail between my legs. "I, um, run for the resort for the Redneck—" Holy hell, he looks scary. His eyes are big and dark. His shadow completely gobbles me up. "You're not going to kill me, right?"

"Just stop," his gruff voice belts out.

I contemplate the two options I have at this moment: fight or flight. My heart is pounding. My eyes are wide, blinking frantically. I probably look like the little mouse who got its tail caught in a trap Pops put in his kitchen drawer last winter when all the little outside creepy-crawlies within a one-mile radius got the word it was warmer in his house. They decided to move in. Their new living accommodations were not well-received. Pops was not pleased with finding teeny oval-shaped mouse poop in the drawers with the silverware, near his cereal boxes in the cabinet, and his sugar bowl on the kitchen counter. Especially so because he thought I had put some brown rice in the sugar to keep it from clumping up as I do with the salt shakers. *Well, this ain't going to work, baby girl,* Pops had said to me one morning holding up his coffee cup under my nose. He poked two little brown rice-turds popping to the surface with his forefinger.

*What?* I asked back. *Mouse poop in your coffee?*

*Mouse poop?* Pops looked at me aghast. *Why would you put mouse poop in my coffee? You're not trying to make me do some weird glooty-free diet like you did with your uncle, are you?*

*It's gluten-free, and no!* I'd exclaimed. *And why would I put rice in a sugar container, Pops? You'd have to dig it out each time you used it. With salt shakers, you have the little holes on the top so the rice doesn't fall through.*

Accordingly, it was the last time Pops dug out mouse poop from his coffee and instead, dragged out three spring-loaded mousetraps from beneath the sink and put one in the cereal cabinet, one on the counter near his sugar bowl, and one in the kitchen drawer. It was the one in the kitchen drawer the little mouse managed to lick off the peanut butter Pops carefully smeared on the flat platform to entice him to the trap.

Pops' cleverly crafted deception worked, but only slightly. The mouse had probably turned, sated with a full tummy when *BAM!* Down came the hammer, and it caught its little tail. When I opened the drawer with a yelp and a hop-skip that mimicked the funky whipping emoji dance on my phone, it ran frightened circles dragging around the trap and banging the four walls of the drawer until I begged a grumbling Pops to release its little tail and set it free in the woods. When he snatched it up between pinched finger and thumb and dangled it upside-down to the shed, the little mouse's eyes were wide and panicked like mine right now.

"Don't do it." High Flyer Hercules must know the look when someone's going to bolt. He's stepping forward. I'm stepping back, wagging my head left and right for a way out.

"Do what?"

"Run."

"Okay." I lie. I'm two seconds from darting under his arm. I fold my arms across my chest to quiet the distrust in his eyes like I assume he thinks I won't run if I have my arms crossed.

He suddenly tips his head to the side, looks up, takes a step back. "You know what? Never mind. You're not who I thought you were."

"No, I'm not," I start, and with the caution of the curious cat state: "But who might *that* be?"

"You're Brandy. You're the one who found that guy who murdered his wives for insurance money." His voice is not deep like Bear's that barrels out sometimes so powerfully that it startles me. It is somewhere between. I think he might be talking low, so I don't bolt. "You were one of them. You were one of Josh Devereauxs's wives. The one who lived." He stares at me. I'm expressionless. I don't know how to answer him. Was he sent by Josh's family to kill me in revenge? "I read about you in the papers. I found stuff online about you. I just thought you were more—kickass."

"Well, that's insulting. I'm tough. I'm kickass," I interject hotly. "And there were two who lived." Oddly, I feel like a newscaster who met a fan closeup and the fan tells her she looks prettier on TV. "I choose my battles wisely."

"No, you're more like—" He rubs his chin thoughtfully. "A wussy. You just thought you were going to die and stood there. How *wise* are you?"

"How do you know I thought that?" Why do I attract these men? "Are you stalking me?" Shit. It almost sounds like I'm upset that my stalker isn't as interested when he meets me face to face. How creepy is that? What is wrong with me? I think I release the behavior-inducing pheromone in buckets that instead of making guys horny, it affects their common sense and makes them mean and stupid.

"I guess I am stalking you. But not for the reason you think." He looks to the right. There's a rumbling sound. Yeah, I hear a car too. His bike is along the side of the road, parked there out of the way. I can bet he is as unsure about being here as me. Hercules looks like he just stepped out of prison and he's casing the resort for a robbery. "Meet me at that bar in town later. Nine o'clock."

"Noooo." I shake my head, and my voice sounds like a swish of whiny wind. "Are you serious? Leave me alone."

"I'll leave you alone if you just hear me out."

He steps back, eyes me hard, and turns. In ten easy strides, he's at his bike and climbing on. I see him wheeling his leg up, distractedly watch his t-shirt rise by his waist. It is a split second, but I narrow in on another tattoo, a frail orange butterfly with wings outstretched forever flying upward. Then, it disappears as he straddles his bike seat.

"I'm not coming," I call out. "You know that, right?"

"I'll pay you," he calls out. His words are nearly sopped up by the growl of the motorcycle and then the softer grind of the car wheeling around the bend.

"Pay me for what?" I watch him start up the motorcycle, wheel it the opposite direction, and zoom away. Faster than I can even unlatch my arms, he's gone. I cringe, seeing the black Land Rover filling the void where he disappeared easing along the roadway. "Shit," I grunt. It's Amelia Vega.

# Chapter 4— The Legend of the Video Camera and Getting Kicked off the Dream Team

There's an alleged amateur sex scandal video drifting around New Alliance with performances by Amelia Vega and a former town police chief. No one knows if it exists or not, this vintage movie from the 1980s. Like the mystery of the Loch Ness Monster, it allegedly shows up randomly and cryptically drifting around the pool of office staff where it secretly gets passed from one worker to another with the same stealth and secrecy expected of any creature of folklore.

Because the camera is allegedly so old, the little film cartridge can't be used in anything else. You can only watch it through a tiny monitor on the side, too small and bright to copy the material to a phone. I suppose that is part of the appeal, barring the obscurity of this movie camera *and,* more significantly, who is bursting through the restaurant doors without a shred of clothing on and chasing Amelia Vega, also naked, down the empty hallway in a fit of laughter—Big Don, the ex-New Alliance cop. Both were married to different spouses at the time. What happens after that while they tussle around on the floor is only known by those chosen few who have been given the opportunity to see the video and, in my opinion, have the stomach to watch.

It has always been my deepest desire to procure that camera, discover it like a lost treasure so I can use it against Bear's mama. I daydream about it quite often and mostly when she is berating me—finding it in an old, dark cabinet in the attic of the resort like a treasure hunter unearthing a pirate's chest filled with jewels and gold and unearthly delights hidden in a cave near the sea.

I'm there right now in my head, musing secretly to myself, reaching into a mental drawer six-times padlocked, my fingers barely alighting on an antiquated movie camera. It's because of what happened after I finished my run at the resort, showered, and got a text message from Amelia Vega: *Brandy. My office. Now.*

I had cringed and dressed quickly, then made the long walk down one bare hallway leading to her office. I know she saw me standing by the road, saw High Flyer Hercules haul ass down toward the main highway on his motorcycle. The door was open to her office. I avoided a knock, simply walking through the entrance.

I didn't recognize the man who was sitting in Amelia Vega's office. He was stoic, handsome, cool, and wearing an expensive three-piece suit. He was also sitting to the right of the desk slightly reclined in his chair. He was tap-tap-

tapping his thumbs on his cell phone. Bear looked up once from his phone. He stared at me like he didn't know me either, like he didn't remember I was the one who knew how to tickle him on the back of his neck just below his earlobes to make the goosebumps spread out on his arms, or who made him groan in bliss with soft kisses on his belly.

I don't know what I must look like to him. Just another woman he could toss flowers at to get them into bed. Local. Hillbilly. Frumpy in my jeans and blouse. It was all I had that was clean. Between training for the Redneck Run seven days a week and concluding my internship at a bed and breakfast in Salt Springs, three towns over, I haven't had a whole lot of time to do the laundry. On my only day off, which is Sunday, I spend the morning cooking a meal at Pops' house for the entire family after church. Then the late afternoon and evenings, I make special diet sack lunches (under the table and probably unbeknownst to Missus Vega) for some of the customers who stay at Boar Mountain resort because their meals are mostly greasy buffet-style. It is Bear's sister, Lilly, who runs the restaurant. She doesn't cook, so they buy all their food commercially pre-prepared from a bulk food product distributor.

Maybe he didn't see that because he was too busy trying to forget I was the one who laughed a little too loud at his stupid jokes that never made sense. I was the one who opened her mouth at the worst possible times when he had business associates over. I always made some dimwitted remark only people in my part of the woods would understand. Who had to turn out the lights when we slept together because I was afraid he'd see the real me and not like it and walk out of my life like men always did to my mama.

"Why would you dress like this for a meeting?" Missus Vega is seated with her elbows on the desk and a pen wagging in the fingers of her right hand. Her auburn hair is perfectly settling across her shoulders, not one strand out of place. She is wearing a suit costing more than every present we had under our Christmas tree last December. I'm saying that recognizing the fact Pops likes to spoil my sister and me with way too many gifts.

Bear's mama works her designer glasses slightly down the bridge of her nose. She assesses the situation with the same cold blue eyes that demand subservience from the lower level staff and she includes me in their social order, regardless I was almost her daughter-in-law. She insists I address her as Missus Vega and not Amelia. Her gaze reaches from the tip of my old tennis shoes to the top of my still-damp hair. "We've talked about your attire, have we not, several times? Your lack of professionalism astounds me, not only with your articulation but with the way you physically present yourself. These are the factors that we cannot tolerate. We have guests here who evaluate us via our staff. We have reporters and journalists who stay here. Proper appearances are critical." Missus Vega sighs deeply and lets her hands rest on the desktop before she rises. She can't stand to look *up* at anyone. She thinks it gives them dominance. "I suppose I can see why they didn't hire you after your stint at Little Bend of Salt Springs bed and breakfast."

"The innkeeper, Sandra Wright, couldn't afford a full-time chef," I reply quickly. However, I know inside they didn't need me anymore and not for lack of the reasons Amelia would imply—that I'm incompetent. I gave the innkeeper the menu and recipes I developed and prepared. I trained her on making each meal. And don't think I'm seething about Missus Vega's criticisms. I am. However, she is Bear's mama. My pops taught me to respect others, and especially those linked with someone I love. If I hurt her, I hurt Bear. With that in mind, I mutter: "It was just an internship so I could finish my credits and graduate. It has ended."

"Is that what Sandra Wright told you?" Missus Vega gives a roll of eyes like that's what the owners told me and was not the truth.

"I can dress better next time." I smooth my shirt with my fingers. "I haven't done the wash."

"*Done the wash*," she repeats dully with a bit of twang like she is trying to match my thick drawl. "My God, Brandy, you don't even know how backward that sounds, do you?" I stare at her blank-faced trying not to appear narrow-eyed sassy like Pops says I look when someone says something mean or spiteful to me. I bite my tongue. "Do you know what people think when you say things like that speaking on behalf of the resort? It makes us look—" She pauses. I know she sees the glare slipping across my eyes, the irritated tip of my chin upward. I wait for her to say we make her look like a redneck resort. "My ex-husband was right when he said if you rub elbows with the mountain folk here, you're going to appear like mountain folk." She glances at Bear who still has not looked up. Tap-tap, his fingers work the phone.

"You *are* sponsoring the Redneck Run," I remind her.

"That's different." She struts around the desk, tall and lithe. She snatches up a folder and holds it up. "And as far as dressing properly for an event, even as small as joining in on a meeting with the staff, there isn't going to be a next time. You are no longer running in the event. We've expunged you from the team as

37

you have broken contract rules. My attorney has written up a letter that will explain it clearly. If you wish to retain an attorney, which I know you can ill afford, you need to understand I will hold this out in court until after the event so it will be a waste of time and money for us both."

Boom. It was like a punch in the belly. I supposed, somewhere in the back of my teeny mind, it had occurred to me I have been standing on the crumbling brim of a high cliff overlooking some huge cavern with Janie, Carrie and the twins behind poke-poke-poking me in the back so I'll take the stumbling step across the threshold and tumble-fall over the edge.

Still, I stutter: "You—you've got to be kidding me. What do you mean?" Just to make sure I understand her. "I haven't done nothing—" I cringe    inwardly    and    correct    myself immediately. When I get nervous, I have to think out every word exploding from my lips. "—a—*anything* to base getting thrown out." I see Bear look up, a slight tilt to his head sympathetically as if he had just watched me battle a giant and I'd pathetically failed with one sweeping blow to my head.

Missus Vega smiles when she hears me stutter, her lips curling upward with a scary clown grimace. It is silent barring a phone ringing down the hallway, soft chatter far away, and the shuffle of feet passing the room. "Up until this point," Amelia shoves the folder at me, "we've endured your lack of enthusiasm and your inability to get to the training on time so you could finish your schooling. We've overlooked your absence of public speaking skills, recovered from the countless embarrassing, ignorant, and backward remarks to reporters, and have compensated for your ineptitude in social situations because you've provided some resources for special diets at the resort. And yes, I do know that you have been sneaking them to the rooms and taking money for them. I have overlooked this as it is certainly against our policies to have food delivered that, most likely, is not prepared safely. But we can't fail to see that you are providing nothing for the team and nothing for the events. You run. *Anyone* can run. I've gotten over seventy applications from professional runners to be a part of the team and two of them, I am reviewing heartily as a replacement."

"I have been working on those social skills. Bear can tell you that—" He looks up quickly as if to deny he had any contact with me. He doesn't catch my eyes. Instead, Missus Vega and Bear share expressionless gazes.

"Beau, can you please go answer that phone." Amelia points to the hallway, waggles the folder so I will take it. Bear rises, slips across the room without looking at me. There is no phone ringing.

Amelia waits until the door closes behind him. "Now that my son has left, I will address one final thing. It has come to my attention you have been sneaking off the property during training," Amelia grunts while I fumble to extract the folder from her fingers. "I took it as just another quirky behavior with you. However, after seeing you making some clandestine meeting with—I don't even know how to describe that *creature* you were talking to along the road. If you are working with some—" she pauses and lowers her voice. "—*kin* to rob the resort or are simply engaging in wanton behavior with that gorilla, it stops here. We cannot and *will not* have this kind of conduct mar our reputation—I will not have my son caught up in some dirty scandal."

"Scandal—?"

"As you know," she interrupts, her voice louder than mine. "We only need four competitors for the run. You were bottom of the list and, as your contract states, your situation with the resort is terminated." She takes in a deep breath and lets it out like a balloon with a teeny pinhole in its latex. "And —"

"—because," I added. "I'm no longer going out with your son. I know that. Maybe I'll do it on my own again."

"What are you going to do?" Amelia cackled. "Try to get your old team back from last year? From what my son's told me, the little Amish girl doesn't have a phone so you can't even contact her and your archer, Bobby Reese, just got out of the hospital from knee surgery. The only way that cousin of yours made it through the ATV run was because he threw mud all over the other competitors. It looks like you don't have a team." She huffs a laugh, tosses a hand into the air. "It wouldn't matter anyway. We learned our lesson with that fiasco. There's a five-thousand-dollar fee that is paid by a corporate sponsorship that goes directly to a chosen charitable organization. I doubt you could procure corporate funding at this point, much less find a team among the rag-tag mountain folk from whom you have descended. Now that said, out with you. Please do not make me call security."

I do as she says. Because she will call security and the cops. She has done this before. Still, I pause just before I leave. "As you sow, so shall you reap."

She sighs and smiles fake-impatiently, folds her hands in front of her. "Is that another one of those old wives' tales you're always coming up with, Brandy?" She sniff-laughs. "Are you threatening me?"

"It's not me that said it. It's God. That comes from the Bible," I explain to her. "It means, what goes around comes around and if you treat people badly, Missus Vega, it's going to happen to you." I close my eyes while I step out of the door (and I'm not proud of the prayer I request next, I'm not). I wished God would send down an angel and lead me to that treasure of a tape so I could get her back so that I could have some vengeance against that old evil witch.

"Well, we'll just see about that."

## Chapter 5—Meeting A Stranger in a Bar Parking Lot

"I didn't think you'd show."

I'm sitting in the parking lot of the Crazy Kettle at eight-forty-five in the evening meeting a stranger. I'm staring up at High Flyer Hercules through a small gap between window and frame on the driver's side of my truck. I'd lowered the window about three prudent inches to the *Bip-Bip-Bip* sound of the switch beneath my forefinger depressing.

His hair is now tied up in a bun behind his head. He's staring down at me unsmiling, dark eyes unreadable. "Better here than on a dark highway," I answer softly. "I get the feeling you'd hunt me down if I didn't show."

For each inch, I cautiously tap it back once and just enough to activate the motor so the power window regulator doesn't take it upon itself and intolerantly open wide. It's a little touchy, that switch. If it thinks I'm being squirrelly or overly cautious about opening it, the mechanisms controlling the power window assume I'm just stupid and make the rational decision for me to open the window wide so the glass disappears completely through the two channels in the door.

There are two banged-up trucks and four aged cars parked at lazy angles near the entrance. My new, loaded, and huge black truck sticks out like a sore thumb sitting here. I'm already self-conscious about driving this beast, but Bear had insisted I needed something other than my banged-up, four-owner Chevy parked in his driveway. I tend to park near the rear of Pops' drive when my family's over as not to appear boastful. I unconsciously do that now, parking in the back of the lot and at the extreme edge where a crooked parking lot lamp splashes a pale buttery yellow on the wet gravel until it reaches the black hood of my truck where it stops cold just short of the windshield. It smells like rain out tonight. That's what I'm thinking. My truck is running, a low guttural growl almost overriding the slow beat of pop music on my radio.

He doesn't say anything to that. Instead, he holds up a thin box to the glass of the window, banging it out of spite against the opening that is too small. *Bip-Bip*. I push the button to roll the window down two more judicious inches with two short snaps. It still isn't enough. High Flyer Hercules rolls his eyes. *Bip-Bip-Bip* I cautiously let it inch down three more jerky stages at a sluggish, bumpy pace equivalent to my Uncle Charlie's electric wheelchair running out of juice while his fist angrily cranks it to the beat of irritated curse words coming from his lips.

*Bippppppppp*-clunk. The mechanism decides

for itself my IQ is probably smaller than it should be to acquire a driver's license, much less work a window with a could-be madman staring down at me. It resolves I want to go the whole distance and opens the window fully. *Crud.* His hands rise once more and shove the box through. I wince. "What is this?" A bomb? A woman's right ear with a note for the cops to find the rest of her before he cuts off my left ear?

"You ever heard of the Stone Cold Creek Murder?" he asks me as I take the box in my hands. It is an old, dark yellow cigar box. The lid is slightly ripped and flipped inward. He rests his massive elbows on the window. His elbows are as big as my thighs.

"No." I let the box rest on my lap. He's close. Too close. One inch and his hand is inside my truck, and I can bet my entire neck fits into his fist. "I know where Stone Cold Creek is. It's about twenty miles from here. It's near Stone Cold Hollow. My school bus used to go past there when the Youngs lived out past the holler. Fire Mountain Creek flooded, so the bus driver couldn't always get around on the main highway. After their trailer burned down and they moved away, the bus driver took a different route when the water got too high. But I remember seeing the sign. I think I was in eighth grade." I'm cautious, but gingerly lift the lid to peer inside before turning my attention back to the man.

"Glad to know that," he says grumpily, shakes his head. "That said, seventeen years ago, they found a dead girl along the banks of the creek in the summer. She was my sister."

I'm thrown for a moment before I snap my head up and take in the shadow that is his face while he leans into the window. "Well, what does this have to do with me?"

"What do you think?" he asks me with a surly snarl of his lips. "I thought if anybody could figure out who did it, you could. They never found who killed my sister."

"I'm not—" I nibble my bottom lip. "I'm an out-of-work chef, not a private detective." I stop. Chef. It still tastes new to my tongue, calling myself a chef. "I mean there are a million other people that are qualified to find out who murdered her. Cops, to name just a few. Did you try them?" I don't know his name. "What's your name?"

"Marcus Freeman," he answers hurriedly.

"Um, I think I'll stick with Hercules."

"What?" He furrows his brow, blinks as if I'd awakened him in the middle of the night by turning on a bright room light.

"When you were at the bar the other night, I decided you looked like one of those wrestlers my cousin watches on Saturday afternoons. So, I nicknamed you High Flyer Hercules."

"My name is Marcus."

"Hercules is easier to remember."

"My name is Marcus. Period." He throws his hands out, slamming the door shut on any further discussion of me grouping him in my personal nickname files between Greek gods and professional wrestlers. "Listen, the cops can't figure it out. They've let it go cold. I heard your story about finding your ex-husband after he was missing. I've been trying to track you down for months. I can't afford a real private detective. Nobody else wants to touch it."

"Why not?"

"I don't know." He says that too quickly and abuts it with this: "There're thousands of cold cases. It's old. New ones are easy. Old ones are hard. Her name was Katelyn."

He's antsy, looking over his shoulder. I don't ask why. I come from a family who barely makes it past the poverty level guidelines to get reduced rates at the doctor's office. Folks like us tend to get few opportunities to go to college or start a business. However, we are the first to be chosen as possible suspects when the store gets broken into in town, or somebody finds a mislaid bag of pot on the floor.

I look at the box. Then I look up at Marcus Freeman. I hate to deny people who need help. Pops always says I'm the kind of person who would take the coat off my back even if it was twenty below to help someone who is cold.

"Well, I can try. I mean, as long as you don't get mad at me if I can't figure it out. You got your information in here—contacts or a card?" The lid was tucked into the box. I try to wiggle my fingernail in to wheedle it open, but it is stuck. "Is there some background to work with?"

"That's what I'm trying to avoid. Don't listen to all the shit others say. I'll get ahold of you." Marcus reaches behind him and tugs something from his back pocket. As it comes closer to the window, I see a brown paper sack. It has been folded over and over into a big cigar. "I'm banking my last dime on you. You have to see *outside* the box."

"Outside the box? What's that mean?" My questioning eyes go back and forth between his shrouded eyes. He's hiding something. "I don't want your money."

He stuffs the sack through the window anyway, turns, and fades into the oozy darkness outside the parking lot lamp. I hear the *grumble-grumble-growl* of his motorcycle starting, then the crunch of gravel to tires before he takes off. It's loud for maybe sixty seconds, and then it fades away to a bee buzz along the old state route.

I sit there in the silence for another five minutes. I stare at the windshield and into the night, watching a few bugs flit and flutter around the light. Then I put my truck in drive and take off the eight miles to Pops' house. It is down one mountain, then along a flat area before I pass the resort and climb back up Fire Mountain.

Right before the turn, my headlights flash on one of the local historical markers. It's slightly keeled to the right. One of my ex-husband's sisters, Crystal, hit the sign last December coming home drunk from the Crazy Kettle. I can still see the ruts from her tires. It's for the Old Stone Tavern. It's old, just like the sign says. And stone. When Pops told me the two-story building was a place for the stagecoaches to stop back in the 1800s, I asked him if it was still open when he was a kid. I thought it was funny. He didn't.

I pull over and stare at the building with its six windows on the upper floor and six below. Millie Piper owns the old building and the property. When her husband, Ivan, died, I started taking her to the cemetery every Thursday so she could sing Amazing Grace over his grave, pour his favorite mug of coffee by his headstone, and talk to him. When Bear and I started hanging out, he came with me until five weeks ago. Now she keeps asking me where that *nice young man* is and why isn't he the one latching on to her elbow to help her across the bumpy cemetery lawn. She tells Ivan's headstone that she's going to sell the tavern. But she never does. I ask Missus Piper once in a while if she'd be interested in selling it to me for a restaurant. She smiles and pats my hand with the kind of patronizing pat-pat-pat a teacher consoles an eight-year-old student who asks to read a book that is far over her age level and asserts: *Oh, sweetie, you're so young. You could never afford something like that.*

It doesn't stop me from dreaming. I think, while I stare at the building, that it might make a fine restaurant and maybe I can be the chef. Then the high beam lights of a semi-truck creep up from way down the highway. I see the FOR SALE. TOWNE REALTY. It's a sign laying a bit sideways against a tall maple tree like Bobby James at the realty office downtown started to put the sign up, then got a phone call and had to leave before he stuck the little metal posts into the hard ground. My heart leaps. *I could buy it!* Then reality slaps me in the face. *I don't even have a damn job.*

I feel a huge lump of heartbreak settling in my throat. It was always a lot easier when it was just sitting there vacant and full of my dreams. Now I'm going to get to watch somebody else toss out my dream and replace it with their own every time I drive by. I'm grieving over a dream that just died. I sigh and make my turn. But the idea of working there sticks in my mind long after I climb up Locust Grove Road and pass Pops' sign that says: MCALLISTER SAWMILL AND TREE CUTTING SERVICE.

I see the low beam lights of a truck barreling down the mountain. It almost runs me off the road when we pass each other. I recognize the truck and wince. Bear. I watch it disappear in my rearview. He doesn't slow. I dare to think what he was doing up at Pops' house. I pause at the peak just before I see Pops' little white frame house tucked into the woods. Then I pull into the lot and slide out of the truck.

The grass needs cutting in Pops' yard. It's ankle high and tickles my bare ankles when I cut from gravel drive to the broken concrete walkway leading to the porch. The lights are on inside. I can see the TV running. Pops is usually in his recliner drinking a beer when I get home and watching the History Channel if my little sister has fallen to sleep. He likes the old war documentaries. Tonight, though, I see him flit away from the window like he's waiting for me. Ug. It's not a good sign.

## Chapter 6—What's Inside the Box

"This is why I told you not to waste your money on college, Brandy." Pops is giving me the mean-eyes when I slink into the front door and plop my purse on the kitchen table. "You got those student loans to pay back. You ain't got no job." His voice is low because my little sister is supposed to be in bed. I know better. She lays in her little white twin bed with fuzzy unicorn comforters and that faces the TV in the living room at night. Kaylee fakes closed eyes and watches whatever Pops is watching which is cartoons because he knows she can't sleep. When she thinks we're all asleep, she tiptoes into my room and climbs into bed with me.

He doesn't want her to know he's an old softy pushover for sad, scared eyes that are afraid to fall asleep because of Mama's monster boyfriends always partying and getting high in the other room. I know. I used to be that little girl until Pops rode in on his four-tired horse like a knight in shining armor and saved me.

Next to my purse is a brown cardboard box that I'm sure is all my stuff from Bear's house. It is silver-duct-taped shut and says BRANDY in scrawled black marker. It was written on the cardboard using one of the indelible markers Bear keeps in a shiny red mechanics box in his four-car garage next to one of his shiny new trucks. The indelible marker is the only thing he knows how to use from that mechanics box. Bear doesn't even grasp how to properly change a flat tire, much less change his oil. But it isn't his cursive anyway. I recognize it as Meghan Reynolds's handwriting. I bet he had her write it on the box on purpose to make me jealous.

"You're home. There's a box on the table. I take it you're in a fight. Again." Pops says with a gruff voice. He scrubs the evening stubble on his chin. "What were you thinking, girl? You have a good man there."

"You mean a *rich* man."

He's got sky-blue eyes. When he's mad, each of his pupils enlarges, and his entire eye turns dark like they did when I made that remark. I know better than to be smart-alecky when he's in a mood. I have the little cigar box Marcus Freeman gave me scrunched up between elbow and ribs. I wiggle it out and plop it on top of Bear's box. I hold up one hand. "Don't say it, Pops. I know I'm a loser. You don't need to remind me. I'm going to bed."

"What you got there?" Pops asks, nodding to the cigar box as I start to pick up the boxes to lug back to my room.

"Something to wash away my sorrows."

"Wash away your sorrows? You ain't drinking, are you?"

"No. I don't drink. You know that," I say with a grouchy voice. "But you don't know me, do you?" I feel that big ball of sad dropping low and deep into my belly making me stupid and angry. "You think I'm gonna turn out like Mama. Maybe I should because it wouldn't make a difference to everybody. Then they'd all get to finally quit holding the truth in like those big balloons full of catsup Kenny used to toss from the roof to see it explode, so he knew what zombie's heads looked like when they burst. I know what they say: *We knew she was going to turn out like ol' Ruby MacCabe all drunk and drugged out and in jail. The apple doesn't fall far from the tree.*" I see Pops' eyes narrow. "You were like everybody else and figured I'd be pregnant with six kids by the tenth grade. You didn't think I'd finish high school or I was ever smart enough to make it through college. You didn't think I could win the Redneck Run last year and most of you think I cheated and I never did win. You don't support me or my dreams. You want to hold me back like you were always held back and squash my dreams just like everybody else squashed your dreams. You want to see me fail—"

"Girl, you are treading on thin ice with your mouth tonight."

"Well, I feel like I'm standing on thin ice!" I yell that which isn't typical for me. I hold my hands out, palms pressed to my temples on either side of my head and wiggle them like my head is going to explode. "My life is skidding out of control. When it stops, that ice is just going to break. I'm going to fall in over my head, and I'll be back to working at Smiley's Grocery again, and that's where I'll be for the rest of my life. Everybody laughs at my dreams. Everybody shatters them. All's I ever wanted was to cook for people! I never wanted to stock shelves. I never wanted to wait on tables. I want to do something more with my life than—this! I'm sick of it!"

Then, I just grab up the boxes and trudge to my little room that hadn't changed much since Pops fixed it up for me when I came to live with him. I slam the door. It's got a twin-size bed with a fuzzy pink throw rug on top of a deerskin next to it, a little table with a lamp, and my favorite chair to sit in—a papasan chair. I kick the throw rug, drop Bear's box in a corner, and plop my butt into the papasan chair.

I let the tears flow, try to wash away that dream. I can almost hear my mama telling me it was just another pipedream, that old house, and I should push my chin up, get a job at the bar waiting tables, and move on. I sob there a good ten minutes before there's a soft rap-rap of a knuckle to my door. I know Pops hates sopping up my emotions almost as much as I hate him doing it. "Baby girl, you alright?" he asks through the door.

"I'm fine," I sniffle.

"You want me to come in? You sad about Bear and stuff?"

It is quiet. "And stuff."

"What stuff?"

"Nothing."

"It don't sound like *nothing*."

"Missus Piper's selling her old house that used to be a tavern. I saw the sale sign. I just wanted it to be mine like you got your lumberyard. I wanted to—" –*make it mine*. I pause. I guess I don't want to profess my true feelings out loud. "It's not a big deal. I'll get over it. Yeah, I suppose it's Bear. He grew on me. I need to cry and let it wash out of me. I'll see you in the morning, Pops."

I know he stands there for forty seconds trying to decide if he should push the issue or walk away. He chooses to shuffle off. I wait until I hear him turn off the lights before I pick up the cigar box and set it in my lap. I shove away the tears with a wet fist. The sound of teeny soft footsteps follows the sound of Pops' closing the bathroom door. I look up, watch my door open mind-numbingly slow. Then it skids to a stop when it hits the deerskin rug there.

"I know you're there, Kaylee. Go to bed."

The door slides a bit more. I see a dark head, a mini-me except for blue eyes. "I can't sleep. I had a bad dream." She slips through, hand reaching up to catch the worn plastic tiara with fake diamonds Pops got her at the New Alliance Dollar Store last year. I know something's wrong when she wears it. She thinks it has magic powers like a shield to protect her.

"You didn't have a bad dream. You never went to sleep. When I passed the door, you were peering through the slits of your eyes." I tap my eye.

"Did Bear hit you?"

"Hit me?" I snap my eyes upward. "No, baby." She's looking at my puffy eyes. "Bear's not like that. He's like Pops and Papaw and Uncle Craig and Kenny. Nice. Only bad men hit women and the other way around. We just aren't going out anymore."

"Can I still go to Sunday kids' choir?" She rocks back and forth. "He's teaching me how to sing." Bear is the choir director at Holy Trinity. He majored in business in college to please his mama but minored in music, his dream. I supported him wholeheartedly except Meghan and Michelle Reynolds are his star vocalists. It always pissed me off, that dreamy gaze he got when Meghan belted out a solo. I can't even belch out a single not-offkey note.

"We'll see," I mutter and jab a thumb to my bed. "Get up there. Go to sleep. I got stuff to do."

"Miss Lila said she'd take me if you won't." Miss Lila is the woman who watches Kaylee while me and Pops work. Lila is short for Delilah. Kaylee's little lips couldn't wrap around the whole word, so she chose that nickname for her. Now it has stuck. "Miss Lila is beautiful. Like a princess," Kaylee mutters dreamily. She's right. Miss Lila is strangely beautiful like one of those too-skinny, too-tall fashion models walking down the runway with sad smiles. She has soft brown skin that Kaylee says looks like chocolate milk and brown hair she always braids down her back.

Miss Lila hasn't been here but maybe ten years. She came out of nowhere and bought a little white house with Gingerbread trim at the edge of New Alliance. If you ask somebody in town how long she's been here, he or she'll get a contemplative glint to the eye and look upward, tapping a chin. I mean, it is like she's always been here. And that's what they'll tell you. She doesn't have family here, and she doesn't have the Devereauxs wild red hair or the skinny stature of the MacCabes or the McAllister penetrating eyes. She's not dark skinned enough to look like the Wellmans and not light olive skinned and wide enough to look like the Gants. She doesn't look like anyone in particular, so they know she's not from here. Miss Lila sometimes gets herded in with the Murphys in a seating arrangement for a wedding for lack of finding someone to associate her with or for lack of finding someone to provide a reason she does something or doesn't do something because that's how we explain things here, we blame our genes and kin. I always imagine her standing at the top of some castle tower looking out glumly and longingly for something that will never come.

"Go!" I snap impatiently at my sister. Kaylee looks smug and climbs up into my bed and pulls the covers over her. It takes some persuading, but I can cajole the lid of Marcus Freeman's box open with a silver nail file. I open the cigar box, peer inside.

"Is this some joke?" I whisper, reaching in and tugging out a picture. That is all that is within the box. I stare into the emptiness after I take the photo in my fingers. I turn my attention to a face staring back at me. It's one of the pictures they take at school with a murky blue background. It's a girl, maybe sixteen or seventeen with the fake school picture smile. She's cute with sandy blonde hair to her shoulders and freckles on her nose. But it is her eyes that catch me off-guard. They are beautiful and wide like one of those Japanese anime cartoon characters. And something within the dead gaze staring back at me is haunting, echoing of something so sad it almost brings tears to my eyes.

"Who are you?" I ask, turn the picture over. *Katelyn Freeman – 12th Grade.* That's what was written in cursive pencil on the back. I say her name out loud, then snatch up my cell phone and complete a search for her online.

"Aw, shit," I curse the word softly.

"Aw, shit," my little sister repeats so softly behind me, I think it is little more than a sigh.

## Chapter 7—Grossing Out Kenny

"I need you to do me a favor." I have a little piece of paper in my hand. I'm standing outside Craig McCallister and Son Lumber and Post staring up at my cousin Kenny through his truck window. He's the *and son* in the business. He was pulling out of the driveway with a load of lumber he's hauling. It's a big truck with an enclosed trailer, so I have to look up, up, up to see him inside. He and my Uncle Craig take down a lot of old barns and resell the siding as reclaimed pallet wood boards to high-end building companies.

Kenny is my first cousin on Pops' side of the family. He's tall and lanky with red hair buzzed up the sides, and he's just a couple months older than me. We're not related by blood, but we treat each other like brother and sister and mostly because we've hung out together twenty-four seven from the time we were four.

"Take a shower. You stink. I can smell you up here." He peers up over my shoulder.

"What?" I follow his gaze behind me.

"Where'd you park your truck?" He waggles his head right to left. "You didn't get back with Bear, did you? I heard about him. You want me to kick his ass for you?"

Bear used to tell me there was more to life than just Kenny whenever he'd come home to an empty house because I was out riding ATVs with Kenny or munching popcorn on Kenny's couch and watching horror movies with him and his friends. I think he was jealous of Kenny. I think Kenny was jealous of him. I always told Bear he was welcome to join us. He declined. I suppose it was a good thing. Kenny and Joey Goodwood were always making fun of Bear. Bear tried to chuckle along thinking the joke was with him and not aimed at him.

"I ran all the way from New Alliance."

"You *ran*?" He leans against the window and wiggles out his wallet. "You that poor? You need a couple of bucks for a ride back?"

"I did it on purpose."

"That's not normal. You know that, right? Aren't you taking this a little too far, Brandy Pandy?" I'm always Brandy Pandy, Brandy Hard Candy, or some other weird nickname he comes up with when he's bored with those two. "Is there some mental illness you have that makes you obsessed with running. Or did you forget that normal people drive from Point A to Point B?"

"Go to hell. I know you've got the database access to do background checks for the employees you hire. Can you look up some names for me?"

"Don't tell me you're getting on some dating site, are you? You that desperate already?" He gives me a snarky chuckle. "I know if I gave

Joey forty or fifty bucks, he'd whore himself out to you for a date."

"You're gross." I grimace. "And I'd have to grow another set of boobies." Joey Goodwood always sits around and talks about sticking his hands up girls' shirts and playing with their tits, and he likes girls with big breasts and big butts so he calls boobies teats like they are cow udders or something. He doesn't care if I'm around when he says stuff like he's got ten different pairs of girl panties in his glove box in the same way a serial killer collects fingers as a prize for his conquest. I suppose in his defense, he probably considers me *one of the guys* because I've always hung around Kenny's friends so much.

"I'll pass. Joey's a creep." I sling my hand up high and thrust the paper at Kenny. He takes it reluctantly and wiggles it open.

"It's wet."

"It's sweat. I put it in my sports bra."

"You're grossing me out!" He tosses it to the dash like it's on fire. "Yeah. But you better not be getting into any trouble again. You're not, are you?"

"I don't know. You can tell me when you look up the names. There are six of them."

## Chapter 8—Stunted Sapling

Katelyn Freeman grew up in Quail Hollow about a hundred feet from the old Dunston Glass Factory that went out of business in 1962. Quail Hollow is about a forty-minute drive from New Alliance and right on the state route. There's not much there since the glass factory died. At least, that's what the web-based satellite view looks like from the online map. The local history site stated most people packed up and left for jobs in Wheeling or Charleston. The land around it got eaten up by strip mining, also shown as huge ugly yellow splotches on those online maps where plants are still not growing. She lived in a modest one-story brick home, once inhabited by the glass factory manager's family, with her parents, both who worked at the Frazee's Food Services on their production line, and her brother who was working odd jobs to pay for college.

In high school, Katelyn played trumpet and was a B-average student. She hated math and decided she wanted to be a third grade teacher the senior year of high school. She had a fluffy gray tiger cat named Tessa, and a life most would say mirrored the typical kid growing up in the U.S. At least, that's what her eleventh-grade teacher told me over the phone when I called to ask her. She had no reservations once I told her I was looking into the murder.

Katelyn had just finished her second year of college in May of 2002. She had returned home and was working the summer at Sunrise Year-Round Camping Resort located at Froggy Waters Pay Lake in the camp grocery store twenty or so miles from home. It was her second summer there. But her life, as everyone else knew it, came to a skidding halt the Saturday night of June 29th when she failed to return from work at her usual time between eleven and eleven-thirty. Her body was discovered three days later along Stone Cold Creek and less than one mile from the campground. A maintenance worker on the township transportation crew had been sent out to clean up a dead deer hit on the road and was dragging the moldering carcass into the tall grass. He noted a lime green flip-flop. He thought little of the flip-flop until two steps later, and he caught just the pale edges of Katelyn's bare heel. Upon closer inspection, he found her lying on her back, fully clothed in a red cami top and white shorts, arms at her sides, and legs slightly splayed as if she had been tossed quickly from a vehicle. Later it was found that she was killed by blunt force trauma to the head. There were no signs of sexual assault.

I dragged out an old corkboard bulletin board my Aunt Jenny had bought at a yard sale and was storing in the rafters of the barn. I dug out a little plastic box of old thumbtacks and attached the picture of Katelyn to the top. Beneath it, I also fixed newspaper clippings and articles I found about her murder. The next morning, I stuffed it under my bed so Pops and Kaylee wouldn't see it.

"The newspapers I dug up online said they had three suspects for a murder of a girl who was dumped here," I am telling Gabe Murphy. We have decided to surpass break-up etiquette and remain friends even though he was technically Bear's friend first. We came close friends last summer when I worked at Little Bend of Salt Springs. He's so mild-mannered—what Pops calls a good-time Charlie—that I'd probably put up a fight with Bear if he claimed him all for his own. He's mid-size with scrubby red-blonde hair.

We're standing on the bank of Stone Cold Creek and on the exact spot where the picture in the Charleston Journal Post showed the paramedics kneeling as they zipped up the body bag with Katelyn's corpse. There is a hill leading into a grassy edge where I'm standing and pine forest on the other side. I parked my truck along a gravel pull-off and walked a hundred feet or so to a place where it looks like folks spend a lot of time fishing. Or living.

"I had a background check done on her," I go on dispassionately. "It was cleaner than an unused Q-tip." Not so for Marcus Freeman. He has a prior offense and a conviction—First

Degree Murder for the death of his sister. I don't tell that to Gabe. It lit Kenny up like a firecracker with questions and accusations. He automatically deduced I was dating the guy when he found that on the background check.

I kick a clear, plastic makeup case. It is already broken, the lid's popped off, and the contents are spilling out. A razor falls out along with a dirty washrag and some mostly-used bars of white soap. I hurriedly kneel, scoop the contents up, and slip it back inside. I set it upright.

"Lord, what are you doing?" Gabe's face is scrunched up, his nose wrinkled like I just touched a long-dead fish bloated on the shore. "Don't touch that trash. Are you crazy, girl? It might have needles or something in it."

"It's somebody's stuff. I didn't see any needles."

"That's junk somebody dumped."

"I don't think so." I stand, nod to the left. "It probably belongs to somebody living here. Whoever it belongs to probably heard us drive up and left really quick."

"Like—" he holds out the word, snaps his head right to left. "—vagrants? Maybe we should go."

"In a minute," I say. "Keep an eye out. Just because they don't have a home doesn't make them murderers."

"You just told me there was a dead girl found

here."

I roll my eyes. "I love how you blended those, dumbass. If I would have said there was a multimillion-dollar house right over the edge of trees, would you have assumed the owner killed the girl?"

"Yeah, probably."

"You're lying." He is. Gabe gives me a lop-sided grin.

"What exactly are we looking for?" Gabe asks, kicking at a plastic grocery bag with something white inside.

"I'm not sure." I poke a finger toward his foot. "That's an old poopy diaper somebody tossed from a car. You know that, right?" He looks up, horrified. "I don't know what I'm looking for, but I know it isn't a poopy diaper."

"Surely the cops have already gone through this creek with a fine-toothed comb for evidence. How long ago was the murder?"

"Seventeen years." I glance up. Gabe is eyeballing the toe of his tennis shoe, working it upward to make sure what was in the bag didn't get on his shoe.

"Seriously?" he asks, rubs the toe of his shoe in the sand to wipe away imaginary poop. He looks up, pokes a finger at his shoe. "Do you see something on there still?"

"I think so. Just a little," I fib. The bag is closed. Gabe takes a few steps forward, dragging the toe of the tennis shoe behind before sizing it up again. "Honestly, I've got no other clues than a few newspaper articles that don't give any details."

"Did you try the police?" he asks me. "I know this entire area is covered by one police station. It's out of Bear Knob. It includes everything from Quail Hollow to Betts Station to—God-knows-where. But Jack Keeling works there. You made him blueberry pancakes all the time at Little Bend of Salt Springs restaurant. He's one of the full-timers."

"I don't like cops so well." I do remember Jack. Little Bend of Salt Springs was the closest restaurant to the police/fire station, so we got a lot of cops and firefighters coming to eat during the day.

"Not all of them are bad, Brandy," Gabe says softly to me. He gives his toe one final scrutinizing gaze and appears to believe the ghost poop is gone. I can barely hear him over the water but look up from where I'm nudging a pop can with my foot. He smiles sympathetically. "I know Big Don gave you a bad time, but there are some good ones out there. You've got to give them the benefit of the doubt."

"Yeah, sure, maybe I'll call him. But, middle-class-white-boy-driving-a-Smart-car, you need to know as soon as someone who is the type of person who is a wannabe-Superhero straps a

Smith & Wesson on his belt and a little badge on his bullet-proof vested chest entitling him to shoot first and ask later, it is a known fact that unarmed black guys and poor white folks start getting hurt."

"Don't be such a rebel. You've always had a problem with obeying certain rules. Jack Keeling's a nice guy."

"To people like you."

"If we didn't have cops, the world would be lawless."

"I know, Gabe," I sigh. He's right, and he's wrong. But the wrong side, I'll never be able to convince differently any more than he can convince me, I suppose.

There are a couple of old buckets turned upside down for seats and broken hooks and pieces of monofilament fishing pole line stuck on driftwood laying on the bank. It is warm out. Already, the hungry mosquitoes are buzzing around my bare arms looking for a snack. I swat them away with an open palm and take in the muggy scent of fast-moving creek water splashing over rocks. It stormed last night. The air is stagnant and clammy from the last shreds of rain still dribbling from the gray sky. What is usually knee deep from one side to the other a stone's throw away, is now rolling hip high.

"I should have known you had ulterior motives." Gabe rolls his eyes, but he's not mad. I did drag him along with me on the premise I was looking for a good fishing spot. His dad is the preacher at Holy Trinity Church in town. Gabe always has a smile on his face, even when he's pissed off at Bear. He's Bear's best friend, or at least while he was growing up. They still hang out once in a while, but now he spends more time with Ben who runs the Little Bend of Salt Springs with his mama, Sandra, where I took my internship. And me, when he flags me down running through town and tells me he needs to talk.

"Well, back at you. Because I know you didn't almost run me over with your car to hang out like you said," I retort candidly. "You either want to tell me something about Bear or your dad is wondering why I've missed the last few weeks of church."

"I guess I'm busted," he laughs. "But it's neither. I haven't talked to Bear. Even though my dad mentioned your absence, he just figured you were still working for Ben on Sunday mornings. Since you left and no longer work on Sundays, Ben's getting complaints from the returning guests and the after-church Sunday crowd that the food isn't as good as when you were there." I snap my eyes up. *Does Ben want to hire me again?* Gabe must read my thoughts, or maybe he catches the hint of desperation and hope in my eyes. He holds up a hand evil-sorcerer style as if to magically wipe away the prospect of a job and dash my dreams.

"Ben was wondering if you could come back and show his mom how to follow the recipes again. She wants to add a dash of this or a pinch of that where there shouldn't be dashes or pinches. It's horrible, Brandy, just horrible. Her muffins have balls of baking soda stuffed in them."

I snicker as he waves a hand in the air with exaggeration and turns his head away in mock distaste. "Yeah, she's like that. I don't think I can change her."

"You made cooking look easy. That doesn't help." Gabe comes up behind me. "If they could afford a full-time chef, you'd be it. They just can't. It's a small operation even when they are full." I don't tell him he's standing where a dead girl's head had once laid. "I believe in you. You changed Bear. If you can make a good man out of an angry, money-hungry jerk, you can teach Ben's mom how to season to taste or at least follow a recipe. Can you come tomorrow?"

I am looking at him with a smile on my face that drops instantly. "I can come tomorrow." I look out past the grass. I see the tippy top of an old tent. "But Bear didn't change. Or if he did, he backslid. It was all a big lie, Gabe. I think we had two good months and his mom was already slipping him poison whisper-hints every time I opened my mouth. She started throwing Meghan in his face again. It will never work with him and me because he won't defend me when she points out my flaws."

"He thinks the world of you," Gabe mutters. "Sometimes relationships require work." He sounds like his mama, Gabby, who finds the bright side of everything. Once I caught her plunging the toilet in the women's restroom at church. Some Sunday School kid must have shoved half a roll of toilet paper down the pipe and then tried to flush. It had flooded the bathroom, and the water was making its way into the foyer surrounded by a horrible smell of sewage. When I came stepping through the door, she just turned to me and wielded the cheap black plunger like a sword with gag-watering eyes and said *I'm trying hard to think that it's Satan trying to make his way up those pipes and I'm God's superhero keeping him down. But Lord help me, it smells like the very bowels of hell in here. I'm hoping I'm not losing the battle.*

He's not kidding about relationships. I spent the better half of last night tossing and turning. I couldn't sleep. I felt like I'd taken money from the devil, himself. I had Marcus' brown bag stuffed back in my locked glovebox with five-hundred dollars and his note that said *This will start you out.* And on the floor next to my bed was my laptop with a newspaper article still displayed on the monitor. It said **Killer Goes Free: Stone Cold Creek Killer granted release from prison.** *County Common Pleas Judge Charles Lee Scott reluctantly granted Marcus Freeman's* *motion for release. Bound by law and a plea agreement struck with Freeman resolving a string of unrelated crimes committed, it guaranteed Freeman's release after three years. Freeman adamantly denies any connection with the death of his sister found dead in Stone Cold Creek, WV. "I was wrongfully convicted. I don't know who killed my sister. It wasn't me—"*

"I know you fight with your sisters all the time." I poke Gabe in the belly. He chuckles and backs up, shoves his hands in his pockets.

"I do. My sisters annoy me. They leave brushes full of hair on the sink, tattled on me my whole life."

"You ever get mad enough to want to murder them?"

"Of course. I didn't, though," Gabe snickers. He takes me in, realizes I'm serious. "Oh, no, not really. I'm kidding. Kid sisters are irritating. I found that tossing the brush in the toilet stifles any fuel for the fire to hurt them physically." Again, he laughs. I laugh along. "Why are you asking such a creepy question?"

"Because the brother of the girl who was murdered here went to jail for it. They were from a nice family. I got on a genealogy site and couldn't find any known insanity in the ancestry gene pool. I couldn't imagine pinching Kaylee, much less taking a baseball bat to her head. And my background is questionable." I sniff the air. "I read that twenty-four to forty percent of murders are from family members. I'd never thought about it until now."

"Okay, we're changing the subject." Gabe shivers. "So, what are your plans now you're not working for Sandra?" He comes up beside me, forces me to drag my attention away from the newspaper article. It isn't like I've been able to find any more information than the vague clue to why they tied Marcus to his sister's murder—he allegedly had been making her steal money from the campground store where she was working. For a month and a half, almost nine-hundred dollars had disappeared from the cash drawers they kept.

"It hasn't changed. I want to be a chef."

"Well, that I know," he says. Sometimes I wish he liked women instead of men. Barring that, he's the prototype of every good guy who ends up marrying the heroine in every one of the Saturday afternoon feel-good movies. He hangs on every word I say. He looks me directly in the eyes right now, inviting me to say more. He kisses well. I kissed him once. It didn't give either of us starry eyes.

"I love you. Will you be my boyfriend, Gabe?" I tease.

"I love you too. But, no, Ben would kill me. You're trying to direct my attention from the conversation."

"Well, I wanted to run in the Redneck Run again. That got dashed. I got kicked off the team. I saw a For Sale sign at the old tavern, and I've asked Millie Piper a hundred times if she'd sell it to me so I can make a restaurant—"

"I think Bear was saying his mom was going to buy that property. She wants to add a golf course and club to the resort. She also wanted to tear down the old buildings on it, put up new. She mentioned it to someone, and the Pipers heard and balked at the idea of seeing their family's farm torn up." Gabe winces when he tells me that. "I mean, what did they expect? They're asking over a half million. Once they sell, they've got no say. Regardless, somebody's going to buy it and probably tear it down. It's old. I'd think if Bear's mom wants to own the property, she'll get it even if she has to say she'll keep the old house. Then she'll tear it down anyway."

"And so why do you ask me what my dreams are, Gabe?" I swallow hard. "Please don't tell me to follow another dream or move and find a job somewhere else. I've sent out resumes everywhere. Nobody wants to hire a chef who went to a teeny community college in the middle of backwoods West Virginia."

"You give up too easily." He sighs. "Did you try to get a loan for the property?"

I look out over his shoulder at the forest on the other side of the creek. There's a tiny, stunted sapling along the edge of the water, alone and barely knee-high compared to the huge pines behind it. I suddenly identify with that undersized tree, always being outshined by Amelia Vega's Dream Team of runners, never being able to grow because of all the rich restaurant owners who can buy the best chefs. "Shit, that's me," I grunt. "By the end of summer, it'll either be drowning six feet under in water or shadowed by the trees so it can't get sunshine."

"Good God," Gabe swivels his head, follows my gaze. "Are you talking about that tree?"

"Uh huh."

"Give it time. That's a baby Sycamore growing on the bank with its feet in the water. That's what they like, lots of water to nurture them. That creek can beat at it for days, and it just loves it in the same way my mom loses herself in a hot bath for hours. In a few years, that thing will be twenty feet taller than the pines and overshadowing them so they can't grow." Gabe sighs deeply. "Go try for a loan before you give up. Just go for it. Don't you remember that old joke about the guy who prayed to win the lottery and didn't win? He got a bit miffed and asked God why he didn't win after he prayed so hard." Gabe waits for me to shake my head back and forth. "Well, this is what God said: *Because you never bought a lottery ticket. Do you get what I'm saying? You got to exert some effort."

## Chapter 9—Risky Paths

I used to find risky paths to run. I'd end up dodging the oil tanker trucks on the highway or sprinting past the NO TRESPASSING signs old Crazy Willy, our well-known local recluse, tacked to the trees bordering his property while he shot at my head and let loose his hounds after me. Sometimes, I'd head straight down the middle of the Fire Mountain View Trailer Park where my ex-husband's sister Crystal lives. There were always rumors, even before Josh disappeared, she wanted to kill me.

Bear used to tell me I run because it releases chemicals in my body called endorphins and they trigger some happy code in my body. It's kind of like getting a shot of morphine. It makes me feel good. I look at it a little differently. It's because I had a lot of stuff I called *maybes* in my head. *Maybe* Mama gave me away because she wanted the best for me. Or *maybe* she was drunk and just forgot where she left me. *Maybe* my ex-husband was alive and couldn't get back to me because he hit his head and got amnesia. Or *maybe* he didn't want to come home. All the jumping over limbs and rocks and straight down the mountain kept those things from creeping in my mind and thinking things better-left un-thought.

I'm breaking out in a dribbling sweat when I hit the state route today. Someone in a little car honks a horn at me. I'm still running because of *stuff*, but this time it is *should-haves* and *don't-want-tos*. I should have just let Bear flirt and carry on with Meghan, let his ego feast on the women fawning all over him and looking for a handsome, rich husband. I shouldn't have followed my dreams to become a chef and instead, worked for the rest of my life at Smiley's Grocery where I, at least, had a job. I don't want to listen to Gabe and take a chance of getting a loan when I get to the bottom of the mountain.

I hear one car jam on the brakes, skid sideways while it tries not to hit me. Ah, the rush! I break through to the sidewalk on the other side, pass Holy Trinity Church and wave at a couple of the Murphy kids playing on the porch. I settle into an even run in front of the drugstore, the gas station, two little shops and—*screech*—my eyes come to a halt. I SEE BEAR. He's hard not to notice while I sprint down the sidewalk. I try not to peer at him standing by a baby blue Porsche and making a gentlemanly appearance opening a door for a woman whose long, long legs are slipping out. I still lose my breath when I get an eyeful of him. He's beautiful. So is Mila, who is rising from the car.

*Mila.* I say that in the same drawn-out, deep voice a villain is introduced in a fairytale. Amelia Vega hired Mila Boucher, CEO of

Boucher-Ankrom Global Marketing for the resort public relations and advertising. Bear told me his mama threw in almost every penny of the divorce settlement she'd gotten when she and her second husband split up to have Mila's company handle all aspects of the resort and the Redneck Run affairs. I secretly believe she must have also paid Mila's company a pretty penny to sever the ties between Bear and me too. If I had to put my finger on it, the moment the six-foot-one-inch creepily perfect redhead showed up three months ago, my relationship with Bear began to disintegrate.

I would liken the budding love of Bear and me as a thousand-piece puzzle about a quarter of the way finished. The box had just been opened. Although Bear and I were both afraid to count the pieces to see if they were all there, we just had a feeling it would come together. We would both laugh gently when one of us made a clumsy attempt to put a piece with another that wouldn't fit. We'd praise ourselves when one matched.

I don't think there were any missing pieces until one day I walked into Bear's empty office to drop off a lunch I had made him. He tends to work-work-work, then gobbles up some fatty, over-salted menu item at his desk from the resort's dining room. In contrast, I focused on special diet foods in college and prepared him meals that both filled him up and tasted good.

He wasn't there. I planned on plopping the lunch on his desk and leaving. I just happened to glance at the huge, white calendar he's got on his desk. Atop, there was a pile of pictures laid out for Redneck Run marketing. I saw some of the girls running. None with me. I noticed pictures taken at a hotel he stayed in for a TV promotion on the event. I looked closer. I could see Carrie and Janie, Meghan and Michelle all lined up in nice dresses with Amelia Vega and Bear like they do for promo pictures. I was absent from the images. I had no clue about this event. Then as my eyes homed in, I let my eyes follow along Bear's sleeve and Meghan's bare arm. Their two hands were latched, fingers twined together.

I hadn't heard Bear's steps down the hallway. I was mesmerized by the sight. When the door creaked open, I turned. I noted, without satisfaction, Bear's face had turned a dull shade of red. *Didn't expect you here, babe,* he'd said. I told him I could tell. *Oh, you saw the pics, huh? They were just some we all took at the conference. You know, the resort conference. We were all there anyway because the girls all work for mom and you don't. You were working at that bed and breakfast.* When I asked him why he was holding hands with Meghan, he also just told me: *Oh, we aren't. Ha ha. It just looks like it.* Then Mila had strutted into the room with a handful of business associates for an advertising meeting and brushed me aside.

*Can we get her out of here?* She had whispered loudly to Bear with a roll of her eyes. Both of them looked at my spandex sweatpants and the tank top. They shared a soft laugh. I left. I knew right then she was slowly and meticulously snapping up pieces of that puzzle and flicking them into the dark, obscure places lost puzzle pieces disappear and are never found.

The sunlight now makes a hard bounce off the hood of Mila's Porsche. I'm blinded. I forget about the little break in the sidewalk I've run across a thousand times before. Of all the moments I've been off in a dream or had the sunlight rip through my corneas passing to the other side of the awning and somehow managed to *not* trip on that little dip downward, this was not the time. To make matters worse, I completely fail to see a third figure following behind Bear. My right foot goes out from under me. Abruptly, I'm smacking into a soft wall of man-chest that has the sweet scent of fresh morning cologne. I keel sideways, flap my arms doggy-paddle-style in the air, and skid clumsily along the pavement on my belly.

"You okay?" The man's voice, whose chest made an inflatable bouncing house wall for me, is unfamiliar. A hand touches gently on my arm. He is kneeling where my body came to a harsh, inelegant stop against the brick of the building. I blink-blink-blink past the sun-blindness at the man hovering near me. Styled

hair, fresh button up shirt, and cargo shorts—
he's city boy and attractive too, his dark head of
hair silhouetted like the little haloed angel on
my Aunt Jenny's Jesus pictures hanging in her
living room.

"I'm fine." I'm so embarrassed at my blunder.
I beg to sink into the pavement. I look up, see
the New Alliance National Bank digital time
and temperature sign with the fluorescent
green numbers blinking at a temperate seventy
degrees. I rise with the help of his hand.

"Mister Gordon, sir, we should continue our
tour." Mila has stepped across the curb in sky-
high heels and a perfectly fitted black sheath
dress barely tiptoeing on the edge of what
might be too sexy for work. Bear once told me
skin-tight little black dresses and sky-high
heels were his biggest weaknesses. The image
of him stupid-gazing me when I wore that sexy
combo for him seeps into my head. I bristled
wondering if he looked at Mila the same way
this morning when she wore that to work. I
simmer. It's not like I left him cold-turkey. His
mama had spent months slowly weaning me
off him. Still, I feel crushed.

Mila is tugging on the elbow of this *Mister
Gordon* with red-lipsticked lips tightly glued
together like an overbearing mama snapping
up her pretty-suited city boy right before he
jumps feet first into a mud puddle with the rest
of the farm kids dressed in t-shirts and hand-

me-down shorts. Oh. *Rush* Gordon. Rush being the nickname of the Midwest All-Terrain Vehicle Organization's founder. And if you ask me how I know this, I'll tell you Kenny used to have a poster of him on his bedroom wall when he was in high school. Rush Gordon must be their pick for the ATV part of the race.

He does leave, but he keeps looking back at me while Mila opens the door for him in the same way a chauffeur opens the door for a customer. I look to the bank, sigh deeply, and hope I've got enough endorphins left to walk through the doors.

# Chapter 10—Heebie-Jeebies at Stone Cold Creek

I don't get back to Pops' house until five in the morning. I pull into the drive slowly and cautiously. I'm wary. Pops' front porch and the living room lights are on. He doesn't get up until six. I know there must be something wrong. Bear parked his truck in the gravel in front of the barn Pops uses as a garage.

I didn't go home after I went to the bank. I'd gone inside, waited a good twenty minutes for over-groomed Todd Bailey, loan officer, to come out shaking the hand of one of the more snobbish worshippers who go to Preacher Murphy's Holy Trinity church, Grant Battaglia, congratulating him on his new SUV. Todd's pasty-cheeked and round-faced with a teeny nose. The tie around his button-up shirt collar is so tight, I can't help but wonder if his head doesn't pop off like a cork pops off a wine bottle when he goes home each night to change into something a little less tidy.

Todd gave me a fake smile and settled me into a chair across from his desk. When one of the office clerks came in and handed him my financial application I filled out for Millie Piper's old property, he gave her the same knowing gaze Pops gives me when Kaylee says she's not tired and doesn't want to go to bed, but her eyes are slowly closing even as she speaks. I knew even before he pretended to scan the documents that I had a big REJECTED written across the top. "Missus Devereauxs, you don't have a job, collateral, or even a backer for this—what do you want to do with the property?"

"Use it as a restaurant."

"You know, about sixty percent of restaurants fail within a couple of years. What happened to the job you had at Don Smiley's grocery? You weren't happy there?"

"Um, I graduated with a degree in culinary arts. My dream is not to work in the retail grocery business."

"Ah, and it is our job to make dreams come true?" Todd scoffed. "Most folks go out and work under a real chef for a while—"

"I've been doing that for five years. I am a *real* chef."

"Right." He gave me an eye roll. Then Todd chuckled and looked past me. "Well, Brandy, you may well know that Amelia Vega has already placed a bid on the property today. It was right before you got here. We're working out the fine details with the Piper family. But you can see where this conversation is going, can't you? You've got five dollars in your bank account, and your family's track record isn't great. The property is worth half a million. I don't see that it will happen. However, we do have a couple of trailers for sale at the Fire Mountain View Trailer Park and Campground."

I left not long after that. My dream, once a big red balloon heading toward the skies, was deflated and reduced to a couple of drab pieces of latex lying in the gutter. I ran back home, took a short shower, fuming. I grabbed an armload of old blankets, one of Pops' razors, a loaf of bread and some meat, and a can of mosquito spray from Pops' cabinet and stuffed them into a black garbage bag. I got into my truck knowing when my day is dark, making someone else's better pushes away that black.

I drove past Mama's old trailer park and sat there for a few minutes and stared down the asphalt-buckled street and the rusted trailers settled there. A couple of women were sitting on porches, poking at their cell phones. I watched three little girls riding their hand-me-down bikes up and down and up and down. I looked at Mama's old trailer and where mine used to be when I lived with my ex-husband. Mine, it was gone, burned up. I want to believe, just for a second, that maybe Todd Bailey's right. *This* is where I came from, and this is where I end up. But I can't. I won't. There's more to life than sitting on the front porch smoking a cigarette, texting somebody else's boyfriend, and watching kids ride bikes up and down the road at Fire Mountain View Trailer Park and Campground.

Instead, I hit the gas and headed on down the highway, the *old highway,* that is. At least that's what Pops calls it because the *new* highway is two fresh lanes going one way and two lanes going the other and races from big city to big city. The old highway parallels the new for a while. Then it breaks away from its younger version, plodding off on its rough course like it has done its job and it is going off somewhere to die deep into the belly of the mountains. It trudges past old towns that were once big but are now small. It runs along Stone Cold Creek on fifteen-year-old buckled asphalt before it goes back and forth between a mixture of gravel for a while, then blacktop for a while, and then almost nothing at all.

I ended up at Stone Cold Creek again, staring out at the still rolling water. I knew I'd be better off just leaving the paper bag full of cash locked in my glovebox and the cigar box stuffed under the seat of my truck until I ran into Marcus again and shoved it back at him. I don't always listen to common sense. I got out of my truck, hauling the black garbage bag full of blankets and food and tucked it behind a wall of grass for whoever was living back there. I see the tops of three survival tube tents held up by the same kind of laundry line Pops uses to hang his muddy pants on outside.

I walked through the brush along the shore, then started along the bank, avoiding the place where I think the homeless camp is located. I don't know what clues I was trying to find. But I've got nothing to go with except one dead girl killed with a blow to the head and discarded at a known dumping site along an isolated roadway. I marched through the tall grass, tossed a couple of stones into the water, then kicked old buckets around that were settled into a pile of rolled carpet, broken orange construction barrels, and a brown recliner chucked from the back of somebody's truck.

I suppose if the random image of Todd Bailey making a pretend crumple of my loan application in his cupped palms behind my back and tossing into his wastebasket basketball-style hadn't popped into my head, I wouldn't have given the ground a swift, angry kick of my tennis shoe. Had he not noticed that I could see his reflection in the cool glass of the room divider while I walked away?

Pop! Something cracked beneath the force of my toe hitting the ground. I pulled my foot back and narrowed my eyes to peer downward at a tiny blue and white unicorn decal near my toes. I would have thought it was nothing more than a sticker attached to a discarded vinyl picket fence panel if I had not also caught the faint edges of glittery peel and stick letters.

I knelt, rubbed the dirt off the plastic. I could barely make out: **DANA PITZER 1983-2001**. When I snapped up a flat rock and worked it beneath the edge and dug the dirt away, I was holding the ragged remains of a plastic cross and staring down at a second one beneath, more shattered than the first, but still intact: **SARAH THOMPSON 1982-2001.**

I looked right to left, searching for some explanation for the placement of the crosses. Maybe they had just rolled downstream from a local cemetery during spring floods. I was intrigued. I pulled out my cell phone and did a hasty search for Dana Pitzer. Three pages in, I found this archived newspaper article from 2011: THIS DATE IN HISTORY 10 YEARS AGO TODAY: TRIPLE HOMICIDE IN GLEN ALLEN. 2001 - *Volunteers and officers combed the area of Old School Road, Bellhanger Hollow for two missing teens searching for evidence that may help explain the reason a local Cold Creek woman was found dead in her home at eleven p.m. A cryptic call for help led police on a wild goose chase for hours along I-79 before a second cell phone call directed them to the Pitzer home. When deputies arrived at the scene, the body of a woman identified as Margaret Pitzer, 53, was found. She was killed with blunt force trauma to the head. More than a hundred tips were received for the two missing teens before the bodies were discovered in their car, overturned in Cold Creek two days later. No vehicles were at the home. The death of the woman was ruled a homicide. It isn't known how long the girls were dead. The homicide remains a mystery.*

I laid the crosses back on the dirt-sand shore and took a picture with my phone. A shiver ran up my spine, cool fingers making a trudge up my back, along my shoulders, and stopping just shy of the nape of my neck where the downy hairs stood instantly erect. I thought of my mamaw, Pops' mama, right then. *Somebody's walking over your grave.* That's what she used to say when somebody got goose pimples for no apparent reason. It was the heebie-jeebies. I felt like I was being watched. I had an uneasy sensation someone was watching me, staring at me, eating me up with cold, hungry eyes.

I shuddered. Suddenly, I couldn't get out of there quick enough. I made a fast pace of my feet along the bank of the creek, up to the pull-off. There was a red Blazer parked next to my truck. My eyes grazed the plates. They had an American Flag emblazoned on them. The windows were tinted. I couldn't tell if someone was inside. I made an immediate exit.

It took me ten minutes to shake the strange sensation. I drove straight to Little Bend of Salt Springs. I promised Gabe I'd go over how to make muffins with Ben's mama again. It didn't matter. I didn't want to go back to Pops' and spill the beans about Todd Bailey poking fun at me at the bank. I knew I would.

## Chapter 11— The Time of Our Lives

I met Ben Wright's mom, Sandra, on the front porch of the small resort and spa. "Well, there she is!" She greeted me like she'd been expecting me. She is a relocated New Yorker. She heartily clings to her old accent with the wistful pining of those who regret leaving their home and will someday return. I like her. She's short brown hair, lots of makeup, jewelry, and pretty clothes. She reminds me of the city girl who moves from a ritzy apartment in New York to a tumble-down home in the country in the old Green Acres show Pops watches. However, her bed and breakfast isn't rundown at all. It is beautiful and thriving and what everyone calls *the* place to go in the middle of nowhere.

She was sitting in a white rocker gently swaying back and forth. Next to her, a thin man with the same kind of bushy, hipster haircut and slouchy hat as her son, Ben, was latched on to a newspaper. He had just made a rustle of it with his hands and placed it on his lap to snatch up a dainty coffee cup with a free hand. He took a sip and smiled politely. I smiled back.

"Oh, *darling*, Gabe and Ben sent you to show me once again how to make those morning muffins." Sandra clapped her hands together and threw her arms out wide. "God bless those boys. But Ben's got ulterior motives. Do you remember Bill Gaynor with *The Time of Our*

*Lives* Magazine? He does the human-interest stories."

"Um—no." I didn't realize she was talking about the man sitting next to her until her hand flapped toward him. My cheeks turned red. He caught my discomfited gaze, shrugged. "I'm sorry, it's not that I haven't heard of your magazine," I backtracked. "My Aunt Jenny's a big fan. She lives for the drama and the star stuff. She collects them like my cousin stockpiles girlie magazines in his closet. But she doesn't hide them. She tosses them on the living room table, then the bathroom when they start getting too tall to see the TV." I threw him a knowing smile. He chuckled and tossed one back. "But whenever I saw you journalists and reporters in person, Bear was always shoving me behind him."

"Bear?"

"Um, Beau Vega," I replied. "Well, up until a few days ago, I thought he was protecting me," I laughed. "I've got a thing about big crowds. I'm scared to death of them. You guys do this big rush forward, and I go woozy and BAM!" I clapped my hands together to give the full effect. "I hit the ground in a dead faint. But I've come to find out it wasn't me he was protecting. It was the resort and the public he was defending. I guess I sound like an idiot when I open my mouth."

"You don't sound like an idiot to me," Bill

said casually. "Just candid. I like that."

"He covered the race last year," Sandra divulged. "Because we sponsored your little team and you won, as part of the winning package, we got free advertisements and a writeup in his magazine. He's good friends of ours now, aren't you, Bill." It wasn't a question, and he must have known that because he nodded. "He brings his family to stay twice a year." She waved a hand in the air. "I'm sorry, you two. Ben tells me I'm unfocused and I am. I start talking and get off the point. Bill wanted to do a story on you." She looked toward him as if getting affirmation. "However, to be quite honest, Missus Vega, she just told him you didn't have time with all the training. He showed up with the rest of the media this week and asked for an interview. Missus Vega was so unpleasant, he left the press conference and came back to his room here completely flustered that you weren't even around. He said something to me, and I told Ben. Bill won't stay anywhere else but here, you know. I hoped you could do us a personal favor and perhaps grant him an interview."

I was taking in Sandra with the half-deaf ear of someone who is only partially listening. Most of the time, I hear about half of what she's talking about because she does tend to ramble. While I was cooking the meals at her bed and breakfast, Sandra would come into the kitchen and try to help and offer her advice, chattering about whatever came to mind. I learned to tune her out so I could focus on the meal and mutter an *uh huh* once in a while as not to hurt her feelings. I guess it became a habit because I realized while she was staring at me, I'd barely heard what she said.

"Brandy? You in there?" Sandra waved a hand in front of my face and gave me a warm laugh. I lied with a bob of my head up and down. "I was telling Bill if the Redneck organizers hadn't added all those asinine stipulations and exorbitant fees this year, we would have sponsored you. But it would have cost us more than our little business to sign up. A quarter million." She snickered. "Why, that's more than I'll make in my lifetime. And—I think folks should know that. I think you should do the interview."

I stopped her with both hands between us. "Listen, I'm not the best speaker for anyone. I would let you interview me, but it wouldn't matter. I got kicked off the team."

"What?" Sandra shifted forward on her chair, made a hearty plop of her coffee cup on a little wicker table between her seat and Bill's. "You're kidding. I just saw that page you've got on the social networks. You didn't mention anything about it."

"What page?" I asked, snapping my head upward. My eyes worked back and forth between hers. I pressed a palm to my chest. "The one Gabe does for me?"

"No, it's about the Redneck Run and Boar Mountain Resort. You've got a big following. *I* follow you." She tipped her head like she was talking to my great grandma who calls Pops by his dad's name and tucks her dresses into her underwear.

"I follow you," Bill agreed. I blanched. Is somebody pretending to be me? Because Gabe is the only one I know who made me a social media site before the Redneck Run last year. It has nothing to do with Boar Mountain Resort. Whenever he comes to visit his parents, he drags along his camera and takes pictures of me running or working or hanging out on ATVs with Kenny. I am an open book. I answer questions all the time, sometimes a little too intimate for me like what kind of underwear I like to run in or the favorite of kids—what do I do if I have to pee in the middle of running long distances? There is no secrecy in my life; it is plastered for all to see except one thing— nobody knows of my romantic relationship with Bear.

"Well, somebody at the resort must do it. I've never seen it. Missus Vega doesn't believe I'm a good representative for the team." I turned my attention to Bill. I couldn't read his expression. "I'm sorry. It wouldn't be much of a story if it was about an out-of-work, ex-runner." I forced a giggle. It came out like a lame huff.

"No," Bill leaned in, set elbows on his knees. His shirt sleeves were rolled to his elbows. He rubbed his chin with his fingers. "I think therein lies the story. It's just you and me, not a lot of reporters shoving a camera in your face."

"I'll do it if Sandra will donate some blankets to a cause," I decided out loud. "There's a bunch of homeless people living up the road off the highway. I could only dig up three blankets from my house. I could use a few more."

## Chapter 12—Shattered Dreams

I came home to an irritable Pops standing at the doorway at five in the morning after I spent the evening and most of the night with Gabe, Ben, and Sandra. Bear is standing behind Pops looking all tired and smug. "What's he doing here?" I grunt. Pops ignores me. He's lugged Kaylee up on his hip. She's tired-rubbing her eyes with one fist, and she's looking from him to me, mirroring his scowl.

"You're in trouble, Bam Bam," she taunts me. She calls me Bam Bam because Pops always leaves the bathroom door partially closed at night with a tiny night light on so Kaylee can get to the toilet. After she takes a pee at one in the morning, she turns off the light. I go in at five to get ready for work or running, and I bash into the edge of the open door. It flies open and makes a bam-bam sound against the bathroom cupboard.

"You're wearing my beads, bratface," I tell her in return while I watch her reach up and fondly pat the Mardi Gras beads I got at the dollar store. She must have forgotten to slip them back into my drawer after she confiscated them from my room last night.

"Did you lose your cell phone again?" Pops grumbles, shifting Kaylee to the right. "I've been worried sick about you! I almost called the police station and filed a missing person report."

"Really? I've only been gone twelve hours," I grunt suspiciously. "I'm an adult, Pops. I can come and go when I please. Even the cops will tell you that."

"Not while you're living in my house," he retorts.

"Not while you live in my house," Kaylee repeats in a growly voice and wags a finger at me.

"Under my roof, you follow my rules even when you're seventy. And my rules say that you call if you ain't going to be home when you're usually home." He mean-eyes me hard. He used to do that and I'd burst into tears and hide under the bed. Pops' fuming gaze was far worse than any spanking any kid ever got. "And *he* was worried about you too." He tosses his head toward Bear who gives me a haughty tip of chin. He thinks he's got Pops on his side. "I called him to see if you had stayed at his house—" Pops' face is angry-red. "—and find out you aren't even dating no more. And you up and decided to get a bank loan for that old house down there. You ain't even got a job."

"You ain't even got a job," Kaylee leans into Pops when I narrow my eyes at her.

"Shut up, Kaylee. How'd you know I went in for a loan, Bear?" I am seething. "You drove off before I went inside."

"Todd Bailey called. He said you looked upset when you left."

"Because he laughed at me for coming in. I would think he has no right to call you about me getting a loan. There are privacy rules."

"He meant well," Bear says. I get the impression he was laughing when he called Bear too. "You don't have a job, Brandy. Todd is right. And—and Pops is right." Stupid Bear, stupid, stupid Bear. He tries to side with Pops against me. Not the smartest thing to do. Pops snaps off his hat, scrubs a hand through his hair.

"No, he doesn't mean well. He called you so you could have a good laugh over it." I turn to Pops. "This had nothing to do with him, Pops, except he is the only one I ever told that it was my dream to buy Millie's old house other than telling Millie." I wait for Pops to groan and throw his hands into the air. He does not, just stares at me. "I wanted to make it into a restaurant. You are the one always telling me going to college was stupid and a waste of time and money. You tell me to make something of myself. I was trying to do that, not be a loser because Bear's mama kicked me off the team. But Todd Bailey seemed to believe our family spent more time failing than achieving—"

"You're not running in the Redneck Run?" Pops takes me in, then turns his head slowly to Bear and says between clenched teeth.

"Because, *boy,* she is the only one from our community representing the team. There's a lot of folks who come to that race because of her."

"There's more to it than that, *sir.*"

"Sir." Kaylee does her best copycat of Bear's deep voice.

I grit my teeth. He's such a suck up. Bear clears his throat. "I'm not justifying my mom kicking her off the team. I don't need to—she broke the rules. She cuts out of training. She doesn't get along with others on the team. She spits at Janey almost every day while running. She makes Meghan cry with the stuff she says to her. But this is not a private discussion. This was a business deal. If you have problems with the decision, you can call our marketing team."

"Call your marketing team?" Pops' head is tilted, bewildered. "I don't even know what to say to that. She was your girl, Bear. You should have supported her, talked to her and your mama if there were problems—"

"Support her?" Bear chokes down a snarky laugh. He looks at Pops with a condescending lift of chin and with a pompous glaze to his eyes. "Well, that's the pot calling the kettle black. Because you spend half the time telling her it was a waste of time going to college. Do you call that support? It isn't. Did you even know she was trying to get a loan? Probably not. I'm sure she wouldn't tell you because you'd laugh at her and tell her she'd never get it.

And support isn't making her feel guilty every time she opens the newspaper to look for a *big girl* place to live instead of a bedroom at your house."

"You've got a lot of nerve telling my Pops that considering you have someone answer for me on some stupid social network!" I scream.

"You need to leave." Pops outraged eyes are like bullets aimed at Bear. I know why. I have edged over, so I'm standing next to Pops. Bear has never spoken his mind to him like this, condescending like he's better than us. "You got no right to stand in my house as a guest and make a judgment on me and my own." He's sizing him up. Pops may not be as big as Bear, but he's protecting his little girl right now. "Get out. Now!"

I jump, startled. Bear doesn't move for the count of three. I almost feel the sweat beading on my forehead. Kaylee's eyes get all cloudy and extra sky blue like Pops' eyes. There's no doubt right then she's more Pops' kid than I will ever be. She's all princess and tiara and follows him around with a piece of his pants' leg clutched tightly in her little fist. I was always kicking his shins when I was her age and sneaking out the window to see Josh when I was a teen. I don't see her giving him gray hair as I did. She adores him. He adores her. I think she might be his spare, you know, the backup miracle kid when your first kid screws up everything like I do.

Bear walks to the couch, snatches up his jacket laying there, and stomps out. "And I want my page removed off your resort site," I growl at his back. "Nobody answers for me, especially dumbass rich people like you."

Kaylee starts yelling at him to *come back, Bear! Don't leave!* He doesn't listen to her. It isn't much more than four minutes later when Pops walks into the kitchen.

"Don't say a word." He eyes me warily when I walk in. "Go to your room or something. Let me think." I know what he's thinking: *What the hell did I do wrong with her? Why's this one so broke?*

"Pops." I start to turn but pivot back around. I realize right then he was wearing his good button down red and black flannel and a pair of new blue jeans. His hair is freshly cut. I'd caught the scent of aftershave which he's been wearing more and more these days. I sit on this a second and wonder if he's got an important meeting this morning. It's more like he was getting ready for a date. Naw. Pops doesn't date. I shake that thought. "It's not your fault. I haven't always made the best decisions. I know that. It isn't because of you. You did everything right. Don't listen to Bear. He's an ass."

"Baby, you heard what I said. And don't talk like that."

I do as he says, feeling seven-years-old when I plop down on my bed and stare at the ceiling. I feel like nothing and nobody all over again with shattered dreams laying like broken glass around my feet. I tug up my phone, search for my name. I see the site that Sandra was talking about, and I take in a breath while I scan it. There's a year's worth of chatter on it, updates, and messages from me that aren't really from me. I feel sick to my tummy because it isn't me at all making the weak replies and sterile responses. I groan and roll over in bed and toss my phone to the wall.

## Chapter 13—Welcome to Mister Smiley's

"Hello! Welcome to Mister Smiley's!" I blare that heartily into the microphone like a rock star shrieks out a song over the applause of the crowd at a concert although I'm just at the checkout counter of Mister Smiley's Super Grocery in New Alliance. It is with a lot more enthusiasm than I feel while I lean casually against the register. I feel my life getting sucked back into the same vessel of lost hope and misery I was in this same time last year.

I should be moving up, not down. I'm a half-dead nightcrawler stuck on a hook that doesn't catch a fish in the pond. At the end of the fishing trip, I'm yanked back off that hook and dropped back into the same old Styrofoam container filled with dirt and the lid closed tightly. At least last year, I aspired to climb out of that container. Now, I feel broke and more half-dead. I know everybody in town is coming into the store and judging me with the same puckered lips of distaste Kaylee gets when she's fishing with Pops and he pulls one of those deflated, mostly dead worms from the container to put on her hook. *Ain't no good ever come out of any of Ruby MacCabe's brood. We all thought this one dug her way out. But nope, she's back to working at the grocery.*

Even if I don't want to admit it, Pops and Bear are right. I need a job. Our hometown grocery is about half the size of the big-city stores. But it is the only place you can get food supplies within a thirty-mile radius, not including the overpriced stale, cheap stuff at the Quick Stop in town. It is also the only place hiring, barring the Boar Mountain Resort. Like the broken and imperfect toys nobody wants on the Island of Misfit Toys in the Rudolph Christmas show Kaylee likes, we're what's left over that *Santa Smiley* offers jobs when we can't get hired at the resort.

Consequently, I applied at Smiley's a week ago and started immediately. Seven days into my stint, I've moved up to the highest echelon of employee status—Check Out Girl. It is much to the disappointment of Gayle Meacham and Margie Prather who felt they were higher in the pecking order since they'd been there twelve years. Both women were vying for the position.

However, Mister Smiley looked relieved when I applied even though I'd taken the long way around the mountain the day I'd stopped into the store in mid-run to avoid the SALE PENDING sign in front of Piper's old place. No one can blame me. The Pipers have hired Pops and half my family to take down the old building, gutting it as part of the sale agreement. *Money is money, baby girl,* Pops had said when I confronted him the other day and called him a traitor after seeing his truck and Kenny's truck parked out beside the building.

*And we need the money to pay the bills. Life ain't always built on daydreams.*

I was sweat-soaked. Mister Smiley had waved a hand in front of his face to fend the odor. But Gayle is always sneaking out the back to smoke cigarettes near the dumpster. She's left the cash register unmanned twice. Somebody's dipped hands into the little twenty-dollar bill holders and swiped a couple of hundred dollars. Margie is related to just about every person in this county, and she gives unauthorized discounts to her family when they come to the store—a loaf of bread here and four full-size turkeys there slide just above the scanner, unscanned and unpaid.

Eighty-something Dora Pingleton with blue-gray hair has spent about forty seconds waiting for the automatic sliding glass door. The doors she's trying to enter, they tend to open just as someone starts to step in, then make a jerky stop before snapping shut again. People take that first step forward with confidence. After the door starts to close, they whip back a bit jaded and wary. Sometimes these shenanigans go on for three or four tries while the worn-out motion detection sensors correctly trigger someone is walking through, then fake-triggers it was just a scam. Up and back, up and back, it's like the first step of the Whip and Nae Nae dance caught in a loop and playing over and over until it finally opens. By then, the customer is just livid and gives me a reproachful glare like just because I'm stifling a laugh, I've got some remote-control device to work the door and humiliate them.

Missus Pingleton finally jumps through with her chihuahua partially stuffed into her purse. She was already shaken, but when she catches my blaring voice from the speakers on the ceiling, she jumps at my deafening roar, startled. I think the whole ordeal is way too much for her. She gets a glazed look in her eyes, and I follow their trail as they climb upward to the drop ceiling above us. It scares the crap out of me for a minute because she has a pacemaker. "I think I killed her," I forget to move my lips from the microphone. My mumble evolves into a roar that echoes through the entire grocery store.

"My God, Shirley," Mister Smiley reaches out and covers the microphone with his palm. He's got fuzzy eyebrows like huge black woolly worm caterpillars straggling across the roads in September. When he gets cross, they wiggle like they are going to come alive, squirm up to the top of his basketball-shaped head, and snuggle into the crown of dusky, fuzzy hair on top.

His hand cupping the mic makes a muddled roar and everyone freezes including Ellen Wells who is sweeping along the aisles. "You said you could handle this until my girls come back. Can you, or can you not?" *My girls* are, of course, the four Boar Mountain Resort Dream Team runners who are usually the Check Out Girls. They get the next few months off for training until September when the Redneck Run is over. Mister Smiley has forgiven me for mouthing off to him last year so I got fired. He's desperate for somebody who knows how to run a register and will not turn him into whatever grocery patrol there is out there that would send him to jail for paying me less than minimum wage until *his girls* come back.

"Say what I told you and that's it. Don't improvise, for heaven's sakes! Just say the rest: *If there's anything our patrons need, they just have to ask our courteous staff!*" he goes on, prompting me with his pink too-puffy lips that spit at me with every word. "*We're here for our loyal customers! Mister Smiley's, where everyone within a forty-mile radius shops!*"

"That seems like an awfully big mouthful to say, Mister Smiley. If ten people come in at once, do I say it ten times?" I sigh in relief as Missus Pingleton blinks back to life, continuing her stride. "You know she is bringing in a dog—is that allowed by the health department?"

"We just pretend we don't see it, Shirley." I guess today I'm Shirley. Mister Smiley never remembers my name. Sometimes I tell him it's something different to confuse him. Yesterday, when I left Pops', I told him I was Candy. Today, I'm Shirley. "She's been a customer for forty years. We allow some flexibility unless the health department comes, then we pretend like we didn't see the dog, got it?"

"Yep. Got it." Mister Smiley gives me a bland purse of lips before his eyes skid slowly toward the doors opening again. Bradley Devereauxs is slipping between the slow-moving entry in a navy-blue hoodie sweatshirt with the hoodie swept over his red-blonde head. He's got hands stuffed into pockets and a backpack over his shoulder. He's my dead ex-husband's youngest brother. He's seventeen. Last I heard, he was living with his always-wanting-to-kick-my-butt sister, Crystal. His mama, Elizabeth, died. It was just a week before her last boyfriend kicked him out of her trailer. Bradley tends to come in with an empty bag and leave with a full one. It infuriates Mister Smiley because he can't seem to catch him red-handed.

"Now that's one you got to watch." Mister Smiley leans in guardedly, nods his head toward Bradley whose eyes stare at the floor. "Keep an eye on him. You catch someone like that stealing something from the shelves, and I might give you a ten-cent raise. I'm giving you the opportunity to grow in this position until my girls come back. Ten-cents. That's a lot, right?" He gives me a nudge-nudge on my arm, a wink, and a nod. I restrain from giving him a nudge-nudge on his arm, a wink, and a nod and telling him: *you're kidding me.* I need this job.

There isn't another in a forty minute drive.

Not twenty minutes later, though, I am helping Ellen Wells stock the candy bar shelves, and Mister Smiley gets on the microphone. I hear: "Shirley, there's a wet spot in the cereal aisle. I need you to clean it up."

"You know it's dog pee, don't you?" Ellen asks me when I groan out loud. "I'm glad you're here now." She follows me through the big metal doors of the back room where the supply cart and boxes of inventory are kept. "Not that I want you to clean up Missus Pingleton's dog's pee, but them girls that you're covering for, they don't do crap," she tells me over my shoulder while I snatch up a roll of paper towels and the mop. "They never have to clean anything up. I'm the one always stuck with it."

She follows me back out the metal doors and to the cereal aisle where I stare down at a teeny yellow wet spot and a tiny brown chihuahua turd. I hand her the mop. "Everybody else said you was all highfalutin with marrying that boy from up the mountain. Not me. I said you'd be back here. You won the race. You showed them. Don't listen to Gayle and Margie. They're just jealous you got the job. I'll let you know when they spit in your bottled water in the fridge. I got your back." I look up wondering how many times they'd spit in my water. She tosses up her hands. "You come back home."

"Home." I kneel and unroll a wad of paper

towels. "Welcome to the Island of Misfit Toys."

"What?" Ellen peers down at me questioning. I don't want to explain the entire story. "Uh oh." I barely look up at Ellen when she says that. Then I freeze. I catch the faint edges of flirty-woman giggles and a deeper, gruffer laugh blending along just as the sound of the automatic doors open and close. It was only a matter of time when they came into the store.

It's Amelia's four highly overrated Dream Team girls sweeping into the store in the same way puffed-up princesses will walk among the peasants in an impoverished village with a piece of cake in one hand while peering snobbishly down at the starving waifs. Meghan and Michelle start on past the end of the aisle, both with arms out on either side like they are playing follow the leader and trying to touch the cereal boxes they pass. They stop swiftly enough that Janie and Carrie smash into them with a burst of cackles. All four latch on to each other and peer down the aisle at me in a fit of high-pitched giggles. The four always act silly-drunk when they are around people, giddy middle school girls playing dumb to please the boys. They proceed down the aisle toward me laughing and whispering amongst themselves with palms cupped to lips. Not once, but twice, I see Meghan turning to look behind her.

"Are you mopping the floor on hands and knees?" Meghan asks as she stops just short of me. She pushes her blonde hair behind one ear and leans over, staring at me. "Ew, what is that?" She gasps and steps back, hauling the other three with her in two exaggerated yanks.

"It's what I'm going to shove into your face if you don't leave me alone, Megs," I say softly, rising slowly. I hold the towel out with the poo, dangle it in front of her nose.

"You can't talk to her like that!" Michelle presses a hand to her chest while Meghan flaps her hand near her nose and turns her head away. "She's a customer. We'll complain to Mister Smiley and get you fired. Apologize to her *right now*." Michelle scolds, pushes my wrist away with her fingers.

"No," I say. "Don't touch me."

"You're jealous because I've got Beau right under the tip of my thumb." Meghan holds out those last three words and wiggles her head. She lifts up her fist, thumb popping out and pointing down in slow motion, an embellished arc before she twists it back and forth like she's smooshing a little bug beneath. "Dollar Store Dolly, you're nothing but redneck trash from the top of your head to the bottom of your feet. And you'll always be poor white trash."

"You know," I interrupt. "There might be a few people who think you shit rainbows and multi-colored glitter, but I know better. It just *looks* like it from the outside. But appearances eventually don't lie. It's fake. I see it. Inside, you're nothing but four gold-digging, vain, cold-hearted piece of crap bitches who don't care about anybody but yourselves. You may go to Holy Trinity every week, but you do it as a cover for all the evil going on inside those little heads of yours. You know what? I'm going to be watching you. Every step you make. I'm just biding my time to catch you. I'm going to be looking for that little bit of smoke coming off your evil feet when they step inside the church doors. One day, you're going to walk into the dollar store you sneak into to buy the little bottles of glitter you eat and food coloring you drink so you poop your phony goodness and—"

"Shut up!" Janey's hand reaches out, pulls back to slap me. "You're nothing but trash, just like she says. Trash! You ain't going to be no better than that drunk, drugged-up mama of yours and—" I stop her blow with a nimble flick of my hand to her wrist, snatching on tightly.

"You don't want to do that, Janey," I angry-whisper in a gravelly voice while she tries to twist away with teeth gritting. "You don't want to start a fight with me. Because one day, I'm going to be that big ol' shark swimming around in the water and you're going to be one of those little fish that follow it around waiting for a bite from the food I catch. I'm going to look down and remember all the crap you four give me. I'm just going to gobble you up."

"That'll be the day." Carrie snickers, but still

looks a little frightened, unsure because I haven't released Janey's wrist. She reaches up and touches Janey's hand as if, by some magic, it will make me release her.

"Let her go," Meghan's eyes are looking from my hand to Janey's now-red wrist. "We're going to go tell Mister Smiley that you started a fight. He's going to fire your butt."

"He would know you're lying."

"Oh, how? It is our word against yours—four against one." Janey finally snaps her wrist back.

"Maybe Amelia Vega is blind to your batshit crazy. I'm not. I got proof—" I turn slightly and point to the security mirror and video camera on the wall at the end of the aisle. "There's a security camera, dummy." I nod toward the camera. As I do, I see a sideways view of Bradley Devereauxs snapping his eyes around shiftily in Aisle 3, next to the aisle where we are standing. He sloughs off his backpack, whips it around, and slides something into the pocket.

"Crud." I watch him slink down the aisle and disappear from the security mirror. I spin back around on my heels. Disregarding the four girls, I push my way between them to make my way to the end of the aisle, assuming Mister Smiley would be at the cash register. He's not. But Bradley is making his way toward the front door, worn tennis shoes stepping up a beat.

I do the only thing I know to do. I snatch up the microphone. "Mister Smiley? Mister Smiley, you are needed at the front register!" I whisper it too loudly. Bradley passes the register. I see his eyes get wide before he reaches up, tugs the front of his hoodie and they fade away into the darkness beneath. "Mister Smiley!"

My voice was booming when Mister Smiley comes red-faced stomping from Aisle 6. I'm jabbing my finger toward the door that is closing behind the hooded figure. "I think he stole something," my voice bellows into the microphone. "I saw him. What do we do?" Somewhere in the back of my head, though, I'm wondering if the ten cent an hour raise for turning in one of my ex-relatives will be worth a butt-beating from Crystal.

Mister Smiley is certainly not in shape. He's got all the signs of someone who is one step away from a heart attack. He's Santa Claus pudgy around the belly. His ankles swell because he sits in his chair too much. When he runs for the door and does the dance back and forth and back and forth while it opens and closes over and over, I see his bald scalp getting redder and redder. I think his arteries might burst party popper style out the top of his head.

I jump to attention and push my hand on the door. I burst past Mister Smiley, see Bradley's hat falling back when he makes a snap of head back to see me high-tailing it after him at a full-out sprint with my grocery apron flying up and down in the wind.

## Chapter 14—Catching A Thief, Kind of

I have to jump the hood of one dingy car whose driver jams on the brakes just past the faded white lines of the crosswalk in front of the store. I blast past two shopping carts. A second vehicle is lazy-parking in the fire zone. I use the bumper to jump over the grocery cart corral giving me a couple of extra steps toward my goal, Bradley.

It's a big black truck I recognize as Bear's dually truck because it has those annoying too-bright LED headlights that make everybody blind-swerve coming down the road toward them. It's also got a custom vinyl decal on each door that says: *Boar Mountain Resort. Find Your Adventure!* It is irritating that the passengers Bear must have dropped off at the front door are the hometown runners for the Redneck Run. Yet, they are too lazy to walk the twenty-odd-feet like everyone else including the people in wheelchairs, from regulated parking lot spaces to the store. Such, I use the side like a board so that it bucks a little up and down. When I cross over, I give a random shopping cart left along the sidewalk a casual kick and the handle smacks into Bear's back door.

I'm a runner. Bradley is a smoker. It doesn't take me four more minutes to catch him, tearing up between a couple old brick electric company buildings in the valley where the town is settled. I work my way up a considerable incline of row houses toward the outskirts of town and where the mountain starts to rise. I stop him with what Kenny calls my *superwoman dive*; he always said it with a lot of sarcasm hanging on his lips. It isn't as graceful as it sounds. When we were kids and we got mad at each other, I used to come rushing for him. I think my depth perception is off a little. I could never judge the distance well between us. I would run up behind Kenny and clobber him head-on, knocking him over.

That's what I do to Bradley, smashing into his back. However, for lack of balance, I grab him around the waist. We both tumble down a slight incline before coming to a rest in a shallow ditch with an old concrete pipe. He rolls on his backpack twice before it wriggles off his skinny shoulders and lays there between us. I jump up, wobble forward to grab the backpack. A dog barks from the subdivision and a couple of cars pass, none slow. Then, I hear the sirens.

He pushes himself to his feet. I think he's going to bolt or punch me. I haven't seen him in probably a year, and he grew five inches and lost the little kid look. Of all Josh's little brothers and sisters, he was never the one who punched or pinched or kicked my shins. He was always the quiet one, and the one everybody seemed to forget because he didn't get into trouble like the rest. And here he is, just like the rest of them.

His lips are curled feral-kitten-style. He looks so much like Josh I'm floored. He's got the Devereauxs freckled nose, deep red hair sticking up a little in the back and blue eyes. I stand there dumbfounded like I'm staring at a ghost. It isn't just that. Now I've caught him, I don't know what to do with him. It appears by the way he's wavering with the grass floating off his jacket he's as unsure as I am.

"You're in big trouble, Bradley. What the hell were you thinking?" I reach out, snatch up the backpack, and out rolls a plastic container of Baby First Infant Formula.

"Crystal had a baby. She ran out of the formula they gave her at the hospital. It's been a whole day." He's out of breath. "The baby's been crying. It's going to starve." Bradley's dancing foot to foot with the panic of a deer spooked by the headlights of a semi-truck coming straight at it. The sirens are coming closer. Mister Smiley must have called the cops. I snatch up the formula and toss it hard at the first place I see which is into the hole of the concrete pipe. I look over my shoulder where the growl of a truck catches my attention. Damn if there isn't a black dually pulled in there already.

"Did he see that?" I turn, eyes wide.

"Probably."

"Okay, stay." I look at Bradley, but it is Josh's terrified stone-cold blue eyes staring back at me. "If you run, it will be worse." I don't get to say more. Bear is getting out of the truck. The cop car, with sirens running and lights flashing, pulls up to the brim. I'm shaken. However, I hold up the backpack and wiggle it a little upside-down while I take four steps to the vehicles. I cringe. It is Dee Reynolds who hunkers out of the door, pushing one uniformed leg out slowly and sliding on his mirrored sunglasses. He reminds me of the sadistic guard in aviator sunglasses on Pops' favorite Florida chain gang movie, Cool Hand Luke.

Where the last town cop, Big Don, was short and his nickname something of a town joke whispered behind his back, Dee *is* a giant. He is also what my uncle calls *meaner than two wildcats with their tails tied together*. He doesn't like the folks from Fire Mountain like Bradley and me. He tends to throw us—the Devereauxs, MacCabes, and McAllisters—all in the same pot like we're different kind of vegetables in a soup that cook well together. Usually, we don't. We may be related by blood or marriage, but we don't hang out together. If there are levels built around Dee Reynolds's caste system in our community, Bradley Devereauxs would be the second from the bottom. I would be last. I not only tattled on his brother, but he's the uncle of Michelle and Meghan, my rivals.

"Okay, so I was a bit—quick to judge," I holler out, wiggling the bag and hoping nothing else falls out. Phew. Nothing. "There's nothing in the bag. I was wrong." And still, I wince. Mister Smiley is slowly pulling up to the curb behind the cop car. That's just what I need, somebody else to lie to right now. "There wasn't anything." I watch as Bear comes around the truck. He always pats the hood when he rounds it. He is expressionless. His passenger side door opens to expose Rush Gordon sliding out. He's taking in the situation.

"Please don't let them beat the shit out of me," Bradley's voice breaks. I see his concern. The wall of big men looks like a pack of dogs getting ready to tear up two teeny kittens.

"And have Crystal, then, beat the crap out of me?" I try to waylay the situation to ease his fears. "On that one, I'll pass."

Rush Gordon makes a point of getting to us first. He outwalked Dee Reynolds (who was making a beeline right toward me with eyes dead set on my face and his fingers tickling his side pistol), Mister Smiley, and Bear by four steps and he's laughing like this whole mess is the funniest thing he's ever heard. He snatches up Mister Smiley's hand and introduces himself. Suddenly, Mister Smiley is starstruck, gushing with admiration, a teenager at a rock concert who just got noticed by the hot drummer. He forgets that I might have tackled a kid who just came in to get a pop and decided not to get it.

I get to act all embarrassed and stutter apologies to everybody for screwing up and thinking Bradley stole something. Bradley fades away, slapping his backpack over his shoulder like he *didn't* steal something even though he did. He disappears. I watch Dee's eyes narrow and follow before he drops them down to me. "You're Ruby MacCabe's girl." That's all he says like he was making a mental note of my infamous family tree and where I fit into the limbs for future arrests. After, Bear says he'll drive me back to the grocery store only a few blocks away. I decline, but he leans in and tells me if he is going to be involved in a felony, he wants to know what transpired. He saw me toss something in the pipe.

"So—what happened here?" Bear looks at me in the back seat from his rearview mirror. "Because you put Rush in a really bad position. He could get into a lot of trouble for lying to a cop." Bear's got Josh's eyes too, although they are brown. It's the slant because they had the same mom, Elizabeth Devereauxs, and his dad was Amelia Vega's husband. He was adopted by Amelia Vega when he was just a baby. He doesn't talk about it. I doubt there are more than three people who know the truth.

"I didn't lie." Rush shrugs. He's got a soft grin. He turns his head so he can see me over the seat. "But sometimes life's like driving on a foggy night, right?" He's got a deep southern drawl, soft, smooth, and sweet like honey. "You're just guessing there's a turn ahead. You don't always have time to slow down and think it out. You've got to use your best judgment and make the turn and hope you made the best decision. Most of the time, I do okay. Other times, I go off the road into the dark." He's got a twinkle in his blue eyes, gives me a warm-hearted wink. "And I find a bit of adventure."

"Well," Bear grunts. "With Brandy back there, if you're looking for adventure on some dark path, you're in for one heck of a ride." I feel my face turn a hot shade of red. My eyes snap to the back of Bear's head. He hasn't been mean-spirited in a long time. Did he realize what he just said? I can't tell. Rush shrugs it off.

"I'm well aware of Brandy Devereauxs's achievements." Rush turns and settles into the seat. "That was the reason I signed on with Boar Mountain for the Run. I like when a deck is stacked against a team. It makes the win that much sweeter, right? Your story and that of the others on your team last year were inspiring to so many people, so many kids. You beat the odds. You made folks believe they can beat the odds too even if they've got no good cards to play. Do you know how often I see places slip in a couple of aces to stack a deck now? Sports for kids are even cutthroat." He looks over to Bear who is quiet, then to me. "And it's no big deal. Do you know that kid?"

I settle back into the seat, drink in his words with uncertainty. I wondered if he knows I am not running in the event. His words implied he didn't. Or maybe he was talking about last year. I look to the rearview mirror and can only see Bear's eyes looking into the windshield.

"Yes, I know him," I answer slowly. I feel as if I'm holding a deck of cards and asking to deal them out, but I don't know the game. Rush is smiling big white teeth. I smile back. "He lives up the other side of Fire Mountain. It was baby formula he took. His sister just had a baby and can't afford the food." I eye Bear. "That's why I tossed it. Officer Reynolds would have sent him to jail." I chew on my lip, imagine that baby crying and crying. "Bear," I say quickly. "I got eighteen bucks in my purse at the grocery. If I gave it to you, would you go to the Quickie Stop, get some formula and diapers?"

"When do you get off work?" He glares at me.

"I've got an hour."

"Sure. I'll be back in an hour with your stuff."

"Can you go up and get Pops' old truck and load it in the back?"

"What?"

"There's no way we're taking this new, monster truck with resort decals displayed all over the sides up there like they're getting charity from the resort or something."

## Chapter 15—Sneak-Dropping Groceries and the Background for a Trip with Bear

Bear picks me up after work in Pops' old truck. He's alone. I make him go around to the passenger side even though he looks good sitting inside appearing all homegrown boy in a beat-up pickup. He's got his sleeves rolled up to his elbows. His hair is windblown because he's got the windows rolled down—the air-conditioner doesn't work. Country music is playing low on the radio, scratchy and with one working speaker on the driver's side.

"I got the stuff." He jabs a thumb toward the back seat while I climb into the driver's seat. I take in the entire back seat filled with well over three-hundred dollars' worth of groceries including a whole ham.

"Holy hell, boy, what were you thinking?" I gasp.

"I overdid it again, didn't I?" he asks. His voice is flatline, soft but deep.

"You are high-cotton, Bear." I force a low laugh, nod.

"That's—*rich*, right?"

No, it is rich *and snobby*. I don't want to fight with him while I put the truck in gear. "Yeah, sure." I want to *be with* him. I want to forget the things I heard about him and Meghan, pretend they didn't happen. I want to pretend he didn't kick me off the team the second we broke it off. Except, I'm not that person. I've seen my mama sitting by the window of her trailer way too many times waiting for somebody's husband or some one-night stand to come back for her, ride up on a white horse, and carry her off into the sunset. They never showed up. Nobody ever put a real diamond ring on her finger, not even Pops. I'm not going to be my mama.

"Yeah, Bear, you did. Sneak-dropping a box of diapers and some baby formula at the door is one thing but dumping half the Quickie Stop on the porch is another."

"I went to the grocery two towns over. I hated to only spend twenty bucks on the drive. But I thought it would look suspicious buying formula at Smiley's considering the situation. Quickie Stop didn't have squat."

"That's not the point. Crystal's family is prideful."

"*Pride goeth before destruction, and a haughty spirit before a fall.* That's from the Bible, Proverbs."

"You want to tell Crystal Devereauxs that quote?" I ask him with an incredulous furrow of my brow. "I dare you to do that, Beauregard Rodriguez Vega. I dare you. But you better have a bulletproof vest on when you do it because she'll shoot a hole right through your chest."

He does not relay that information to Crystal. Bear is silent. It's a drop-and-run. Bear unloaded everything on the porch. I watch him peer curiously at the half-sister he's never formally met and probably never will. "We don't need no charity," she grunts hardly coming out the door. "Take it back."

"Then look at it as a gift, Crystal," I grumble back, just as distastefully. This is the proper etiquette we must follow, a sparring of equally poor who must feign they are negotiating junk that would be better tossed in the trash. "I'm not taking it back. It got dumped at Pops' for Kaylee. She's too big," I lie. She knows I'm lying. "Use it or give it away. I don't give a rat's ass. You're just the closest neighbor. I'm not lugging it around all over this mountain to see who wants for something. Pops said to give it away. I don't have time to play Santa Claus."

"*I'll* give it away."

She won't. We both know it. Bear doesn't. He brought it up when I started to take him back to Pops' to pick up his truck and be on his way. I wave it away with my hand. He tells me he's got nothing to do and he'll ride along wherever I'm going. "If you take me up there, I won't get out. Take me with you." I sat at a stop sign, the crossroads tapping my finger on the steering wheel. I should go left, take him to his truck. But I go right.

I'm gripping Pops' steering wheel with both hands. My arms are shivering and jerking with every jarring rock beneath the worn tires. "If you stay in this truck after I asked you not to, I'm going to pretend you're not here." Driving his old truck up and down graveled mountain roads is like my Aunt Jenny and me juggling and trying to move my papaw's jumbo jigsaw puzzle from the kitchen table and up the stairs to his bedroom when he got the flu last January so he could continue piecing it together. I feel like at any second, it's just going to explode and collapse into a million pieces.

"Fine." Bear folds his arms across his chest. "Where are we going?"

"I'm not answering that question." I'm not. I don't want to answer it because I don't want to tell Bear that I'm researching Katelyn Freeman's murder. It will just be one more task he'll decide is too difficult for me to achieve. Maybe it is. I tried to call her parents and ask them questions. I simply said: Hey, *my name is Brandy and I'm trying to find out information on Katelyn for*—and bam! Her daddy slammed down the phone so hard, it nearly busted my eardrum. I think they couldn't offer much anyway. I was a teenager. I never told Pops anything.

Then I had made a little detour yesterday after heading over to my Aunt Jenny's house on my way home after work to drop off six of the megapacks of toilet paper they had on sale at Mister Smiley's. One of the benefits of working at Mister Smiley's is that I get a fifty-percent discount off the bent, dented, and overstock groceries. Missus Smiley accidentally ordered sixty cases of Sashay Ultra Soft Luxury Toilet Paper. It's one of Aunt Jenny's favorites. I bought her two cases.

After dropping off the toilet paper and realizing I was only about twenty minutes away from Quail Hollow, I got the sudden inspiration to stop at the Quail Hollow Police Department and look up Jack Keeling like Gabe suggested. I called Gabe. Gabe talked to Ben. Ben called his mama, Sandra. Sandra called Jack. I set up an impromptu appointment to meet with him.

Jack has a state highway patrol haircut, buzzed high and tight and shaved to the skin on the sides. He's got a teeny nose and laughing eyes. Ben's mom is charmed by him. Sandra used to make sure I prepared a double batch of blueberry pancakes for him. Although he's not handsome, he's somewhat of a smooth talker and always tucked a five-dollar tip in my pocket when he left the restaurant.

He's thin, maybe a little too thin. I couldn't help but wonder if he's like Crystal's mom who started a meth lab in her trailer seven years ago this November. See, Crystal's mom was smart by any standards. I suppose Elizabeth Devereauxs's IQ was through the roof. My aunt told me she went to high school with her. Elizabeth was so smart that the teachers were afraid to teach her because she also had a mouth on her and would make fun of them if they got something wrong. But growing up on the side of a mountain with a drunk daddy, a mama who stripped at the Kitty Cat Gentleman's Club, and nobody to show her how to fill out college applications in the 1970s didn't get her the best foundation for higher education. There was no way she could get a student loan. The odds were against their family from the start. They couldn't get jobs at the resort, didn't farm, and were the whipping boys for anybody who broke the law when the cops couldn't quite pinpoint who did it. In all honesty, Crystal's mom would be considered savvy if her business had been running a franchise of gas stations throughout the Midwest instead of making meth in her trailer and dealing drugs. Regardless, while Elizabeth Devereauxs was smart enough to develop a successful, lucrative business, she wasn't smart enough to *not* dabble in meth herself. She died a few months ago from an overdose.

Jack sat me down in a stuffy interrogation room reeking of a detective who dabbled in filching small enough amounts of narcotics from local drug busts from the evidence lockers at the station as not to be noticed by the other cops, but just enough to keep his addiction at bay. That's what I thought when he slapped a navy blue 3-ring binder down between us. He looked a lot like Crystal's mom the last time I saw her, pale in the face and skinny. He patted the binder with one hand, let his fingers play on it one at a time.

"The big question is—what is this sudden interest in Katelyn Freeman?" he asked me. "Are you writing a book?" He seemed to think this was funny and chuckled. I huffed a laugh along.

"I'm looking into it for a friend," I told him.

"And this friend—?"

"Asked me not to divulge his or her name," I answered.

"Well, let me be direct. If you talked to anyone in this office seventeen years ago, they would tell you it was a closed case. We knew who committed the crime. Marcus Freeman murdered his sister, killed her dead with not one, but twelve bashes of a baseball bat to the back of her head. She wasn't dead the first time, must have screamed or cried out to him. She wasn't dead on the second hit. By the third, she was out cold. After that, it was overkill. Freeman was arrested for it and placed in jail for the rest of his life. Case closed. However, after a few years, this monster who murdered Katelyn was released from prison. By then, we had no new evidence, and it became what was called a cold case. However, we all know who did it. It is not cold at all. All the evidence we had kept in the office was lost in a fire nine years ago. This information is all that remains.

Case closed."

I was listening intently, watched his hand slide the binder toward me slowly, then slowly pull it back. I found it strange that all the evidence was lost in a fire. Did they not have a fire safe locker to store it? Over and over, he teased me, each time giving me a lop-sided grin. "What do you want to know, Brandy Devereauxs, who makes the bestest blueberry pancakes in the whole world?"

I hesitated. I wasn't sure how to take this man who was sweet-smiling me one second. Then, next, he's baiting me in the same way Kenny tries to drag me down with him when he's in a bad mood and tells me it looks like I got *hit with an ugly stick* just because I woke up with my hair sticking in the air. "I don't know. Everything, I guess. I read all that in the newspaper. I don't know what to believe is true or not.

"You don't believe what I'm telling you?"

"I was implying I was not sure the *newspapers* had the correct story." The conversation was awkward. I wished I'd never came to the police station while I was sitting there. "There are some things that aren't clear— like the location where the murder took place." I offer gingerly.

"They don't mention it because we don't know. We took samples from over twelve cars and trucks from friends and families of the

Freemans. We found no blood residue. We think she might have been dragged into Stone Cold Creek and beaten to death there."

"Okay," I went on. "What led you to believe it was the brother and why not anyone else? What was his motive?"

"Listen," Jack Keeling sat back, crossed one leg over another. "I'm just going to say it. I like the Wrights. They give all us enforcement officers a good deal on food when we go to their restaurant. They are nice folks. Sandra gave me a call and asked for the favor. But I'm not going to do anything to help that monster if that's why you're doing this. He is going back to jail. I guarantee it. Is that who hired you? Or is it somebody in his family?"

"I'm not at liberty to discuss my client—"

"If you don't tell me certain things, why would you expect that I would offer up information? I, personally, was the detective in charge of the team investigating the murder. He was freed because of flawed evidence. I am continuing to collect evidence—"

"And maybe I can help you out with that," I offered. Then I poked a finger at just the edge of the blue binders he was still caressing with his hand "Can I look at your binder or not?"

"You can see some of it, not all. Because it is still considered an open case, there is some information, confidential evidence, that we are withholding in the case. We need to protect some witnesses also." Jack Keeling had allowed me ten minutes with the binder while he hovered overhead. I took twenty-two pictures with my phone until he looked up at a clock in the hallway and said it was time for him to attend a meeting. It was the same moment, the page flipped. I saw a horrifying image, a closeup of Katelyn's head, hair splayed to the side and the scalp and part of her forehead bloodied and bashed. I could barely see her nose and one half-closed eye staring into nothingness. I couldn't help but gape at it. She was dead. It was gory with marks like someone had taken a kitchen meat tenderizer mallet and buried it into the side of her head, whacking it over and over and over like it was nothing more than a boneless chicken breast from the deli fridge. A baseball bat? No, I've seen meat with those same bruises. I think Jack Keeling's not telling me the truth.

"No, you can't take a picture of that—"

He didn't know I did. I nodded, tucked my phone back against my chest. Then, the meeting got strange.

"During the investigation, what was the reason you believed Marcus Freeman killed his sister?"

"It was drug-related."

"He was looking for drugs or dealing them, and she wasn't paying?"

"She was stealing money for him to pay for

his habit. That's all, Brandy. That's all I'm allowed to give you."

I stood up and thanked him. I have never heard anything bad about this man. Ben's mom dotes on him almost like he's her son. But as I took a step toward the door, he grabbed my arm firmly and gave it a little shake like he was reprimanding a child. "Be careful who you invite into your home," Jack whispered hotly near my ear. It was almost a threat. "Shrewd people can fool you in many ways. Satan wants nothing more than to find an open door."

I hit the front glass doors nearly running, the sunshine poured on my face and nearly blinded me. I blinked past the light, saw a red Blazer just like the one that pulled into the gravel next to me at Stone Cold Creek the other day. I followed the hood of the vehicle to a small sign directly in front of the parking space. It said: *Parking for Bob Keeling, Sergeant*. Then it occurred to me I've seen that Blazer a third time. It was the night in the parking lot at the Crazy Kettle when I met with Marcus Freeman. There was a red Blazer near the front then. They must be following him. Now that they saw me with Marcus, I wondered if they were trailing me.

"Hey, don't let them get to you." The deep woman's voice had wafted along with the thick scent of puffed cigarette beneath the small awning where I was hovering between its darkness and the patch of sunshine just one step away on the sidewalk. She was standing in the smoking area for employees. There was an industrial outside ashtray/garbage can near her right elbow. "It's been a slap in the face for the force since they released Freeman."

I had turned, ready to take my next step. I was staring at a fifty-something woman with one arm crooked and fingers pressing a cigarette to her lips. She had city worker clothes—a white blouse and blue pants. A nameplate on her right breast stated: Jayne Ward. "It's the anniversary of Katelyn Freeman's death tomorrow—June 29th. We don't got a single cold case in this town. But folks wanna make her murder up to be one. Things get a little edgy here about this time."

"A little?" I furrowed my brow. "He was a psycho."

She chuckled. "Yeah, you did come through those doors like someone was chasing you. But there's always a local news station that calls for updates. It wasn't ten minutes after you contacted us, Joyce Acres with the Daily Regional called. She wanted to do an interview at Froggy Lake. It gets them all riled up."

"At the campground there?"

"Naw, the lake—far end by Stone Cold Creek. Somebody sets up a cross and flowers there every year on the anniversary."

"The newspapers say she was found on the bank—a pull-off. The story of a worker finding her was really detailed," I challenge her story. "I saw a picture of them bagging her body."

"Well, because that's what they thought early on. She was killed closer to an old shelter where the creek and Froggy Lake are close together. Police think she was dragged to the other side by the pull-off to hide her body in the grass, head officers in the wrong direction. She was killed closer to Froggy Lake, then dragged up toward the road."

"You don't know who leaves the flowers?"

"Don't know. Don't care as long as they don't call Joyce and make a big thing about it again. Five years ago, somebody saw the flowers. People started talking and remembering those flowers have been put there since that girl was murdered." She stubbed out her cigarette in the ashtray. She leaned in toward me, cigarette-and-bologna-sandwich-breath wafting toward my nostrils. "That's public information. But here's my opinion on the murder. Freeman was high when he did it. I think Katelyn wouldn't steal that money and told him she wouldn't do it as he was taking her home. He threw Katelyn out of his car. While she was walking, he chased her down and ran her over and dumped her at Cold Creek like she was trash. You know that's how it got its name. It used to be Cold Creek. But everybody said he had to have a stone-cold heart to murder his baby sister."

## Chapter 16—The Mysterious Flowers

I didn't believe her. I think Jayne Ward is like my Aunt Tony who always has to outdo a story told to her. If you tell her you accidentally got an extra order of fries with your McDonalds, she got six burgers for free from Wendy's. Then when Aunt Tony realizes her story might get back to her husband, Charlie, and he'll start asking where the other five burgers went before she got home, she starts back-pedaling and waving it off like it was nothing.

That's why I am heading down the state route with Bear after dropping groceries at Crystals. We're heading toward a little town about fourteen miles from Quail Hollow and a well-known, twenty-dollars-for-six-hours-of-fishing lake. I've got a couple of poles, and bait, and now Bear, who will whine for the next four hours about mosquitoes, and being bored, and his time better spent at work. I want to determine the identity of that *someone* who sets out flowers and a cross. Maybe this person can give me more information.

"Do you have your fishing license?"

"Fishing license?" Bear shakes his head back and forth. "No. Why?"

"Because we're going night fishing."

"It's only seven. I've got a ton of stuff to do."

"I'm not turning around. You should have

thought of that when you refused to get out of the truck, big guy," I declare. "I can let you off somewhere. You can call your mama or one of your girls, but I'm going fishing." He sulks at my words. I pull into a gas station and poke my finger over his lap and toward the big sign that says: Joe's One Stop. I tell him: "Either call somebody to get you or go buy a license and make yourself legal." He over-sighs, leans back in his seat, and eyes me hard. "There's no cell phone service here. I guess I'll have to fish."

"Most people overlook how much line plays a critical role in the success of catching *big* catfish at night," I'm telling Bear with my elbows on knees. He is looking at me intently, nodding once in a while. It's thirty-five minutes later. We plop on a couple of white paint buckets where Froggy Lake abuts Stone Cold Creek. The light is fading on the horizon. We walked about a quarter mile around the lake and stopped another four hundred feet from where the owner told me the cross is located. "Best secret fishing spot around right there. How'd you know about it?" I fibbed and told him I heard it from my uncle's friend who came here. I know for sure he thinks something is up.

"You've got to have a good line, you understand?" I go on. "Me and Pops use Big Cat monofilament line." I tap the string on my pole with one finger. "You see, Bear," I look left to right suspiciously just like Pops did when he told me his secret, lower my voice, "It's not too thick, not too thin. It's right down the middle. We like to throw heavy baits and sinkers, and it can carry it well. And those ol' catfish, they can tell the difference, they can."

I point to the small plastic container on top of Pops' tackle box. My eye is on the road running past. I am waiting for a car to come through. The cross is placed at the point where a shelter sits on a dead end. I didn't want to park there in case it would scare the mysterious bequeather-of-flowers away.

Bear opens up the little plastic container, dips his fingers inside, and pulls out a little pale gob that looks like a battered mushroom right before you plop it into a fryer full of hot oil. Then he brings it to his nose and gives it a curious sniff-sniff that ends in a head turn and stifled gag. "Holy mother of God, this stinks." Bear wrinkles his nose and snaps his head back and stares at me horrified.

"Why'd you stick it up to your nose like that?" I grunt impatiently. "It's supposed to stink. It is chicken liver, beer, corn flakes, garlic powder, and parmesan cheese. It's catfish bait."

"Because it looked like one of your battered mushrooms. I thought it was a snack."

"Good thing you didn't just pop it right into your mouth," I mutter. I close my eyes for two seconds, take in a long, soft breath as if to remain calm. Then, I open them again to stare at Bear, expressionless and silent, eyes unblinking to the count of five. It's my signature expression, albeit lazy, to let him know he said something utterly stupid. He picks it up, tosses it back at me with: "Meghan never looks at me like that."

"Go to hell." Now I know my shitty expression morphs right then to surprise, then hurt. "Why would you say that?" I huff, then let it pass. "It doesn't matter anyway. She has an IQ of fifty. She's like a bottle of beer, empty from the neck up. So, it doesn't surprise me."

"I shouldn't have said that."

"It doesn't matter." It does. My heart feels like he just punched it. Any other time, I would get up and leave. I can't. I've only got this little timespan where I might be able to get even the most minuscule bit of information from this mysterious person who leaves flowers at a possible place Katelyn was murdered. "Just put your bait on the hook and toss it in the water."

We sit there for about four minutes, knee to knee, elbow to elbow. I watch Bear fumble around like he does when he doesn't want to do something I want to do. He opens the tackle box, closes it. He gets out his phone, pretends to text, text, text. Then he sits back and wiggles the rod. He bangs the end of the fishing pole on the ground, then twirls it like a sword. I ignore him as not to fall prey to his pettiness. Then

Bear stops and scrubs the hair on his head.

"I have never gone fishing before, Brandy. I don't know what the heck I'm doing."

Oh. I've already baited my hook, tossed the line into the water, and decided Bear was the biggest whiny baby I'd ever known. I had plopped down with my finger on the line, waiting for a tug-tug. I guess I was so distracted by how I was going to approach someone dropping off flowers, I didn't think to ask him if he had fished before. I should have known that's why he was side-peering at me. He was trying to watch what I was doing.

I peer over at him. I think Bear believes I'm going to laugh. I don't. Instead, I grab up his fishing pole. "When I took my first culinary arts class, I sat down in the back," I tell him. "I was scared the professor would ask me something, and I wouldn't know it." I point to the container of livers and wiggle my fingers so he picks one out. I watch him while he does, trying not to gag. I find the hook on the line and hold it out to him. "You got to slide it on, twice if you can. We don't want it to fall off, but we also don't want the fish to swallow it. If the catfish is small, we toss it back. If it is big, I'm making catfish for Sunday dinner." He nods. I go on. "Back then, I knew Pops didn't call a spatula a spatula. He called it a *pancake tosser.* That's the kind of stuff I grew up with, and I didn't want to look stupid and get laughed at for saying a skimmer strainer was *that thingy Mamaw uses to catch the fish in the tank when she can't find the net.*"

He chuckles while I guide his hand to stab the liver into the hook. I tell him to stand up. I come up behind him, gently take his arm (which is no mere feat because he's taller than I am) and I show him where to hold the fishing pole and how to press in the thumb button to release the line just after he hauls it back and wheels the pole in an arc toward the water.

Bear holds the pole out to the side and looks like his life depends on this one cast of his line out into the water. "So, Bear," I say softly. "I sat back there with the crowd that talks and chatters and doesn't listen to a thing. They played on their phones and never listened to a word the professor said. I did that for nearly two weeks before I got up enough guts to sit in the third row and dread the moment he picks me out among the crowd." Bear is listening to me intently. I sigh, nod at him. "Go for it."

"I was waiting for the end of your story."

"Oh." I shrug. "That was it unless you want to know the truth. The professor finally called on me one day. He asked me if I'd read the lesson for that week. I had studied it all night and like twenty times the next morning. But you know how I am. I freeze in crowds. When he asked me what another name for a colander was and I just went blank and stuttered: *My pops always called it a strainer thingy.* Everybody laughed like I was making a joke. I swore I'd never go back to that class. I was done with college. I was out. But the professor said, in front of everyone, that it was correct. It was a glorious day, that's what my Aunt Jenny would say. I felt smart, and I moved up to the front row. I suppose the moral to my story is that even if you cast your pole and your hook goes three feet into the water and sits there, tell me that you're fishing for the ones up close. I'll tell you that's a good idea. It's warmer there."

Bear eyes me carefully. "Is another name for a colander really a strainer thingy?"

"Not really. The word my professor was looking for was *strainer skimmer*. I think he saw the look of fear in my eyes. He knew I was going to bolt, not come back. What teacher wants to lose a student?"

Bear nods. He brings his arm back and casts. The line makes a wide veer upward and over our heads, works its way in a perfect arc. Then it lands about a stone's throw out. *Plunk*. "Well, I guess you didn't need that talk," I grumble half-heartedly. "But now we sit and wait."


I wouldn't have noticed her if a flashlight had not bounced along the water. It was a beam of light not much bigger than the shimmer of moonlight creeping through the curtain of clouds. But it busted across the little expanse, caught on the tan grass on the other side.

"There's an outhouse around the corner. I've got to go use it," I tell Bear who is quietly settled down on the grass. He starts to rise, asks me if I want an escort. I curtail him with a shake of my head. It has been quiet except for once in a while, one or the other pops up with vague chitchat. We avoid talk of the Redneck Run and work. We dodge anything having to do with Millie Piper's place or us. We don't speak of what might have been or could be.

It is unusual, but not unexpected. I think we are in that dead zone between trying to move on and not wanting to move on. I hop up from the bucket before Bear can object. "I'll be right back." I snatch up the mini flashlight from Pops' tacklebox and tramp along the grassy shore until I get to the bend of the lake. There's a rugged bridge at the dead end that leads over a spillway and to a marshy area where the shelter house stands. I creep across the bridge and to a trail leading to the place where I can see a dark form almost blending into the wall of pine trees beyond.

I nearly trip over a small cross and a bouquet wrapped in plastic. The flashlight bobs toward me. The beam momentarily blinds me. I suppose it isn't until this moment that I realize I've not thought out how I am going to approach someone in the dead of night in a dark area and ask why he or she is leaving flowers where a murder may have taken place.

Or how they know this is the spot. Or if they are the murderer.

A gasp is cool, clean, and female. The trample of grass and leaves lets me know she is suddenly sprinting up the hillside from wherever she secreted herself along some path. In and out we weave, into the darkness, past tree trunks.

"Stop," I call out. I can catch up easily. As we climb the path, I'm gaining. The mysterious woman is breathing deep, hard. "Please stop!" I call out. The crunch of feet to pine needles and last year's autumn leaves pauses. I stop. The moonshine creeps in and out.

"What do you want?" It's a groan, a wheeze of breath.

"My—my name's Brandy." Again, the light flashes over me. It lingers at my head. I'm looking up the path three steps away. "I'm just trying to find out why you leave the flowers. If you know something about Katelyn."

"You're the girl who won the Redneck Run."

"Yeah."

"Did the cops send you? How'd you know I was here?"

"I went to the Quail Hollow police station. They wouldn't tell me anything. Nobody will tell me anything. When I was walking out, this lady named Jayne Ward—"

"Who?" She's out of breath, huffing. I can see

a tall, willowy form. She has long hair, a white t-shirt, and blue jeans. When the moon shines through, I catch her face. She's in her early thirties with pale blonde hair and wide eyes.

"Jayne Ward was her name."

"I don't know her. Why would she tell you about me?" She puffs frantically. "Did she know it was *me*?"

"I don't know. I don't think Jayne knew who you were. She just said somebody leaves flowers every anniversary of Katelyn's murder. I have no clue why she told me about this, but it is the only thing I have to go on. I'm trying to find out who killed Katelyn."

She's the first person who doesn't blurt out that everybody knows who it was—Marcus Freeman. She wavers there, then takes two steps down the steep incline. "Why are you trying to do it?"

I hesitate. "He told me not to tell anyone, this person who I'm working for." I finally weave around the truth.

"It's her brother, isn't it?" she asks, then looks up, doesn't wait for my answer. Maybe she knows by my silence, I won't say. I hear a huff-huff like she's starting a sob. "Does he want to find me—kill me? Is that what this is all about? Is he going to kill me?"

"Kill you," I repeat. "Why would he do that?"

"Because he found out I'm not dead."

## Chapter 17—It's All About the Timing

Bear always has the worst timing. He always used to forget to knock loud on the door when he wanted to use the bathroom when my mostly-deaf grandpa was visiting. When no one replied within only two seconds, Bear'd storm in on Papaw in mid-pee at least once a week. Papaw would always grumble: *There's something wrong with that boy* when Kenny did something weird like leave his car door open in the rain or Pops would disappear into his shed for a long time. But he said it so much about Bear that I think most everybody was starting to believe him.

Therefore, it isn't surprising that the precise moment the woman says she's supposed to be dead, I hear him holler out my name from the path I had come. It is far off and deep like the cutoff howl of a wolf. The woman's eyes nearly bulge to two golf ball size orbs of white, and she makes a raspy hoot. She leans into the hillside, nearly stumbles, rights herself. I see her hand flap to her lips before she starts to turn. "Please don't let him kill me!"

"It's not Marcus Freeman!" I hiss. "Don't go! Tell me what you know. Why would he kill you?" She doesn't answer. But Bear's fever pitch shouts make me wonder if there isn't a pack of coyotes swarming around him. I see her make two skip-steps. I hold out my hand, a vain attempt to stop her. She'll have nothing of it. "My name is Brandy Devereauxs," I call out to her back. I'm torn. I want to chase her down, but Bear calls out again. "Please find me. Call me!"

I scramble back down the path toward Bear. I call back to him. However, it isn't until I return to the same place that I left him that I find he had never moved at all. His voice had just carried across the water to our ears.

"I—I think I've—I've got a fish!"

"You've got to be kidding me," I tell him flatly. "You yowled like a cat getting eaten alive by a dog." I can feel the downy hairs on the back of my neck stand on end in irritation. I'm wondering if I can't just swing around and run back toward the woman, try to catch her still. No, she's far gone, I'm sure. Bear, however, is staring at me with wide eyes.

"Why aren't you reeling it in?" I ask him, stopping short of where he is pacing up with the pull of the line toward the creek, and then back when the fish seems to tire. I decide it looks more like the fish has a man on the pole than the other way around and I tell him that: "It looks more like the fish has you."

"Ha ha, it does!" he announces loudly. I start.

"Then reel it in."

Now Bear isn't an idiot. He's college-educated, quite bright, and can play the piano (My Aunt Jenny always tells me a guy's a great catch if he's smart enough to play a musical instrument because she read it in one of her magazines that people with musical training had high IQs). But there's something that happens when you put anything that has to do with the outdoors in his grasp. He goes nature-stupid. He completely totaled Kenny's ATV into a tree that was thirty feet off the path. He yowls like my little sister screams when she gets stung by a bee if a wasp is even crawling on a window ten feet across the room. And right now, he's holding the fishing pole in both hands and taking steps back, trawling it in, then walking forward letting the line pull back out.

"Reel it in?"

"That—wind it towards you." I point to the fishing reel handle. I hold up my hands into the air, feigning holding the pole in one hand and winding the little handle of the fishing reel with the other. He's nodding, watching my hands intensely and finally pats his way along the fishing pole handle until his right hand gets to the reel. Bear pushes his tongue to his lip in concentration and starts to turn the handle, tugging and pulling. He finally gets this huge catfish up to the bank, and it is flopping and floundering. It is the biggest catfish I have ever seen in my entire life.

"Holy hell!" I announce, already seeing it well-blackened with a piece of lemon on an ivory plate, buffalo-grilled in aluminum foil and plopped on a paper plate as Pops likes it or sautéed with gently steamed veggies meticulously settled around it. I'm imagining twenty great challenges on cooking it myself—

"Don't get stung!" Bear rips away the sweet scent of cooked fish. "God, I don't know CPR!"

"They don't sting, goofball," I grunt back, looking up at him. "Where'd you hear that?" He's standing overtop it similar to Pops standing victoriously over the trophy buck he brings in during hunting season each year. But the difference is, the dang fish isn't dead. I know there's no way in the world he's going to wiggle the hook out.

I fall to my knees and wrestle the hook out of the fish's mouth. I've done it a hundred times fishing with Kenny and Pops. I can roast this puppy in parchment and tomatoes and a sprinkling of special spices. I can— "Damn, woman, go!" Bear is prancing above me and pumping his arm up and down, a pro wrestling coach spurring on his best wrestler in the ring.

"Hand me the fish stringer." I'm straddling the fish, knees muddy, hands a little bloody because the fins have these little sharp spines. I'm going to cook it Cajun-style, maybe, and that gives me goosebumps just thinking of it. I look up, almost catching the scent of it smoked. Bear stops long enough to give me a questioning gaze. "It's a little blue and white rope. I'll push it through the gills to string it."

"What? Why? Won't that hurt it?"

I suppose I'm furrowing my brow in confusion, tipping my head. "Dammit, Bear! Don't be an idiot. It doesn't matter. We're going to eat this one. It's the biggest catfish I've ever seen, and he's not tired. I am!"

He's slow-motion reaching for the tackle box. He's flopping his hands on it, looking at the fish, looking at me, looking at the fish. I am so wrapped up in mentally preparing this fish for a meal, I overlooked the fact he's nature-stupid. Does he even understand that the food he eats was once a live animal? "No, Bear, do not look it in the eyes. It is a stupid fish. Like— like the steak you eat. It comes from a live cow. Like eggs. They aren't baby chickens." I see it though. "Please, don't, Bear." I swear, I see those two lock eyes because for one moment the hugest catfish in humankind comes to a complete stop.

Bear hovers near the tackle box, pauses and looks down, soft brown eyes taking in the fish. "No, don't do it," I whisper. "It's like the chicken you eat. It *was* a bird." But Bear makes this soft murmur much like a mama kitty purrs to its newborn kitten. Then (and by all means, it was just coincidental BAD TIMING) the catfish burps up a soft catfish grunt.

"Shit!" I hiss when Bear looks up at me. He's got this sad-puppy gaze. "Please, Brandy." It might as well be Bambi gazing wide-eyed and miserable the moment his mama got shot. "You're kidding me, right?"

He wasn't. Twenty minutes later, I'm driving with my eyes set to the windshield. I'm a bit surly. I still see the image of Bear walking slowly and with much decorum into the knee-deep water and gently swishing the fish back and forth while I stand by his side shivering, holding my cell phone up to his face so he can follow the video on the proper way to release the fish (safely and responsibly, as the caption read).

"Are you still mad." He's side-peering me timidly.

"No." I don't turn. "I mean, I could have fed my entire family with that catfish on Sunday morning. I'm tired of making turkey every single Sunday morning, Bear."

"They aren't going to starve. That was my first fish." His chin is high. I see a bit of smug and confident in the set of his shoulders.

"It should probably be your last because you know you can't adopt them like a kitten, right?"

He lets that roll off him with a grin. "I caught a fish. I kind of rate in some cultures, you know? I mean, in some civilizations, catching a fish, hunting down a meal is becoming a man— a warrior, a real man bringing home the bacon. Then you can take a wife and make a family."

Except he didn't bring home the bacon. He

released it back into the wild. He looks over at me, and maybe he can read my mind. He is now quiet and sullen. "I'm sorry, Brandy." My shoulders fall. My eyes dance over to his. He's looking more humble than egotistical. "Don't be sorry. Yes, you did catch a fish. It was probably a record. And it was probably the best thing you could have done. Old Grampa Catfish will live another ten years and mate and produce more big catfish like him."

"It was a male?"

"Yeah, Bear," I lie. Hell, I don't know how to sex a stupid catfish. I cook them. I eat them.

"That's good. But when I said I was sorry, I meant about fighting with you. I miss you, Brandy. I miss the adventures. I miss this." He waves a hand between us. "For just a second, I felt like I rated with your family. I know how your pops and Kenny and all your uncles hunt and fish. I always feel like they look at me like I don't make the grade. I wasn't good enough for you because I was too soft or something—not a warrior, not worthy."

"Well, mighty warrior, I can fend for myself. I don't need a knight around—" Especially one who would have me starve to death because the fawn he was going to shoot for our meal was too cute.

"I know that." He shrugs, looks away. "I'm tired. Just take me home. I'll get my truck tomorrow."

I missed him too. And for some stupid reason, I fell into his senseless, great warrior speech. I drive him to his huge cabin on the mountain. I linger there in Pops' truck while he gets out. He does have a bit of feral fish scent mixed with mossy creek and pines outdistancing the aroma of black smoke spewing from the muffler. Bear lingers near the passenger door too, looking at me with his brown eyes and mussed hair. We are different, Bear and me. He's city. I'm country. He's fastidious. I'm easy going.

"When I caught the scent of your skin coming off the woods tonight, I couldn't think. There's something about you, Brandy. You take my breath away." He smiles longingly. I fall into it, tap my steering wheel.

"I took my wet tennis shoes off and drove back barefoot." I nibble on my lip, look at him softly. "I don't want to walk across the pebbles from your driveway. But if you can carry me, I'll hang out a bit, Bear."

Hang out. We barely make it past the front door. He carries me like a baby even as he fumbles with the lock on the door. He pushes it open, sets me down. He passes me into the foyer. It smells like new wood and some freezer meal he must have microwaved. Bear stops, turns in the dim light. "Are you coming inside?"

Our eyes meet. Lord, I love him. Everything else wipes away—replaced with this soft, sweet excitement rumbling below my belly button. Being here, being with Bear right now grasps me in its warm, tight fist. It feels like home and so right, so very, very right. I run to him, three steps, and take this two-footed lunge up, up, up. I'm teeny, athletic and agile. He's none of the above except maybe city-boy, training room ripped. He manages to surprise me. He should never have caught me at the perfect moment. His arms—man, they are strong and muscled, a bulging swell just above the cleft of his elbow when he takes my weight. We should have slammed together, my chest to his flexible belly. I should have slid to the floor like I hit a soft wall. I don't. His belly is firm, taut. It should have been awkward and eye-opening. It wasn't. He catches me in midair easily. He's been working out more and not just in a training room. I wrap my legs around his waist. He holds me up by his hands beneath my rear.

"God, I missed my wild mountain girl," he tells me softly. I feel just a kiss from his lips on my forehead. It is soft, sweet, tender. I look up. I'm squeezing the shit out of him. He's got a boyish grin on his lips. Those lips that curve, barely hide a smile. Those soft brown eyes that crinkle at the corners and make my belly bounce. I reach up, slide my fingers around his neck, tickle the downy hairs just above his collar. I know him well enough that he gets goosebumps when I pull myself up and rub my lips across his before I press into him, kiss him hard. I leave one hand around his neck, pull the other to his jaw and cup it, tugging him toward me again for a kiss. Then, I've got both my arms around him. My legs are sliding down. Bear has turned. He's pressing me against the wall, not too tightly so that I feel crushed and feel like I need an escape route.

I feel him unleashing his jeans. He releases me long enough to drop my shorts, my panties. I catch the scent of Bear, of all those wonderful scents of musky cologne and *my* man. He leans over and pulls me to him again, bare flesh to bare flesh—our scents mingling. We are as close as two lovers can be, pressed to each other and kissing, kissing, kissing before we come together. He groans. I groan. Then that sweet feeling overcomes me, the one I never felt with anybody else. It pours through me, and I let it fill me up before I sigh.

"I miss this," I tell him softly and later while we are lying in bed, me lying atop his open arm. "Bear, I miss this so bad." I think he might be asleep. He doesn't answer for a second.

"Me too, Brandy. It was fun tonight. I'm a mighty warrior whether you think it or not. We're good together, right?" I sigh for my answer. I think he has fallen to sleep. I wait for his breaths because that is what I love most about being with Bear, lying there stuffed next to him, feeling safe and loved.

"Can I ask you a favor?" I hear him whisper

in my ear. I don't turn. I think he wants me to reach around, tickle the top of his head and roll my fingers over and over through his hair as I do sometimes to help him sleep.

"Yeah, Bear."

"I was wondering," he says in a sleepy voice. "Can you do me a favor and not tell Rush you're off the team?"

Silence. Did I hear him right? I've got my arm wiggling out of his embrace and almost around to his head to play with his hair. "What?"

He stifles a fake yawn. "You're probably not going to run into him, but if Rush asks if you're still on the team, can you tell him you are?"

"Why?"

"I don't know. I get the feeling Rush chose us over some others because of—that."

"What's *that?*" I ask and Bear shrugs and tells me he doesn't know. I think about it, let it lay cold and dank in my head. It's all about the timing, I suppose. Maybe Bear's better at it than I thought. Whether it was Bear walking in on Papaw in the bathroom because maybe all along he was tired of waiting and it wasn't just an accident. Or enticing me into a promise while I'm still sweet after sex. Twenty minutes later, I hear the sound of his sleeping breaths. I push myself from the bed and leave feeling used like a rummage-sale item that got bought at a sale and was found to be broken, then tossed in the trash.

## Chapter 18—Allie Blankenship

Her name is Alison "Allie" Blankenship, the tall woman from the Froggy Waters Pay Lake who had bucked from me. She vanished seventeen years ago, and it appears into thin air. I found an old missing person poster for her online. It was an advertisement in a newspaper and copied to a social network post for an account belonging to a woman named Jenny Young-Blessing.

It said *Alison "Allie" Blankenship. Presumed Dead. Missing since July/August 2002. Age 19. 5 ft 8 blonde hair, shoulder length. Four-door blue Buick found on Union Street, Mt Pleasant. A reward is being offered for the arrest and conviction of the person(s) responsible for her disappearance or her safe return—* On the post, Jenny had written: *This was my best friend in junior high. Allie lived two doors down on Franklin Street.* There were six images of Allie also on the post at different ages. They matched the woman's face I saw last night. I made a copy on my printer and added it to the cork board by Katelyn's name with a question mark. I looked up the Youngs on Franklin Street on the online tax plat map. Sure enough, Allie's parents still lived next door.

Upon further searching, I also found her disappearance coincided strangely close to Marcus Freeman's arrest, just three weeks later.

Sunday morning at seven-thirty after I ran and showered, I drove past the sturdy brick house on Franklin Street with a tidy lawn. It was only ten minutes from the very spot where Bear and I fished. A slim middle-aged man was standing in the driveway in a middle-class Sunday suit and tie and leaning into a car. I slowed, worked my courage up in three huge inhalations of stale air in my truck.

I pulled to the curb and got out while the man curiously paused with a hand on his door. He peered cautiously at me when I rounded the back of my vehicle. I told him my name, said I was researching Katelyn Freeman's death. I asked him if he knew Alison Blankenship and if he was her father. His cheeks turned a green-pale. I didn't realize there was someone in the passenger side of the car until I heard a woman's velvety voice purr: *Bradley, tell her we don't know anything.*

They didn't ask if I knew where she was or if I had seen her. That would be normal responses to a stranger walking up to you, asking about a missing family member, especially one offering an award for her safe return. Instead, they told me if I did not leave, they were calling the police. Bingo. They knew she was alive.

I chewed on that the rest of the morning, and while I'm carefully drizzling the last of the thick brown sugar and maple syrup glaze to the ham I'd pulled from the oven only moments earlier at Pops'. I have a crowd watching. Usually, I don't unless I'm making cookies and the little nieces and nephews want to lick the batter. My family's been eating my cooking since I was twelve. They don't care about the process, only the result. Today, that outcome is maple glazed ham initially smoked along with savory scalloped potatoes, sweet baby carrots, lemon green beans with almond breadcrumbs, and Aunt Jenny's favorite potato biscuits. Oh, and cut hotdogs with mac and cheese for Kaylee because that's all she's eating right now for breakfast, lunch, and supper.

The crowd includes Bear and Rush Gordon. Rush has an entourage of eight unfamiliar faces who had traveled with him this week because he doesn't like to fly. They all look like Rush, wearing upscale outdoor clothing, what Kenny calls Urban Hillbilly. It was Rush's idea to come up Fire Mountain Road. Bear had mumbled being sorry about it all. I ignored him, turned my back to him. He's acting like the other night didn't happen. Oh, and I'm saucy about it.

Along with Rush and his traveling buddies is anyone in my family who has seen Kenny's poster that's been on his wall forever. I feel sorry for Rush because they are all weird-smiling him the same way stage-struck teen girls push to the front at a boy band concert. When he and Bear came rolling up the hill in ATVs, everyone flocked to the windows like a murder of crows homing in on a hawk that had swooped into their territory. "Who is that? Who is that?" they all cackled and cawed.

Since Bear was in the lead ATV (he tends to drive an ATV like my half-blind mamaw sluggishly urges her archaic Buick into town with her foot pumping the brake pedal instead of the accelerator pedal) the entourage was moving sluggishly and stopping, starting, stopping again, and spitting out stones all over the place. Nobody local goes ten miles an hour up the mountain in a long line like one of those tours they give on standup motorized scooters in New York City. So surely, these were OUTSIDERS. It was probably more frightening and exciting than seeing an alien spaceship land on Pops' old barn out back.

Kenny came swooping to the front and cried the shrill alarm: "Holy shit! It's—it's Rush Gordon! It's RUSH GORDON, International ATV Champion of 2017!" Then they all poured out on to the porch to my Aunt Jenny cawing and scolding him harshly for his curse word, the rest squawking and carrying on while I threw back my head, groaned. I didn't have enough ham to feed an army.

"That smells ridiculously delicious." That's Rush leaning over, one arm on my shoulder while I lug out the ham. His nose is in the air, eyes closed. "It smells like Easter at home. My gramma made ham since as long as I remember, sweet with maple syrup and honey. Makes me homesick."

"This would have been a meal of fresh West Virginia catfish if Bear had not felt a sudden desire to become an advocate for gamefish conservation." I look over my shoulder to Bear who is smiling apologetically.

"They are the most valuable members of the population," Bear rapidly asserts. "Big fish make big baby fish. Big fish are healthier. If you toss back the little ones, only little fish genes are in the pool. I helped the environment. I don't need to justify my decision."

I am guessing he knew, at some point, I would confront him in public about his little indiscretion. He probably spent six hours looking for some validation to hide the real reason he set the darn fish free. He's a softy.

"The catfish would have fed my entire family." I turn to Rush and wave an oven-mitted hand at him. "I hope you all are hungry. It is almost time for Sunday dinner at the McAllister's." Bear takes a moment to scoot everyone to the living room. Rush deliberately lingers where he's leaning against the cabinets, looks to where his people and my people are spreading out in the living room.

"So how well do you get along with the Vegas?" He jabs a thumb toward the living room where Bear reluctantly disappeared. "I mean, other than the event." I realize right then, he has no clue Bear and I were engaged or were more than simply associated because of the Redneck Run.

"Well, you know how Amelia is, I suppose."

He laughs, bobs his head. "Oh, yeah. That said, I meant to ask." He pushes out from the cabinet and lowers his voice, leans into me while I ready to pull the casserole off the stove. "Did a guy named Jim Bakersfield get ahold of you?"

"Jim Bakersfield," I repeat, taste the unfamiliar name with a slight shrug of my shoulders noncommittedly. "No, why?"

Rush whips out his wallet from his back pocket, tugs out a business card, and hands it to me. "He's a billionaire entrepreneur. He's got his hands in everything including the mass sporting events like long-distance running. If he hasn't owned it, he's going to own it. He owns a multimillion-dollar golf resort and sporting complex a few hours away. He's the one that provides a lot of preseason practice areas for the semi-pro baseball players."

"What's he want with me?"

Rush peers out into the living room. "He's looking for competitors for the Redneck Run." I hesitantly take the card from his fingers, look hard at his eyes. "He called me too. If you want to be a part of the winning team, you might want to give him a chance."

"Are you?"

"Are you?" he asks me.

"Why are you telling me this?"

"Well, long story short, I asked Johnny Remy who works in maintenance why you weren't out with those girls running. Beau told me that's just not how you practiced. You were a wild card. Johnny, he said it was all a big lie. They kicked you off. I've got to be honest, there's a few of us who came along here because we like the way you play. I don't sign contracts. I go where I want to go when I want to go. I don't need this financially. Getting the promotion would be nice. People like you, Brandy. They like what you stand for—"

"Who likes me?"

He laughs like I'm kidding. "Amelia Vega is making a big mistake letting you go, a big mistake. Say the word. If you like Jim Bakersfield's way of playing cards and you want to win, I'm with you."

## Chapter 19—The Threat

"Is that why you're here, so Rush thinks I'm still on the team?" I corner Bear after dinner while I'm jamming my foot into the raggedy, mucky boots I use to ride the ATV. I'm old jean shorts, a camo t-shirt, and a glare on my face. I'm hop-skipping in the foyer, trying not to whisper too loudly. "I've got a million things to do tonight, Bear. I've got to do the wash—" I pause and pretend I'm his mom and do a haughty tip of my head. "I'm sorry. I have to do the *laundry*." He doesn't think I'm funny. "I've got to make some of my mail order to-go meals. I don't want to be up all night preparing them."

"I'm not the one who asked to go riding up here. It was Rush. I thought Kenny would want to meet him," Bear yell-whispers back. "I'm doing you a favor. You don't have to take us up the mountain."

"Doing *me* a favor?" I laugh sarcastically. "Kind of like whoring yourself out the other night so I don't tell him I'm off the team?" Bear is seething. I see his eyes narrow, his jaws churn. "And yeah, I do. Pops says I do. He doesn't want a bunch of yahoos up there tearing up his deer feeding stations and drinking." Almost everybody else has milled out with the excuse of other things to do. It's not the usual. Most of the family stay until eight or nine on Sundays. Pops has decided he

165

doesn't want Bear and his pals rambling around his property without *proper* supervision, so Kenny and I get to babysit. "Did it not occur to you that my family might say something? Or someone from work? I think he knows I'm not running for you." I pause, don't want to betray who told Rush the truth. "I also want my page off your website. I told you that."

"You're still under contract. Your entire team from last year is on our lineup for P.R. for the event this year. You're all extra players sitting on the bench like any sport."

I swing my head upward. "Benched," I grunt scathingly. "That's a nice way to put it."

"We can't take you off. You just aren't running like Bobby's got his name on the team, but he's not shooting. Nor is Kenny running the ATV competition. You're all still under the binding agreement. I think we pay you a couple of hundred bucks for nothing else than using your pictures and names. It's easy money."

"Well, *unbind* me. I don't want any part of the event."

"It's not like you're going to run for anybody else. It costs us to have the attorneys pull up the info and take it off." He says hotly with a snarky twist to his lips. "And if you do, I'll make you a deal. We'll take you off." I stop and stare at him hard, one foot partway in the boot, pushing back my hair with my hand. I wish I had a superpower and it was firing flames from my eyeballs because that is what I would be doing right now, shooting Bear with flames so big his head would explode.

"You think I'm not good enough to compete, do you? You think I was just lucky last year."

"I think you have a hard time following rules. I think it's easy running wild through the woods and the trails and the old roads without getting timed. Nobody knows when you stop or how fast or slow you go. I mean, every time our folks tried to time you, Brandy, you'd disappear. Therefore, I don't know."

"But you *don't know*."

"I do know there was some question last year that you took a shortcut through the woods and set Willy's dogs on the other team."

"You know I did *not* take a shortcut."

"No one runs that fast, Brandy."

I do. "Why are you so mean Bear Vega? Why are you suddenly this person I thought I knew and now you're a stranger?" I hiss. "I've done nothing to warrant all this!"

He does this huge eye-roll that I know means the conversation is over as far as he's concerned. "I think you and your family do."

"My family? What are you talking about?"

"Oh, you'll know soon enough."

"That sounds like a threat."

"It could be interpreted like that." What's that mean?

## Chapter 20—Flabbergasting

When I was seven, I heard the word *flabbergasting* for the first time. The way it bobbled awkwardly off the lips like a clown clambering into the open end of a cannon, then being shot back out, it screamed a certain circus-like disbelief and shock. It embodied the mood one pretty summer Sunday afternoon in church when I was in first grade. Snooty old Missus Robinette, who was always scolding me with a cluck of her tongue for wiggling my bony bottom on the splintery, rough wooden church pew or kicking the back of her seat, turned suddenly and twisted her head around to give my Aunt Jenny a warning gaze because I dropped a hymnal.

When Missus Robinette turned, she let out a long and drawn-out stuttering fart that echoed like a piece of cloth being slowly ripped. It was much to the horror of her husband who always fell into a blissful sleep five minutes into the sermon. Her flatulence was so loud, it awakened him with a start. In a vain and mostly sleepy attempt to cover up the grand finale of her scandal, he had shouted a hearty AMEN as if he was giving a shout out to the preacher's fine telling of some verse. However, the timing was off. His words came *after* the indiscretion. It appeared to those listening that he was praising his wife's generous offense.

To make small of her scandal and push the grave indelicacy off to me, Missus Robinette had harrumphed loudly and chided my aunt. *You need to keep that wicked child under control!* My usually quiet, bashful aunt had sat straight up and snapped back quickly and loudly: *I don't think her disruption, Judy, was as flabbergasting to the rest of the congregation as your own!*

Much in the way the rest of the church was shocked and amazed at Missus Robinette's slip and my aunt's valiant response, I would be flabbergasted today. Pops has six or seven trails running to the top of Fire Mountain. Three are rugged paths meant only for deer hooves, people boots, or thick-treaded ATV tires. The sun was getting ready to set when we got to the peak, a bland pale peach settling overtop the other mountains and making the fog lifting from below look like pink cotton candy. They oohed and aahed, Bear's pack when we got there. It smelled of damp pines and smoke creeping up from a campfire below.

When we all get to the top, we dismount and stare out over the horizon. "You see that over there?" I ask them, pointing to the mountain straight across. You can't see the resort with the trees all leafed up, just a ball of light from the parking lamps making a cool beam above. "That's where the resort is, tucked into the trees. It wasn't always called Boar Mountain. A long time ago, we were all the Fire Mountain range. Back in the 1800s, there was a coal company here. If you hike down the mountain, you'll see old foundations from the homes, twenty or thirty of them on both sides," I say softly. I watch as heads turn toward me to listen. "When the Civil War broke out, this mountain, Fire Mountain, was mostly made up of my Pops' side of the family, the McAllisters. They were southern sympathizers and fought for the south." I point over to the other mountain. "But just over the hollow where it's Boar Mountain now, it was my mama's side of the family—the MacCabes, Pipers, and the Picketts. And when the war broke out, they decided to fight for the north. Now around here, there was some fighting between the families. A Pickett shot a McAllister, and a McAllister burnt down one of the Piper's pig barns. Then one night, there was a fire. Nobody knows where it started—maybe lightning, maybe somebody's twelve-year-old smoking a pipe for the first time in the hay barn. But it blazed a path up Fire Mountain, then started its way down the hollow and up the other side to what's now Boar Mountain. Most anywhere else, folks would have just watched their houses burn down because there wasn't anybody to help them and all the water was way down in the creek between the two mountains. It was too far away for ten or twenty to hand bucket by bucket up. But for some reason, Jonas MacCabe called out to his ten or so boys, and they made their way down to the creek and up the other side and started handing buckets up to the McCallister boys. They put out the fires over there, then came over here and stopped the burning. Now it wasn't easy, but after that, the folks from the two mountains became one big family and started New Alliance down below." I sigh and try not to look at Bear. He knows the story, knows that his mama, Amelia, was the one who broke up these two mountains again. I don't say that. Instead, I nod toward the hollow. "They say Fire Mountain's a ghost town. I suppose to some extent, those who say that are right. My mamaw used to tell me they'd see little lights coming up the side of the mountain some nights. She said it was the ghosts of those folks who used to live here reminding us that although we're all different, deep down inside we're all the same."

"That's beautiful." It's Rush whose voice breaks the silence. I smile at him in the dimming light. "I believe in ghosts," he tells me. "I want to see the lights." I do too, but up this high, I can get cell phone service. Pops calls and tells me I need to take my grandpa home, so I opt out and let Kenny take charge. I see Bear staring at me, eyes strangely set hard on my own. I turn away. It makes my chest feel heavy, my heart sad. How can I love-hate somebody so bad? I want to turn back the calendar to March or May and figure out what I did wrong to make him so angry at me by June. I can't, so I make my way down the mountain to Pops' house.

I suppose things that change my life always seem to happen when I least expect it. When I'm blindly walking around and patting the walls trying to figure how to get out of whatever dark tunnel I'm bumbling around. Like April and May slid past me unadorned and thinking everything was just fine with Bear when it wasn't.

Pops' dad, my papaw, is the only one left at the house. I hear the door squeaking open when I come into the dusky shades of the lawn after parking my ATV. He comes out and meets me at the stairs in the light of Pops' porch. I can barely see him taking the steps a bit sideways, one at a time, leaning hard on his cane. "Hey, ornery," he says. He's a big guy, and a bit keeled over nowadays. He always scared the crap out of Bear because he's a bit surly and questioned everything he did. Bear was always *yes-sirring* him and *no-sirring* Papaw. He's overprotective of me, the one who got all teary-eyed when I walked down the aisle for college graduation at Fairview State Community College a few months ago.

"Hey, Papaw, where is everybody?"

"They all went home. Your old Pops drove your aunt home." We climb into my truck and ramble down the mountain. It's almost dark. I flip on my signal to turn right. Papaw raises a finger and points to the left. "That way."

"Huh?" I mutter, confused. I do what he says, and swing left. "Right there," he tells me, pointing to the bit of light spraying off a porch at the old tavern. "Looks like your Pops stopped in to grab his tools or something. I want to ask him if he remembered he's supposed to cut that old Redbud tree down in front of my house tomorrow. It's all crookedy since Kenny backed into it with his truck." I follow his finger and pull into a graveled lot. I don't want to do it. I'm a bit saucy he's helping get the old place ready for the sale. It's like I've got a double-broke heart losing this and losing Bear at the same time.

There are lots of trucks there past the wrought iron fence and gate we drive through. Papaw tells me to get out and run inside and see if Pops can come out to the truck. I grumble and amble deliberately slow up the stone steps, taking in the sweet scent of damp stones and the trees bursting full of summer leaves. It's probably the only property in the valley that was never skimmed down three layers of earth by logging, never cleaned clear for coal. It's like a little oasis amid a desert and along the state route leading into Main Street in town. It's filled with the smells of the creek running out back and tall grasses and a little freshly mowed lawn. It's cool and dim on the porch.

I'm not sure if I should knock on the door or

not. I don't. I push open this huge oak door and burst inside, waiting to see Pops looking guilty for collaborating with the enemy. He thinks I haven't seen them parked down here. I have. I avoid it when possible.

The home has belonged to one family for the last one-hundred and fifty years. It's been unlived-in for ten or so years when Millie's husband started getting too rickety to care for it, and they moved into a little retirement brick ranch in town. I expect most of the walls taken to bits, pulled down as they work from the inside to the outside demolishing the building. I'm wrong. It is just the opposite as I come face to face with everybody who had been up at Pops' house eating my Sunday ham, now down here standing with big wide grins smeared all over their faces.

"What's going on?" I ask. They all give a roaring SURPRISE so that I startle and take a swaggering drunk step back. "Surprise, what?"

"Baby girl, this is your place." Pops steps forward. My eyes waver to him, a little dizzy with doubt. "I bought it." He turns to take everybody in with a hand. "We all went in together on this old place." He's holding out a navy-blue packet with Harrisburg National Bank in gold letters on the top.

"How—how?" I stutter.

And Pops smiles. "It don't matter. It's yours, all yours. We've been working on it since I got the loan. It just needs some final touches approved by the county. Now don't just stand there and look goofy. Do what you did on that Redneck Run thing last year and amaze us all."

*Flabbergasted.* I can't describe my feeling of fall-to-my-knees shock and amazement any better. Later, I walk around the house and peer at all the incredible work they had done. The carpets had been torn out, the wood floors sanded and stained. The kitchen is gutted, and new professional equipment carefully added along with freezers and my appliances from Pops'. "Brandy, why are you crying?"

"It's everything I ever wanted, Pops."

"I know that. That's why I did it."

"But at what cost?" I ask him. "Where'd you get the collateral and the deposit?"

"Well, your papaw had some retirement. He paid part of the down payment along with Uncle Craig and just about everybody either helped rebuild it or tossed in some money."

"None of us, altogether, has as much money as it took to buy this. I know."

"Aw, I put the farm up for security. I got over twelve-hundred acres of prime property."

"Oh, Pops," I grunt, my hand going to my lips. "What if I don't—what if—?"

"It ain't gonna happen. You're gonna make this work. Baby girl, I know you think I doubt you. But I don't. I don't."

# Chapter 21—A Mixed Message of Knives and Flowers

The Fire Mountain Redneck Run didn't start out as the professional tourism-promoting event it is today. When the Crazy Kettle owner, Hensley Peters, first got the idea thirty years ago, the competition wasn't anything more than a mud bog ATV race and a bunch of drunks sledding down McAllister Hill in old bathtubs prettied up with chicken wire, tissue paper, and homemade cardboard signs looking like floats in a Fourth of July parade.

I tell that to Jim Bakersfield from the Resort at Two Bridge Falls when he calls me two days later. I'm lugging my commercial mixer up the steps to my new restaurant—I realize, then, I haven't even come up with a name for it. "Um, what was I saying?" I mutter. "Oh, and I think they had some shooting event where they used sawed-up shotguns to shoot at foam deer targets. Then after some drunk got shot in the leg, the local women's bible study group had the cops put a stop to that one."

He laughs and says the Redneck Run is all they talk about in his neck of the woods when the time rolls around for the event. He tells me, they all talk about me winning last year like I'm some folk hero. I told him with a giggle: "You make me blush."

"I was talking to Bill Gaynor with *The Time of Our Lives* magazine when he came out to do a piece on our golf course. He said you're on hiatus right now. Is that a rumor or not?" He doesn't wait for me to answer. "Because I want you on our team. I've *got to* have you on our team. What does that mean to you?"

"I—" I swallow hard. "I just bought a restaurant here in New Alliance. I'm still working mornings at the grocery store. I honestly don't think I'll have time."

"Good. I don't take *no* for an answer. I want you to come up, take a look-see. I think we can cut a deal to make us both happy. Gift me— bring me a batch of cookies."

He's like a hard burst of wind, Jim Bakersfield. He blows in and then hangs up two seconds later without even a goodbye. I'm staring at the phone like I got caught up in that whirlwind. Now it is still and quiet. I sit there a moment, watching cars roll down the state route. One honks. I wave lazily. I've been trying not to sit too long because I start thinking, feeling anxiety creep up at the extent Pops went through to get me this property.

It's Pops thought, I suppose, to have the restaurant good to go by the time of the Redneck Run so getting kicked off the team doesn't weigh heavily on my mind. He's got no clue how much is involved with running a restaurant. I think he believes we can plop down a couple of tables and I'm good to go. The basic kitchen, waiting area, and dining area are ready. There are permits and licenses to obtain, marketing, equipment and furniture to buy, and a simple initial menu to make. I've got the background. I've got the tools. I've got the experience. I've got it all in my head, I have to make it happen and not think about all the restaurants that fail in their first year like Todd Bailey at the bank predicted it will.

I know he's right about the probability. I took the restaurant management classes. I know the odds that thousands of dreams are dashed every year by businesses that fail. Todd Bailey is like a fat rat lounging shrewdly in the shadows beside a mousetrap with a little chunk of cheese sitting on it. He's waiting for a little mouse to come up, unsuspecting and reckless, setting off the trap because Pops didn't go to his bank for the loan. Then when I'm smashed beneath the trap, that fat Todd Bailey rat is going to swoop in and safely steal the cheese.

I can't fail. I have to succeed because if I don't, my family is going down in a spiraling ball of fire because of me. That piece of cheese is Pops' property. He will lose his farm. Papaw will lose his retirement. Uncle Craig will lose his house. Amelia Vega will be wagging her forefinger at me once again, telling me how much a failure I am.

That's what is still grinding through my

head while I stand in MY grand new KITCHEN and stare at my appliances I've been collecting over the years, usually nestled on Pops' old counter. Now they are sitting on a brand-new state of the art stainless steel counter that wraps around the wall Pops managed to buy scratch and dent at a warehouse. It's not a tight workspace. It is its own room, the size of a small living room with a stainless-steel kitchen island and a lamp/fan atop with places for pots and pans to hang. Between the dining area and the kitchen, there is a double oak door Uncle Craig found at an estate sale. It opens wide to a small area where staff will pick up the meals and wider to almost half the room if I want folks to be able to see the cooking in process.

Bear pulls in with his big truck a couple of hours later. When I part the doorway and peer out, he's standing at the threshold of the bottom step with the same puckered lip uncertainty Kenny wavered at the door of Holy Trinity Church the first time he went with Aunt Jenny after she found the girlie magazines hidden under his mattress.

"What?" I huff. The short hair on top of his head is sticking up. He's nervous and has been running his hand through it. His brown eyes look darker than usual which also means he's irritated. He's gained a few pounds, so he's not eating well. His jacket is wrinkled. I'm not sure what that means. It is new to me—

"You know Pops went to the bank in Harrison. He bought this property right out from underneath our investors and us." Bear is pucker-lipped with aggravation. "I just got done with the meeting. I hope you're happy." I step out the door. I'm still dumbified, that's what Kenny calls it, overwhelmed and scared shitless. I'm trying to wrap my mind around the idea that a dream that was easier to dream than making come-true is right under my feet.

"Let me get this straight, Bear." I have a pen in my hand. I stick it over my ear. I lean against the doorframe, uninterested. "Your dreams are more important than mine because you're rich, is that it? Or is it because you're prettier, more sophisticated, polished, and schooled?"

He scratches his head. "I'm not talking to you when you get like this."

"And that's why we're not together, isn't it?" I chuckle sarcastically. "Because you can't see my side of the story. Fine. Goodbye." I push away from the doorframe, start to turn. He lingers there. I can feel him staring at my back. At this particular moment, I don't care.

"No, I'm not done talking to you."

"You just said you are finished. I'm done," I reply with a snarky wiggle of my shoulders. "Go away and whine to Meghan. She's your new feel, isn't she? Leave me alone." I hear his foot on the step.

"My sister runs our restaurant. It is ten

percent of our profit. This will hurt us."

"Then you should have hired me to prepare the menu and meals. Nobody likes the food."

"That's mean."

"No, it isn't mean. It is the truth. You buy the food premade, Bear. It tastes like the frozen meals in the freezer section of the dollar store." My back is to him. I tap my fingers on the frame of the door and turn my head slightly to take him in. "And no, it was mean of your mama to never hire me to make a dessert or two once in a while or bake special meals for her customers instead of me sneaking around to do it. It was mean of you to never show up for the candle-lit suppers I made especially for you night after night after night. It was horrible to find out from somebody else you were screwing Meghan. It was mean of you to kick me off your team, not yell at those bully girls who harassed me constantly, and not stick up for me at all. I can tell you a thousand more mean things you've done to me, but why bother? I'm done with you. I'm finished with your overbearing, meddlesome, over-bitching, could-have-been-monster-in-law. As long as you're here, I want you to know I've been contacted by another agency to run in the event. I'm going to do it."

"What?"

"Let me tell you something, Beauregard Vega. I honestly believe that this whole relationship between us was nothing but a way for you and your mama to get in cozy with everybody in New Alliance and Fire Mountain. It was what you're always calling a *good business move*. You pretend as if you've changed from that asshole who moved back here and somehow managed to get a soul after hanging around me a while. Folks see you with me here. They give you discounts on everything. You become a part of the community, look good to everybody. I'm your go-between for your employees that you think are beneath you. That is until your kind come around—the rich, pompous jerks who think they are better than everybody else. Then you pull Meghan out and shove me away and tug her in beside you. Nobody knows you and I were a couple."

"You'd never go anywhere with me either. You were always hanging with Kenny."

"You never asked." I tap my chin. "Hmmm, you and your mama kept that pretty quiet, the trips out of town with your new girl. Because God forbid a redneck like me from the mountains would ever fit in with your self-aggrandizing, superior, arrogant crowd."

"It goes both ways, Brandy. Do you know what it's like to see you and Kenny exchanging eye rolls whenever I said I wanted to ride ATVs with you guys? Do you know how hard it is to sit in that house on Sundays and listen to everybody's stories from *way back when* and not be a part of it, not be the one who wiped out down the mountain on his butt like Kenny did? Or how everybody thinks we never worked for a dime and all this fell in our laps? You call us pompous. But your world, they make the rest of us feel like outsiders. You and your family are the pompous ones." He turns on his expensive shoes and stomps to his truck. I assume he's leaving. He opens his door and leans inside. Then he stands upright just as I head inside.

"Hey!" He yell-growls. I look out. I think he's going to shout at me. He's got a mid-size box in his hands with flowers slapped on top. He walks to the porch again, this time stopping with one foot on the bottom step. His face goes expressionless. "Listen, congratulations. Do you want this or not?" I'm not quite sure what to say. I step on to the porch, down one step. Bear juggles the box in one hand and shoves a bouquet at me with the other.

"They are irises." He pokes a finger at the purple petals flowing outward. "I asked Faith at the flower shop what you give—a—a friend to congratulate her on something. She said irises signify hope and courage and admiration. I think that was it." *A friend.* Right. My heart careens downward and lands like a bad egg from a two-story building in my gut. Splat. He nods to the yellow mum. "The yellow is optimism." He contemplates the thought with a rub of his free fingers to chin. "I wish you well."

I take in a whiff of the flowers. Bear holds

out the box. "I realized while picking this out for you, how much I don't know about being a chef, Brandy." He does his signature *huh-huh-huh* chuckle even if it is bland. "All those times I sat in there and watched you make stuff, I guess I wasn't thinking about the appliances you use or the food you were making as much as—" He contemplates his words, stops self-conscious. I see his cheeks turn a burnt red. He makes an impulsive thrust of the box upward. "There was one thing. I think of you cutting up the food into portions for me. Regardless, best wishes for a successful restaurant."

It is well thought out, his gift for me, but a mixed message too. Knives and flowers. Is he pointing out some direct connection between our relationship? I'm not surprised it's expensive. It is three of the Takahashi brand of chef knives, the most used, the highest priced.

"Good God, Bear, I—"

"It said online it's the most important tool a chef uses."

I stand there unsure. For this moment, he reminds me of the Bear that was *between*. Not the petty, narrow-minded, arrogant man from last year, and not the one a few weeks ago who sat there playing with his phone at the resort, callous and snobbish while his mama cut me down with her words and kicked me off the team. It's the one who got off work early to meet me at Pops to watch old movies with a bowl of buttered popcorn in his lap and an arm over my shoulder. It's the one who bought a hundred teeny roses, walked them into the bedroom, and made a heart on the bed.

"I've got to go. Meetings." He gives me a wave of a hand.

"Oh, I've got some of your meals in here if you want them. I made enough to last the—"

"I probably shouldn't." He forces a smile, pulls a shield up over his face. Then he's the Bear on either side, the mean, arrogant one again. "Meghan might think I'm getting a little *something-something* on the side."

*Arrgh*! Bear knows I hate that saying. He knows I connect that to Mama's already-taken, one-night-stands on the weekends. I keep a straight face. I'm good at that. I'm also good at working up a head-tipping, sweet grin that's hard as hell to read. It comes from an ex-husband who was easy with the fist. "Oh, no worries about that, Beau," I say. "My new guy would shoot bricks at you if he thought something was going on." *My new boyfriend. Why'd I say that? And how do you shoot bricks?* I look at a fake watch on my wrist, work up a look of mock alarm. "I'm supposed to be somewhere in a few. Thanks for the gift and good luck to you. I also wish you the best." And I hope they fall off a cliff too.

"The one who rides the motorcycle?"

"Huh?" I blink. "Oh, yeah. Yeah, it's him."

## Chapter 22—Love at First Sight

Is there such a thing as love at first sight? I am standing on the banks of Stone Cold Creek lugging another black plastic garbage bag full of Mister Smiley's day-old bread to empty tents. It's my usual drop-and-run. I'm not so sure it does any good. For all I know, raccoons are dragging the stuff I bring off into the woods. I continue to collect stuff. In my head, I've concocted this whole idea of a scrawny woman with a starving baby picking through the trash somebody else left here. Her eyes brighten with the thought of the double-double chocolate chip cookies I made last night to bring here.

But the raggedy tents are gone today. It looks like a tornado ran through. Blankets, rolls of toilet paper, shirts, pots, and pans are scattered around. I'm perplexed enough to stand there, not heeding footsteps behind me.

"You must be new at this." The voice comes from nowhere. I jump so hard, I lurch forward and heave a grunting gasp. "The cops came through and sacked the camp. I guess somebody complained."

"Oh." I'm charmed. Why? I don't know. He's just cute. His eyes are bright, smiling, and baby blue. He's got those little laugh lines at the corners of his eyes. I've never done this before, been what my mamaw used to call smitten—

infatuated by an attractive face. I'm muddled by it.

"I'm so sorry. I parked a mile away to avoid the police. I came back to grab something for someone." It's a twenty-something man in a clean t-shirt and jeans. He is thin, freshly showered, and shaved. I'm assuming he's not among the tent community. "It's alright. I'm not going to hurt you or drag you away. I'm with the Jamestown Community Church. You don't look familiar. I was bringing lunch, but that got disrupted. You probably shouldn't be here so soon. The police are still rambling up and down the road clearing out folks. I can take you to the shelter or the clinic if you want." I had remained silent until then, watched his eyes fall to the black garbage bag clutched in my fingers. Oh, he must think these are my belongings. "You were lucky. You got all your stuff before they came, huh?" He smiles with heart-shaped lips.

"I, um, I'm not homeless."

"It's okay." His voice is soft, gentle. "It happens. We're all one step away."

"No, no." I shake my head, hold up my sack. "I was bringing food and some day-old bread and stuff because I saw the tents one day. And cookies. I bring cookies."

"You're Girl Scout, then."

"No."

"No, I mean, that's what Charlie calls you.

Girl Scout. Because you bring cookies all the time."

"Oh, maybe, I do bring chocolate chip cookies and some homemade protein bars. I made a bunch with peanut butter. My pops' friend, Miss Lila, she said I shouldn't because some people are allergic to peanut butter." I'm rambling and don't know why. I go on for another thirty seconds while he smiles patiently. Then, I give up, hold out my hand. "I'm Brandy."

"Oh, I know you." He steps forward, shakes my hand.

"The Redneck Run?" I ask. He nods.

"I'm Zane Powers." A mosquito buzzes past my nose. I swat it away. "I'm doing mission work here for the summer, studying to be a minister or youth counselor. I'm stuck between which to choose. I'm from Tennessee. Maybe I'll see you around here again, Girl Scout." That's what he says. My heart jumps. "Hopefully not in a tent. But boy, Charlie loves those cookies of yours. I can take them off your hands and make sure he gets a few—"

## Chapter 23—Shelly Holcomb's Story

There's something about the cigar box that draws me to it. I've always liked a mystery. I used to hide Pops' slippers and leave him little yellow Post-It Notes around the house so he could find them. It's more than the picture of the young Katelyn staring back at me. I stare back at her. I wonder if she blew bubbles on her back porch and if her first kiss was at a dance or a first date at the movies. I'm curious if she shared secrets with a best friend in high school.

Bill Gaynor corners me on the front porch of the restaurant while I'm thinking that. He's standing there with his huge camera and smiling a big-toothed smile. I'm a bit flustered. I've been thinking about Zane Powers, even did a little search for the Jamestown Community Church which was what I was doing when I heard Bill's car pull in.

"I hear from Bakersfield he's courting you for the race. I also saw that you mentioned the same on your social media. *And* I heard some rather exciting news from Ben Wright. You bought this beautiful restaurant." I stood there speechless, knowing he had probably flown in from whatever place he was doing a story. "I would have hoped that you would have told me this and I didn't hear it from the grapevine. But bygones. The story is going to print. I need an update. Lord, you work fast. It is hard to keep up. Let's get a shot so I can get this story to print on time." I hurriedly pose for some shots, unsure of his motives. I ask him. He says that folks want to know what happened to me after the race. I smile, make a silly pose, then hold out my arms. "This."

When I run the boxes of meals to Sandra and stop in to pick up wood so my uncle can make me a sign, I also stop in the little town of Pittman. It is here that 35-year-old Shelly Holcomb, who worked at the Sunrise Year-Round Camping Resort camp grocery with Katelyn, lives in a modest one-story house alongside a whole town of homes pressed up against a mountainside. I knock on the door. She answers. She's a big woman, tall and thick-boned. She's short blond hair and pale eyes and lips. After my little spiel about looking for information about Katelyn, she stands at the door for a good three breaths. Then she makes a careful sweep of what I can't see through the raggedy screen window and yells that she's going outside.

"Who are you again?"

"My name's Brandy Devereauxs—"

"I've heard that name before."

"I ran the Redneck Run last year."

"Yeah." Suddenly, she brightens up. "And you caught your husband who'd married a bunch of women. I read that in the newspaper." She wiggles a finger at me, tells me to follow.

"I'm not sure I can tell you much more than I told the cops back in the day. It's been, what, fifteen or twenty years? I can't remember yesterday most of the time." She chuckles. We wind our way to the gravel drive and come to a standstill, facing each other. "She worked her usual shift that night. The normal campers were coming and going, lots of old people with their grandkids and families. I remember she asked me if I could take her home. I couldn't. I was working until midnight. She got off at eleven. I watched her leave about twenty minutes after her shift was done. Her brother was late. She walked out the door. I told the cops I always assumed it was her brother picking her up like usual. But I was busy, didn't look out. That's all I know. My shift got done a half hour later. I left."

"You never saw her leave with her brother?"

"No."

"Who worked after you?"

"Roddy, the owner."

"Did you see her steal money from the campground?"

"Katelyn?" She laughs, looks upward at the puffy white clouds hovering above the trees.

"You're kidding me. She was like a church-girl; all smiles all the time and doing things by the book. I imagine if she found a buck on the floor, she'd be chasing people down to figure out who it belonged to."

"Why'd they say she stole money?" I tug on my lip. "I read two newspapers that stated she was stealing money from the campground registers and giving it to her brother. The cops told me that too."

"I read that too. But half the stuff reporters put in the newspapers was a bunch of crap. And have you met the cops in Quail Hollow? They'd come down once in a while to the campground to check the plates for what they called *known drug dealers*. Roddy Graham, he was the one who owned the Sunrise campground. He said it was private property and probably illegal as hell to be sniffing up and down the camp roads. But he let them do it. Roddy got this funny look on his face when they were there like he didn't trust them. They dragged a couple of folks out of there a few times, said they had warrants out on them. But, if anyone was stealing money, there was no way they'd know how much or even notice it was gone."

"What do you mean?"

"Roddy was kind of grouchy, but a nice old man. His wife had died a year before I started working there in 1998. She did all the books. He didn't have a clue about taxes and keeping inventory. He was always snatching money out of the register over our shoulders for groceries or to buy gas for his trucks or whatever he needed to buy for the store. If the bottled gas guy came in, he'd grab a wad of cash and pay him. I don't ever remember him making out a receipt to show what he took out. At the end of the day, he just had us count what was in the register and leave a hundred bucks worth of change for the next day. I don't even know what he did with the cash he took at night." Shelly shoves her hands in her pockets.

"Why would the cops base an entire motive on Marcus Freeman murdering Katelyn for drug money if she wasn't stealing? Where would they come up with that?"

"I think they heard talk. I never saw her take any money. I don't know where the cops got that information. There was never chit-chat about anything like that. I knew all the gossip."

"Did you ever meet her brother, Marcus?"

"He came to pick her up lots of times if her dad had to use the car. His car was always breaking down." She gets this little smile on her lips. "He was a big guy."

"Did you feel uncomfortable around him?"

Shelly scratches her forehead, waves a bug away with her hand. "I don't remember anything like that. I mean, it's been a long time. He just waited by the door, said hi to me. He complained about having to pick her up all the time. Katelyn always bragged on him, said he was working for a contractor to get enough money to go to college. He wanted to be an EMT or a fire investigator or something."

"Did he come in that night and say hi?"

"No, it was busy though."

"Did you know Allie Blankenship?"

"Yeah, I remember that name." Shelly's eyes roll. "She worked at the campground for about a year and a half. Katelyn liked her. I didn't. Allie was always trying to fix Katelyn up, get her to go party and stuff. She quit not long after Katelyn was found dead."

"Why didn't you like her?"

"Nothing big. She was just always trying to get me and Katelyn to go to The Coffin off the state route and we were underage." Shelly shrugs it off. "It was full of old guys. She was trying to fix me up with a couple of guys that were like forty."

"Did she act strangely between the time Katelyn was murdered and the time she quit?"

Shelly nibbles on her lips, taps her foot on the ground. "No. Not at all." But she won't look me straight in the eye when she says that just like my little sister won't keep eye contact when I ask her if she was getting into my stuff in my room. Kaylee will give me a resounding *no*! while she's standing in a puddle of my underwear she's dragged out of my drawer.

## Chapter 24—The Stalking

I noticed the banged-up Ford truck following me about ten minutes out of Pittman on the four-lane divided highway. I passed it at a junction. It was stopped between the lanes at an intersection with black smoke chugging out of the exhaust. I took it in like I do everything I pass. It was white and worn out and had municipality plates. I caught the silhouette of a man inside. He was wearing the same kind of yellow safety crew t-shirts Kenny wears on his contracting jobs when he has to flag traffic. It has orange and gray reflective tape and patches along the front.

I turned my attention back to the highway and the trees and the GPS map that was showing me I had eight miles until I needed to make my next turn. The truck pulled out directly behind me, stayed in the right lane with me. When I flipped on my signal and turned on a backroad that cuts through the mountains and heads a more direct route toward New Alliance, it continued behind.

The backroads are buckled asphalt and sometimes just the marble-size gravel the townships toss out on the roads in winter to keep folks from slipping right off the side and down the embankment. I have to speed up, slow down, almost come to a grinding halt at hairpin turns. At the bottom, the road is covered in a layer of tan dried mud, small broken limbs, and pieces of white Styrofoam cups and old green soda bottles from the creeks overflowing last week. When I ease up the next mountain, they're covered in slippery last autumn leaves.

I don't think much of it at first, the truck easing up behind me. There's no pull-off or driveway to slide over so the driver can pass. The dim light of day is fading to a gray hue and then to a quarter moon of dark which leaves me driving a little slower because there are no edge lines. The lights of the truck go on, then off, then on again. I think, at first, the driver is just flicking the truck lights because it's starting to sprinkle and he grabbed the lever for the lights instead of the windshield wiper arm. Maybe he wants to pass. Maybe, he's stalking me.

BOOM! That's the sound the truck makes at the tippy top of one steep hill. BOOM! The front of the municipal truck bashes into the left rear of my truck a second time. I jolt, feel my truck buck forward and skid sideways in the pebbles on what is barely a shoulder. It is unexpected. I'm stunned as my truck makes a wiggle to the right. It careens down through the darkness, trees and brush skidding and squealing along the sides until I come to a jarring grind at the bottom with the front end of my truck sticking out at the turn in the road below. I can't see a guardrail. I can only see my lights shining slightly upward into the night sky.

Now my foot is desperately tapping the accelerator until I realize I don't know where it will lead me if I move forward. I feel my heart pounding, hands shaking, legs trembling. I hear my rear tires spinning, catch the scent of burning rubber. I'm terrified one tire will finally catch and send me bursting forth again, and this time I won't be so lucky when I break a guardrail and head blindly down into the darkness of some deep overhang. I've got no choice but to slip out of the truck and peer into the dark, see where I am. I snap my eyes upward. I don't see the truck lights not a stone's throw away. Or anywhere. I think, but I don't know for sure, that it must have turned around and left.

I open my door and step outside listen to the crunch of gravel beneath my feet, keys jingling in my hand. I close the door softly, wag my head left to right to take in my surroundings. I see the shadow treading around the curve. Shit. Close. The figure is too close for me to jump back in without knowing where the road is heading. He's swinging something slowly back and forth, back and forth. "Hey, little girlie-girl, let's play—" It's a bat, a baseball bat.

The shine of guardrail is barely on the other side of the road. I click the remote to lock my door, and it sounds as loud as a shotgun—*chunk-chunk*. I slip along the side of my truck back to cool doors, slide into the brush, and up four steps of the hillside. I scrunch down to a squat. Does he know where I am? I don't think so. He is coming for my truck, silently stealthily. My mind is mush from this unexpected turn of events. Why did I get out of the truck instead of staying inside?

His truck is parked above on the road. I slip along the side of the hill in the brush and up the hillside. The wet from the drizzle makes the leaves mushy. Only the sound of rain pattering on the roof of his truck comes to my ears. I can see, from this vantage, below. My truck is facing toward the roadway in the direction I was heading. It is slightly on the hill. I can see where it pushed aside brush and trees to get to where it is.

My heart makes a new and steady beat, hard and rapid while I watch him look into my passenger side window, step back, wag his head back and forth like he's searching for me. Bam! Bam! Bam! He's got the baseball bat in hitter mode, over his shoulder and swinging hard. I watch him bang the windshield of the truck. Not hard enough to break it. The alarm goes off loud and resounding. I jump, cringe.

Bam! Bam! Bam! He hits it again. I don't know how to stop him. Bear is going to kill me. The registration and the insurance are still in his name. A dribble of sweat tickles along my forehead, fades to my cheek. It is cool, moist. I tiptoe to the bumper of the truck, take in the license. It is nondescript. The door is open, a radio making a steady hum of country music. I'm drawn to the open door. It smells like beer and cigarettes and twenty years of dirty-booted, overworked maintenance crews climbing inside. What am I doing? I am stuck here. He might have a gun. I see a six-pack of beer, three cans gone, three cans full. My cousin, Jake, works for the county. They frown on eating in the car while driving, won't allow smoking, and it's certainly against any rules to carry an alcoholic beverage in the vehicles, much less drink one inside. I let my fingers work to the open beer can in the center console and pick it up with the sleeve covering my fingers and spill it across the seat and carpet. Then I pop, pop, pop the last three and let them fall across the seat. I hear a deep voice below yell out. I hear the sound of boots clomping up the road and close my eyes. With one lug of my wrist, I release the emergency brake. The vehicle makes a soft roll forward. Then it gains some momentum while I heave with my shoulder. I listen to the tires crunch on gravel down the road. And then, to the angry bear-bellow of my stalker as his truck ambles driverless down the mountain.

## Chapter 25—Breaking News

The breaking news in the morning paper on Wednesday states that a couple of unknown drunk teens hijacked a truck from Sandstone Falls Village Transportation Department near Quail Hollow and had taken a joyride ending in the totaling of the vehicle. There were no injuries. The teens were not apprehended, but there was beer found within the vehicle abandoned after careening down over the brim of what locals called Owl Hollow. There was a short comment by the department head, Jones Ripley, how the teens managed to get into the fenced-in lot with a padlocked gate. Artie Lambert, who had worked for the crew, was the last to leave the maintenance barn. Coworkers, Joe Sutton, and Tim Burke, had clocked out and left only moments earlier. Artie Lambert had seen Burke's truck still sitting in the impound and assumed the man was still in the offices. But Burke's vehicle wouldn't start, and Sutton had offered him a ride.

Lambert, believing Burke was still inside the building, had gotten into his personal car and driven out of the lot leaving the gate unbolted. Three hours later, he and his brother had passed the lot going into town and noted the gate was still ajar. Lambert also noted with some curiosity, one of the village trucks was missing and was sure he passed the vehicle coming back into town. He turned on his heels and found the stolen vehicle off the road fifteen miles away which they were trying to extricate from a twenty-foot drop when police arrived at the scene. The state patrol are investigating the theft but did not comment.

I also assume Artie Lambert had no clue I had called the state police three miles down the highway. Shaking, I told the cop who arrived an excruciating twenty minutes later, a drunk driver had been following me wearing city crew clothing in a white truck. He had run me off the road, then gotten out of his vehicle to chase me down on foot. I had hidden in the vehicle until he left. They took a report. I went home.

# Chapter 26—Brandywine and Going All Crazy over Marcus Because he Doesn't Have Time for Trivial Fluff over Cookies and Milk

Mama used to tell me she gave me my name because when I popped out of her, the first thing she saw was my big tan-pink eyes the color of her favorite drink, Brandy Alexander. Pops said she told that to the nurses as a joke when they came in to fill out the birth certificate, and even the doctor laughed, so she kept going with it and started telling everybody that's how I got my name.

Pops said before she got hooked on the beer, she wasn't so mean, and could light up a room with her jokes. Not so now. The only things Mama lights up are her cigarettes and dope. Regardless, he didn't think that was how she came up with *Brandy*. He said at one time, they used to have a small vineyard in the bottoms at the Piper's where my restaurant is going to be. They made brandy from the wine. There was still an old mural painted on one of the barns when I was first born that said BRANDY WINE SOLD HERE.   SWEET. BOLD. DARING. When Pops' high beam lights flashed on it the night he was rushing her to the hospital for my birth, Mama told him it was a sign. I was going to be like that—sweet, bold, and daring.

I nervously burst out with that to Marcus Freeman when he pulls his motorcycle into the parking lot of the restaurant at lunchtime and slowly slides his leg over his bike like I'm a rabid pup running from the building getting ready to nip at his heels. I'm usually an open book, and more so with people who make me nervous. I start spurting out stuff, sometimes nonsense to anyone but my family and me. I can't tell if he wants to kick me away. He's got that aloof stare that sets me back a step and wondering how stupid I sound.

"I got my new sign." I sound too frantic. I slow my words. "I guess I'm just a little excited. Sorry." As if he cares. I guess I did run out fast. I was deep into working on my menu items. When I heard him pull in, for a teeny moment, I thought it was Bear's deep-throated truck—the old *Bear*, the one before Mila *Bear*, the one-who-used-to-get-excited-about-my-stuff *Bear*.

Not willing to backtrack, I point to the sign Marcus passed coming into the gravel lot out front. His eyes follow cautiously. Pops took a piece of an old oak from our mountain he cut down. He took it to his friend's house who makes signs and had him engrave *Brandywine Restaurant and Tavern. At the Foot of Fire Mountain.* We hung it out by the road today on a pretty lamppost with COMING SOON on a recycled metal real estate sign underneath it. Gabe, who has a degree in marketing, says he'll be my *advertising account executive* if I cater a couple of meals for his mom's bible study group, and if I get rich and famous, I tell everybody he got me there. *And, oh, by the way, can you come back one more time and show Sandra how to make that honey-dipped bacon thingy?* He also said I need to start promoting the restaurant even though it isn't finished.

"Nevertheless," I'm telling Marcus while I wave him inside, "that's what we're calling it."

"I stopped to see if you found anything."

I blink at his expressionless face, feel disappointed and a bit shortchanged like I used to feel when I'd be sitting in bed and watching the best part of a movie and Pops would come into my room, flip off the TV, and tell me it was time to go to bed. "Yeah," I grunt flippantly. "I found what one person tells me is completely different from what the next person tells me. That your sister was murdered at Stone Cold Creek or—or it could have been at Froggy Pay Lake. Oh, and I found that somebody wants to stop me from helping you enough they'd kill me. Now can you greet me like a normal person, say *hi, Brandy* or something first?"

"Kill you? You're kidding. What do you mean by that? Do we need to have a conversation? I'm paying you to do a job for me. I can do without the chit chat and trivial fluff. I don't have the time or the patience to banter around like two little girls at a sleepover. You either do the job or not. If not, I'll go elsewhere."

He hurt my feelings. I let my own face go slack. I march to my truck purposely, swing the door open wide. Then I snatch up my keys laying on the seat, unlock my glovebox. I dig out the brown paper bag and stomp back over to Marcus with my arm extended, but far enough away he can't reach my hand when I drop the brown paper sack between us. "Bam! There. Go elsewhere. I don't particularly like being inside every cops' radar within a two-hour drive because they know I'm rubbing elbows with a man they *still* consider a murderer. I don't like being hunted down by creepy old men in big trucks on dark roads with baseball bats and me with no clue why they are chasing me, only the vague impression that it is linked to the fact I'm asking questions about something they don't want to be asked." I take in a long breath, let it out. Marcus looks like he is going to speak. I give him a mean eye and stop him with my palm out. "And I know if my pops finds out I'm getting my hands dirty again with what he calls gumshoe detective work, and he does not say it with a proud tip to his chin, he'll know I've been making bad decisions just like my mama always did. I happen to like chit-chatting about what you call *trivial fluff over cookies and milk* or whatever else whether you like it or not." I pivot on my feet and walk back inside, slamming the door shut behind me. I can hear him driving off. I don't care.

## Chapter 27— Trivial Fluff over Cookies and Milk

It isn't a half hour before the sound of the motorcycle comes grinding back into the gravel lot again. I let out a deep and exasperated breath. It isn't unlike the way Kenny hard-sighs when he finds out Preacher Murphy (with his short sermons filled with everyday anecdotes Kenny can identify with) is going on a church mission, and his substitute is long-winded, two-hour lecturer James Hill who makes eye contact with Kenny when he tells everybody the eleventh sin is cussing.

"I stopped at Mister Smiley's down the street and got milk for you and one for me and—" Marcus busts right through the door, letting the outside screen slam hard behind him. I'm leaning with my elbows on the center counter and look up guardedly. He slaps down one of the teen magazines that Mister Smiley keeps behind the counter by the cash register. "If you want, there's a fun twelve question quiz on page seventeen about which type of Disney character matches your personality." Then he makes a point of pushing back that wild hair from his face. "I would suspect, from what little personal contact I had with you, I don't have to open up the magazine to weigh in on which figure matches your feisty Chihuahua-like disposition, princess. I could whittle it down to two characters: one, the sassy red-haired Celtic one and the crafty cat with the sword and boots. Regardless, somebody found a plastic baggie with little bits of pot in Janey Mills' locker from last year. Did you hear that? Ellen—um, Ellen—who works at the grocery—" He pauses thoughtfully and looks up to the ceiling.

"Wells?" I add the last name with a questioning, but wary set to my eyes.

"Yeah, that's it. She told me that it must have fallen out of Janey's bag in her locker. She also said Frankie Little, who drops off ice, said gas is cheaper here than in Wheeling."

"You're chit-chatting," I declare skeptically while Marcus opens a plastic grocery sack. I peer inside, note factory-made chocolate chip cookies. "I accept your apology."

"I'm not apologizing. I'm un-quitting you."

"You can't do that. I'm the only one who can un-quit." I tip my head inquisitively. "Is that a word *un-quit*?" I also give the sack a shove toward him. "I make my cookies, thank you. Would you like something to eat?"

"I'm not hungry. I don't have time—"

"And we're back to not chit-chatting," I remind him. "You have to understand if you stand in my kitchen, you have to eat. That's the social culture I grew up in. I'm going to make you something because you look like my Pops when he hasn't eaten—all tetchy and holier-than-thou." I see he is getting impatient again.

Redneck Run II – Shine    Shay Lawless

"See? Tetchy."

"Let's talk creepy old men with baseball bats, and the reason your truck out there has a gash down the side and dents on the hood."

"Let's eat and talk about the crazy man." I twist around, make a swift retrieval of one of twenty-two spiral bound notebooks I have carefully placed in a small workspace behind me. They are a collection of recipes I've made over the years. Like an artist's portfolio, these are a collection of my culinary works of art. "Let me guess," I say promptly. "You look like healthy portions of salmon and brown rice."

"Fast food cheeseburgers, three large fries, and—"

"Not on my watch!" I hiss, walk to the refrigerator and grab the salmon dish. I pop it into the oven.

"By the way, you're my fake boyfriend," I announce.

"Are you trolling for a date?" Dark eyes stare me hard when I lean back again, elbows on the counter. He's scooted up a bar stool from across the room. He rattles me. Marcus Freeman's gaze is intense, penetrating straight through me. He can see through the shell I won't allow others to see past. I force back a shiver, instead grunt up a stupid giggle that sounds more like a snort. I want to pull my eyes away. I won't. Pops says I have too much headstrong in me; I'm willful and won't back down first. He said I could have spent a lot less time cooped up in my room in teen-timeouts if I had simply swapped out my signature unyielding stare along with the grand finale snarky head waggle with a fake teary-eyed sorry gaze.

"No—no, of course not." I have a difficult time keeping up the glare.

"You got some guy bothering you?"

"No. I mean, yes and no. My ex-boyfriend and I broke up a few weeks ago. He's got a girlfriend already, maybe two. I got a little stupid and said I had a boyfriend—"

"Me?"

"That's what he assumed. He thinks I'm basking in misery over him."

"Are you?"

"Yeah, but I didn't tell him that. I'm still knee-deep in ill-feelings, regret, and wrapping his t-shirts in pillows at night and propping them up in the bed next to me." Marcus looks a little scared which kind of scares me because he's ten times my size and the one who everybody thinks murdered a girl. "I don't wrap up his t-shirts in pillows."

"Okay, that's good."

"I sleep in them."

"Holy hell," he gasps.

I laugh. He laughs. "Then the guy who works the security gate at the resort *and* the guy at the gas station asked me out. The gas station guy is somewhat of a local legend. I hear from my aunt's card table gossip on Sundays he's slept with every woman from sixteen to sixty within a forty-mile radius." I shrug. "Not me. You're my excuse, big guy. You're not going to have to tell anybody. But if it comes up in conversation at any point while you get gas at Quickie Gas, I didn't want it to throw you for a loop. I told the guy I'm going out with a guy that looks like Hercules. You're the only one around fitting the bill."

"I'm probably twelve years older than you." He's not pulling his gaze away either. I'm fascinated. It's like he realizes I've drawn a sword, await a battle of the headstrong. Now, he's pulling out his weapon of choice, a daggered tongue. I narrow mine. He narrows his.

"I'm not fishing for a boyfriend. I met a guy. I'm thinking about asking him out. I'm not sure I'm over the last one—but do you believe in love at first sight? Never mind, I was joking. But he's got these eyes—"

"The love-at-first-sight-guy?"

"Yeah, they are always laughing. I mean, I've only seen him once. But they were laughing then. I've never met anybody like that except my friend, Gabe. Whatever." I sigh deeply. "Everybody always figures I'd turn out like my mama looking for a daddy figure and stripping at the local club."

"How long are we going to keep up this battle of wills, this staring contest?" Marcus says flatly. "I've got to be honest, I used to have them with my sister. I never lost."

"You started it with that snarky look, then the gaze. I'm not turning away. I've won nine times out of ten with my cousin Kenny. I'm a sore loser, a really sore loser."

"Can you at least answer why we're doing this?"

"You started it."

"What? Not wanting to sit around and gossip?"

"No, I'm way past that. You started the staring contest," I mutter. My eyes are burning. "In a roundabout way, you implied I wasn't good enough to ask you out."

"I didn't say that."

"You just blinked when you said that. I win," I lie.

"Bull."

"Damn. That ploy works on Kenny," I mutter. It always works on Kenny even though I've done it a thousand times. "Okay, so we're doing this. What are the stakes; what's the point?"

"I have no idea in hell why we're doing this, and every penny I own is in that paper sack."

"Do you know anybody named Artie Lambert? Think hard. I think he might have been the one to run me off the road last night. I don't think he was trying to scare me."

*Blink-blink.* "Bam, again!" I cry out in victory when Marcus snaps his eyes wide, then closes them. I pump a fist into my palm making a slapping sound. "I won."

He ignores my victory cry. Marcus settles into his chair, pushes elbows on the counter, and folds his hands together. "We went to the same school, best friends until eighth grade." Marcus looks like he's swallowed a pill that's too big and it is sticking in his throat. "He went one way when we got into high school. I went another."

"Which *ways* did you two go? Like the dark side and the light?" I feign swinging a Jedi lightsaber.

"No, he played football. I played drums in the band."

"You look more like the football type. Last night, the guy who chased me down looked more like the sits-in-front-of-the-tv-and-watches-football kind of guy."

"Once you go to jail, your type changes. I was chubby back then." He shifts uncomfortably. "Artie—I don't know what route he went."

"You think he would have chased me down randomly?" I ask him. "You know, because I'm so cute," I tease, blinking my eyes rapidly, flirty. "Or maybe he's warning me. I talked to Shelly Holcomb right before. Is it coincidence or did she call him because they are involved? It was like he was waiting for me, knew I was heading that direction."

"I remember Shelly. She and my sister were pretty close in the summer."

"Then she really downplayed their friendship which is strange, toned down Katelyn's death like she couldn't even remember how long ago it happened." I hold up a finger. "Hold that thought." He's all sullen until I bring the salmon out, put it on a plate with a buttered sweet potato, and baby carrots. I hear his belly growl like it's whining, trying to convince him to eat it. I tug out another spiral notebook where I've written down the information I've collected so far. "Listen, I know you don't think I'm doing anything. I am. I'm not a cop. I don't have information at my fingertips. It's like wading through a pond and trying to catch a fish with my hands. It's hard. It's been a long time. People—forget. That said, I need to ask you a couple of hard questions so I can wrap my head around this," I say in the same cooing voice Pops soothes Kaylee while he rocks her after she's had a bad dream. "Just answer them, and we'll move on."

"Okay. I can't think of a reason Artie would have anything to do with this. He was shitty once he started hanging around football boys. Alone, he was okay. They were like a pack of wolves. Together, they'll bring a deer down and eat it up. By themselves, they usually sit back and watch the world go by their territory."

"Yeah, well, that's what I'm wondering isn't happening with your sister's case," I tell him softly, catch his eyes again. "A bunch of wolves. Everybody is afraid of them." He pokes his fork into the meat and takes a bite slowly.

"Regardless, I know what you're going to ask, Brandy. No, I didn't kill my sister. We got in fights, but we hardly even yelled at each other unless I accidentally walked into the bathroom while she was in there." He rubs his face. "No, I didn't do drugs. I didn't even smoke pot back then. I was too busy working and playing video games. All my friends from high school either got jobs or went to college. My parents couldn't afford tuition. I was trying to get enough money saved to go in a couple of years. My life was either work or playing games."

"Okay, so I need to fill in a couple of blanks." I roll my pencil down a timeline I've gotten so far. "I've got Katelyn going to work and being there until eleven."

"Midnight. Katelyn was working with that other girl that night until midnight. Then they'd close the store."

"Shelly told me Katelyn worked until eleven."

"Not so." He pushes his fork into the meat, gives me a nod and wane smile. "See this is what happens. Everybody's got a different story. Mine, I was playing video games at home by myself that night. I didn't want to leave to pick her up. It was a pain driving over there. I had to get up at four again the next morning for a job in Wheeling. We were sharing a car. I had to use it during the day for my job working for Long's Carpets. Jerry, the guy who owned it, paid me under the table to help rip out the old carpets, install new ones. When I got done, it was my job to pick Katelyn up if mom and dad were working at Frazee's. Some days I was working fifteen hours. That was one of them. I called her and asked if she could get a ride home. She said she couldn't. It was a stupid question because nobody lived our direction. But in normal circumstances, it was just a way to show I didn't want to pick her up, but I would. I always did. It was a way to annoy her, I guess, show her how I felt about it." His mouth screws up at the corners. "I knew we didn't have a choice. It didn't matter. It just irritated me we had to share a car. I guess I blamed her. She got better grades in high school so Mom and Dad figured she was the one they'd invest money into going to college instead of me. Nobody else ever drove her home. I drove up there to pick her up by midnight. I left at eleven and was probably twenty minutes early. I was tired and mad that I had to pick her up. She was gone. The building was locked. There wasn't anybody around. I drove around the campground looking for the guy who owned it, but it was like a huge party there with all the campers. I drove up and down the roads thinking she got mad and walked. Then about three in the morning, I went home. I tried to call my parents at work to see if she'd called them. She hadn't. Mom and dad got back around six. I'd fallen asleep waiting for them. Bad thing to do, I know. But it was the last thing on my mind that anything would ever happen to her."

Marcus Freeman starts to talk, really talk. He tells me about the nightmare of being dragged into the police station over and over again, harassed and thinking they were trying to help his family find his sister. He had no clue they were trying to pin the murder on him. Then when he did, he couldn't remember what he told them or didn't tell them, or what was right or wrong answering questions under duress.

The cops began manipulating his words, making him repeat things, so it looked like he confessed. He just wanted to go home and pretend it didn't happen, go and pick up Katelyn. His parents backed him up, but always blamed him for not picking his sister up on time. They started to build a wall which Marcus said he added to it. He was in jail for three years. By the second year, they stopped visiting. He hasn't talked to them in eleven or twelve years. "I told them it was my fault. When I did, the cops ran with it. I meant it was my fault I was late picking Katelyn up. My last words to her were: *God, you're such a pain in my ass*."

"I say that to my cousin, Kenny, all the time. He's like a brother." I sigh, reach out and swipe a carrot from Marcus' plate, pop it in my mouth. "An annoying brother who is always in my stuff." I want to cry. It is sad, makes my heart ache, his eyes looking up at me, the angry swiped off for the moment. I reach out my hand, let it slide across and pat his wrist twice, pull away. "It's the way we communicate, like saying: *You're a part of my life. I guess we're just going to have to deal with it.* It's kind of like *I love you* in a brother-sister kind of way."

"But he's still around. Katelyn's not."

"I know."

"I'd give a million bucks to turn back time. I'd give a million more to fly away somewhere nobody knows me, knows my story."

"Like your butterfly," I say, patting my side. He looks at me with his hard-stare again, all closed up like I just don't get it. But I'm getting the feeling that hard stare is just a wall like my own he puts up when I've peeked a bit into his soul. "I probably can't say anything to make it right," I mumble. "But you're talking to the woman who sat in a bar every week waiting for her dead ex-husband to come back to her. I should probably get a tattoo that says *STUPID* in big, fat letters on my forehead for how long it took me to realize he was just an ass."

## Chapter 28—Bear VS Marcus

"I'll be right back."

Bear's out in the driveway of my restaurant inspecting the rear end of the truck where there is a huge imprint of the Sandstone Falls Village Transportation Department front bumper. He must have come from a meeting. He's still sporting a suit coat and dress pants, and it is a good seventy degrees outside. He paces around one side, hand out and finger rolling along the scrape from the back door to the hood.

"Are you alright?" he asks me, looking up while I make my way around the wooden wheelchair accessible ramp Pops is building along the side. His eyes roll from the top of my head to the bottom of my feet. "I got a call from the police. Said the truck had been run off the road. The vehicle registration and insurance are in my name," he adds as if to justify the reason he was discussing the truck with the police. "Cam Bowers with New Alliance Insurance will be out to take pictures."

He stands up straight. I see him looking over my shoulder to the doorway. "Is that *him*?" Bear adjusts his tie, looks back to me.

"*Him*?" I ask. Marcus is exiting the door. It is just five steps from the porch to the drive. He stops short of the truck.

"Sweetie, I'm leaving."

*Sweetie*? Why the hell did he address me like that? He's looking at me. I'm looking at Bear. Bear is looking at Marcus. "Uh." That's what I say. I'm not sure why nobody is moving. I swallow hard. "Marcus, this is Beau Vega." I wag a hand at Bear, then make a whirl of my hand toward Marcus. "Beau, this is Marcus."

"Her boyfriend," Marcus says boldly.

I make a crazy swing of my head around to Marcus. "What?"

"Is this the guy from the gas station that's been bugging you?" he asks.

"No," I say that with the same grunt-choke I made last week when I swallowed a bug whole while I was running.

"The security guard?"

"No."

"The love-at-first-sight-guy?"

"No!"

He gives Bear one of his intent, pokerfaced gazes before looking back at me. "You're okay?" he asks while I nod my head dumbly. "I'm taking off then," he says without offering a viable explanation to the status of our relationship. "We'll do this again. The lunch was great. You need to add just an inkling of salt to the carrots." He holds up finger and thumb and almost pinches them together. With that, he gives me a wink and hops on his bike.

"Now you're a food critic?" I snap at his back.

Crap. I didn't get around to asking him about Allie Blankenship. He turns enough to waggle his head. "I don't—" I start to say *need to add more salt.* But he just gives a sly smile, takes off in an insulting spray of gravel pelting Bear's truck and silences my retort.

I turn in the calm after the motorcycle fades away, fold my arms protectively over my chest. "I'm sorry about the truck. I'll get some extra hours at Smiley's and pay the deductible or whatever it costs." I rock on my feet. Why am I nervous? "I was going to try to get another truck, you know, because—" Because I can't say we're not going out anymore. "Then you wouldn't have to make payments and all. I'm not sure what to do now."

"If it's totaled, then you can get another truck on your own, how's that?" Bear looks up. I try to see his eyes. I feel like something is dead inside there. "My mom suggested it would be a good idea for you to buy your own vehicle since we are no longer getting married, gift or not. I should take the truck."

"Now?" I feel a little dizzy. "I—I don't have a vehicle. I don't know if I can afford one with the building and my student loans and—can you give me a couple of weeks?"

"You should have thought of all that before you bought the land from underneath us, huh?" Bear used to have this mean grin when he was a kid. I see it working up. "Maybe your new boyfriend that might be—what did you call it? Oh, *shooting brick mad* if we were doing something, can cover your bills like I did."

"I can care for myself, fight my own battles."

"Or maybe you should have thought about it before you announced to the world you aren't on the team, huh? Do you know what a public embarrassment this is?" He wheels around and stomps to his truck. He reaches into the open window, pulls something out. This, he brings over to me, hand extended, and shoves it toward my chest. I look at him, look at the magazine. It is a copy of *The Time of Our Lives* magazine. I narrow my eyes, peer at the cover. I blanch. The cover is a picture of me standing in front of the old barn out back. "Is this a joke? Where'd you get this?" I ask Bear. I yank the magazine from his fingers, take a closer look. "God, I didn't even have lipstick on."

"That's what you're worried about?" he seethes while I snap my gaze up to him, eyes angry. "I know you know all about it. I talked to Gabe. He said that Bill Gaynor had been out a couple of times for the story."

"So?"

"*So* everyone is pulling out advertisements with the resort. We've lost sponsorships and two competitors for the event in the last six hours." He reaches out and spanks the magazine with his fingers. "Because of this. Because of you."

## Chapter 29— Resort at Two Bridge Falls

Jim Bakersfield from the Resort at Two Bridge Falls is delighted to meet me. At least that's what he tells me when he leads me down the maze of hallways to a conference room. He sent a car to get me. I took the four-hour ride in a black limousine watching TV with his assistant—a dark-haired and almost too-handsome man who knew how to lead a conversation.

"I read about you in Backroads Runner magazine from September of last year," he had started, smoothing back his hair with his hand. His name is Phoenix Drew. He looks exotic with too-white teeth and baby blue eyes like the summer sky. He should be sitting in a bamboo beach chair sipping cocoanut/strawberry tequila with a dark-haired beauty on some South American island. "Is it true you run about twenty miles a day?"

"More if I have time. I've got workout benches in my Pops' garage that I use now I'm not working out at Boar Mountain Resort. Nothing fancy." I was sure I had seen him on a commercial for men's underwear and made a note to myself to perform a search online later to see if I was correct. I was dying to tell Kenny I may have met a famous underwear model. He'd laugh himself right off his ATV. Phoenix was all gentleman and stayed by me the entire day, keeping up the conversation when it lagged with anyone. He was good at centering the attention back to me. I have a way of manipulating the conversation so I'm not the center. Phoenix Drew would not allow it. God, I love even saying that name. I mean, who is born with a name like that? I was so excited that I let him have one of the nutrition bars I made for Jim Bakersfield instead of the cookies he'd requested. I thought it more fitting for a man who was hosting a sports team for the Redneck Run. He liked it, asked for the recipe. I eagerly gave it to him.

Jim also tells me he's got his marketing staff waiting to meet me. "Be prepared. They are dying to meet you. You're a superstar."

"No, I'm not. At least not where I come from." I'm wearing a black sheath dress. It's tight, but not too tight to not pass as business attire. At least that's what the advertisement said in the online catalog when I bought it.

"We'll change that, my dear." He thinks this is funny. "I think you'll be surprised. You're quite a celebrity. I work fourteen-hour days, seven days per week. Don't have to. Want to." He waves me down another hallway. It smells like lavender in here and the savory scent of fresh wood. Everything he says is in short spurts, a faucet flushing out air in the pipes. "This is it. This is Two Bridge Falls. I fell in love with it at first sight. Three years ago. I bought all the stocks. It's mine, all mine." He stops, turns. "I'm rich, you know. Don't think I fell into it. Not inheritance. I earned it writing books. Have you ever heard of the Jace Taggart series? Ten books. An ex-military man hired as a private investigator. I wrote them all."

I can't walk away from the feeling I'm unfaithful. It's not just to Bear and the resort, even though they kicked me off the team. It's also to Fire Mountain. If Jim Bakersfield wants me, I'll be running against the team, running against my hometown.

"And here we are—" We burst through two doors. I'm staring at two tables filled with business-types, all in their thirties, and all sporting teeny laptops, but poking their fingers on cell phones. It looks akin to any one of my college classes. They all look up like Jim's the professor and I'm a guest speaker. I cringe, try not to freeze while they all set down their cell phones and rise, start clapping their hands with smiles on faces.

"Damn, you must be one heck of a boss," I mumble nervously. Jim has his hands in his pockets and throws his head back and laughs. "Brandy Devereauxs," he says over the applause and throws his hand out. He turns to me and leans in. "No, that's for you. I cut the crowd that wanted to be invited by a hundred. A little bird told me you're anxious around a lot of people."

That was my introduction to Jim's team, his

investors, and team members. If he described my reaction in his terse words, he would say it was: *Overwhelming. Empowering. A hold-on-to-your-seat-ride.* I left with a sore hand from signing autographs on forty posters from last year and a head-spinning cocktail hour (he knew I drank ginger-ale) with local celebrities.

"I know for a fact you're not getting this kind of treatment from the Fire Mountain team," he told me right before I left nearly five hours later. "You come run with us. I guarantee a head-spinning, wild ride. I'll make you a winner if you make me a winner. You'll make me lots of money. I'll pass that on to you. Sign on the dotted line."

"Well, here is the hitch. I'm interested." I've been treated so well today. Jim introduced me to several of his runners. They were excited to meet me. He's taking in ten, he said, mostly for the marketing aspect. There aren't any stipulations as to how many he has listed, just how many will run, and that does not have to be final until the day of the race. "But I was told I'm still under the Boar Mountain contract."

"Tell them to sue you. I'll take care of the rest."

I did sign with Jim Bakersfield. Before I left, I was looking at the little space I post things for my social networks. I typed out: *I got fired off the Redneck Run Team for Boar Mountain. Now I'm with Two Bridge Falls.* And I sent it out.

## Chapter 30—Preacher Thinks I Shine

Most of my family goes to the Fire Mountain Holy Gospel Church, also known as Fire Mountain Community Church, or That Church Up Top the Other Side of the Mountain depending on who you ask. It isn't as big as what my Aunt Kim calls that swanky Holy Trinity in New Alliance with the *real* preacher.

It has grown from an old white schoolhouse with wooden church pews, a lop-sided podium, and hand-me-down hymnals to piggybacking a big metal pole barn where a food pantry is set up by Holy Trinity's Preacher Murphy, open from two to four in the afternoon on Monday, Wednesday, and Friday. Most folks from around the area are too prideful to take handouts or follow the signs announcing: *FREE WARM MEAL*. I tell the preacher that when Mister Smiley makes me take my truck up on Friday and drop off the expired groceries, open-box diapers and toilet paper. Bear used to pick them up. For some reason, he's stopped.

"I know there are more needy families in the community than this." Preacher Murphy and his son, Gabe, look alike except the father has gray hair and a few lines under his eyes. He's standing by himself at the door in the vacant pole barn. He wasn't surprised to see me. I'm assuming he suggested my services for this mini-vacation from being Cash Register Girl.

"Where are they?"

"Well, some don't have cars to get here," I tell him, lugging a box of toilet paper in my arms. I hand the box to him and walk back to the truck. "Like Crystal Devereauxs who just had a baby. Me and Pops have been taking stuff to them."

"Oh, I guess I should know folks better."

"Preacher, I've known folks here since I was knee-high to a grasshopper. You've just started to get to know us." I grab another box. He takes in my words like he is drinking a tepid cup of tea he wished was hotter.

"We've been here way over ten years."

I don't tell him he's contending with folks who've been here a couple of hundred years comparatively. "Some are embarrassed to ask for a handout. Maybe if you ask them to volunteer and give them some food for working because—" I lower my voice. "You say the church can't afford to pay them with anything but food. Look like you feel bad and they're doing you a favor for taking food."

"That's an idea. But as you can see, they wouldn't have much to do." He juggles the door with his elbow, pushes it back so I can come through, then follows me to a worn, white table. "I'd hoped to get this started. It would run itself. But nobody's volunteered." He's right. The room is nearly empty except what I've brought in, a crockpot with something that smells of chili someone at church probably provided, a couple of loaves of sandwich bread, a cooler with lunchmeat, and a table full of homemade cookies. "We used to get large donations from the resort, enough to pay much of my salary. That's why the Trinity Churches allowed me to stay in a smaller community, because of this funding. The resort has cut us dry. It's hard times, honey. Amelia decided their money would be better spent hiring a new marketing team and a new assistant manager to help out Beau. They took a big loss last year. They're trying to recoup losses."

"Yeah, like laying off his cute little housekeeper who comes in twice a day to clean?" I say slyly to the preacher. "The last time I was there, Jaylin who works at the resort still cleans Bear's already spotless cabin."

He gets a sour purse to his lips. "I'm sure the Vegas idea of a loss is different than most of these people who rely on donations for support. Folks are living on canned beans while they dine on caviar up there. I heard the Vegas made millions last year. My son told me a slight fluctuation in that income was traced to Amelia—poor investments and bad choices centering around the Redneck Run last year made for a lot of explaining to investors."

I turn, and we walk back out to the truck. "Gabe didn't say anything about this to me." I step from bright sunlight to the dimmer yellow lights of the building. "What's going to happen to the church, to you? To this?" I let my eyes wander the room, take it in.

"We've put off telling the family and congregation until last week," Preacher Murphy tells me. "It's still sinking in for all of us. We're all hanging on for a miracle, I suppose." He chuckles softly. "I'm being transferred to a larger congregation as an assistant pastor in Charleston."

"The church will close down?"

"It'll go up for sale. The community doesn't have enough to fund it." He smiles. "It will be an adventure for all of us. Perhaps some religious entity will buy it, continue God's work here." He isn't as okay with this new venture as he appears. "We were blessed to have the Vega's financial support as long as we did."

"It was probably the only thing Bear liked doing, being a choir director. You know that, don't you?" I ask Preacher Murphy. He grabs up two warm apple juice boxes from one of the bags and offers one to me. It is stifling hot in the building. We take them outside to drink. He shakes his head a little. "He told me that. His degree is in music. He felt obligated to take over for his dad at the resort."

"I doubt it was his decision," Preacher says.

"I wish I could say that about our relationship. I saw it coming with Meghan. I knew it was going to happen. He knew, in his heart, I wasn't as good as her." I frown.

"You are, Brandy. Why do you think I had him put a Band-Aid on your knee last year when you fell at church?" He chuckles maybe a bit sadly. "He was wrestling with doing the right things versus the wrong things. You have a good heart, a good soul. Did you ever tell him you didn't like it?" Preacher Murphy asks.

"What? And take him away from the only thing he got to do that he loved? That's the only thing that keeps him here, you know. Not his mama, not me—" I look at Preacher Murphy and hope he can't see my eyes tearing up. "He had a high paying job somewhere else. He stayed because he got to direct the choir at New Alliance. He loves your church, loves working with Meghan and Michelle in the choir. He always looked up toward the ceiling like he saw straight through the beams, pink insulation, and metal roof to heaven when they hit just the right note. He said they sang like angels shining down from heaven. I want to shine like that."

I abruptly make an excuse to use the rickety bathroom and wipe away tears with my wrist. It isn't long before cars start to arrive. I help Preacher Murphy make sandwiches, sack up dented vegetable cans and banged up diaper boxes. We make small talk while we work. There are twenty cars parked in the lot and more coming up the mountain road. Mister Smiley has left eight messages on my phone to *GET THE HELL BACK TO WORK*. I have his ringtone set to the growl of a mountain lion roar sped up so it sounds like a chipmunk hitting a high note and then giggling.

Preacher Murphy reloads my truck with boxes of diapers and food for Crystal and a few more families I'll pass on my way home tonight. He pats the cab as I leave as if I'm driving a carriage and he's urging the horses to move forward. "You know, Brandy, you shine in your own way," he tells me, "brighter than anybody I've known. Don't exchange that shine for one that you think might look prettier to someone else's eyes." He leans back, makes a hurried look over his shoulder at the small line forming again at the door to the church. "There's a scripture in the bible that says something like that—" He lets a smile beam on his face. "And don't look at me like that. I deserve to give you a mini-sermon. You've missed church the last few weeks." He waits until I succumb to his furrowed brow. *Let your light so shine before men, that they may see your good works and give glory to your Father who is in heaven.* He nods. "Others see your good deeds. There's a little song that is supposed to be suggestive of those words. Harry Dixon Loes wrote it. You remember singing: *This Little Light of Mine* in bible school?" I nod, hear another round of chipmunk giggles on my phone with another round of Mister Smiley mean-texts. "Look it up. Keep shining."

## Chapter 31—This Little Light of Mine Ain't Shining

*This little light of mine. I'm gonna let it shine.* I don't shine as bright as Preacher Murphy thinks. *This little light of mine. I'm gonna let it shine.* I know that song all too well while it belts out verse after verse in its sing-song taunt over and over in my head two days later. I was trying to outrun it like I do all my problems when I sprinted on a fresh deer trail along the tree-hidden side of Boar Mountain. *Let it shine, let it shine, let it shine.* There was a reason Mister Smiley was binge-texting me. Jim Bakersfield sent a video production crew out to get pictures of me doing what I do outside the Redneck Run. Suddenly, I'm in the spotlight. *Hide it under a bushel - NO! I'm gonna let it shine.* Surprise! It was great for Mister Smiley who got loads of free advertising. But for me, as Amelia Vega has never been discreet, I am a stuttering idiot in front of the camera. I am going to be PUBLIC ENEMY NUMBER 1 in New Alliance for conspiring with an enemy. *Let it shine, let it shine, let it shine.*

It won't go away. It just gets louder. It doesn't help that my little sister must have heard me humming it and started belting it out in the kitchen this morning until I screamed at her to stop with my hands to my ears. But the song has a story for me. Pops didn't yell at me for yelling at her because I've always felt a need to help folks. Aunt Jenny says it's just something sweet inside my heart. It's like a big air hug. I may not be able to physically wrap my arms around folks, show my love with a warm embrace. Instead, I do nice stuff, squash the living shit out of them with kindness.

Pops is a less flowery. He says it's because I got to see the hard side of life when I lived with mama. Never-the-less, it was May 4th of my third-grade year at the teeny Fire Mountain Elementary School, an old one-story brick building that smelled like crayons and finger-paint and toxic asbestos dribbling from the ceilings. Missus Moffatt, the choir director, was putting on the spring concert and everyone was aflutter. She had chosen a multitude of songs for the children to sing, none of them would be my very favorite song in the world that we sang at the Fire Mountain Community Church and was in the old hand-me-down hymnals we got from the Methodists in Wheeling, page 535. *Won't let Satan blow it out. I'm gonna let it shine.* When the thirty-six people who made up the congregation, mostly my family who bickered mildly during the week, finally joined forces on Sunday mornings to sing that song, it sounded like an army of saints raining down sunshine against the devil himself. On the days we sang the song, there wasn't a person in the crowd who didn't get saved, even if they'd been saved twenty times before.

I had stuffed the hymnal in my jacket and brought it to Missus Moffatt. I demanded we sing that song. I guess I figured if that song saved all thirty-six people at the Fire Mountain church over and over then certainly everyone attending the concert, heathens or not, would be brought to their knees before God at the elementary school. I could save them all.

Be it as it may, I showed up with the hymnal tucked beneath my scrawny arm for the spring concert, my chin held high and wearing a little blue dress, white leggings, and the haughty airs of a mini traveling televangelist ready to bring the house down. I was prepared to save the souls of everyone in New Alliance including surrounding communities like Bellaire and New Castle, should the need arise. Mama had never come to any of my life events. For Christmases, she never showed for the morning opening of my presents even if invited. She never giggled at me tripping over my basket to collect Easter eggs, never showed at parent-teacher conferences, never helped me pick out a prom dress. For all those times she failed to attend my ups and downs, the ins and outs, she decided to come dead drunk to this one. Of course, I didn't know until I held the hymnal aloft just like the preacher did at church on Sundays, jerked the mic from fifth grader, Sierra Graham, and Mama stood up from the rickety metal chair and started cheering me on in her baby blue thrift store shoes, a black leather minidress, and red tube top. Then she fell over in a crash and bang, screaming for me as they dragged her out. *Let it shine, let it shine, let it shine.*

You can see, then, why I wrestle with that song even more so when Pops tells me I need to forget that past, let it go. Kaylee had been working hard with Bear so she can sing it at the last church service before they close down Holy Trinity Church. I asked him why he didn't stop them from doing it. He said Bear didn't know anything about that specific song. But it didn't matter anyway. Bear had officially stepped down as choir director as not to cause more conflict and friction amongst the congregation.

"From what your Aunt Jenny heard," Pops said to me over his newspaper. "Half the congregation was ready to form a lynching mob for Missus Vega and Bear after hearing about the loss of funding for the church. The other half just started wheedling out and going to other churches." Such, Bear had called Pops this morning so he could break the news to Kaylee. Could I have picked a worse time to yell at her? "By the way, I just read the resort was burglarized this week." He lays the newspaper flat and points to a picture on the front page of Amelia Vega with mouth open addressing a police officer. "Somebody stole money from the safe, including cash and valuables from customers staying there."

"It doesn't surprise me. Security's been cut."

"I'm beginning to question your rationality, question my decision to put my entire world and your family's world up for collateral when you are hanging around with ax-murderers. I should have thought you learned your lesson with that stupid ex-husband of yours. I hope to God you're not getting into trouble."

"What do you mean ax-murderers?" I hiss at him. "Who told you that."

"Bear. He's worried about you. I'm worried about you. What the hell is going on in that little head of yours?"

"Here's a thought," I snap. "Why don't you call up Bear and adopt him too, huh? Since you seem to be on his side."

"Here's a thought for you, Brandy," he gruffly grumbles. "You've got room at the restaurant to set up a little bedroom for yourself. Why don't you do just that."

I wince. He's changing, morphing just like everyone else around me. He had Chuck Williams Trash Company come in and clean the front yard of mowers and old car parts. The grass is mowed all pretty and the front porch painted with two wicker chairs he bought at the flea market.

"Is that what this is all about?" I yowl. "Get rid of Brandy? You've got my replacement. You don't need me anymore!" I jab a finger at Kaylee who sticks her little pink tongue out at me.

"It isn't like you're easy to love, Brandy, is it?" Pops roars at me. "You and your running like a scared doe from the headlights every time somebody wants to show affection. I don't think I once saw you holding Bear's hand. It took two years of coaxing before you sat on my lap when you were little. I can't believe that man put up with you as long as he did."

"You got room to talk. You *put up* with Mama."

Pops huffs a mean laugh. "Yeah, I did. Do you realize what you just said? You're right. You're starting to act like your mama."

"I am not her," I grunt bitterly. "I will *never* be her." I just stood there, silence between us. Pops could have whipped out an AK-47 and started firing it at me and hurt me less.

"Well, good luck with that." He knows my worst nightmare. He just tossed it into my face, bare and cruel. I walk slowly to his refrigerator, open the door. I reach inside and pull out a can of beer set inside. Then, I pop the lid and force down a sip, refuse to gag. "Go to hell if that's what you think. Then so be it." I've never said anything like that to him. He rises from his chair, mouth set. "Get out of my house." That's what he says. He stomps across the room, grabs the beer from my fingers, and slams it against the wall. "GET OUT!"

## Chapter 32—A Sweet Gesture

I've got nothing but a stupid mattress, bare and settled on an old iron queen bed frame at the Piper's house. When Millie moved, she left the furniture. There are five rooms lacking sheets and blankets but containing bare beds and empty dressers and closets. I'm lying in bed, and even on a warm night, I'm cold.

"Bear?"

I got a call. It startles me even though I'm wide awake in this new and strange environment. I'm not used to new. I've not lived in many different places—Mama's trailer, Pops' house, Bear's cabin. Never alone. Never. I'm terrified. I'm alone.

"Your Pops called me. I'm not telling you this, but he was too proud to check on you, knew you'd know the sound of his truck. But he's worried."

"I'm at the Piper's house."

"I know. Look on the porch. Take the phone."

Bear is quiet on the other end of the phone until I get to the bottom of the steps. My teeth chatter. It's more out of the fear I get when I've got to do something new than the chilly air. I feel a coolness in the foyer, and it embarrasses me that he might have heard. "It's cold here."

"I know. It's in the valley. I walked the house when we looked at it to buy."

"Oh." I swing open the door and look down. "That's the blanket from your bed," I say softly. I see a red and white blanket there and something on top. I kneel, tug it up, and it is Bear's old sweatshirt I like to wear to bed. Something else falls out. Socks. The big thick ones without holes in the toes that come to my thighs. I take a sniff of the shirt automatically and loudly; I know he must have heard it. "And your shirt."

"I thought you might be cold. Pops said you went off in—I think he called it *a huff*."

"Thanks, Bear."

"I owe you, Brandy. How many times did you keep me from eating at two in the morning when we first met? Go to bed and lay down. I'll stay with you until you go to sleep—"

## Chapter 33—Pointing Fingers

"Here. You need to know this. It's about your new boyfriend. I haven't said anything to anyone yet. I wanted you to see it first." Bear had almost driven past. I see him stop, back up, then pull into the drive. He thrusts an envelope at me. It's as if he didn't even make that sweet, sweet gesture for me the other night. I mean for three hours, he stayed awake with me on the phone while I tossed and turned. "Open it."

I know what he's got. Still, I open it and tug out a thick wad of copy paper. I flip through absently. "So?"

"So?" He scoffs at me, brown eyes narrow. "Are you crazy? Do you have a death wish?"

"Why would you do this?" I stare at the paper, then look up to Bear furiously. "This is none of your damn business." Where is the man who sang a silly song that he made up for me one hour into my dozing?

"It is my business. The resort got robbed. I've got a good idea who did it. By the look of all those wild tattoos, he's been in prison more than once." Bear shifts in the seat.

"Hold on." I wave a hand between us, chuckling sarcastically. "Stop there. I'm trying to connect the dots. You are basing the robbery of your resort on the one clue you have—tattoos. Did you see a map tattooed on his back that showed a trail from the getaway car to the resort safe?"

"You're taking that out of context."

"You're linking the robbing of the resort to this man by his appearance." I shake my head.

"It's the type of tattoos common on criminals. And there's more—"

"Well, he has a butterfly tattoo just above his waistline and almost to his belly." I wiggle up my shirt a little, poke a finger at that sexy place just above my hipbone. "What does that say? He's a sexy robber?" I sniff slyly, lick my lips and part a sweet smile like I've seen more than that butterfly on Marcus. "Bad guys don't put butterfly tattoos on their bellies." Bear's jaws had been working hard. His hair was blowing in the wind. He was mad for nearly two breaths, seething mad. Then he belches out a laugh.

"You know how goofy that sounds?" he jeers. I can't help but remember sitting on the back porch of his cabin with him early fall of last year, me in one chair with a light blanket around my shoulders, him in another staring out to the pond with wisps of fog curling above it. A gust of wind blew through. I giggled, turned to keep the dusty spray of old autumn leaves from creeping into my eyes. When I shifted my head, I looked at his face—bristle-bearded cheeks and warm, brown sugar eyes. He was watching me intently, so intensely. My God, he was beautiful with a bit of a grin settling on his lips like he was getting ready to tell a joke and couldn't stop laughing inside long enough to begin. It wasn't that I just realized it. Well, maybe I did. Maybe for the first time, I saw him for who he was as he reached out and ever-so-gently touched my cheek. *You are the most beautiful woman I've ever seen, Brandy.* I stared at him. *Inside and out.* He stared at me. It was probably thirty seconds. I had moved over, straddled his lap, kissed his lips. They were soft and cool and bristly from his beard. He had grasped me around the shoulders, pulled me so close I thought I couldn't breathe. We had made love right there on the back porch with the mist finally rambling upwards and blanketing us in its embrace.

"I knew I saw him somewhere before."

"Huh?" I snap from my memory.

"I did some homework on him. The state police gave the vehicle report to the Quail Hollow cops who called me immediately. Does the name Jack Keeling ring a bell?"

"You're assuming this man, Marcus Freeman, is the man who stole stuff from your resort?" I lean forward, press a hand to his window. "And Bear, I have to assume, since I'm—" What did his mama call me? "—among the rag-tag mountain folk, it automatically makes me a thief too? I'm just guessing, but I bet this is some payback for buying out the

Piper property before you could get your hands on it. Or is it because I signed on with Jim at the Resort at Two Bridge Falls?"

Ah, that got a spark. "You—*what*?"

"Oh, didn't you hear? I'm running for the Resort at Two Bridge Falls. I figured you'd seen my posts online."

"You're under contract with us. You can't."

"You broke the contract when you kicked me off the team. Jim Bakersfield had his attorneys look into it. I don't have to honor it. Sue me." That's what Jim said to tell Bear. Then I let the tan folder sail across the expanse between us and into his window. He catches it clumsily against his chest. "Just for future reference, I'm not stupid because I come from here. He is not my boyfriend. He has hired me to do some work. I did not rob your stupid resort, nor did he. Nobody cares about your castle on the mountain especially when you turn your back on everybody here."

"If you're running against your hometown team, I'd say you are the traitor. You have no idea who you are siding with, Brandy. Bakersfield is—"

"He is what, Bear? Watch where you point fingers. He is no meaner than you. *You* kicked me off the team. *You* never stuck up for me with your mama."

"Did you ever stick up for me around your friends?"

## Chapter 34—Mighty Mosquito

I can't run fast enough. Jim Bakersfield gets a puzzling twist to his lips when he tells me that three weeks later. I respond that I'd never completed any qualifying standards on a regular track, much less on a certified course. I run in the wild West Virginia woods on mud and dirt, over limbs and ankle-breaking roots, through sharply-honed thorns and an occasional branch swatting at me.

To make matters worse, every time I run with his top four runners, they line up and make a fence I cannot get around. They don't hide this discourtesy as I try to weave my way through, calling out to each other in abrupt *left* or *right* depending upon which side I am trying to pass. I know for a fact Bakersfield watched this happen today and stood on the sidelines laughing about their dirty deeds.

"Does that mean I won't run in the event?" I swipe a towel over my sweaty face. I'm tired. I didn't sleep well last night. Pops is still irritated with me, so I tossed a bunch of clothes in garbage bags along with some blankets and a sleeping bag and lugged them to my restaurant. There are still bedrooms upstairs with un-sheeted beds and empty drawers and closets. I took the biggest room and made a little place to sleep. I pouted most of the night thinking Pops would show up all apologetic. He didn't.

I'm a little down too. The open-air, flat cinder track is like running in a vacant desert. I was up against runners who were all sinew-muscled, model-skinny, and as computerized and unresponsive as robots. They are a pack already. I call them Uppities because they act like they are better than the rest of us. I'm the outsider. I try to joke with them before the gun goes off. They stare at me with annoyed gazes. One of them said with a deep accent: *She like a little mosquito. I will swat, swat, swat her little butt away.* I told her mosquitoes are mighty. She laughed, slapped her hands three times to demonstrate what she would do to me, then dusted me on the track. *That's how it is done, Mighty Mosquito.* That's what she said beneath her breath when I finally caught up. *You are fat, American, and can't even win on your own track.*

In fact, besides the Uppities, I felt like one of those tiny mean and dark fairy creatures who flit about tossing hurtful spells like a mosquito homes in and bites the soft flesh of a bare arm of the heroes in Bear's role-playing tabletop game, Hero Diaries of a Rogue. He plays it every Friday night with his geeky buddies. Bear always raises his voice to a squeaky higher pitch when one of those petite fairies attacks his ne'er-do-well band of rogues with superhuman abilities (His name is Javelin Hawk and has super strength and carries a scythe). The other runners are just like one of the chaotic super demons who come after

Bear's rogue band, God-like and beautiful compared to wee me while we rounded Jim's professional track.

"Well, you won't qualify for our A-Team. Or even the B-Team, the backup, in endurance. Maybe don't eat for a few days. We can try it again. That's what these athletes do. They don't eat. They only run, run, run. Starve. Starve. Starve." He pokes a forefinger toward a woman who continues running. "Like her." Every muscle in her body shines off her skin. I don't envy her. She's creepy-skinny. My Aunt Jenny would sit her down and give her a damn good talking-to about putting pride and winning before a healthy body. "It's not genetics, like most think. Americans are fat," he goes on with a bit of bored detachment and his sentences even choppier than usual, looking for a way out of talking to me suddenly now I'm not his poster child. "They have a low BMI, Body Mass Index—measure of the body size. They have a higher height to weight ratio. You need to get taller, too. Ha ha."

"What's that mean?" My heart is laying in a puddle on the cinder at my feet. This was my redemption from getting kicked off Vega's team. "Am I off the team?"

"No big deal. It's alright." He pats my shoulder. I cringe. He looks disappointed in me. "I guess we'll add you to the list. You won't receive any compensation like lodging or transportation or payment."

*The list.* No pay. Nothing. I feel let down. I suppose I realize right then if my family had not given me that restaurant on a platter, I'd be nothing but working at Mister Smiley's register for the rest of my life, never living my dream. I couldn't do that by myself. I can't even win a race against *real* runners.

"Does that mean I don't get a ride home?" I only know one person on the team. I can't call Pops for a ride. He's working today. "Do you know if Rush Gordon is here today practicing?"

"Who?" Jim Bakersfield asks. "You mean the racer. No, he isn't with our team."

"You had him give me your card to contact you."

"No. I never contacted Rush Gordon. If I'm correct, he's on the Boar Mountain team." He'd jogged off after one of the winners in my little run, left me standing there alone, a Christmas pup from last year replaced by a cuter and younger pup. He's lying. Or is Rush Gordon the liar. I try to shake it off. I can't. It just doesn't make sense to me.

## Chapter 35—Bobby Reese

Bobby Reese was in the first Fire Mountain Redneck Run around 1967 way back before the local tourism ruined it by making it what he calls a Rated-G fancy schmancy sightseeing attraction. They took his Rated-PG/R occasion away from the Crazy Kettle where Bobby told me he and his buddies would shoot at animals on the front of old hunting magazines tacked to a bale of hay. They had a parade of floats made with old bathtubs and toilets on wheels and a mud bog where ATVs made a run-through.

"My favorite were them pretty girls mud wrestling." Seventyish Bobby is telling me from his bed at Grant's Rehabilitation and Nursing Center. His coffee-colored face looks more olive than usual, his wrinkles more pronounced. He makes a whistle between the hole where his two front teeth used to be. "Damn, those was the days. Those women, they was sleek and lissome promenading in that mud with their pretty titties waggling up and down. They was as perty as any of those dancers on TV."

"We should do it like they used to. Make it fun to play, fun to watch." I let my shoulders slump. "I don't like running for Bakersfield's team. It's not a team—I mean a *real* team where everybody's working together to win. Everybody's competing against each other so they get more money. It's more like work."

"That's the way sports is now," Bobby replies. "It's a business. My grandkids stopped playing ball in middle school. They was good. Said it weren't fun no more. They play basketball by themselves at the high school. Still do. Them sports owners don't care. The players don't care. They'll abandon their fans in two shakes of a lamb's tail if they get paid better in another city."

"I let my town down not running for them."

"You got sucked into the business. Ain't no fault of your own. Until the fans stop paying and the stakes stop getting higher, there ain't nothing going to change it. What a waste some idiot sitting on the couch watching a game instead of playing. That's what it is now."

"Maybe I'll start my own Redneck Run next year. You can be the archer again."

"I'd be up for it. Doc says I'll be up and running in a couple of weeks. I been practicin' until I got my surgery. Ain't no bad knees gonna keep this old man down. See that nurse?" He wags a wrinkled, brown hand toward the hallway where a chubby woman in white scrubs is passing out medicine in little white paper cups. "That's Rhonda. She gets jealous if I'm not chasing her up and down the hallways." He leans in, gives me a big smile. "You gonna come to sneak me out for the races so me and the boys can watch?"

I laugh. "I'll see what I can do."

## Chapter 36 —The Taking of the Legendary Video Camera

I know everything I can know about Katelyn Freeman except what happened to her between midnight and the time they found her body at Cold Creek three days later. It would appear a huge void. However, because of the decomposition of her body, the coroner believed Katelyn was killed only two to three hours after she left her job. Taking that into consideration, I only needed to find out what happened between the hours of midnight and three in the morning.

I find myself drawn to the cases of Dana Pitzer and Sarah Thompson who wrecked at Stone Cold Creek a year earlier. *And* with Dana's mama's death. These are the only violent female deaths in the area barring a suicide and a wreck on the highway involving a woman traveling through the state. That's three women found at the creek. I counted at least twenty-nine creeks in the vicinity of Quail Hollow encompassing over one-hundred and twenty-three miles of shoreline. Why would there be three bodies found at nearly the exact location and within ten feet of each other all within a year and a half? I decided to add these three to my evidence cork board to one side of Katelyn Freeman.

I just got off an eight-hour shift from Mister Smiley's Grocery. I'm rotten-angry. Not only do I feel miserable and a double-failure between Boar Mountain and Two Bridge Falls, but I've also got a new twist added to the mix. I still can't sleep because Pops hasn't raised a finger to come down and make sure I'm not dead. He's still mad. I'm embarrassed I told Bear I was ONE OF THE CHOSEN from that team. For the first time since I was three, I don't even feel like running. And I don't. I'm throwing myself into solving this crime I probably can't, but it is better than being a loser at everything else.

I had just pumped gas into an old banged-up work truck I am borrowing from Kenny and Uncle Craig until I can figure out how to get another vehicle. A towing company came and took away the one Bear had gotten me. Next, I'm heading to Owl Hollow to meet with a local Amish farmer who is going to supply my meats and seasonal vegetables. It is Martha Hershberger's family. I went to Fairview State Community College with her. She swam for my makeshift team last year. Kenny's also got a huge crush on her which, due to a certain bartering system, let me borrow his truck if I mentioned his name to her. If I get him a date, he owes me one.

"Brandy, can you come to the register inside?" I blink up at the gray speaker above the gas pump. It's Buddy Webber's nasally voice who usually runs the register.

"Why?" I ask snippily. "I don't have time to fool around. Some of us have to work." He tells me I won a free drink of my choice. I'm stupid enough to believe him.

"Hey, Brandy Devereauxs," he calls out when I come through the doors. "Just go get your fountain drink from the machine, then come up here so I can scan it." I don't look up when I work myself to the slushy dispenser and grab a mid-size cup of cherry slushy, my drink of choice. I also eye the candy rack and pick out the cheapest candy bar because I feel strangely obligated to do so since I'm getting a free slushy. I don't particularly like to have eye contact with the pudgy, frumpy-dressed man at the cash register, nor his skinny, bushy-haired and smiling-too-widely sidekick shoving gas station chicken legs from a portable fryer to a pan beneath a heating lamp. I'm afraid he will think it's a first date. He used to take pictures of me eating popsicles when I sat on the curb outside.

There are a few people coming and going. I weave and adjust my stance to avoid them so they can check out.

"I guess you heard I've got something for you."

"A slushy?" I cringe while I hold up my cup, look up, and see him staring at the little opening in my blouse and right to the tiny cleft between my breasts, unconcerned I caught him leaning forward to do so. "So, what did I do to win this delectable treat?" It unsettles me. Buddy's always creepy-flirty. You know—*you let me know when you're looking for a little something-something. I can help you out*—he would say pointing toward the chocolate candy bars but eyeing me up and down. Since he found out Bear and I aren't dating, he's started sniffing around for information about me from Kenny's friends.

I slap the candy bar on the counter between us like I'm putting up an electric fence between. Buddy leans over and wriggles something out from beneath the counter and gives his sidekick a knowing gaze. "Feast your eyes on this." He plops an ancient video camera on the counter, leans in on pudgy elbows.

"My eyes are seeing an old video camera worth five bucks at the flea market. I'd hardly gobble it up." I stare at the ancient and dinged video camera and take a sip from the slushy straw. It must be from the 1970s. "I don't need one. Don't have money for one. You can get a new one for fifty bucks on the auction sites." I nudge the candy bar closer to him on the counter. "In a hurry. Got to go."

"You won't get one like that." The sidekick comes up beside Buddy, folds arms across his chest. He smells like B.O., bubblegum, and cigarettes.

"I'd say someone who just got jacked by Old Lady Vega would offer up just about anything to get their hands on this little piece of equipment." Buddy has this strangely twisted smile to his lips, almost evil. It doesn't register at first, the magnitude of the object before me. Then I blink. Is it the much hunted, highly coveted video camera holding all my vengeance dreams in its grasp?

Goosepimples rise up my arms, tiny bumps that scatter up to the nape of my neck sending the hairs standing on end. "Cripes." I'd been holding my breath. "Where did you find this?" I breathe out. "Is this the camera with the video of Missus Vega running naked—?"

"The one and only." His sidekick, who I've named B.O. and Bubblegum, says like he's sipping hot coffee from a mug. "The stuff of legends—Blackbeard's mysterious buried gold or Montezuma's lost treasure. The jeweled crown King John misplaced trying to cross a marsh. This little camera is worth more gold than you can imagine. It's been said it was this very video that pushed Big Don over the edge and into corruption. It is the one that sent Judge Patterson to kill himself over his wife's infidelity. It might be cursed. The video is so sought-after, it has been called Boar Mountain's Lost Crown of Jewels."

"I wouldn't go that far," I whisper. I reach

out, start to roll my finger along the handle.

"No, no, no," Buddy coos softly to me, reaches out and gently draws it slowly back and just out of my reach. "Something like this should remain a shrine. But I could probably turn it over to you for a small fee—" B.O. and Bubblegum chuckles heartily. "Imagine what leverage it will give you, huh? I've heard what you've said about that woman and her son. I got buds up there in the kitchen and a brother who cleans the pool. They tell me your jokes about the Vegas. You're funny."

"Not me."

"The mouse in the weight room? That was you, right? That went viral online," Buddy tosses out. "The time when Beau Vega fell down the steps. You synchronized it to music online, up and down, up and down?"

"I saw that one," B.O. and Bubblegum laughs with a wheeze. "It was hilarious. I liked Beau Vega's face plant on the track and the belly flop in the pool. What a dumbass."

I'm looking back and forth between them while they hash out a few more. "I didn't do all those." I am lying.

"Right." Buddy snickers. "Nobody's *ever* the ringleader."

"Listen, I've got twenty bucks." I stand up straight, reach into my blue jean shorts pocket and wrestle out four five-dollar bills crumpled and stuffed within. Buddy reaches out, gently touches my hand. I'm dizzied at the realization that everybody knows about my little jokes on Bear. I mean, I expected a laugh from the staff who I hung out with because the Dream Team shunned me. I didn't expect that *everybody* saw them. Or maybe I did. Maybe—I wanted Bear to feel the same kind of pain I was getting from those mean girls and his mama.

"I wasn't thinking about money. I was thinking about a little something else," Buddy snickers.

"Huh?" I'm befuddled.

"You know—a little *something-something*," he whispers with a sultry air. "Robert can cover for me. And you can have this icon of regional folklore all free and clear." He jabs a thumb toward the little door leading to the obscure back room and suddenly comes up with a British accent. "A little rendezvous in the back room, my lady, if you might. You and me." He bows low. "To sweeten the deal, we won't tell anybody your mama stole a case of beer out of the refrigerator this week and offered up a deal if we didn't turn her in to the cops."

My cheeks suddenly burst into a hot shade of tomato red. I snap my head upward, take in full eye contact. "What?"

"You screw me *and* maybe my buddy over here in the back room and—"

It's been an up and down ride this week, huge belly-jumping highs, and ass-slamming-on-the-ground lows. Then this belly punch. I feel the sweat on the slushy beneath my fingers—this cherry-slushy-slut-bait to lure me inside doesn't taste so sweet to my lips now.

"Don't you ever say anything about my mama." One second, I'm standing there with the cherry slushy in my fist. The next, I am lobbing it like a water balloon at B.O. and Bubblegum who takes it like a shotgun shell and falling backward to avoid the impact with arms flailing in the air, red cherry ice splattering bloody murder on his chest and groin. I'm jumping on to the counter and hovering over those two men. (Well, that was the not-so-carefully-thought-out plan. I made it to my knees. It was more a crawl than a superwoman hurdle.) I hover there with arms out to my sides and legs slightly splayed like a heavyweight wrestler readying to dive on her opponent trying to balance and backtracking the second I see the fear creep into those eyes.

"Don't you ever forget, I am a Devereauxs, MacCabe, and a McAllister, all wrapped into one, you hear me? I came from this mountain. I live on this mountain. If I have to, I'll die on this mountain. I'll drag your sorry asses down with me. Just so you know, Webber, that's not one kind of mean, that's three Fire Mountain families that have passed on all different kinds of mean. You don't ever say anything bad about us, or by God, I will rip your throat out with my bare hands and—" Buddy snickers. That's all it took for me to freefall on him with my fists flailing at his face and my knees jamming into B.O. and Bubblegum's gut while we topple to the floor in a very confined space. I kick, I bite, I jab my elbow into soft places. I rise slightly to jump twice on Buddy's chest. They can hardly move in the teeny space between counter and wall. I feel hands jerking me upward and off him swiftly. My fists are bloody and sore while I am stood upright, urged backward in two baby steps to the side of the counter by the fryers. "Stop it!" That's what B.O. and Bubblegum was yelling when the stranger's hands released me. I reach out, snatch up the video camera and hug it to my chest.

"Put it back."

"Come get it," I say with a snarky twist back. "I dare you, Buddy Webber." He doesn't move. Nobody moves. This man standing next to me who had snatched me off him is wavering there like he's not sure if he should call the cops on Buddy *or* me. "Okay, if I ever hear of you saying something about any one of us again, I'll come after you. I'm not going to be alone next time. If I ever hear of you trying to get a woman to pay for her slushy or a candy bar with sex, I will personally make sure you will never have sex again. Do I make myself clear?"

"Holy shit, he did what?" Somebody is coming through the door. It's Rocky Baxter who owns the stone quarry out on the highway. He stops, rolls up his sleeves. He looks from the man who had pulled me off Buddy and then back to me.

"Liar! She tried to steal a candy bar," Buddy grumbles.

I sigh and twist my head like Kenny does when he cracks his neck like most people crack their knuckles. "Well, how about I call Officer Dee." I whip out my phone from my back pocket. "Let's see what he says about the situation." I hold up the video camera. "I'm sure he'd have a few questions as to where you got this, huh? I'm sure his brother would wonder the same."

"Take that video!" Buddy screams. "It's frigging cursed. Just take it and don't come back to this store!"

## Chapter 37—Bloody Carpet at Margaret Pitzer's

I race out of the gas station, enveloped in victory, the apprehension Buddy Webber was going to call the cops, and cherry slushy residue on my shirt and hair. The triumph prevails twelve miles down the highway when no sirens follow my trail. Reveling in the sheer magnitude of this unexpected plunder, I feel like a leprechaun sitting on a pot of gold.

I reach out, gently touch my prize. Goosebumps. I imagine holding the camera up, wiggling it a little beneath Amelia Vega's nose. In a 1920s gangster voice, I'll say something like: "Ah ha! Now look who has the upper hand. This ought to teach you to be mean to me." I'll carefully turn the camera on, display just an inkling of the scandalous videotape. I'll pause, like they do in the movies, drawing out the moment. I'll have a crowd—yeah, all the staff at the resort she bitches at and rides like they are dogs. I'll watch her eyes go from witchy-cruel to puppy-dog begging. *Please, Brandy, let me have the video*, she'll plead to me dropping to her knees and folding her hands in front of her chest. She'll suddenly seem small and inconsequential. *I will give you anything for that tape for I know what you went through to get it. The journey must have been hard and dangerous! I beg of you, give it to me. I'll buy you a new truck,*

*I'll give you back your running position and fire those other dumb women. I didn't like them anyways. Nobody did. They are small, smaller than small. They are stupid and dumb anyway. I'll wait on you hand and foot—* Okay, the last part was a bit carried away, but it left a warm smile lingering on my lips when I pull along the curb outside the concrete pad of the driveway that belonged to Margaret Pitzer eighteen years ago.

I park along Main Street in Glen Allen Ridge. The road is on an incline. The hood of my truck sets downward. I'm staring at the two-story tan house that's seen better days. It's got a saggy porch, three windows on the first floor, and three windows on the upper level. I don't know why I'm here. It's not going to tell me its story. I hear a tap on the back of my truck. I turn in my seat, watch a man rounding the driver's side before stopping at my open window.

"Hey, you here to see the house?" He's about six and a half feet tall and gangly, the sandy-haired man bending to stare at me with a big smile and loads of freckles. He's chuckling because a woman behind him is poking and tickling a bit of bare, pink skin just above his belt that is sticking out as his shirt pulls forward. "Quit it, now," he says to her and she giggles. Then he turns his head to me. "A.J. Jackson. I've got the key. Barb gave it to me. You look familiar. Do I know you?" He sniffs a laugh because the woman doesn't quit. She's pinching his skin and he slaps her hand away. "Barb said to tell you they'll take any reasonable offer." He brings up a hand and wiggles the key at me. I want to lie and tell them a hearty *yes*, because I know if they know the real reason I'd like to set foot in that house, it would be a no-go.

"Well, maybe, maybe not." I scoot around in the seat, try to figure out how I can convince them to let me inside.

"It's the murder thing, isn't it?" The woman with him looks thirty-something. She's blonde hair, blue eyes, and wearing blue-jeans.

I'm still swiping at my shirt, little flecks of red on it. "Aw, no, that's slushy. I spilled it on me at a gas station."

"No," she says, giggling and dropping her gaze to my shirt. "The house. Everybody thinks it's haunted."

"Okay, honestly, yeah." I pull the knob to open the door. It sweeps out with a grinding scrape of metal and then a yowling screech. "But I'm not looking to buy." I hop out, shut the door, and lean against the hood. "I'm doing some research on the Katelyn Freeman murder that happened north of here. The story with the Pitzers came to my attention."

"You're the girl who won the Redneck Run, aren't you?" A.J. points at me. "Damn. I *do* know you. I saw you race. You was covered in mud."

"That's me. None other," I agree with a smile.

"Damn, again!" A.J. mutters. He's taking me in, a bowl of hot chicken noodle soup on a chilly day. "Can I get a picture with you? My mom's not gonna believe me."

"Sure." I smile. The Private detectives on Aunt Jenny's crime channel always flirt and smile and barter to get what they want. "I'll tell you what. You let me get a look in the house, and I'll let you take ten pictures." I suppose, though, there's a fine line between flirting and acting like a fake politician which I know my smile turns out to be. "No, I'm just kidding. Have at it. And—" I whip out my phone from my back pocket. "I've got a page I could post us on. Come here. I'll take a shot too."

We take a couple of pictures of us smiling. I turn to him. "The case I am working on is just up the road on—"

"Cold Creek, right?" A.J. answers for me. "

"Yeah."

The two eye each other, lounge there for a minute, faces void of the smiling eyes and lips. Then the woman tells me her name is Melissa. She was friends with Dana Pitzer and grew up here. "We were best friends. Her mom and my mom hung out together. You know, movie nights and Saturday cookouts. Let me get my mom. You might want to talk to her. I know she'd like to get the case back open, that's what she always says."

"I can call Barb and see if you can go inside,"

A.J. says, looking right to left warily. "Because you're going to want to see something."

"This is where they found Margie. That's what we called Margaret. She was all balled up like a baby asleep in a crib." Those words come from 55-year-old Maureen Thurman, Melissa's mama while she points to an old linoleum floor in the living room. She curls her arms to the chest and drops her chin to her fingers. Maureen tells me she was 37 at the time, a single mother who worked with Margaret Pitzer at a shoe factory outside town. Margaret and her husband, Gil, had split up three years earlier. He was about fifteen years older than she was and the principal at the local high school. He had an affair with one of the teachers at the school. When Margaret found out, she kicked him to the curb. The school board, they fired him. He took a job in Toledo, Ohio and hired his new girlfriend as a teacher there. Margaret cried on Maureen's shoulder for days after and that's when she helped Margaret get a job at the mill. Then they became close friends. They shared rides to work, shared days off together. "She was laying on her side with blood pouring out her head. God, it was all over the place like someone had gotten a bucket of red paint and tossed it on all the walls." She goes on to tell me an aunt of Margaret had rented the home until two years ago, then decided to sell it. They'd had no buyers.

The room is bare barring bits of trash here and there from the last renter who left. "I was watching TV. I heard screaming," Maureen tells me. "I mean, those two used to fight—Margie and Dana. We'd hear them yelling at each other. Then they'd work it out. It was mama-daughter stuff, nothing big. Dana wanted to stay out late. Margie wanted her home by eleven. They'd yell. Dana'd go up to her room or come running over here all mad. But nothing more. That night, though, it wasn't just one scream. I know it was all of them screaming at once. It was like the sound kids make when they take that first downswing on a rollercoaster, you know a bunch of screams." She goes down on one knee, points at a little orange stain. "That's blood still. Can't get it out." She shakes her head and rises. "I called 9-1-1 the minute I heard it. The first couple times, the call wouldn't go through. Then, I had to look up the county number, and nobody was in at the police station. I ended up calling the fire department directly. By then, the screaming had stopped. I'd say it was fifteen minutes that passed. The EMS working told us to stay in the house. Lock the doors."

"The neighbors on the other side came running out. Nobody answered the doors at the Pitzer's," Melissa says. "They came over here. We thought, well, maybe it was just a fight. We didn't hear guns or anything. It didn't look like anybody was home. While we were talking, the garage door opened and Margie's car came flying out. Dale Baumgardner, that's who lives on the other side, bolted to our front door. He thought he saw a man's head in the lamplight."

This whole time, A.J. has been silent. Then he waves a hand at me. "That's not all. Follow me." While we're going up the carpeted stairs, Melissa is quiet until we get to the top. She turns, runs her hand on the banister. "Dana and I used to get pillows off the bed, sit on them, and slide down the steps when we were kids." She forces a wane smile. "I hate coming over here. I hate it. We weren't hanging out much anymore in high school," Melissa tells me softly. "We grew apart. Her mom went through a lot of boyfriends. Dana changed in tenth grade. She was smoking pot and drinking and hanging out with all the partiers at school."

"I told folks there was something funny about that boyfriend of hers," Maureen divulges. "I told the cops that. They didn't take my story seriously."

"He wasn't a *boyfriend*, mom. I keep telling you that." Melissa eyes her, irritated. "It was Tara's step-dad who was coming over here. Every time Margie Pitzer left, I'd see him coming down the street, looking for her car to see who was at home. He wouldn't come near that house before Missus Pitzer's husband left. Mister Pitzer wasn't the principal when Tara's step-dad was in high school. He was the football coach along with Sarah's dad, Johnny Thompson. Tara's step-dad was like some wonder boy on the football field in high school. He ended up getting kicked off the team for drinking. I think some people were passing around the rumor that Tara's step-dad was getting Johnny Thompson and Gil Pitzer back by killing those girls for giving him the boot."

Maureen nods solemnly. "I heard that too. But Margie liked the men after her husband left, that's for sure," she says. "She always wanted me to go out to The Coffin. That place was a dive. I thought it might have been one of those men she picked up who murdered her. Never thought it was those girls."

"The Coffin." I remember that name. That's where Shelly Holcomb said Allie Blankenship would always want to drag her after working at the Sunrise campground. "What was Tara's dad's name?"

"It was George, I think," Melissa starts.

"Walter. It was Walter Fee," A.J. pipes up while he comes around me. "He wasn't Tara's dad. He was her *step*-dad. Tara always made that clear." We've reached the top of the stairs, and Melissa stops. "You guys go. I don't want to be up here at all. I feel sick."

"The owner always covers this up with a bed," A.j. mutters. I'm not prepared for what I see when I walk into the room. A.J. wiggles off a baseboard easily with his fingers. Then, he proceeds to grab a handful of carpet and rip it upward and away from the wall. "Look." He steps to one side and walks it down.

"Shit, is that—blood?" I ask him. I am staring at what looks akin to two human-size, aged puddles of blood that must have soaked through the carpet. There isn't any carpet pad, so whatever or whoever bled up here did so a lot, and it was soaked straight to the floor and akin to the amount of blood I've seen come out of one of Uncle Craig's pigs he slaughters each year. What once stuck tacky to the bottom of the carpet and floor, now peels away and trickles between like crumbly red glitter.

"Yep. We found it last year when I was helping one of the renters move in."

"What'd the cops say? They didn't see it on the carpet when they checked the house after the murder?" I whip out my phone, take a bunch of pictures while we talk.

"They hardly did shit about the murder. They didn't even come to the house until the next day. The cops came out, took pictures," A.J. gripes. "It was what you read in the papers. They said Dana and Sarah beat Margie and ran. They wrecked going too fast. They found beer in the car. And yeah, the cops came and looked at it. The guy in charge just stood there and said it was too old for testing, but they made a big deal of putting some in a baggie and carting it off. Now you tell me if it doesn't look like two people were murdered right here!"

"That is like so freaking weird," I say. "Maybe I watch too many crime shows, but don't they usually have detectives working on stuff—"

"Here? In Glen Allen Ridge?" Maureen laughs, scoffing. "We don't have any cops here. We don't have a mayor or even our own school anymore. We have to send our kids to Northridge for school. We have to rely on Quail Hollow or Northridge cops to come here. Sandstone Falls puts down gravel on the roads if they have extra when it snows. Our fire department consists of A.J. here and a 275-gallon tote tank he hauls in the back."

"Knowing what you know," I say, turning to the three as I leave. "You don't think those two girls would have killed Margaret?"

"Nope," Maureen shakes her head. Her daughter and A.J. both wag their heads back and forth too.

"I think Mister Fee had something to do with it," Melissa discloses.

"Yeah and maybe the local cops know it," A.J. says. "You know, a whole bunch of them used to hang out together over at the Fee's house. Once Margie was murdered, it stopped."

"It did," Maureen agrees. "Walter Fee stopped walking up and down this street. He's still here and works at the dollar store. But he takes the long way around now, doesn't come past here."

## Chapter 38—Gushing, Crushing, and Making a Fool of Myself

"I was driving past. I thought I'd stop in and say hello." This is me trying not to sound like a gushing middle school girl with a crush on the most popular boy who probably doesn't even know I exist. "You remember me?" I'm also lying. I went forty miles out of my way to get to the Jamestown Community Church and Shelter to see Zane from the pull-off at Stone Cold Creek. I don't have time for crushes. I've got a restaurant. However, I've convinced myself I've got a little hole gouged in my heart and this is as good a place to get it Band-Aided. I don't know why I treated *shelter* like an exclusive VIP dance club with a guest list. I brought a stack of blankets, six dozen cookies, and a sack lunch for Zane as a way to bribe the doorman.

At a front desk, I'm directed to a common room. Zane is sitting with hands on knees talking to a man in a raggedy t-shirt who is leaning toward him. A TV set is blaring on one wall. Zane looks up at me: "Hey, back—Girl Scout?" It ends like a question. I probably shouldn't have dropped by unexpectedly. Embarrassed, I blurt out with: "I looked up Tennessee foods because I thought you might be homesick." My hands are full juggling the blankets, so I have to bob my head up and down, nudging the sack with my chin. "It's

Nashville-style hot chicken on a buttery toasted bun. I re-dipped it in oil. It's got enough Louisiana hot sauce and cayenne pepper that I'm surprised it hasn't caught the bag on fire." Then while the two gape at me, I make a hearty *hyuck* laugh-snort. Then I stand in silence waiting for either to say something. Zane rises and pats the man's arm. "You'll excuse me?"

"I'm sorry about that." Zane pulls me to the side of the room. People are staring at us. I assume they are coming into the shelter for the air-conditioning. "I wasn't expecting you." I assume I walked in on a heated conversation because the man to whom he was speaking is rising to leave. "I was just ministering to him, trying to get him to stay."

"Surprise?" I spurt out. I drop the blankets on a table and balance the plasticware full of cookies so I can hand him the chicken. "Here. Give me a call or something." I see the man working toward the door. "Your—person is leaving."

I left about three minutes later while Zane dashed to find the man he was tending. It wasn't until I started around the corner of the building that I realized I didn't even leave him my number. I banged my head on the brick wall wondering if I should turn around. "Stupid, stupid, stupid," I'm muttering when I hear the glass door swing open.

"Hey, Girl Scout, I don't know your number."

## Chapter 39—Love Smack

"Pops, do you think we treated Bear like an outsider?"

I'm leaning on the frame of the women's restroom door of the restaurant after checking the mailbox for the fifth time. It has been twelve days since I ran an advertisement in the local newspaper for staff hiring. The mailbox has been empty of applications. Pops says maybe I need to run the advertisement again or put up some fliers. But I see the look in his eyes. I think people know I'm running for the other resort. I'm a traitor to the town. There was, however, a little note from Bear in the mailbox and a plastic container filled with store-bought chocolate chip cookies. The note said FROM BEAR. He confuses me. I don't know why he would give a chef premade cookies. I nibble on one anyway.

I hold the container out to Pops when he looks up. He shakes his head. He and Uncle Craig are finishing up on the restrooms. They have to be to code. He acts as if nothing happened at all. But he brings four quilts, three blankets, and all the stuff on my dresser shelf in a box. He also drags along Kaylee and Miss Lila, who today looks like a movie star with big earrings and new highlights to her hair. Miss Lila is snooping around with her hand latched to my little sister's hand, strolling from room to room and pretending to be adventurers looking for hidden gold in a castle. "This is lovely, just lovely," she keeps declaring. When she brings Pops and Uncle Craig cups of hot coffee, I see this weird proud admiration well up in her gaze, and she dotes on Pops' work like he's the only one in the world who can wield a Phillips head screwdriver. Pops' cheeks turn a humble tomato red. Uncle Craig hides a grin.

"Did you hear what I said?" I repeat. "Did we treat Bear like he didn't belong?"

"Bear?" he huffs a laugh. "Why do you say that?"

"I don't know. It was brought up." I don't tell him I thought about it a lot last night while I listened to the unfamiliar noises at my new home. The sound of the creek water scurrying toward a little waterfall behind the building, the freezer and central air conditioner running downstairs, and cars zooming down the highway. Occasionally, a semi-truck would blast through, and the driver would see the lower speed sign, hit the Jake Brake with the same sound of a gun going off.

"You keep looking at the phone," Pops says. "You waiting for a call? Maybe a boy?"

"I don't know. Maybe."

"When we going to meet this new fellow?" Uncle Craig asks. "He's nice to you, right?" I see him peer at the bruise on my cheek from wrestling down Buddy Webber at the gas station. They remember my ex-husband and his free hand.

"Yeah, he's nice. Maybe too nice."

I am, for the first time, alone. I think about things I don't want to think about. I worry about messing up with the restaurant. Zane called last night and apologized. We small-talked for an hour about nothing personal. I chattered way too long about running and my restaurant because he said that was the best chicken he'd ever eaten. Maybe it was. Maybe it wasn't. I get the feeling he tells folks what they want to hear, not really how he feels.

I worry about everyone laughing at me because I thought I could outrun those women at the other resort. I don't know why I thought they'd treat me differently than Amelia's Dream Team. *Mighty Mosquito*, they called me and whipped fingers in the air followed by smothered laughter. I wished I was. I'd sting them right in the middle of the back where you can't reach to scratch.

Then, I remember Bear sitting between my Papaw and Aunt Renae a lot with his arms folded and staring at the TV. I remember him faking laughs at memories we brought up about each other. He wandered around a lot while I cooked, bouncing around from one cluster of aunts and uncles and cousins with that unsure fake smile on his lips before he'd come into the kitchen and plop down at the empty table behind me. I didn't think anything of it, figured he could fend for himself. Maybe I'd felt a little indignant about it, resentful he never stuck up for me with Meghan.

"Well, it don't matter now, does it?" Pops looks up from the floor where he's holding a pipe. "He's out of the picture." I don't answer. I think it does.

"No, I suppose not," I say anyway because Pops is still looking at me. He seems satisfied, looks away. "I'm going to make lunch. I need you to try out some menu items." I ordered all my meats, and Mister Smiley is going to supply the fresh vegetables I can't get locally.

"That'd be great, hon, I'm hungry." Uncle Craig looks up. I smile at him. He smiles back. I've been thinking a lot about what Pops said, about what Bear said. *I'm a hard woman to love.* That's a hard pill to swallow. Nobody's ever said it out loud before. I don't want to be unlovable. Still, the idea of holding someone, hugging someone fondly because it means something to them kind of makes me feel dizzy and— vulnerable. Mama always pushed me away. Sometimes with the toe of her foot if her boyfriends liked to see kids fall on their butt.

I make my way to the kitchen and start to work on chicken noodles because that's what Uncle Craig likes. Kaylee and Miss Lila make their way into the room and plop down at the counter watching. "I don't know how I'm going to do all this," I mumble while Miss Lila tugs a paper and pen from her purse and sets it out for Kaylee to color. "Until I just saw Kaylee here, I forgot about kid meals." I look at the paper and nod my chin toward it. "I've still got to hire servers, even if I'm starting small. How do you do it? You're like a magician, pulling stuff out of nowhere at just the right time."

"It's my job, being a nanny. I've been doing it for a long time. You'll get it. This—" she waves a finger into the air and makes a circle. "—is all new. It's like any job. You'll bumble through until you get it just right. There's always a learning curve. I would forget baby diapers and even the baby bag when I first started." She gets a faraway look to her eyes. "Oh, and I once got to the park three blocks away without the baby." She laughs and winks at me. I can't tell if she's kidding or not.

I wonder how Pops can afford a real nanny. I know he put in new floors for her. He has been wearing aftershave and singing in the shower. Hell, he's been wearing button ups and nice blue jeans without two-year-old oil smudges on the knees. And the house is suddenly swept and tidy. Oh. Shit. It occurs to me right then that they are the closest thing to a couple I can think of without holding hands or kissing when one or the other leaves. "Are you—dating Pops?" I ask her, cutting right to the question.

"Does that bother you?"

"I don't know." I'm cutting up celery. It's fast. Chop-chop-chop. I'm watching her eyes watch my fingers, the knife blade. Kaylee isn't listening. She's working the crayon hard with her little fingers. "It's always been just him and me and then Kaylee."

"That's what he said he was afraid you'd feel like. You're a family. I'm—" She struggles with the words, leans over Kaylee and guides her fingers while she spells her name at the bottom of the paper. "I don't know."

"An outsider?" I am watching her, feeling tired and a little grumpy. I don't know why I suddenly feel like I want to hurt her, make her go away. I want Pops to be happy. Then, I feel it, the cut across my middle finger. It isn't big, but the knife is sharp, and blood starts to gush from it. Miss Lila jumps up. She knows what she is doing, snatches up a towel and guides me to the sink. It stings like Holy hell, but she stops the blood while Kaylee watches intently and without even a pout.

"I think you'll live," she tells me, pulling a Band-aid out of her purse and gently wrapping it around my wound.

"I guess it is better thinking that he kicked me out because he wants to hang out with you than what I worried about all last night and that I'm a hard person to love," I say out of the blue. "I mean, you and him liking each other would be better."

Miss Lila sighs, squeezes my hand with her fingers. "All better." She nibbles her lip, looks like she wants to say something, stops, then sighs again. "Okay, so it upset your Pops. I'm just going to throw this out at you like a stranger on a bus. I know your mama hurt you. Your pops told me that. Can I say something? I mean, maybe this will help you with the next guy. The guy that isn't Bear. See, inside, I think you feel like if you show someone you love them, you're giving them power—the power to hurt you. Such, you don't let them. It's easier to detach yourself. No love. No hurt. You avoid relationships."

I stare at her with my lips already curling into snarky. She doesn't know me. To think my pops discusses my issues with her, exposes my vulnerabilities with a stranger irks me. "Listen," I start to say, but heed her finger shushing me a moment. "Love-smack coming."

"What?" I look up, confused.

"It's what she calls it when she's telling you something you don't want to hear," Kaylee mumbles while she taps her crayon on her paper. "Like telling me I got to go to bed and not letting me watch cartoons like Pops does."

"What she said." Miss Lila bobs her head up and down, jabs a finger toward Kaylee with approval. "You see, I had to drink away a lot of men to learn that after losing my husband in Afghanistan in 2004. I didn't want to go through that again. I didn't want to toss my heart out there and have a part of it taken again. Judge me if you want. Get mad at me if you want. I see me in you. You can reverse the whole thing. If you don't, you're giving your mama the power over you like I gave a wonderful, but dead man, power over me." She doesn't look up. She focuses on something I can't see on the counter, rubs it with one finger. "I think I owe it to you to tell you that. Because you made your pops a patient man who isn't afraid to throw his heart out again and again and not give up on people like us. Not everyone is like that."

## Chapter 40—Little Mosquito is Gonna Get Swat

I'm sitting on the video camera like a chubby kid sits on a suitcase full of candy at fat camp. For the past week, I've pulled it from the little dresser near my bed where I secret it at least twice a day. I've held it in my arms, a treasure of fancy-schmancy fantasies of how I'll bring down Amelia Vega playing out in my head. It would probably be one of the greatest scandals of New Alliance if it got into the wrong hands if for no other reason those who hate Amelia Vega could use it against her.

I'm thinking about that instead of the crowd at the Resort at Two Bridge Falls. Jim Bakersfield set up a fund-raising dinner for the event and invited local celebrities, stars, and politicians. He sold tickets for five-hundred dollars per plate. In the afternoon, he invited about a hundred kids with the regional Care Together Youth Foundation to tour the resort and have use of the outside play facilities and soccer field afterward. Between, they were bustled past the long line of Jim's staff and team. The interaction was carefully planned to occur about the time of arrival of the high-roller paying crowd as they passed huge signs telling them that a portion of their donation would be given to local charities so that all or part of their big-ticket meal was tax-deductible.

For these, it is a packed house, booze is flying, and my heart is racing with all the folks who want to meet us. We are settled in temporary cubicles made from portable office panel partitions. Each of us has unique free stuff to pass out to guests, and we autograph picture postcards. Bakersfield hired a popular country music band to play. I'm completely overwhelmed and happy to hide behind the twenty other competitors for the four events Bakersfield's lined up for pictures. They come in waves, people wanting to meet the previous year's Redneck Run contender who won the running event. They don't ask where Bobby and Martha and Kenny are from last year's race. I never liked the focus on me. They take pictures and chit-chat insincerely. They aren't my kind of people. They are rich and shallow and inclined to say I am the reason they paid to be in this event, then turn and say the same to one of the Uppities in the cubicle next to me.

I'm so overwhelmed when the tide starts to ease away, I slip out through a side exit I'd been eyeing with the same enthusiasm as a mouse eyes the hole in the wall he will escape through when cornered by a cat. I had presupposed it was a backdoor with a step and maybe an isolated and empty back parking lot for staff like the resort at Boar Mountain. Instead, I find myself in yet another jam-packed event—the resort playground swarming with a couple hundred Care Together Youth Foundation kids.

Turning, I grab for the door, give a big push. I faceplant. It is locked.

I hear a giggle. I'm standing at the top of a grated steel walkway and look down. My eyes are still adjusting from the dim lights inside to six o'clock bright sunshine. I blink. There's one boy in an electric wheelchair looking up at me with thick glasses. A second boy is scrunched up on a step, skinny elbows clutching skinny knees. He peers at me, then turns back to studying something on the ground. A third, a little girl of ten or eleven with thick, brown hair and a patch over one eye says a little too loudly: "Did you think this was the girl's bathroom?"

"What?" I ask.

"You've got to talk louder, she's deaf," the boy in the wheelchair announces with a funny purse of lips. I say: *what?* loudly. The little girl punches the boy in the arm. He grunts, laughs.

"I'm not deaf. I've got my hearing aids in. He's just a shit."

"You're the third person that's done that, come out the door looking for a restroom." The boy in the wheelchair is holding his arm and rubbing it. "You're the only one that got stuck, though. Everyone else caught the door in time."

"I was just getting some fresh air."

"And now you're stuck with the freaks," the little one staring at the ground tells me.

"The Freaks." The boy in the wheelchair seems to agree, although his words falter. "One look at us and the last two out here got crazy eyes and almost killed themselves getting back in." He thrusts out his hand. I take the three strides down the steps and grasp his fingers, pump them gently up and down. "I'm Zach. I have cerebral palsy."

"I'm Brandy," I greet him. "I'm here because I won the Redneck Run last year, might be a third-rate runner this year, and I don't like crowds, so I came outside."

"It is social anxiety. Grant has that too." He points to the floor gaper. "We know who you are. You were one of the resort people."

"I run for the resort."

"Big shit." The girl rolls her eyes.

I slide down close enough to sit on the cold concrete. "How come you aren't out there playing?" I poke a finger toward a group of kids kicking a soccer ball on a field.

All three give me dirty stares. "Really?" The girl blinks at me hard three times with the one eye not patched. "Don't patronize us with do-goody stuff. We realize our limitations."

"Then why are you *here*?" I ask. "If you don't want to do this stuff, why'd you come?"

"Why are you out here with us?" the sassy girl taunts me back. "Same reason. *They* made us come."

"Maybe the door locked behind me, but I'm glad for it right now." I lean back, close my eyes, let the sun shine on my face. "I'm tired of getting picked on because they say I'm a stupid hillbilly. Out here, it's nice. You haven't pointed out I talk funny. Being with you three cynical brats in the fresh air is better than being with a whole lot of those people in the stale air inside."

"Isn't it the Redneck Run you're doing?" The girl spits. "That kind of makes you a hillbilly. You sound like one."

"Shut up, Elizabeth."

"But I am the only one competing who can truly categorize herself as being a hillbilly and redneck. The rest are all as city as taxi cabs and high-rise apartments. I don't mind being backwoods. I recognize who I am. But I don't define it as a limitation. It is the culture I grew up in. I want to show people that being backwoods and redneck doesn't mean I'm unsophisticated, poverty-stricken, and stupid." I mean-eye the little girl looking at me. "I'm not. I do mind people calling that to belittle me. Or Mosquito. They call me *Mighty Mosquito*. It isn't because they think I'm powerful."

"It's an insult?" Elizabeth's wary gaze drops.

"Yep."

"Mighty Mosquito." Grant pulls his gaze from the floor, peeks cautiously up, and smiles. "Only female mosquitoes bite people, did you know that? They can detect your sweat a half football field away. They stick their proboscis into your skin and move it around until they find a vein, then suck out the blood."

"It sounds like a superhero to me." Elizabeth decides. "A woman is bitten by a mosquito and gets superpowers."

"Like what kind of superpowers?" I laugh.

"Sucking the lifeblood out of bad guys and making them run slow," Grant pipes up.

They think this is funny. I eye the fence around the play area and point toward it. "That's where I run here. Do you guys want to look at the track by the fence? I can show you where I wiped out the other day—"

By the time we get to the fence, peering over to the other side—the area declared off-limits to the public and Jim Bakersfield's multi-million dollar complex he calls the Golden Field of Glory, we gain the entire group and the youth leaders. I hesitate as Elizabeth comes up and slides her hand into mine. "We're all just stupid kids." She tells me. "If you say something stupid, it'll be forgotten tomorrow because somebody else will say something stupider. That's what my mom tells me."

She smiles up at me after her too-wise words for a ten-year-old, pokes her hearing aid a couple of times. Zach whizzes past us in his wheelchair, reminding me of Kenny zooming up the mountain on his ATV. He whispers: "Mighty Mosquito." Then comes up beside us like he's making sure he's in with the cool kids.

I see the gate open, and we file through, an

army of kids with wide-eyes staring at how huge the track and field is. I tell them about the Redneck Run. I'd always been terrified of crowds since Mama made her drunken debut at my choir concert. For the first time, I realize these were all individual kids and not a mob waiting to laugh at me, judge me. I tell them it doesn't matter where you came from or even where you are right now; it's where you're going and how you shine like little lights inside.

It makes me feel a little powerful. Probably too much because I lead my little fan club around the track. We do a little jog around it to show how challenging even one lap can be and I do eighteen the days I drive here for meetings. While we file back out and I say my goodbyes, I see one of Jim Bakersfield's Uppity A-Team standing by the entrance to the resort. She's slyly opening the door for me, eyes following.

"You, Mighty Mosquito, are in big shit trouble if Jim finds out you took those children and ran wheelchairs and dirty shoes on his priceless track. Only runners are allowed on it. Nobody else. It is forbidden." She smiles a flash of white teeth, a wolf's snarling growl coming after. And I can only think that now, his A-Team and B-Team members are the only ones on a first-name basis with him. I have to call him: Mister Bakersfield. "Little Mosquito is gonna get swat." She slaps her palms together. She's probably right.

# Chapter 41—Staking Out Marcus Freeman

I park outside the dumpy subsidized housing apartment settled between Apple's Used Cars and a car wash open 24-hours. It is a one-story motel tucked into a corner and in an L-shape. It's blue and drab with dingy, beat-up cars parked in front of every door except for one space in front of Apartment 12B which holds a motorcycle. It belongs to Marcus Freeman.

I borrowed Aunt Jenny's car to sit here. Marcus doesn't recognize the white Honda Accord parked at the Russ's Pizza and Carry Out. He doesn't even eye it cautiously when he passes within inches of my tinted passenger side window to go inside the eatery. I watch him through the bay window. He immediately goes to work behind the counter in the open kitchen pulling pizzas out of the oven, cutting them with a knife, boxing them up in white cardboard cartons. He disappears behind the register once in a while to check out a customer.

"This is a far cry from being an EMT or firefighter," I tell him stepping up to the register. "Unless you're expecting this place to catch on fire."

"What are you doing here?" His gaze is guarded, angry when his last customer strolls to the door. He doesn't even ask how I knew that was his dream job according to Shelly Holcomb. "I don't want—" He drops his voice, waves a hand in the air encompassing both me and the restaurant. "—these two things to overlap. You need to go. I need this job."

"I ordered the thick crust with black olives and pepperoni. It's under the name of Brandy D." I point to a young man dribbling mozzarella cheese on an uncooked pizza. "Paul took the order twenty minutes ago."

Marcus turns, calls out to Paul who bobs his head up and down, then snatches a pizza box from the warmer above the ovens. After he lays it on the counter, Marcus hard-stares me, leans in even closer. "This deal does not include a relationship, you understand that?" he whispers harshly. "You don't need to invite yourself into my life. The only interaction I want with you is you handing me the newspaper that tells everybody on the front page it wasn't me who murdered my sister when you solve the case. I want to walk away from this when it's done and not look back. Don't come back here again."

"I want my pizza," I tell him flatly. I hand him a twenty-dollar bill I pull from my jean pocket. Marcus takes the money and gives me my change. I grab up the pizza without expression, pivot on my feet. I march toward the door feeling infuriated. "Did you need anything else?" He calls out gruffly from the register.

I mull it over a moment. "No. I've got it on my own."

He ticks me off. I tuck the recruitment brochures for Emergency Medical Technician and Fire Science from Fairview State Community College into a little band on his motorcycle. I know he must see me do it. I salute him with one of my signature middle finger waves from across the parking lot. Then I take off too quickly for him to chase me down.

I'm two miles down the road when my cell phone rings. The caller ID says Road Rager. It doesn't take a detective to figure out who that is. I pick it up. "You embody your cell phone ID," I say without allowing Marcus to speak first. "You are aggressive, angry, insulting, and if you continue to *ride* my ass like you do, I'm going to jam on the brakes. Boom."

"What did you mean that *you've got it on your own*? Answer me."

"It means I got a guy who may have murdered three women and walked. If he did, he dumped two of their bodies in the same place your sister was found dead. I wanted to see if you knew him, that's all. I'm staking out his house tomorrow—"

## Chapter 42—Birds of a Feather

"You know, you're a pain in my ass. You tell me not to bug you, not wheedle my way into your life, and here you sit." I shift in my seat. I look over at Marcus who is sitting in the dark cab of my truck with me. It's hot inside. Rain is pattering lightly on the windshield. It leaves teeny, round mirrors on the glass dribbling to tears floating down the window.

"Why are we here, then?" He looks around at the old maples lining buckled sidewalk of this block of houses on Pierce Street in Glen Allen Ridge. We are a few streets over from the Pitzer home where Margaret was murdered. "This is thirty miles from where my sister was found."

"That house over there belongs to Walter Fee." I point to a white-wood home with paint peeling off. It's one-story with shutters torn off and grass knee-high next to the drive. "You told me on the phone you'd never heard of him. Maybe you've seen him." And here's a real head-banger—Marcus has never heard of the name *Allie Blankenship* before, although he admitted it seemed like there was a different girl working the camp store every week; they all blended together. He never heard his sister mention her name as she did with a couple of others at work. At least, that's what he told me along with a *why did she say I'd want to kill her?* Marcus reaches up and swipes at the smudged window.

"Don't do that."

"What?" he asks.

"Don't wipe the window." I reach up, snatch his arm away. "He might see it and wonder what the hell we're doing here. I'm trying to look like a parked vehicle, empty. Otherwise, that old lady who has been peering out the window three houses down will call the cops thinking we're casing a house to rob." I make a hard sigh. I keep thinking about Artie Lambert who ran me off the road. I wonder why the state cop hasn't called me with an update. "I want you to take a look at somebody, tell me if you recognize him. His first wife says he goes to work at the dollar store at ten. He stocks the shelves." I shift. There's a rip in the vinyl backrest of the seat. It is tearing into my spine.

"Why don't we just go to the dollar store and buy a candy bar or pop?"

"*One*, I didn't want him to notice us, maybe recognize you. Because—" I hold my hand out toward his chest. "You stick out in a crowd with all that hair, tattoos, and muscles and—" I size him up. "I'd say piratey looks." I pause while he lets this soak in. "*Two*, I wanted to see if you'd ever been here. I wanted to talk because that house we passed that I pointed out, it was where Margaret Pitzer was murdered. Her daughter and a friend were found dead on Stone Cold Creek fifty feet from where your sister was left."

Kenny did another round of background checks for me. Two were for Melissa and Maureen Thurman who came out as clean as paper plates fresh from the package. The third search was not so spotless—Walter Fee has seven run-ins with the law, including three domestic dispute charges with his third wife, Tara's mother. Neither Tara nor her mother would return my calls. With a little research and a couple of inquiries, I found he was a person of interest in the murder of his second wife, Kimmy Evans-Fee, although they could never get enough evidence to arrest him. I called his first wife who divorced him only seven months into their marriage at age seventeen. She described him as narcissistic and a sociopath with no remorse. He was both manipulative and conning. She was a naïve eleventh grader. He was a part-time police officer in his late twenties at Betts Station nearby. He would come to her school every day and drive past her house, stop her when she was out in the yard or riding her bike. She was flattered by the attention. Her parents were not so smitten and forbade her to see him. She did anyway and was pregnant within three months. By that time, she realized the extra hours he was allegedly taking at work was spent stalking another young girl, Kimmy Evans. She was found drowned in their bathtub at home after they were married and around the time of the other murders.

I divulge this to Marcus who is staring hard at the windshield. "You think it was him stalking my sister?"

"Not sure," I answer. "Maybe he has nothing to do with it. Regardless, this is crucial—*do not* get out of this vehicle and start harassing him. Do you promise me you will not? I will drive away right now. Because if it isn't and he calls the cops, I may never be able to find more information. I need evidence which I'm collecting now. There are eighteen sexual predators in a six-mile radius of this truck. There are probably ten more people between here and where they discovered Katelyn's body who have criminal records and who could have murdered her. It's a guess because I can't knock on every door and ask. I'm trying to whittle out everyone who might have done it. Whoever remains, I'll dig deeper."

"Okay."

"Okay?" I ask. "That easy?"

"No, Brandy." I hear him swallow hard. "He came out from behind the house. Jesus—" I was spending more time talking than looking. A shadow is approaching the truck. Did we lock the doors? Maybe he'll pass. The man is medium build with a slouched walk. He's holding a lopsided, broken umbrella. I feel my heart beat-beat-beat hard in my chest. Marcus is silent. I am silent. The patter of rain makes pinging sounds on the roof of the truck. I slowly, cautiously bring my hand up to the door locking mechanism. I don't want to hit it if I don't have to—it sounds like a pistol shot. Ten seconds pass as the figure approaches the truck on the sidewalk, then it disappears in the darkness. I freeze, realize the air in the cab is tepid, stale. Both of us are facing the windshield and keel forward slightly at the same time the form disappears. Unexpectedly a flashlight sprays across the seats, a face pressing to the passenger side window.

I gasp with eyes wide and hit the door lock. CHUCK-BOOM! It fastens. Both of our faces are pale and terrified as our heads wheel to the right. We stare there in silence as a hand swipes the glass, face pulls away. I turn the key and the truck starts. I hear the sound of Marcus's door handle moving. I kick the accelerator and make a jarring jolt from the curb and out along the wet pavement.

"You know, you're like a big moose in a chicken suit, right?" I try to kid Marcus when I slither down a back road. We're both shaken.

"Okay," Marcus huffs softly. "There are creepy guys, but he was horror-movie-disturbing. My first inclination was that he was going to reach through the window with a clawed, green hand." He scrubs his forehead with his palm. "Brandy, I don't know about this. I think I've dragged my mind through every hell my sister could have gone through. Rape—"

"I thought she wasn't sexually assaulted."

"I don't know. The cops had so many secrets. Do you think we'd know if someone did?"

I pull the truck over in a gravel pull-off in the darkness. "Walter Fee's first wife told me he's related to Jack Keeling with the Quail Hollow Police Department. His brother, Bob, is the one who is in charge of the station there. Walter is Bob and Jack's half-brother. They have the same mother. They both worked at the Betts Station police department until it closed and Quail Hollow became the headquarters for the area. I was told by neighbors of the Pitzer family who were murdered that they could not reach the cops the night of their murder and they didn't even show up until the next morning to check out the site."

Marcus is staring at the windshield wipers still cranking back and forth. "I don't know how it all ties together."

"Where were all the cops that night if they weren't investigating the calls people were making for the screams at that house?" I pose to him. "My mamaw used to tell me birds of a feather flock together," I divulge tapping my finger on the steering wheel. "You know, people who have the same interests, they stick around each other. But she was always quick to add that when something went wrong—*birds of a feather flock together—until the cat comes.*" I shift in my seat. "Two months after Katelyn was murdered, Walter Fee was *let go* from the police force. But right after, people in that town also noticed that all his cop friends that used to hang around his house stopped coming there. It was between the time she was murdered and the time he was fired. You think that's why all his bird friends scattered? Do you think they were afraid a cat might come lurking around— you know, like a reporter or the FBI or someone in their police force that wasn't involved?"

## Chapter 43—I'm a Harder Woman Not to Love

Bear is sitting in his truck in the restaurant parking lot at six in the morning. I didn't hear him pull in. I didn't sleep at all last night. I got an e-mail from Jim Bakersfield's attorney stating I'm walking on thin ice and I'm most likely going to receive a fine for leaving the event and also breaking the rules and taking the kids out to the track. It seems doing so is as treasonous as harboring a Russian spy in the United States. There are certain rules about anyone but the home team seeing the facility practice areas. No one is allowed without proper written permission. I fell into a deep slumber around three, then dreamed of Jim Bakersfield's hand reaching out of a graveyard and while I innocently ambled past, he grabbed my ankle and pulled me under the earth.

I'm still in my sleep shorts, tank top, and bare feet when I open the door and step outside waiting for the mail, waiting for at least one waitress application to come in. Now, my heart is making a total 180 degrees jumping with joy. I wish it wouldn't. It puts a smile on my lips I have to hide. He lingers inside his truck. I think he is finishing a text. He looks up, pushes open his door, and snatches a white plastic garbage bag from the back of his truck. He holds the bag aloft.

"I know this must be some statement, but I hesitate to guess," I muse. He smiles slowly at me while I take it from his fingers. It is heavy. I let it fall slowly with my hand to my feet.

"No statement. I found these stuffed in a back corner in one of the offices we seldom use. Thought you might like to have them." He must see my questioning brow furrow. "They are letters to you. You know, from admirers of the Redneck Run."

"From who?" I ask like he didn't tell me.

"Fans. I guess they've been collecting dust. I didn't know about them until I stumbled on them." He shifts. He's dressing down today, just a button up and khakis. "How's it going? I mean, at Bakersfield's resort."

"I'm not allowed to say." I don't announce that sarcastically, and I don't think Bear takes it as such. I want to look in the bag. I don't. I sit down on the step. "Did you find out who robbed the resort?" I ask. He shakes his head, doesn't divulge more.

Instead, he forces a smile: "I took some more diapers and baby formula to Crystal. She said you've been taking stuff up every week from Mister Smiley's. She asked why I didn't know that. I told her we weren't going out anymore. She said I was an ass." He waits for me to agree with her. I don't. It occurs to me that Elizabeth Devereauxs was his birth mama even if she never held him in her arms. I wonder how her death impacted him. It isn't the first time that thought entered my mind. But now, looking back at the path he's been walking from Point A to Point B over the months since her death, he has been attaching to Amelia like he's afraid he'll lose her too. "You're not going to tell me she's right?"

"No. Crystal comes out on the porch and takes the stuff I give her as if she'd rather be dealing with the devil than me. We don't talk."

We stand there in silence. A car drives past. I listen to the wind blowing through the trees. It is cooler this morning and smells like more rain. "Um," Bear tosses out. "The restaurant looks nice."

"Thanks."

His phone tings in his pocket. He takes it out, says he has a meeting. He hesitates after he gets to his truck door. My heart aches. I want to make him stop. I can't. He lingers right before he starts to get in, leans his arm on the door, halfway in, halfway out, a sexy pose I'd like to capture with my phone camera, but I won't. "You know I said you're a hard woman to love, Brandy. I was right. But damn, you're a harder woman *not to* love." Just like that, he gets in his truck and drives off. I listen to it fade away, and I sob quietly into my hands.

## Chapter 44—Two Birds, One Stone

Men. Men. Men. Men. To think I'm complaining about having too many of them, but one's making me feel guilty because I'm trying to let go and can't—*Bear*. Another is making me feel guilty because *he* wants to let go but doesn't want to hurt my feelings—*Pops*. A third is mad because I don't hang around him as much because I'm busy—*Kenny*. The fourth is mad because I'm not some network TV crime series detective who solves a crime in less than an hour (take out the commercials) every week—*Marcus*. Lastly, we have Zane Powers. It seems I can't do anything right with him.

"You shouldn't have left the fundraising event," Zane tells me. "Bakersfield was right."

"You're kidding me, right?" Six phone calls. Six nights of chit-chat. Now he's my life coach? And on the seventh day, he is here at Pops' for Sunday dinner plopped on a kitchen chair while I dice carrots for a wild turkey Pops got last hunting season. I can't help but see him make a slow swing of his head, eyes rambling from one end to the next and taking in the living room when he enters, appraising the value of the house and appearing sorely disappointed. Pops doesn't seem to notice the disapproving gaze Zane gives the 1980s TV that my uncle keeps banging with his hand to get it to work. Nor does he say anything when Zane gives the worn couch, with the dip in the middle and Kenny slouching between, a criticizing eye. When we splashed by the twelve kids filling water balloons in the kitchen and slopping most of the water on the floor while they burst past, he jumps back and acts like they shot him.

Pops likes him, gives him a big handshake. Papaw doesn't mention a thing when Zane coolly eyes his old boots and Confederate-emblemed hat. He gives him a pat on the back. My aunties like him. Aunt Jo says the little parlor game table full of women on the back porch have come to a rousing conclusion he looks like Donavon Blake on their soap opera. Not so with me. I must be broke. I'm falling out of love at first sight. The longer he judges my family, the less blue and sweet his eyes look, the less sexy his heart-shaped lips appear—

"Brandy, they trust you; rely on you to represent their organization," Zane goes on, hand cupping chin thoughtfully, while he sits on the chair Bear used to sit on and assesses my situation like he has any concept of what I'm going through at the Resort at Two Bridge Falls. *Chop-Chop-Chop.* My knife cuts at potatoes now. I wrestle with a somewhat defensive feeling. That's BEAR'S TERRITORY. "I understand you wanted to encourage those kids, but maybe a bit of your ego made you feel it was more important to believe you were inspiring those children." He prods me gently with his finger.

"Do we have a bit of an ego, do we?"

Do I? I'd never thought about it. No, I don't. "I expected you'd back me up on this one considering you do social work for a living."

"I'm saying," he drops his voice, sweet and soft, "you should have talked to the owner first before taking it into your own hands. Sometimes wanting to feel like a superstar makes us do things to please ourselves, right?"

I'm curiously offended, hurt. "I don't feel like a superstar. I'm probably not even running in the race. There are lots of runners."

"Oh, I thought you said you were running for Resort at Two Bridge Falls. I saw your picture on their site."

"You looked me up?"

"Sure. I thought you were stalking me." He laughs. "I'm just kidding." I'm not so sure he is. I saw the way he looked at my hand-me-down truck. "That resort is slated to win, up and down the wall—all four competitions."

"I don't know so much about that," I say. I sigh. Zane's right. I feel like I'm letting everybody I love down. They all know. They don't talk about it. I see it in their eyes, a disappointed glaze, although Pops says it's just that they are tired from working their jobs and helping me get the restaurant started.

I let it go. A couple of my aunts come into the kitchen to help me finish the cooking and Zane disperses somewhere, probably shaking hands like he's a politician. It isn't until after we eat and the dishes are put away, Kenny asks if we're riding up to the top of the mountain like we always do. I'm still a little indignant about our conversation, Zane and me. I slip into my old closet and dig out a pair of ripped up camo pants and the kind of white tank top Kenny calls a wife beater. Then I pull on my slouch beanie and come out to the living room.

"You want to go riding?" I ask Zane. He is making that smile at me, sweet and—maybe I recognize it now for what it is—fake. It's the kind of face posers put on to hide their real feelings like when he thought I was homeless standing there at Stone Cold Creek with my life in a black plastic garbage bag.

"Riding?"

"Me and my cousins ride ATVs after dinner."

"Um." He looks around, shrugs. "Brandy, I'm just submerged in this kind of stuff all day at the shelter. I kind of need to get *out*."

"What does that mean?"

"I don't know. It's just overwhelming. Let's go somewhere upper class, you know? Get dressed up. I'll walk the mall with you; hold your purse while you shop."

"Who do you think you are, a prince? You too good for us because we don't live in castles?"

He's taken aback. "I'm just not used to all this chaos."

*All this chaos.* "Yeah, I think you do, Zane." I hold out my arms, look down at what I'm wearing. "All of this—this is me. This is what I'm about. I'm not always dressed up and rubbing elbows with resort people. This is my home. These are my people." He doesn't answer, doesn't appear to be looking for the right words to say. When his lips finally part, I hear a shuffle by the door.

"Are you coming?" I know Kenny heard the conversation. He's leaning against the kitchen doorframe, bear-rubbing his back up and down to get rid of an itch. His face is expressionless, but he's furious. I see his eyes tearing holes through Zane. Zane doesn't know how lucky he is I'm between him and my cousin.

"Yeah. You know what?" I look right at Zane. "You go to the mall. I'm going to go to my redneck thing."

"You killed two birds with one stone today, Handy Brandy." Kenny chuckles while we hop on the ATVs five minutes later and without Zane. I look over at him. "What?"

"You got rid of two posers in a matter of thirty minutes," Kenny says smugly. "That Zane dude and Bear. Nice job." He sees me look up, questioningly. "Yeah, Bear walked in, saw you rubbing up to the poser and turned around, walked out. There were about six seconds I thought he was going to blow a gasket, punch that guy. He didn't. Two birds. One stone."

## Chapter 45—Under Bakersfield's Thumb

"Whoa, whoa, whoa!" Jim Bakersfield shouts across his Golden Field of Glory. Fifty people are milling around. Everyone watches him direct his attention toward me while I swipe a towel across my face after finishing my first run. I see all eyes on me. I'd just called out aloud: *Red Rover, Red Rover, Brandy's coming over!* The women refused to move out of my way so I could get past them on the track. I go right, and they move right. I go left, and they move left. They are a solid wall, don't budge.

"What are you doing out here?" he asks me, wagging his head from side to side with exaggeration. "No, no, no. You don't belong here." My face turns beet red.

"I'm running like always."

"Well, no, you are not. Did you not get my e-mail?" He watches me shake my head back and forth. I didn't. A parent sent in a video of me talking and walking with the kids on the track. My performance played out like one of those inspirational and emotionally branded shoe commercials that run during the Olympics and it went viral over several major news stations. I was too busy last night answering e-mails and questions on my social network. "If you like working with kids so much or at least more than being a part of a team, then—"

"I don't. The kids wanted to see the track."

"And you knew better to walk out in the middle of *the* biggest event of the season and try to outdo my premier runners with your marketing tactics. Now I know why Amelia Vega didn't bitch when I poached you. As your punishment for misconduct—walking out on your team, embarrassing me in front of investors, and costing me twelve-thousand dollars to fix a ruined track, you're *not* going to be considered an automatic qualifier. For the next month, you will *not* be racing to qualify."

"What's that mean?" I ask him. "You already said I'm not running in the event."

"You had a chance to increase your odds through a point system." He says. "The best times got the highest points, but you still got points. It placed you in the runner up B-Team or C-Team. At the end of the event season, the points added up to money. Now that you have free time from qualifying, you will be volunteering to meet with all the dumbass groups calling me after seeing your little show."

It isn't about the athletic contest, the tourism dollars it brings into places like Fire Mountain, or that it shows the fun of fitness to him. It's like we're all gladiators in a barbaric fight-to-the-death arena, struggling to get to the top. When we get to the peak, Bakersfield, for his cruel amusement, tosses another weapon to our opponents to stop us. Well, me.

## Chapter 46—Hugs

Pops is standing at the bottom of my steps at eight o'clock that night. It stormed, and the landline phones went out about seven. I hear him opening the door. I know his plunk-plunk-plunk steps by heart. He has a limp from breaking a leg falling out of a tree when he was twenty-two and chainsawing a limb off somebody's tree. "What the hell did you do to Aunt Jenny? What'd you do to make her cry?" he demands furiously. "I want to know!"

Aunt Jenny put up the curtains today at the restaurant while I showered after my run. She hadn't scolded me for breaking up with Bear or said a thing about me running for the Resort at Two Bridge Falls. She small-talked and let me feed her lunch—her favorite, my secret recipe tuna fish and bacon on homemade croissants. She told me that Kenny asked Martha on a date and the two are going to the movies tonight. Then she asked why I was so quiet. I told her I was tired. She started to hold my hand, knowing I wasn't telling the truth. She realized her mistake and pulled away apologetically.

Aunt Jenny was the one who sat with Pops and me those first terrifying days and nights I went to live with him at the end of three-years-old and almost four. It was she who went to Mama and persuaded her I was better off being tucked into a bed at night with Pops reading me a book than being locked in a room in a playpen with the TV on so Mama could have an all-nighter party in the rest of the house. It took seven pictures of me with bruises and threats to call the local children's services, three casseroles, two-hundred dollars, and Aunt Jenny's color TV to convince Mama. It was Aunt Jenny who figured out if Pops rocked me facing outward and read to me, I would finally fall into a blissful sleep after sobbing from worry about my mama being alone.

While Aunt Jenny inspected her curtains one last time, I went upstairs to dry my hair. I felt alone. I wished I could have told her how I failed again, made another stupid mistake. Or maybe she'd finally tell me I made too many mistakes. She'd stop loving me and turn her back on me as Mama did over and over again. I wondered if Katelyn Freeman or Margaret Pitzer or Dana Pitzer or Sarah Thompson felt alone before they died. Were they scared all the time of everything like me? I hated myself for not hating my mama for making me this way and instead, taking the bad things she gave me and using them to hurt others. Unlovable. Untouchable. Afraid to love. Afraid to *be* loved. Afraid to be forsaken because of something stupid I did. I thought about Elizabeth's hand slipping into mine when I was at Resort at Two Bridge Falls. *We're all just stupid kids* like it was easy to overcome my fear. *If you say something stupid, it'll be forgotten tomorrow because somebody else will say something stupider.* How simple. How sweet.

I was overcome with something warm in my chest. I wanted to push it away. It was both cozy and painfully uncomfortable. I don't want to be unloved. I want to be touched. I don't want to be pushed away. I'm terrified they'll have power over me like Miss Lila traced my steps to that particular fear. I walked downstairs. Aunt Jenny was adjusting a curtain rod and turned. "Sweetie, what's the matter?"

"I just—you were the first one to make me feel loved. I wanted to thank you." She'd hesitated like she thought maybe I'd finally gone bat-shit crazy, those little threads holding all my insanity inside had finally been plucked from the material and let loose the wacky. "Thank you," she said with a confused smile.

"I was thinking. I mean, I was sitting there all by myself and was thinking I'd try it out, you know, finally the hugging part. It's been long enough. I wanted you to have the first, because—you know, you were the first." She just stood there confused at my jumbled words while I walked up and threw my arms around her shoulders. "A hug." I counted to three, let her hug me back, started to pull away and then just let her hug me in return for as long as she wanted. Then when Pops came barreling through the door an hour later after Aunt Jenny had gone home, I did the same to him.

## Chapter 47—Meeting at The Coffin

Cops have it easy. They can force people to come to the station and coerce statements out of them. They have personal and criminal information at their fingertips along with evidence. They knock on doors and intimidate witnesses into divulging possible suspect's darkest secrets or whereabouts just by implying that they are involved in whatever deed the suspect committed if they don't cooperate. They lie to get confessions, evidence, or to get someone to rat on another person.

I'm not so lucky to have those strategies, psychopathic manipulations, and restricted records while I bumble through my amateur investigation. I do, however, have one tool they don't. People don't trust cops. And I'm *not* a cop. Hence, I am meeting with Ferris Cartwright whose information had been given to me by Marcus. He bet me twenty bucks I wouldn't get a thing out of Ferris. But if I was digging at the bottom of the barrel for clues, witnesses, and information, he was worth a try.

Therefore, I put on my hottest little black dress. I'm trying to do my best to pay for my gas via the wager. We're sitting at the bar they call The Coffin. It is dirtier, darker, and more closed-in than the Crazy Kettle. That's how it got its name; the bartender told me whipping back his long hair with his hand—it feels like a coffin inside there. He also asks what a beautiful girl like me is doing in a shit joint like this. Then he stops, twists his head around and points a finger at me. "You were on that team that won the Redneck Run last year, aren't you?"

"You can recognize me in this light?" He laughs and nods toward the wall to his right. I squint, cringe. It is one of the marketing posters Gabe made last year for the race of me in a teeny pair of jean shorts and a tank top, posing Backwoods Barbie style against Kenny's ATV planted carefully in front of a big sign that announced REDNECK RUN. COME GET SOME. Pops about killed him for that one. "I see you in this light all the time," he tells me, leaning in. "You signed it for me last year. I had to move it back here under glass. Creeps kept touching it."

"Great," I mumble discomfited and feeling vulnerable.

"Yeah, lay off her. She's here with me."

I turn to see Ferris Cartwright ambling up. He situates himself on the bar stool next to me. I know him because Marcus described him to me as this guy who used to be *shaped like a giant pineapple and as green-pale as a zombie because he was a professional gamer, didn't go outside, and played ninety hours a week as a video game beta tester.*

"You're with Cartwright?" the bartender gives me an unsure roll of eyes. "You know he's a vampire, right?"

"Go to hell, Reisner. She's asking about Katelyn Freeman, trying to get the cops off her brother's back." He tugs the neckline of his t-shirt like he's adjusting a tie and says with a bit of grandeur. "I've got information for her."

"I might be able to get some more." The bartender pretends to sop up some beer with the same kind of blue cloth Pops uses to wipe his hands after changing the oil in his trucks. "I got some buddies that used to hang out with those boys that everybody says did it."

"Really?" I say cautiously. "What boys?"

We settle into some seats. "I know where Marcus Freeman was that night. Everything's up here. I remember everything by what game I was playing when things happen," Ferris tells me, prodding his temple with his forefinger while I get paper and pen from my purse and start writing. "June 29th, 2002. Viral Race. It's all up here. I probably could tell you exactly where he was the whole time. I've had three friends. He was one of them, although mostly through gaming." He shifts in his seat, rests an arm on his knee. I'm facing Ferris. He keeps a careful distance. "You have to understand, when we were in middle school, high school, and just graduating, the internet was scanty at best—dialup. Especially where we lived. At the time, there were racing video games I was trying out for Secure Ames, a video gaming company that went out of business in 2014. They called it Viral Race, a mix of zombies and cars where you drive the cars, take out the zombies by running them over. I got two copies, gave one to Marcus to play. We were supposed to be playing Viral Race from eight o'clock to eleven when he got home from work. At eleven, he would leave to pick up his sister, so he got there early even though she got off at midnight. His mom and dad were worried they'd close up the camp office and she'd have to sit out there in the dark with all those guys partying out there." The bartender is on the landline phone. I can see him leaning in and calling someone. He gives me a thumbs-up which I am guessing means he's got someone else to talk to me.

"But at ten-forty-five, I got cut off by my mom," Ferris continues. "She had to use the phone, so I got off. I remember my aunt needed a ride home from bingo at the fire hall that night. A neighbor had to drive up the road to tell us my aunt was trying to get ahold of Mom and the line was busy because I was using dialup internet. After she was done, I called Marcus and we played for another ten minutes, planning when he got back, we could pick up where we left off. Then I saw Marcus pass my house like ten minutes later in his car heading there. He was spot-on time as usual." He taps his watch. "He usually gets back at twelve-thirty. But twelve-thirty rolls by and nothing. Now, this is weird for him. Nothing's open after eleven but the bars and that gas station up by the Froggy Waters Pay Lake. I know something's wrong. Then about fifteen minutes to one, I get a call. It's him. He's calling from that gas station. He tells me he's trying to call his house to see if somebody else gave Katelyn a ride home, but he'd left the dialup connection on, and he was getting that weird busy signal it gives. He asked if I could drive over and see if she was there. I left and—" He pauses, eyes me carefully. "I told the cops this. They rolled their eyes. I went to Marcus' house. I knocked on the door because I saw shadows inside. I figured it was his mom or dad. Then somebody said something like *oh, shit, it's somebody at the door!* and started giggling at the window at the right of the front door like they knew I was there and they were trying to hide."

"Do you think it was Katelyn?"

"Yeah, I do. I knew Katelyn's squeaky voice. She'd answer the phone all the time. She was nineteen going on twelve, you know? She was meaner than shit to her brother and always got away with it around her mom and dad." The bartender wags a hand toward the door. I look up, see the front door part in a spray of light and three men walking through. They are bantering back and forth, and I look back to Ferris. "You know who was with her?"

"Nope. I do know that whoever it was had a little yellow car—"

"A yellow Chevette?" He nods. I swallow hard. That's Shelly Holcomb's car. She lied to me. She said she watched Katelyn leave that night and worked another hour. She said she wasn't with her. Why would she lie unless she's somehow involved or knows someone who is?

"I mean, it was bright yellow like a canary," Ferris goes on. "I sat around the corner and waited. I was mad and knew Marcus was driving all over and freaking out thinking his sister was walking down some dark road. She wasn't. They drove past me. There were three people in that car. In the light of a street lamp, I saw a blonde girl driving. As sure as you're sitting here, I saw Katelyn in the passenger seat. She had on this red tank top thingy with little straps and was laughing at me. Then there was a shadow in the back. It looked like a girl with a ponytail."

"You're talking about Katelyn Freeman, right?" A man in flannel shirt and jeans introduces himself as Robert Beedle, holds out his hand. I shake it. He's Pops' age, as are the other two who have walked up with him. "Oh, yep, now I recognize you. Thought Reisner was making it up to get us here for a beer, him telling us he's got that angel here off his poster." He smells like aftershave, and his dark hair is slicked back 1970s-pretty. I'm hoping he doesn't ask me out for a date. He looks up at the bartender. "We decided you went nuts, thought your redneck angel finally sprouted wings and flew right out of the frame."

"Quit flirting, old man." A man behind him gives him a soft arm punch. "She's not here to play spin the bottle—are you?" They all think this is funny, laugh. "I'm Bob Huffman. You can write it down and use my name. I don't care."

"Barb Hensley saw him that night." The third man scoots up beside me. "You can use my name. Allen Dunn."

"Huh?" I wheel around to face him.

"Barb Hensley saw Marcus Freeman that night. At least she said she did and she couldn't be here but told me to tell you that. We worked sometimes at the gas station down the road from the Sunrise campground. It's the Quail Hollow Express Gas, but most people called it the Froggy Lake Gas Station. Mostly it was when a guy named John-John Emory was a no-show. And he was a no-show that night. I know Barb worked that night because she told me Freeman stopped there and borrowed the phone because the payphone in the parking lot wasn't working. She'd told me he might come back and try again if he didn't find his sister."

"He tried to call her at home. Then called me." Ferris watches me writing, scratching in their names. I've got my phone on, recording the conversation.

"Barb watched him driving up and down Nelson Road slow like he was looking for her like she'd walked. That's what Freeman told Barb too, and that's why she let him use the phone. He was really upset, said his mom and dad would kill him if she was out there walking around by herself," Allen tells me. "She told me to tell you he seemed to be genuinely concerned, not like he was faking it or anything. He told her Katelyn had done that before, started walking if he was late. But he wasn't late. He drove up and down for a couple of hours, then stopped back, asked Barb if she'd take his number and call if she saw her."

"Why didn't she say something to the cops?"

"Why didn't anybody say anything?" Bob Huffman sniffs a laugh. "Either nobody asked, or they didn't want to get thrown under the bus. If you say something, you're in cop radar. I think a few folks tried anonymous tips, but whatever happened from them, I don't know."

"Tips, like what?"

"Like everybody knows after The Coffin would close up at one in the morning," Bob tells me, "all those guys, they'd all go out to Froggy Lake and party whether they had to work the next day or not. It'd be Davie Wharton, Slim Singleton, John-John Emory, and the Keeling boys, and Artie Lambert."

"And Walter Fee?" I ask.

"Yeah, Walter was in the mix," Allen replies

confidently. "All the old local football boys. They hassled Mike Bridge who was camping when he said he saw a yellow car picking her up. He was sitting at his campfire. The cops impounded *his* car to check for evidence, tore it up along with his pop-up camper."

"That was a helluva pop-up trailer." Bob shakes his head. They all nod in agreement. "It was almost like anybody who said anything got a finger pointed at them. Everybody thought the cops did that to Mike Bridge like a warning to everybody else to shut up."

"There was a little blonde girl who worked up at the campground that had a yellow Chevette. She was always trying to get me to sell her beer." Allen Dunn prods the counter by my arm. "Shelly *something*. Don't know her last name. She worked there a long time."

"Roddy fired her for taking cash out of the drawer."

"Who do you think murdered Katelyn?" I ask, cutting to the chase. "Maybe she's with Shelly, and they take off in her Chevette—"

"The only person who might be able to answer that question is Danny Brown," Allen looks to the other men. Each is bobbing a head.

"Yeah," Ferris sniffs a sarcastic laugh. "But good luck getting anything from him."

"Marcus said the same thing about you," I chuckle. "And you're talking."

"Yeah," Ferris mumbles. "Well, *I'm* not dead."

## Chapter 48—Batshit Crazy

Martha Hershberger is holding hands with Kenny on the front porch when I come home from running up the mountain and back down. They both unlatch and fold their hands across their chests as if I'm a middle school chaperone at the spring dance and just caught the two beneath the bleachers making out. She's got long, dyed pitch-black hair that goes all the way to her butt and eyes naturally as big as golf balls. Today she's wearing knee-length shorts, a cute striped blouse, and pink flip-flops which is odd for her. "Where's your Amish dress-thingy?" I ask and then pat my head. "And your hat? I almost thought Kenny was holding hands with somebody else."

"I'm going English today."

"Can you do that? Just be Amish one day and Born-Again Christian the next?"

"I bounce back and forth. Everybody knows I'm confused because Mom's one thing and Dad's the other. It's kind of an accepted fact that our family is weird like that. We kind of get shunned by both sides."

"That's interesting," I decide. "You know if you two have kids," I tell them while I stop at the bottom step to catch my breath. "It's going to be a born-again-Christian, Amish and Baptist-slash-Holy Trinity."

"Geez," Kenny huffs. "Brandy-Not-So-Dandy, why would you say something like that?"

"Because when I first brought Bear to Pops, you told everybody that God was on Bear's side because he came with the preacher to apologize to me for yelling at me before church."

"Because you're Satan."

"I'm glad you're so progressive, Kenny," Martha beams at Kenny, "that you believe Satan is a woman."

"Cripes." I wrench my eyes away from them. "What are you doing here anyway?"

"Pops thinks you're going crazy with all the hugging stuff. We're here to check on you."

"I'm fine." I linger, rocking back and forth on my heels. I look at Martha. "If I could have put together a team this year for the Redneck Run, would you have done the swimming?"

"Of course. I took some lifeguard classes at the college this year just for fun." She's running her fingers through Kenny's hair. He's leaning in like a coddled kitten getting his chin rubbed. "I'm fast. At least that's what they tell me. They wanted me on a swim team."

"Maybe next year."

"Maybe."

"As long as she doesn't go bat-shit crazy on us before then," Kenny snickers, referring to me.

## Chapter 49—He's in a Relationship and I'm Busted

Bear never changed the code to the security gate at his cabin. It is dark except for three little electric flameless candles flickering in the upper windows. The safety lights go on when I pull in, but when I poke in the number: 6652, the gate opens wide to welcome me into the property's embrace like an old friend. No one is home. I hoped I could get in and out without anything more than dropping off the legendary video camera and fading away into the night unheeded. I'm in a too-dressy-to-be-lounging-around-New-Alliance little black dress and swanky high heels. But I concluded the other day I'm going to have to stop force-feeding getting dressed up if I'm going to run an upscale restaurant in a small, dingy town. I mean, who wants to be served fine dining high-end entrées by a woman in old jean shorts and sweaty wife beaters? Nobody.

You might wonder why this change of heart from the wicked leprechaun holding her fingers out in front of her, evilly tapping them together with a leering smile while she contemplated the many ways she could destroy her enemy, Amelia Vega with her pot of video gold. It is pure, simple guilt and something I hate to admit—what my Aunt Jenny calls *pining for a lost love*. Or maybe everybody is right—the damn video camera is cursed.

My stomach has been churning since my hands laid to rest on the camera. It's the same anxious feeling I get when I pass Preacher Murphy on the street, and I haven't been to church in a couple of weeks. It's the jumpy sensation that used to linger when Pops knew I was lying when I told him I'd done my homework and I didn't. And the hurt look in Bear's eyes when I knew he had to stay late after work, but I still gave him the suspicious gaze a jealous wife gives an unfaithful husband.

*Cursed.* Jim Bakersfield is true to his word. He has filled up the days I was working out and running at Resort at Two Bridge Falls with talks with small interest groups. There is one good thing coming out of it—what he laughed and called *immersion by fire* for my social anxiety. I honestly believe he thought I would just quit when faced with one of my biggest fears. He doesn't know what Pops has known since he took me in so long ago—I'm stubborn and willful. I've managed to stutter and stumble my way through eighteen groups so far. When I drove my truck back, I ran out of gas because I'm short on money and had to have a kind trucker give me a can full of gas to get me home. To make matters worse, he recognized me, took pictures of me smiling with him, and I know my image is going to show up somewhere in the social networks as the winner of the Redneck Run from last year who can't even afford gas, she's so penniless.

Because I can't run at the track those two days and I do the meet and greets for ten hours, I have to run at eleven o'clock at night. Such, I tumbled over a NO PASSING sign that someone had hit and dragged to the highway edge last night. I ended up with a bleeding skinned knee. And *cursed*. I happen upon Bear's social network and saw he was—IN A RELATIONSHIP with an exclamation and three smiley faces.

But here is the grand finale. I'm standing on Bear's front porch trying to decide a safe place to leave the video camera, knowing I'm not doing it as a kind gesture. I don't want him to be IN A RELATIONSHIP with an exclamation and three smiley faces when it isn't with me. I know Jaylin still does Bear's housecleaning and she is also still working at the resort and would most likely be the next Leprechaun more than happy to sit on the pot of gold of Amelia Vega's indiscretion. I hesitate thinking maybe leaving it out in the open might be a bad idea. I see the flash of high beam lights coming up the driveway. The lights go from high beam waist-high to red and blue up high. "Shit." A flashlight gushes across the carefully manicured lawn, spews out on to the toes of my high heels and then to my bare knees, and face.

"Hands on your head!"

## Chapter 50—Her Butt's Too Big

"That makes twice you've gotten away with it." Dee Reynolds is leaning into me just off Bear's front porch. "Third time's a charm." I'm staring at the ground. He knows how angry it makes me, his tapping at the handcuffs fastened to his belt. I'm shaking. Bear got here just in time. One more second and I think Officer Reynolds would have laid me flat on the ground with a knee in the small of my back.

He jabs a thumb toward Bear who is running up to the house to turn off the alarm that had started up. "You make one step out of line, and I'll get you bagged and tagged like a ten-point buck in hunting season. I'm watching your scrawny MacCabe ass."

"*Devereauxs*," I return. I know correcting cops annoy them. I look him directly and furiously in the eyes. "If you are packing me in with the MacCabes and Devereauxs, you're walking a tightrope considering your brother got kicked off the police force for misconduct. With that point in mind, I want to think you'd empathize with me."

"You got a mouth on you."

Bear is coming down the steps hurriedly. I see him waving to someone in his truck. It lurches forward cautiously new-driver style while Officer Reynolds hands Bear the paper sack. The officer had already rifled through and peered at the video camera. "Here's what she had. Is this something stolen or—?" I think the revelation hits Dee Reynolds then. He whips his head around. "Is this the camera stolen from the Quick Stop?"

"It wasn't exactly stolen, per se. It was swiped from somebody else. I confiscated it like when you impound drugs." That makes little sense. "I would call it bartered merchandise."

"You came here to blackmail Beau Vega?"

"Where did you get that out of the conversation?" I eye him coolly.

I hear the truck door open. Three sets of eyes rise to take in Meghan Reynolds sliding slowly out of the truck. "Hi, Uncle Dee!" she calls out, and her voice chirps childlike. Officer Reynolds gives her a lazy wave. She comes up beside us smelling like cotton candy and grape slushies. No wonder Bear likes her. He loves candy.

"I was bringing it to you, Bear," I say. "It's the video of your mama."

"That's what the fight was all about?" Bear inquires. "The owner called me in and asked me to identify you."

"Did you?" I look up blank-faced.

His eyes fly to Officer Reynolds, then back to me. "I couldn't tell if it was you or not."

"It was pretty obvious it was her." Officer Reynolds inspects the video camera. "This is the video the staff took of Missus Vega and my brother?"

"My daddy?" Meghan whispers, sour-faced. Officer Reynolds shifts his eyes to her.

"The legendary video, none other." Now I've got three sets of eyes staring at me. "I stopped in to get gas. Buddy Webber, who works there, told me he would give it to me if I had sex with him in the back room." Silence. "I didn't," I interject quickly. "That was the fight."

At that moment, I see Meghan look at me, look at the video camera grasped tightly in his fingers. "It's not true! Daddy told me it wasn't real!" Officer Reynolds's radio makes a loud scratchy sound. I hear dispatch calling him. He releases one hand from the video to bring it to the radio at his shoulder. With the stealth of a spider jumping on its prey, Meghan rips the camera from his grip in one swoop, brings it high, then with a slight angle, tosses it right at my chest. I instinctively wheel to the left. It still bangs off my arm before falling with a smack to the mixture of gravel and grass at our feet. "I hate you!" she screams at me. She sobs and runs toward Bear's cabin, her arms flailing wildly.

"Am I free to go?" I turn back, don't even rub my arm where it has the same pinchy-ache I'd feel when Kenny would jab his knuckle into it when I called him a dweeb. I know there is going to be a good-sized bruise tomorrow morning. I'm not giving her uncle the satisfaction of seeing me in pain. He leans over, snatches it up. I watch him tug out a tiny video cassette and start pulling the tape out and out and out. "This ends here."

I don't wait for him to finish. I know Bear's going to go inside and console that bitch. I've seen him do it before even when we were engaged. It hurts. I make my raggedy gate across the grungy pebbles. My ankles are wobbling in my heels with each step.

"She didn't mean to do that." That's Bear coming up beside me, no difficult feat while I'm easing across the stones. Officer Reynolds's radio is going off again. He walks past Bear with a wad of the tape in his fingers and gives him a friendly pat on the shoulder as he leaves.

"There's a trash can down there. Stuff it in. I'll burn it." Officer Reynolds does as he's told, opens up the plastic garbage can, and drops the tape inside after peeling it from his fingers. "I'm buggering out. They need me out on Simms Road."

Bear nods. "I'll get Meghan home."

"What do you mean *she didn't mean to do that*, she did." I watch Officer Reynolds get into his patrol car. I start to open my door. "Don't defend her." Bear reaches around me and pulls the knob.

"Yeah, you're right. I didn't mean it that way. It's a sore spot. She probably thought you did it to hurt her. You are competing against her. She didn't hurt you, did she?"

"We poor white trash don't bruise so bad."

"Stop it! I know better. You don't show it. You'll probably get in your truck and cry all the way home. Don't you think I know that? But it isn't that she hurt you physically. She hurt your feelings for being mean. You're just not a baby about it. You suck it up and probably shouldn't. Do you think I want to go in there and listen to her blubber about herself for hours? Her eyes get all puffy, and she snots all over the place. She starts looking like your grandpa's million-year-old blind hound that slobbers and spews stuff out of his eyes and nose and butt when he gets excited. I don't want to go in there. I'd rather be in that truck with you any old day listening to you rant and knowing you want to cry so you sock me in the arm instead."

I giggle. I can't believe *he* said that with his arm waving toward the cabin. He pushes it away with his hand and hard-sighs, watches me laughing. "Thanks, Brandy. I mean a hundred thank yous." He puts on a smile, then lets it drop. "I never knew how to approach you before when you did stuff like this. I'm not mean, it's just you don't show a lot of affection. I know it ticks you off when I try to give you money or pay—"

I walk right up to him like I did to Aunt Jenny and she was all stupefied for three seconds. I take in two little breaths, stand up on tippy-toes. "You're going to have to lean over for this, big boy," I say.

"Lean—over?" he asks. But he does slowly, questioning and tipping his head to one side in the same way he does when Kaylee has a secret to tell him. I'm assuming he thinks I'm offering up some classified information. When he's close, I wrap my arms around his shoulders and press my face to his chest. He stands there, half-keeling. I know he's unsure, so I goad him a bit with: "You have five seconds to hug me in return for as long as you want. However, I'm begging you to please do it even if you don't want to for at least ten seconds because I'm in the initial and fragile stages of testing this theory a friend of Pops' offered me."

I feel his hands slipping around just beneath my shoulders, sluggishly at first waiting for me to lurch back, stiffen, and run scared-rabbit. I grasp, at this moment, an image always comes to mind when I feel trapped. It is of some obscure childhood nightmare of Mama sweet-talking me toward her from someplace I'm hiding. I know I'm in trouble for something. She's drunk, wheedling me out. I smell beer on her breath. I crawl from my hiding place to her smile. It turns into a huge grin, a fanged monster that slaps me over and over. It is always so swift, that vision, from start to finish maybe one second. It is one big ball that flashes. I usually pull away. This time, I wipe it out, focus on Bear's breaths, in and out, in and out. I concentrate on his arms in this sweet, unsure embrace. I force it over the old and enjoy it for what it is, probably our last embrace but a good one, *a great one*. Beautiful and sweet, smelling like his aftershave and my Loves Bittersweet Breath Perfume blending.

When we're done, it is silent between us. We're close. I don't step back. He doesn't either. I catch the scent of Bear—of overpriced aftershave and the sweet musky scent of his skin. I peer up at him as he straightens his back. It's probably not awkward until we linger and I say: "Um, thank you." But he's gazing down at me, silent. I realize I'm going to burst into tears. I don't understand this wonderful-horrible ache in my chest like I've got to say goodbye.

"Bear, are you out there?" Meghan calls from the porch. It shatters the strange quiet between Bear and me, a spell broken and torn asunder, blown to the wind, lost. I don't want him to see me cry. "You better get back to your IN A NEW RELATIONSHIP-smiley-face." I use air quotes dancing in front of me.  I try to pitch the focus somewhere else tossing my arm toward my truck. "I should go."

"Her butt's too big."

"What?" I ask, catch Bear's face in the moonlight. I can only describe the expression as this longing look of a little Victorian girl reaching upward wistfully toward a baby angel on Aunt Jenny's churchy wall pictures in her living room. He has tears in his eyes. "Her butt's too big," he says again, turns. "If you don't know what that means, ask Kenny."

## Chapter 51—Clues from Joyce Acres

I remember Jayne Ward from Quail Hollow Police Department mentioning a reporter named Joyce Acres with the Daily Regional. The newspaper/TV station is pretty big by our small-town standards. I find out when I look it up online and see the five-story building.

On what my Aunt Jenny calls a hotter-than-heck day, I am talking to a city-wide women's fellowship at noon and by two o'clock, a preschool class. I drop off a box of special diet cookies in the mail for Zach because when his mom friended me on a social network, she mentioned kids with cerebral palsy need more calcium for their bones and he hated taking the meds. But by four o'clock, I am sitting in the office only six blocks away with Joyce Acres who is eyeing me curiously.

"What is your interest in this particular story?" She is almost as dressed up as me in my little white dress, a devilish red pair of pumps, and matching lipstick. But her golden blonde hair is perfectly laying on her shoulders, an unmoving waterfall getting a thick mist of hair spray by a makeup artist for her news segment in ten minutes.

"I've been hired to look into Katelyn Freeman's death."

"I know who she is. Who hired you?" She

waits for an answer. I start to whip out my usual reply, and she nods before I start. "It's alright. I'll tell you what I know if you let me be the person interviewing you if you solve the case. I asked for an interview with you about the Redneck Run several months ago. Amelia Vega wouldn't grant it."

"I'm not running for Boar Mountain Resort any longer."

"Tough loss for them—sponsors dropped them when they lost you. You're with Two Bridge Falls resort."

"Yeah, and probably not running. I'm just an old poster on walls waiting to be replaced by this year's winners."

"You like that position?"

"Hell, no. But every night I go home, I still run. That's what I want to do, just run. I don't need the crowds screaming my name. I don't need the money. They've got a whole new set of rules. You have to be rich to have a team. Not like last year, when local sponsors could hold the reins." I wave it off. "Now, where were we? I was asking you if you had anything on Katelyn Freeman—"

It appears Joyce Acres knows a lot about the murder. She was too young for the initial news coverage, too green. It wasn't until the case became cold after Marcus Freeman's release, she got to do the short blurbs and updates and also began to find glitches in the case. She told me that police withheld information using the excuse that it was an open case. The weapon used to kill Katelyn, a baseball bat, was lost during a fire. Still, there was some question if she was actually murdered with a bat. The local medical examiner said it was a Louisville Slugger baseball bat found near the creek several weeks after Marcus Freeman was taken into custody. It had Katelyn's blood. And it had Marcus' *touch* DNA on it—residual skin cells and just trace amounts which also included at least three other men's DNA. Simply shaking someone's hand can leave you with small amounts of their DNA on your palm or fingers.

"So, any one of those cops could have shaken Marcus' hand, then touched the bat." I nibble my lip thoughtfully.

"Yep," Joyce answers. "That wasn't even brought up back then in court. Nor did they run tests on the cops to rule them out as being in contact with him. Here's the kicker. A forensic pathologist was brought into the court and testified a bat could not make the wounds found on Katelyn. It probably wasn't even the murder weapon. He felt it looked like some kind of hammer. I feel a person working in the county was covering for someone they knew."

"Walter Fee or Danny Brown?" I ask her. She got a soft smile parting her lips.

"Those names came up." It isn't a question.

"Yes. Right now, I'm focusing on Danny

Brown. What's the story?"

On the night of June 15th, 2002 and nearly two weeks before Katelyn was killed, a Caucasian male in cowboy boots, jeans, and a t-shirt walked into the Quail Hollow Express Gas. He was between the age of eighteen to twenty. John-John Emory, a manager, was getting ready to close and had just turned off the outside lights. He noted that although it was a warm evening, the young man was wearing a thick jacket and was sweating profusely. He also thought it strange when he walked through the doors, and he announced: *My name is Danny Brown.* He brusquely told this alleged Danny Brown the cash registers were closed-out for the night and he had already turned off the gas pumps. Danny Brown told him he wasn't there to purchase gas. John-John told him if he had exact change, he could get a candy bar or what he needed, but it had to be fast. The man said again, that wasn't why he was there. John-John stated Danny Brown repeated his name and then he proceeded to take a gun out of his coat pocket and shot himself in the head. It was nearly a year later rumors began to start that there may have been some love triangle between Danny Brown, John-John Emory, and Katelyn Freeman. John-John was questioned with his attorney and vehemently denied accusations of an affair with Katelyn and that he had something to do with Danny Brown's death, then Katelyn's murder two weeks later.

"He had no identification on his person. There was no car found at or near the gas station. It was like he came out of nowhere," Joyce continues to tell me. "To this day, we don't know if Danny Brown was this man's real name. There is no evidence he knew Katelyn Freeman." Then she chuckles softly. "There is only one minor detail I found while snooping around. At the time, gas station surveillance cameras weren't used much at the small stores. However, that station had three alleged gas drive-offs within that week and a small amount of cash missing from the register all occurring when one manager worked. It was the reason John-John was called into work that night. The owner, Dale Taft, set up a video camera in the parking lot without telling a soul because he thought that it was John-John stealing the gas. In that video, the camera caught the faint view of a yellow car pulling in ten minutes before Danny Brown arrived. There were several girls inside. One was another employee who wasn't working that night—"

"The car belonged to Shelly Holcomb."

"You've done your homework," Joyce bobs her head up and down. "He also said there were at least two other girls inside—"

"Was Katelyn Freeman one of them?"

"Maybe. Someone was in the backseat."

"And the missing Allie Blankenship?" I ask. "I saw her at Froggy Lake. There's a cross there, and she puts flowers on it at the anniversary of Katelyn's death."

"She can't stay hidden forever. She's the key. I mean, who hides like that if they didn't do something wrong or know something went wrong." Joyce looks up as a man waves to her and gives her the *ten-minute* ten-fingers-up sign. She turns back to me. "A neighbor has seen her come and go from her parents' house. The longer she's in hiding, the more she shows up. Arthur Smith is the neighbor's name. Over the years, he calls me if he sees her show up there, for all the good it does me. I can never get there on time. The cops refuse to follow up."

"Why?"

"You tell me." She gives me a knowing nod. "And if you do, I'll love to tell the world." She stands and stretches her arms over her head. "By the way, since I've worked on this story, I've gotten death threats."

## Chapter 52—Guy-Code

"Kenny, what is guy-code for *Her butt's too big*?"

"What?" Kenny, Uncle Craig, and Pops are hovering outside, waiting for the building inspectors to do the final walk-through of the restaurant. Kenny is lingering near the wheelchair accessible ramp. He keeps tugging nervously at his chin. All of them remind me of three boys awaiting their punishment in the hallway outside the principal's office. Uncle Craig keeps peering into the windows. Pops has marched into the restaurant six times, then turns on his heels and marches out. After, he takes off his ballcap, slaps it on his knee, returns it to his head.

"Why are you asking me such a stupid question when the fate of your entire career is hanging by the balance here?" Kenny asks in a hushed, forced voice. "This guy can make or break you with one code violation. If one pipe is corroded or one electrical outlet is waggy—"

"Waggy, what's waggy?" I ask, crinkle my nose.

"I don't know. Broke or not—working. Why are you *not* freaking out?" He scratches a skinny, tan arm.

"I don't know. Because Aunt Jenny, Pops, and Uncle Craig think *you*, the Golden Boy, can never do wrong."

"Yeah, they are right." He gets a smug twist to his lips. "The Golden Boy."

"Answer my question. What is guy-code for *Her butt's too big*?"

"Did some guy say it about you? Because you don't have a butt. It'd mean he was blind."

"No, Bear said it about Meghan to me."

"You're still hung up on him?" He gives me this brotherly shake of his head and a hard sigh with the same patient glaze to his eyes I have seen fake TV doctors give to fake TV family members whose loved one, who has been in a coma twenty years, has finally died. Such, I return with the fake TV family member stare, a mix of relief, grief, and a little anger that he seems so lackadaisical about the whole thing.

"I don't know," I mewl. Yes. I am.

"He must still be hung up on you. Guys don't say shit like that to one girl about another girl unless they like the one they *aren't* criticizing." He leans into the railing. "I've seen him put up with all sorts of stuff with you."

"He puts up with *me*?" I think it's the other way around. I think Kenny might be a traitor.

"You need to listen to yourself around him, Brandy Hard Candy. You chatter and chatter about the stupidest crap I've ever heard and on and on and he sits there and listens to you with a goofy smile on his face." Kenny exaggerates a groan. "That's not normal."

"But he always lies. He's always telling me I look pretty when I look like hell—you know, like when I go to bed with my hair wet, and it's sticking up in the morning, and I'm not wearing makeup." I bite my lip a little.

"Yeah."

"Yeah, what?"

"Yeah," he mumbles, pushing away. "I'm not talking about this stuff with you. You're like— *stupid.*"

"What do you mean?"

"I don't know. Most girls pick this stuff up. You like don't have that coded in or something." He knocks a knuckle on my head. "And I don't particularly like talking this kind of stuff with girls, much less my cousin. It's not right. It's disturbing. Men have secrets." He makes this bizarre groaning sound like he's getting ready to explode and knows it. "Alright, one time. If he tells you another woman is butt-ugly like she has a big butt or a big head or hands that look like feet and true-to-life she's gorgeous and probably perfect for him, it means he likes you better. Now go somewhere else—" Just then, the inspectors come out. They huddle in, a cluster of baseball umpires deciding the fate of a player's maybe-foul call. Then they break up, one coming forward and thrusting some papers at Uncle Craig. "You're good to go. Good luck in your endeavors."

## Chapter 53—He. She. Me.

Their vehicles are parked side by side in the parking lot of Boar Mountain Resort. One big black dually and one little red compact. I watch Bear step from his truck where I've slipped along the old pipe and under the bent fence I used to sneak out while I ran the track. It's dark out except for the parking lot lights that dim in the early morning. And drizzly. A misty bit of air and fog are creeping up from the valley below. He's wearing training pants and a tight t-shirt—only the best and most expensive. He walks over to the car, opens the driver's side door. Meghan eases out. She's wearing stretch pink track leggings and a gray muscle tank, so her tiny bulge of arm muscles shows. "Thanks, Beau," she replies softly, looks at him coquettishly, her lips forming a purse. She lingers there. He takes a step forward, turns.

"You coming?"

She pushes away from the car, hits the little lock button on the key. The hazard lights flash twice and the car makes a loud honk-honk when it is secured.

"You know you can turn that off," Bear turns to tell her, "so it doesn't make so much noise."

"You know I like to make an entrance." She giggles. I watch them walk side by side to the door. Bear keys in the code to unlock the door.

He opens it and Meghan ducks under his arm. *Like I used to do.* He laughs when she does it. *Like he used to do with me.* He scruffs his hair. That's a trigger for me when a guy works his hand through his hair. Bear knows that. It's almost like he knows I'm here and what comes next whenever he scruffs that hair. They disappear inside. My heart is flat-lining.

I'm sitting here wondering if just inside, he turns to her and stops her with his huge bear-paw hand on her dainty, unmarred arm as he'd done to my arm riddled with growing-up-running-wild-in-the-woods scars and Kenny-scars (he was a biter when we were little). *Meghan, I never thought a woman like you could ever love a man like me.* He'll tug her back ever-so-gently, push the hair from her eyes while she looks up at him. Eye contact. Yeah, that boy has it, and he'll look right into her baby blues, and she'll fall into his chocolate browns. He'll notice she doesn't have that little dent on her forehead the same as I do, the repercussions of more than one collision with trees, limbs, and rocks running the mountains. I mean I'm damaged goods, she's not. He'll sigh in relief because she's so damn not-broke. He wants to break her, though, like a stud horse wants to ride the prettiest pony in the pasture. He'll give her that boyish grin and tip his chin up, and a little to the right with hot-guy swagger.

He'll splay his legs a bit, put both hands on

the wall on either side of her shoulders. She feels trapped, but not like I would feel it—wedged in, confined, stuck. She enjoys feeling overpowered, a virginal maiden overwhelmed by the embrace of some naughty, muscled knight fresh from the battle, wrought with sweat and who has just conquered six scoundrels (with less than honorable thoughts for her welfare should they have won). He's won the right to take her. She's willing. Such, she'll roll off her top straight down to what he thought was going to be a sports bra. It isn't. It is two perky bare breasts rising and falling and making his own heart skip a beat. He'll notice her shoulders don't tighten for a fraction of a second and he'll relax, lean in and kiss her on the lips—hard once, then three soft pecks like he always did to me because he knows what makes a woman's heart go thumpity-thump-thump-thump. He'll keep going farther, find those little places around the nipples she likes kissed. He did for me.

Bear will slide his hand down to her bottom, lift her and she'll wrap her legs around his waist. Then, and unlike me, she'll slide her arms around his shoulders and let her lips touch along his ears and neck and shoulders, tasting the salty bit of sweat there. And he'll grunt in pleasure and lay her down, missionary style and crawl slowly on top, a lion scrambling over his mate. He'll keep his weight off a bit with his hands on either side of her head, and she'll wiggle her hands up to his shoulders, place her palms on his skin to feel each one shift as he works them hard to please her. And to please herself, she'll move her hands down and feel the muscles of his back and his butt working, working.

I watched Bear one time straddling a piece of wood to get to the trunk of a tree after Pops showed him how to cut it down with a chainsaw. The sawdust was flying on his arms, sticking to the curly hair just above the place where his long-sleeved shirt was pulled up, and his skin was exposed between elbow and work gloves. He was wearing safety glasses and steel-toed boots. His muscles were flexing, and he was concentrating heavily on the tree he was taking down. I'd never been more turned on by a man than that moment. I want that back. I want to be her. I want to be the woman who is lying next to him on the floor right now, sated and embraced in that tight grip that he always wanted to give me, but I couldn't take.

## Chapter 54—Breaking In

"What are you doing here?"

I'm standing barely inside the doorway of the huge weight room at the Boar Mountain Resort in the wee bit of darkness only twenty minutes later. It is still slightly ajar, held open by a rubber door jam. The lights are on, but only with an adjusted warm glow. Bear is laying on his back on an Olympic free weight flat bench, shoving barbells into the air. He's alone.

"I don't know." Oh, I do know. I'm watching him come and go. Honestly, it's not to catch him doing anything. I miss seeing him. I know—crazy. "I was just wondering if I had a big butt too."

"What?"

Ug! That was quite possibly the strangest thing I've ever asked a man. "I don't know. I mean, I left some clothes here." That's a bald-faced lie. "I need them back."

"I brought those back months ago and gave them to your Pops. It's a brown cardboard box with your name on it." He isn't convinced. I can tell by the bored expression.

"Oh, I didn't look inside."

"Maybe you should." He sits up, scrubs a towel over his bare arms and chest. Wow, they are muscled and shiny and sexy as hell. He is looking right to the left. He's wearing charcoal gray warm-up pants, and his legs are splayed on either side of the bench. "How'd you get in?"

"I used my old codes."

"How'd you get past Evan? You need to be careful about that. Your past exploits may be misconstrued as breaking and entering."

Skip the question about getting past Evan. But fast forward to what he meant by *past exploits*. "Past exploits. What does that mean?" I spit out, come into the light.

"He means it has just been questioned where you came up with the money for the property you purchased out from under his mother."

I blanch. I didn't hear her coming through the door behind me. The floor is expensively wool-carpeted. I wheel around, blink at Mila Boucher standing in the open space between door and frame. Her deep red hair is carefully bound on top of her head in a little bun. It is pulled back so tightly that her eyes look wily, cat-like—one of those two-thousand-dollar Himalayan cats who has just happened upon a little velveteen sack of catnip. "I'll call security—" she purrs, pulls out her cell phone.

"No, it's fine." Bear's back is to her, and he turns his head, drops the towel in front of him. He pushes his hands on his knees with elbows out and turns his attention back to me. "Someone broke into the resort, Brandy." His lips are unsmiling, his face rather blank. I took him by surprise. "He or she stole money out of twenty-six in-room bank safes during our biggest fund-raising event *and* our main safe, which had thousands of dollars of cash, on a Sunday evening before we could make a bank deposit. Our office manager must have never reset the administrator code which can open any one of those safes at any time."

"How would I know how to do something like that?" I address Bear, not Mila. I realize she's got Meghan at her heels because I see the shorter woman behind her peering past her upper arm.

"I don't know," Mila says slyly. "Who *was* your accomplice? You and a gentleman on a motorcycle were seen casing the building lot from the staff entrance. Then you were dismissed from the Redneck Run."

Bear holds up a hand to stop her words, rises. "Enough. Brandy didn't steal anything. I told you that, Mila. I told my mother that. Let's not start more false accusations." He points to the door. "Brandy, I'll walk you out."

"I called security, Mister Vega. Your mother addressed this issue." Mila holds up her phone in a well-manicured hand. "You are not to associate with her. You can't escort her anywhere. She said those words specifically. If you are seen with one of the runners from another team, it could be misconstrued as consorting with the enemy. She could throw the race. Regardless, it is protocol to call security immediately if we see anyone of dubious character or acting suspiciously. I think we have our thief, don't you?"

"I'll walk her out, Mila. There is no reason anyone would know she is here but you, me, and Meghan." Bear gets up, walks over to where his t-shirt is hanging lazily on an elliptical. "Call off the hounds." He turns and says to her. When she stands there, he leans forward and raises his voice. "Now. Or I'll do it myself."

"How'd you get in?" he asks when he opens the door.

"I'll never divulge my secrets," I say in a husky voice, trying, but failing, to sound like some secret spy.

"What was that supposed to be?" he chuckles softly. "Do I need to call Reverend Murphy in to do an exorcism? I swear when I saw the security tape of what you did to the dude in the gas station, I saw your head spinning in circles and your eyes turning bright red like the devil, himself, was inside you."

"You saw that?"

"Everybody within a hundred-mile radius saw it."

"Yeah, I would compare my wrath more to the revenge dealt out by one of the teeny-weeny Shade Idyll Fairies in that goofy role-playing game you like." I sigh, shrug. "They tend to get by holding on to the seat of their pants. When I jumped the counter, my knee hit the credit card processing terminal. I lost my balance and fell over the other side on top of Webber and knocked the breath out of the jerk. Not that he didn't deserve it for insinuating I was not a proper, modest young lady."

"I heard. It looked like that proper, modest young lady was pounding the fire out of him."

"I was trying to get up." I look up at Bear, and he is furrowing his brow as if that is not quite credible. "Okay, maybe a little. Then when I got up, I kept tripping. What is it you say when the fairies hit? Ping-ping-ping!" I let my voice rise like a high-pitched chipmunk.

His eyes narrow inquisitively. He doesn't say anything. He probably didn't know I liked listening to grown men pretend to be superheroes. "Never mind." I shrug.

"You know what a Shade Idyll Fairy is?" That's what he gets out of the entire story.

"Yeah." I try to shrug it off. "You used to talk about them in your Hero Diaries of a Rogue game thingy."

"*Game thingy*," he chuckles, rubs the scruff on his chin. "You used to say it was geeky."

"Yeah, maybe. I mean, I guess." I pause and sigh. "Whatever. I mean, it makes me mad that the women warriors like Tabitha of the Moth Clan and Rhonda—"

"Rhoda Silverhawk."

"Again, yeah, whatever. But neither were worthy enough to be in charge of her *own* guild, you know? A *man* hero had to be in charge. Always." I stress that with a groan and my hands in the air. I catch a bit of the rain on the asphalt. It reminds me of early morning runs here. I kind of miss it. "You completely just dissed their ability to have warrior code because they are female." I lean in, give him a knowing glare. "Yeah, they were good enough to be among the exiles. Yet, you would stop every one of them before entering a territory instead of trespassing, you know? Because you were scared they'd get hurt, right?"

"Well, I guess. We never have anyone who wanted to play them and stick up for them so they could get a bigger part." He wags his head like he's shaking it off. "I didn't even know you were listening. You were up there playing video games on the couch when we played. You could have jumped in."

"Yeah, well, you have to be invited. It's like a closed club." I look over my shoulder. "Isn't that always what you guys say?" The sun is coming up on the horizon over Fire Mountain. I turn. "Or maybe you didn't, I just felt it. Maybe like you felt on Sunday mornings hanging out with my family."

"I liked that."

"They can be socially awkward if you're not blood." He doesn't answer. The sun is coming up, pouring red-orange light down the canopy of trees along the mountainside so it reminds me of a huge cauldron of fiery lava poured from the skies. It is stunning, although in family folklore is not a good sign: *Red in the morning, sailors take warning*. My mamaw always said red skies meant we're in for a storm.

"God, you're—beautiful."

I turn when Bear says that, baffled and surprised. He snaps his head away from me and stutters: "I mean—I mean, *that's* beautiful—fire on Fire Mountain."

"Right." I nod. We stand there for maybe five minutes watching it rise above the mountains. Silent. "I should go," I say. I'm not sure if I should have divulged my secret access at the culvert. He will probably have it filled in. I do anyway. It is either that or sprinting down the road and maybe running into Amelia on her way into work. I start to walk.

"Why'd you come, Brandy?" he asks my back.

"I don't know." I see him come up by my side and we take the walkway over to the outside practice running area. I point down to the hole in the fence. "Here is where I take my leave, Javelin Hawk." I toss my hand to my forehead, woeful-princess-style.

"Crazy wild child of the woods," Bear whispers and his voice blends with the breeze sweeping up through the valley, cool and smelling rain-sweet. "Like a dark fairy, she flies—"

"—in through the night window, she blinds my sleepy eyes. With her light—" I smile, then give him a mock, wary stare as I inch toward the cavern of my exit. "Are we back to this again? Are you testing me, Vega?"

"I think I am. How'd you know that? You're like freaking me out." He leans over, knocks my forehead with a knuckle. "Brandy? Brandy, are you in there?"

"Stop!" I playfully slap his hand away. "I know it because it is the beginning of the Hero Diaries of a Rogue. I've heard it a thousand times. You guys sound like a bunch of freaking satanic cult members getting ready to sacrifice a baby or something. It is kind of hard not to hear. You all are loud and—make the *stupidest*—" I draw that word out. "—decisions. I mean, who uses a banded guild sword to fight Dargon's Royal White Dragons? It's preposterous. You have to use silver. Guild swords are bronze. When I see you all making such stupid mistakes, I got to sit back and access the situation and laugh. Then I worry a little bit that I'm going to rise from the couch and land on some sacrificial sarcophagus and be that something that is getting sacrificed."

"You know that—stuff?" He seems aghast. "So—so how does a dark fairy fly?"

"Charcoal. Dark fairies are all female fighters less than three feet, and if you leave ashes in your fireplace, they can conjure them up to make wings. If I was one, I could destroy you."

"That'd be a joke. So why don't you come sometimes?"

"Oh, I warrant an invite now?" I scoff easing closer until my feet start to slide a bit on the gravel slip. "One hug and I'm in?"

"Well, an initial invite. You have to prove yourself worthy and physically fight your way into the group and then you get a formal letter of—" He notes my offended gaze. "I'm just kidding, Brandy. But you do start little like one of the fairies."

"I certainly can identify with them right now. They call me Mighty Mosquito at Resort at Two Bridge Falls."

"Mighty Mosquito?"

"Yes. Because they've swatted me down to nothing. I am a fourth-rate runner on the team during the event. I'm a political Appalachian poster child for demographic purposes, the actual poverty-stricken redneck on the team."

"I saw his list of main runners. You were on it."

"Maybe, so are twenty-six others on paper who have some background related to race or ethnic group or level of wealth some politician is representing and who Jim Bakersfield is holding hands with politically. He's got some Olympic marathon runners from another country who do this for a living and altogether weigh ten pounds. I went from one set of mean girls to another. Mean girls, I might add, is representative across all boards of race, color, creed, or national origin." I yawn. I'm tired, and it isn't even light out yet. "You don't honestly think I stole that money, do you?"

"No, of course not." Bear stands while I hunker down to slide to the culvert. "Everybody's pointing the finger at everybody else because they think it was an inside job—done by someone working here. You didn't just help prove any innocence by knowing the passcodes."

"It'd be kind of stupid if I robbed the place and then showed up." I sigh. I can't tell if he is telling me the truth or not. I swear I see some doubt in his eyes. I slough it off, smile. "Hey, it goes both ways. Here's an invite for you. If you care to step out from your responsibilities and your board game anytime and are up for a real adventure, you're welcome to ride along."

He doesn't latch on. I'm not sure if it is because he wasn't quick enough when I slide, butt-first down the hillside to where it levels or if he didn't care to join along. I hear him say: "Oh, by the way, no you don't have a big butt." I disappear into the sunrise. He disappears from my sight.

## Chapter 55—What They Didn't Say About Danny Brown

"He was shot in the head, but it wasn't suicide." Pops' Miss Lila was showing me a picture of Danny Brown's death certificate on an online genealogy website she uses, helping me fact-check what Joyce Acres told me. "That's what the Certificate of Death says here: *gunshot wound to head*. I'm reading it exactly as stated, Brandy." She plopped her laptop on the counter in my new kitchen and wheeled it around so I could see. My hands are covered in flour. "The certificate says *name: unidentified*. However, it was scratched out, and Danial William Brown was scrawled above along with a picture of a man paperclipped to the certificate. "There's nothing here that says anything about suicide."

"I was told it was suicide."

"Whoever told you this must not have seen the death certificate. It wasn't added until recently." She points to a little date added icon. It is from June. She also tells me it looks like Danny Brown's brother posted the information recently after he positively identified him. They found out who it was through fingerprints entered into the FBI's Fingerprint ID System. Danny had a history of mental illness. He was homeless at the time of death.

"Brandy, did it ever occur to you to ask local

police about the incident?" Miss Lila reminds me of my special recipe sugar puff cookies, sweet and pretty inside and out and not one single bite of bitter within. One day, someone will make her mad. Out of her head will come a rainbow and she'll burst into an explosion of multi-colored marshmallows and powdered sugar and lemon drops without the sour inside. "They can be so helpful in this type of research. You said you were doing it as a genealogy project for someone?" Yes, I fibbed. But revealing I was hanging around with a man who had been charged with murder and I'm trying to wade my way through a sea of depraved criminals to find the real killer of his sister might raise a few red flags eventually leading to multiple explanations to Pops.

"I don't trust cops."

"They are the ones who take an oath to protect us," she reminds me. "I wish you would place your trust in them. They are the first ones there when we need them." She goes on to tell me her little story of how they were there for her blah, blah, blah. I don't remember much of what she said. I was chewing on the idea that somehow, somebody knew his name before they positively identified Danny Brown. "What do you think?" she asks me. "If I set it up, will you go? You catch more flies with honey than vinegar. Why don't you make some cookies?"

"Uh, okay." Huh? What'd I just agree to do?

## Chapter 56—Caterpillars

"Did you leave *this* at my door?"

Marcus is standing on my front porch. We all looked up when he pulled in on his motorcycle. Gabe, Ben and I are working on a website for the restaurant. Ben gets this funny twist to his lips. Gabe notices, glares at him. I watch Marcus march to the steps, hold up *this*. "Yes, I did," I say. "*This* is a butterfly starter kit complete with a mesh terrarium and plants." He lacks for words. A soft wind blows through the trees. Marcus softens, but only after he eyes Gabe and Ben's curious gazes. "You raise them and then release them."

"So where do I get the butterflies? Do I order them online?"

No, we have to pick caterpillars off the milkweed plants on the side of the highway before the township mows and wipes them out. It's what Miss Lila tells me on the phone who joins us with Kaylee scouring the countryside like kids on Easter morning searching for eggs in the backyard. It takes five hours to find six pinky-finger-size striped caterpillars. We're all sunburnt. I watch Marcus let one caterpillar ramble around his fingers while we put them in the cage. "So, what happens now?" he asks.

"We wait for them to form into a chrysalis, then emerge. Then you'll let them go."

## Chapter 57—Bribing Cops

I'm standing where no Devereauxs-McAllister-MacCabe has ever stood based on their choice and without a police escort and only Miss Lila's advice (which finally sank in) about offering flies honey to entice information from them. It's kind of like a hockey player entering the penalty box and settling in even though the referee didn't give him a penalty. Except I have homemade donuts and cookies eagerly eyed after an initial shocked silence in the New Alliance Police Station.

It is the old one-story elementary school. It still smells like kindergarten in here—dry erase markers, ancient mimeograph copy machines, and grimy linoleum floors. I feel no different than my Uncle Fred's little parakeet he lets loose to fly free around the room for a while. It finally flutters back to its cage and hops inside, too stupid to know Uncle Fred's going to shut the door, lock it in again.

Gabby Murphy used to volunteer here. I expect she's too busy packing up the parsonage for their move to a new church. I would feel safer if she had my back. I'll have to do with Jean, a pudgy woman with too-thick blush and glasses. I remember her well. It was Jean who called me whenever the police found an unidentified male body between the ages of twenty and thirty. I was the only one among my ex-husband's relatives who would make the trek to see if any identifiable features, markings, or personal belongings found on or with the body matched Josh's when he was missing and believed dead. Just the sound of her voice makes me cringe, a residual backlash that I don't think will ever fade away. I ask if I can see Dee Reynolds and she narrows her eyes suspiciously before I flip open the lid of a white bakery box with assorted homemade donuts and cookies that look like police badges with fondant handcuffs.

It's a ten-minute wait with me going from desk to desk offering up my sweet bribes to win Officer Reynolds over. When I finally make an uncomfortable sit on a vinyl chair in his office, I'm greeted with a flat-lined gaze. "Would you like a cookie or donut?" I ask Officer Reynolds, offer the box toward him with both hands and let my purse slip to the floor.

"I do not accept gratuities," he says, but I see him look out to his officers nibbling on my sugary handouts. "And they should not either. What is it you want? I hope none of your kin is in trouble again." I plop the box on my lap and sit there awkwardly. I let it sink in, that stab but I don't wince at the pain. I tread carefully. "I had someone ask me to do some research on a murder."

"The Katelyn Freeman case."

"You know?"

He delves into a metal basket on his desk. "I have received a call from Bob Keeling of the Quail Hollow Police Department." He holds out a report, pokes a finger at a name on it. "That's you, I suppose. It's a formal complaint. He's afraid you are impairing his department's ability to work on the case and damaging his credibility. I firmly advise you to stop."

"Is that—law?" I ask incredulously. "If you say I have to stop doing it, do I have to stop?"

"I can *advise* you to do so."

"What happens if I don't stop? Can you arrest me?"

"Keeling believes Marcus Freeman is unequivocally the man who killed Katelyn. He tells me that the evidence collected, both circumstantial and direct, was irrefutable. He was charged and convicted. Keeling and his people are the experts in this situation, Missus Devereauxs, and should be respected in this conclusion. Keeling was the police officer in charge of filing criminal charges against Marcus Freeman. The prosecuting attorney meticulously examined his investigation. The case is now in our jurisdiction including the site of the murder and the surrounding towns this side of Quail Hollow like Sandstone Falls and Glen Allen Ridge. Their department is small. Their coverage is huge. They cannot afford the manpower and the cost of major court cases. We took over a chunk of their area."

"No kidding," I whisper, then look up. "One of their maintenance crew ran me off the road."

"I'm aware of that."

"I found that Danny Brown, who allegedly committed suicide, was listed recently as a homicide by the coroner."

"And that is pertinent, why?"

"I don't know yet. That's why I came to you. I figure you know everything about this detective stuff and maybe you could teach me a few things, tell me what I need so I can prove it wasn't Marcus Freeman."

"We discussed the issue. I'm advising you to stop."

"But I don't *want* to stop. I *don't* think Marcus Freeman killed his sister."

"What evidence can you offer to make me believe otherwise? You've got to give me something."

"That's what I'm asking. What do I need?"

"You've got to build a case." He sits back in his chair, not one of those expensive ergonomically correct leather ones, but a 1980s gray vinyl one with the wheels on the bottom. He folds his hands at his belly. "You've got to get circumstantial evidence or direct evidence."

I set the box of donuts and cookies up on his desk carefully, flip open the lid, and give it a nudge-nudge toward him. I carefully reach into my purse and take out a small binder with lined paper and pen. "What's direct evidence?"

"Direct evidence is when you've got a witness who *directly* saw whatever disproves or approves a fact and that person can testify that they saw it. Like somebody walking down the street who witnesses a woman getting shot and can testify who shot her."

"How do you know they aren't lying? It seems too easy. Anybody can say they saw something."

"They have to be credible, have no personal interest in the outcome of the trial. If the witness was the brother, they might be considered biased. Or if a witness tells the story six times and it changes each time, they lose reliability. If someone isn't trustworthy, an attorney might bring someone in court who can contest the respectability of the witness."

"Do you *have* to have witnesses?"

"Well, not necessarily. A video of the crime being committed is direct evidence. Something you don't need to reason out and directly leads to a conclusion. There's no guesswork. A confession is direct evidence—"

"Does that happen a lot, someone just confessing?"

"No. I'd get it in writing if you're capable of meeting in person just in case the witness chickens out. The odds of getting this type of evidence are low, especially in cold cases."

"What else?"

"Well, there is circumstantial evidence. Something that's assumed or implies that a suspect is involved. It provides a general idea of what occurred." I am writing like crazy as he speaks. I look up, and he goes on. "The suspect hated the victim. People knew about it. The DNA of the suspect was on the victim. It has to be reasoned out and connected. Believe it or not, fingerprints at a crime scene are circumstantial. You've got to connect it to the suspect being there at the specific time of the murder. Just so you know, fingerprints cannot truly identify a murderer, although they link it all the time on TV shows."

"I read in a newspaper fingerprints were found on the scene. It was a big deal."

"There can be some characteristics of a fingerprint at the scene, but *other* people may share this characteristic. In the last training I went to, there was a great discussion that there's no scientific basis supporting a fingerprint as a concluding factor to match a suspect with a victim."

I tap my pen on the paper. "If there was something that I had to get for you or any other officer to take this seriously, to rethink Marcus Freeman, what would it be?"

"A confession by the murderer or a credible witness on the scene that would challenge the belief it was him." He reaches out, tugs the box a little closer, and peers inside. "It's a cold case, fifteen or sixteen years old. If you can find something like that, I'd be incredibly surprised." He takes out a cookie and studies it, turns it in his hand, and takes a bite. "But miracles do happen, I suppose. I mean, amazing things do happen. Look at this right here." He waves a hand at me. "This is possibly the first time a MacCabe has set foot in my office without handcuffs."

"Pops is a McAllister. I'm not blood, but he claims me."

"Not blood?" he chuckles. "Hell, you look just like him when he was a boy. Hotheaded too. I played ball with him in high school. If we started to lose, he'd get mad and hit that damn ball out over the school building." He peers at the bakery box. "You know you are stereotyping, assuming cops like donuts."

"You just singled me out as a MacCabe. Fair is fair. However, in my defense, I brought donuts for the historical value. I read donut shops were about the only shops open in the wee hours of the morning in the cities for cops working the night shift. That's all that was available for them to eat."

Officer Reynolds chuckles. I almost jump. Big Don made that same laugh last year when he shoved me down on the ground at the bottom of the hill at Boar Mountain and impounded my car, ripped it apart. "Listen, that was a nice thing you did for my brother and Amelia Vega, handing over that video camera. That said, I'm going to tell you to watch your back if you pursue this." He shifts, reaches into a drawer and pulls out a tablet which he opens and studies a moment. His fingers stretch out, snatch a single blue Post-It Note from a pad on his desk. He snaps up the pen from his breast pocket, jots something down on the Post-It Note and slides it over toward me like I did with the bakery box. "There's been a few calls about a certain truck sitting outside the Bradley Blankenship home. The tags come back to a Craig McAllister. I'm assuming that's you."

"Yes."

"It is also the last home address of Alison Blankenship listed in NamUs, National Missing and Unidentified Persons System."

"She's not as missing as you think."

"You know where she is?"

"I've seen her."

"Adults have the right to be missing. However, if she has committed a crime, that does not apply." He pauses as if he wants to say more. Strangely, he doesn't. "Regardless, I told Brad Blankenship the street is public. The truck was not registered to anyone convicted of a crime." He catches my eye. "Try their phone number. I do not savor the idea that someone is falsely accused of a crime, nor that someone is hiding so they can withhold information so that person was accused in the first place. That said, Danny Brown's case has been recently reopened per the request of his family since he has been properly identified. His body was exhumed and reassessed. It was not until the coroner took a closer look with the help of newer forensic testing that this new conclusion came to light. I reckon, Brandy Devereauxs, you are as stubborn as your mama and hot-blooded as your daddy, a volatile mixture in my book. I see you running past here just about every day, saw you run last year in the race. You don't give up like most folks when the odds are against you.  That's a good thing unless you add it to the mix your mama and daddy poured into you already. It's like adding a match to the ingredients of explosives. Boom."

## Chapter 58—Stalking Allie

"Hi. This is Brandy again. Just calling to see if Allie has shown up. When she does, have her give me a buzz." This was call number thirty-three. Thirty-two of these were left on an answering machine. The first, I reached her father who hung up the phone on me after I told him I knew she was alive. Through voter records, property records, and online data vendors, I've found their phone numbers and I've left messages at both work and home. I've also sat outside the Blankenship's house for three nights in a row. I've gotten no replies.

However, while I sat there lounging, I did find out through a simple call from an officer in the New Alliance Police Station that Artie Lambert and his brother were pulled over in his brother's truck after he had run me off the road. The officer gave both men a standard field sobriety test. The brother passed. Artie was considered legally intoxicated with a roadside breathalyzer test; however, he was not driving at the time. The officer had the white truck Artie had used to run me off the road sent to a police force impound where it was found to have the same type paint on its bumper as my own. They also were able to find both alcohol on the seat and floor mats and a half-smoked joint in the ashtray.

## Chapter 59—Discombobulated

Amelia Vega is at Resort at Two Bridge Falls on Saturday morning. It is mid-August and only three weeks to the event. I should have recognized her black Land Rover parked at the drop off zone beneath the porte-cochere in front of the resort waiting to be taken by the valet to the VIP section of the parking lot. I didn't. My mind was on other things this morning. Bakersfield left me a message three days ago that I am to start reporting to the track again. My punishment is over. I forgot my employee entrance coded security pass to get past the security lock on the staff doorway in the rear of the building. I was able to sneak inside the front without being noticed.

However, walking into the resort from any opening is akin to trying to get past border patrol from Mexico to Texas wearing a fluorescent orange hunting vest and waving a Mexican flag. I know any of the staff will snitch on me to Bakersfield to gain Brownie points. It's a cutthroat world here. He's got security and valet and a front desk attendant. Each will slit the other's throat with a bored smile to the lips to keep from losing a job. That said, Jim Bakersfield has gotten raunchy mad at me twice in the last week for parking Uncle Craig's old rattletrap truck alongside the undented and loaded midlife-crisis-mobiles so expensive,

Kenny always calls them *pimped-up land yachts*. The staff keeps catching me coming in with the luxury resort customers dressed to kill and me in my worn-out running clothes. A quick buzz to Bakersfield and he's angry-marching to escort me in the back door.

Consequently, I slink into the empty locker room quietly. It's dark while I get my shoes from the lower locker and my personalized track clothing from the upper locker and then dress. I put off turning on the lights; maybe nobody will notice I'm late. I'm usually by myself anyway. I think it is another form of psychological warfare headed by the Uppity A-Team members, making me feel left out. I'll use my loner existence to my advantage, pretending I left the track to use the restroom.

Bam! The lower locker swings back hard enough I know it was all-out kicked by someone's foot pulled back and waled not once, but twice. As it crashes into my left shin and upper ankle the second time, I yelp and wrench my leg in reverse in a trippy marching step backward. I tumble over the bench in the center and flip over on my right shoulder and back. The air is knocked out of me for ten seconds. I lay there staring at a bobbling shadow opening the door and leaving toward the track.

My eyes freely search out the culprit, lay some blame on the other runners. None of them want me here. I've become a scapegoat. If there is a Styrofoam cup laying on the ground or bottled water tossed in the grass, fingers point to me for the cleanup. I am beginning to think the only reason I was told to return was so they have someone to pick on.

"You're really late, Mighty Mosquito," one of the Uppity A-Team members calls out a little loudly, so everyone turns. I glare at her. "Probably because someone tried to kill me in the locker room." My tangerine eyes accuse her deep brown eyes of the insult. Her hair is short and braided. She taps one braid with her finger and narrows her eyes to tiny slits.

"You accuse me of something?" She pulls one bony arm up and lets her fingers alight on her flat chest. "You should watch yourself." She laughs and runs off.

The trainer tells me to stay off my ankle, and I should get x-rays. I am the one laughing then. Who can afford x-rays? He tells me to head to the hospital and then probably home to rest it. I sit on the bench for a while wishing I was running, then limp out the door.

Bakersfield had already zeroed in on my deceit early afternoon after an attendant questioned the reason that an old truck was parked among the luxury cars. He catches me slinking through the front foyer, escorts me past the paying customers, and lays into me in his office. "You injured yourself? Was it on the track? If you had gotten here on time, it probably wouldn't have happened. You were late again. You were supposed to be in here two hours ago. You know the rules. And what the hell is with this?" He seizes a television remote on his desk, points it to a TV on the wall. With a flick of his wrist and a tap of his thumb to a button, I'm staring at myself on the screen.

*Driven. Heroic. Humble. What is the drive behind great athletes? Not the sports figures getting the multi-million-dollar salaries whose only sacrifice will ever be a personal injury on the field. Not those whose faces don the pages of the who's who of sports magazines. We're talking about the true athletes, the heroes. Those who overcome challenges, sacrifice their time and money for the betterment of those around them. It is these few who are worthy of our admiration.*

"I don't know." I don't. They are all pictures and videos of me that anyone could have taken.

"I do. It is a TV commercial. You are in it. It has been blasted all over Kingdom Come and back again."

"Isn't that what you wanted, good PR?" I hiss at him. "Isn't that why you sent me out to a million groups to talk about the Run?"

"I need good PR from my A-Team runners. I sent you out to meet with the nobodies and the losers. Why would I want to be associated with poor white trash like you? You've got no right doing this while you're under contract with me. From now until you run, I own you; you know that, right? You are a waste of my money."

"You *don't* own me. *And* you haven't paid me a cent to be on this team and make all your sales calls for you, knocking on every small interest group door from here to Tennessee who, I might add, are not nobodies." Oh, no. The hair on the back of my neck rises, and I feel the Mama-side of me coming out, the MacCabe bit of *don't give me shit or else*. "No, nobody owns me." That's when he reaches out his hand. I'm not sure if he planned on just setting it on my shoulder or not. He lets it alight there just above my breast. "Oh, yes, I do."

"You do not own me nor will you ever possess any part of me," I say slapping his hand away. "And if you do *not* take your fingers off me right now, I will personally break every freaking one of them, one by one. I will file sexual harassment charges."

"I would recommend you don't. You will be here two hours early next Friday, or I will personally sue you for everything you own." What the hell? This guy is crazy. The rest was all blah-blah-blah and me telling him in the not-so-nicest way to *screw* off with my finger in the air.

Accordingly, I was slightly discombobulated when I pushed through the doors of the building. I'd turned and slammed the door in Bakersfield's face. I didn't see Amelia Vega exiting the building until I'd wrestled my keys from my purse. As I'm weaving my way through the parking lot and catch sight of the truck, I see Amelia Vega getting into her car.

"Well, look at you." Amelia Vega is stopped at the rear of her vehicle almost as if she is waiting for me. "I heard you had joined the other team. You've lost weight." She's wiggling her car keys on a multi-colored key fob. "Contrary to popular belief, there wasn't anything on the video you gave to Beau. The tittle-tattle wasn't true." *Tittle-tattle*. I roll my eyes. She can't see it. She'll say anything so she doesn't have to owe me for offering up the video. "There's no proof it existed, and it can't be immortalized as a New Alliance urban legend any longer. The tape is destroyed."

"I need to leave." I turn, take a step.

"How does your family feel about that, you going against the hometown team?"

I come to a halt, one foot planted in front of the other. Someone honks far off. A breeze is blowing hot air on to my cheeks. "I would suppose they support the idea considering I wasn't going to run at all for any *hometown* team. Because there isn't a *hometown* team this year, is there? You took that away with all your sponsors and advertising bullcrap. There's only a Boar Mountain team that in no way represents the good folk of New Alliance."

"Hmmm." There is a too-long lull. I cringe. She is contemplating raising her imaginary sword and digging it into the small of my back. "*Are* you going to run here?" Ah, there's the jab. I feel the thrust push past the backbone and deep into my already shattered ego. "Because last I saw, you weren't even listed as one of his team members on his marathons. You know, even these small competitions can require a significant amount of negotiations. You should have hired an agent. The agent would have probably deliberated in your defense so you ran regardless and could cash in on sponsor money. But you didn't just like you didn't bother to hire a lawyer for your shoe endorsement and—well, let's say you could have made a pretty penny. You didn't."

"But you did, didn't you?" I swivel around, face Amelia. She raises her chin. It's a defense characteristic, a shield I've found annoying since it appears she is looking down her nose at me. She's got a pursed-lip cocky smile. I draw my weapon, raise it high and thrust it toward her. "You cashed in on your little advertising cash cow, didn't you?" I pat my chest. "Me. Not Meghan. Not Michelle. Not Janey or Carrie. None of them could outrun a turtle. They are mean and self-centered. It shows in interviews. How many sponsors did you lose when you kicked me off the team? How much money did you take last year that should have been paid to me? Go screw off, Amelia," I groan. "It was about a hundred thousand dollars. But you won't see it just like you wouldn't see yourself running naked down that hallway at the resort with Big Don smacking your butt. I saw it with my own eyes." I lift my hand, poke two fingers at my eyes. "And I can see with my own eyes that your dream team will never win against this resort. If you pretend you don't see it and pretend the money didn't exist, then you think dumbshit hillbillies don't see it either. But we're not dumbshit hillbillies and we do see it. You use us just like you used me last year at the end of the run, all weepy and begging me to tell everybody how good your resort was instead of the truth about all the crap you did to me to keep my team and me out. You had it planned all out so you didn't have to deal with folks like us again this year. Well, screw you." I turn to leave, then once again pause, swivel. "Oh, I forgot my standard exit for bitches I don't like." I raise my hand and flip her off.

## Chapter 60—Bear's Little Lights

"*This little light of mine, I'm gonna let it shine*—sing with me, Bam Bam." Kaylee is a cappella singing in the passenger seat of the truck. She's watching herself in the windshield working up a smile to her fake audience.

"No." She's got a new violet car seat Miss Lila bought her and a little fuzzy book of farm animals clutched in her hands. She's like a prima donna stuffed in there, a little diva with her hair prettied up in braids tied with violet bows. When I picked her up so Pops could *get some work done*, she said to me: "Violet is my favorite color. Miss Lila says it stands for creativity, wisdom, fierce energy." Yes, she paraded those big words out of those little lips.

Work, my ass. He and Miss Lila were giving each other more flirty gazes and coy smiles than two middle schoolers trying to feel each other out at their first dance. It is dark outside and quiet in here for just about thirty seconds. I hear Kaylee huff one, teeny sniffle, then: *WAAAAA!* It turns into the kind of yowl Pops' old tomcat makes when I step on his tail. I flinch, feel an adrenaline surge all the way to a tingle in my wrists, and nearly set both passenger side tires into the gravel of the road.

"Jesus, Kaylee, you scared the crap out of me!" I hiss at her, heart pounding. She gives me this teary-eyed glare, puddles brimming beneath her eyes. "I miss Bear!" She kicks the glove box with one foot, then settles into a sob so loud, I have to pull off the road. I let her roar for three minutes, then hold up my hand. "Stop. I'm begging you." I watch her mouth open for a second round of yowls. "We're going to make cookies at my place. How's that? We can play restaurant—"

"No! I want to see Bear's house. Miss Lila drives me past when I miss him."

"Drives you past?"

"Yes! You know, you *drive*—" The little brat holds out her hands in front of her like she's holding a steering wheel, wiggles them, and stares ferociously at the windshield. "Like this. Can you do that, Bam Bam? Can you?"

"Are you going to be sassy because, no I won't. You're a brat. Pops spoils you."

"Me? He bought you that big house."

"True." I nod, agreeing. She deflates, sniffs, and her lip puckers. "Okay." She rolls her eyes extravagantly. "I'm *sorry*," she says with the airs of someone not sorry, but knowing they are going to acquire what they set out to get. "Now, will you *please* drive past Bear's house."

I relent. She tells me like a mini-rap singer, between bouts of crooning her song and while we drive down Fire Mountain, that she was going to sing in the new children's choir, except there isn't going to be one anymore because the church is closing down. As we work our way up the far side of Boar Mountain toward Bear's cabin, she becomes quiet, staring out the window in the darkness, nervously kicking her feet. By the time we're easing past his cabin, she's leaning forward with her fingers clutched to the car seat in the same way my fingernails bite into the safety bar holding me into a roller coaster seat and right before it heads downhill.

"Phew." Kaylee falls back into her seat and points to the cabin. "The lights are on."

I do see the lights, the three flameless candles flickering in the upstairs windows I'd seen when I dropped off the video that night. "Is it bad if the lights are out?" I ask slowly, wondering what the repercussions would be if one wasn't flickering there after all her drama. Thank God, they were on.

Kaylee doesn't turn her eyes away as we ease past, her neck craning until the cabin is gone from sight. "Well," Kaylee says softly as if she is carefully picking out her words. "Bear said we have to do good things and it is like a light. The light is our spirit." She pats her chest. "We let our light shine. People will see it and do good too." She looks over, relieved. She rubs her fist on her snotty nose. "There is one for me and you and him because me and you always remind him there's good, so then *his* light shines. I'm scared because if he isn't around us no more, his light's going to go out."

## Chapter 61—Kaylee's Big Institution

"What are you doing?"

"Nothing." The answer is short and curt. I'm not convinced. Kaylee doesn't realize she's a miniature version of me. I catch her with my cell phone hiding under the kitchen table and eyeing me with the same disproving gaze I used to give Pops when he'd catch me unlatching the door at age sixteen to sneak out at night. I know she has either texted all my contacts with a picture of me sitting on the toilet because I told her it was bedtime or she's trying to get a nosy sneak-peek of my pictures to blackmail me.

Kaylee wiggles out between the chairs on the far end of the table and stands there with her hands behind her back while my eyes get smaller and smaller like Pops used to do to guilt me into divulging some truth.

"Kaylee, do you have my phone?"

"I'm going to go brush my teeth and go to bed."

Okay, that isn't normal. My little sister pivots on her feet and pads out of the restaurant where we had made cookies and up the stairway. She stops just as she crosses the threshold, leans back, and silently and guilefully peers at me with no contrite. I bend and examine the shadows under the table knowing she is watching. Sure enough, my cell phone is laying there slightly exposed as if she had tried to hide it beneath a small carpet there and stopped, interrupted by my inquiring eyes.

"I have an institution." That's what she tells me.

"You have what?" I kneel, stretch my arm out, and grab hold of the phone. I waver there, suspiciously scanning the screen.

"Miss Lila says I have a big institution for a five-year-old."

"No," I return, hearing the ting of a text. "Miss Lila says you have a big *imagination*. It's when you've done something you shouldn't do, and she's defending your actions to Pops. What did you do on my phone, Kaylee?"

"Nothing."

Nothing, my ass. I poke the text button to expose her deceit. The text says: *I love you too. Are you okay? Do you need to talk?* Shit. *Who* loves me too? Aw, crap. Bear. My eyes skim upward to see what could have possibly obliged him to text me with those particular words. We are kind of in a no-text zone in our used-to-be-relationship. And there I had it: *I lov yu* typed with a chubby five-year-old finger.

"Kaylee!" I shout and hear her feet patter to the stairs and bolt up the steps. "You little brat!"

## Chapter 62—Hostage Situation

"She locked herself in the bathroom." I'm jumping up from where I'm kneeling in front of the upstairs bathroom door. I didn't hear Bear come into the house. I'd unlocked the door earlier. I see him ease up to the top of the stairs in full office meeting battle array—suit, tie, leather shoes. "I hope you're armed with tactile hostage equipment; the bulletproof hostage and crisis negotiator vests." My knees are sore from hunkering down and begging, pressing my cheek to the worn wood and trying to sneak a peek. Bear's face is lacking expression. "I'm sorry to bother you. She won't come out." Maybe he's mad. I had to use our emergency code—*bang bang* to get him from his meeting.

I don't think there is any medicine in the cabinet and I don't think a five-year-old is stupid enough to dip her head into the toilet bowl upside-down and drown herself. Still, I don't know. Kenny and I did some pretty hair-raising and dangerous things when we were this age including trying to bounce off the trampoline after running down the slanted roof above the kitchen at Pops' house. I only imagine Pops and Miss Lila would kill me if I couldn't watch Kaylee for one single night without some major catastrophe and trip to the ER.

I looked up the FBI's negotiating strategy online. It said to listen, empathize, and convince her to see things my way. Not difficult, right? Wrong. It has been forty harrowing minutes of begging, cajoling, and singing to Kaylee during her hostage situation. I've tried every strategy available—bartering and negotiating. It's like haggling with a Kamikaze pilot who's already left the airport.

"We have to compromise, Kaylee," I whispered at the crack between door and floor.

"No!" That's when I broke out in the third verse of *This Little Light of Mine* to Kaylee.

"I'm kind of at my wit's end," I mumble now. I feel my cheeks redden. He had to hear my off-key, half-yelled, harmonization with my little sister who is blackmailing me at this very moment. "She said she wouldn't come out unless you came to sing her to bed."

"But it sounds like you were doing a wonderful job of it already. Your little sister doesn't need me." He narrows his eyes, looks upward. "There should be a key above the door." He reaches up over my head to the little outcrop on the top of the doorframe. I hear the scrape of metal to wood. Sure enough, he brings down a little hooked door key with a flat end. "How'd you know that?"

"Everybody keeps an emergency key up there." He sighs. *"Bang bang*, huh?" He looks down at me, and chocolate brown eyes flatlined while he stands there, doesn't say anything about Kaylee's text. "You know I did eighty down the mountain thinking—" Then he cracks a grin and gives a silly eye roll. *Bang Bang.* It was the third of October last year. He'd been in meetings all day. I'd been working at Sandra's all day. I got home, alone and horny and made the mistake of watching a cowboy romance on the women's network. I'd found my old county fair cowboy hat and then ran to the dollar store for a plastic toy pistol with a holster. I had gone to his house and undressed down to nothing but fire red panties, a black bra with red lace, and that holster around my waist. I donned the cowboy hat and took a come-hither picture. I texted Bear with the shot. *BANG BANG. My head on the headboard. Before the bad guys come.* Bear pardoned himself from a meeting with the excuse of a family emergency. He was home in ten minutes.

He sees me reflecting, confuses it with a lack of words to answer him politely with a rejection. Bear adjusts himself appropriately, knuckle-knocks the door. "Kaylee, I have the key to open the door. If you nicely open it yourself and promise me you won't do this again, I'll sing you to sleep." We can hear the pad of bare feet across the floor, the squeak of knob turning and then the creak of old hinges. "Are you mad?" One eye peers out.

"I am a little mad," I say.

"I'm not talking to you, *Bam Bam,*" Kaylee grumbles. "I'm talking to *Bear.*"

## Chapter 63—Pops' Cat and Me

Bear and I sit down on the porch steps after Kaylee falls asleep. I look at him. He looks at me. We both look away. I stare at my hands. He's got something in his hand, a folder he offers up. "These are applications and resumes. I found them plopped on my desk. They were addressed to the restaurant. Someone has been stealing them out of your mailbox. Most are from our dining staff wanting to apply for waitress jobs at your restaurant."

"Who?" I ask. He shrugs, shakes his head. I take the folder in my hand. "Is your mom on the rampage again?"

"No more than usual." He sniffs a laugh. "The last one who quit working mentioned you were our only liaison *between* us and them instead of us *against* them."

"I think they might like working there if you acted as if you cared. Do you ever eat lunch with them in the breakroom, buy them coffee once in a while?"

"No. I should." Bear deep-sighs and changes the subject. "I also have two grocery sacks of letters. Don't you tell fans you're running for Bakersfield?"

"No. I don't like him. I talk about the old Redneck Run and how much fun it used to be before all the rules that made it open only for professionals." I sigh. "I'm going to be honest. I didn't write that text you got."

"I haven't been getting a lot of my texts and e-mails, so it surprised me. I'd somehow accidentally blocked half the people on my contact list including you and Gabe. Gabe called me the other day and asked why I wasn't answering him." He rests his elbows on his knees, peers over at me, catches me peering at him. "I thought you might have drunk-texted me. Then I saw the picture."

"Picture?" For a second, I'm standing on the edge of a cliff, lose my balance, and I'm feeling like I'm going to fall over the edge. Shit! Did Kaylee take a picture of me sitting on the toilet or worse? He whips out his phone, starts to snicker. I lean in, take in the face of my little sister who is now sleeping soundly upstairs. It must have been the exact moment I caught her texting, and a finger or palm slipped across the little icon to take a picture. She's looking down at the phone with lips in a wide O and her eyes as big as her fists. She had started to whip her head around; her hair is slapping her cheeks. She had no clue she was pushing the button to send the text message.

"I suppose it was better it was sent to you than everybody on my contact list," I determine aloud.

"Yeah. I should probably delete it. I don't want to. It's cute as heck like you two singing.

You've got a good voice, Brandy, when you're not silly." He must see my curious gaze. He snaps his phone away, stuffs it in the breast pocket of his t-shirt. The top pokes out a silver hue.

"Of course, I do," I tease him. "I didn't get the chance to sing a solo in Missus Moffatt's choir concert just because I was pretty. I was gonna rock it, *This Little Light of Mine*."

"That was the one your mama showed up drunk."

"Yeah." I drop my smile, look at my hands. "No biggie."

"Well, the world has missed out on a beautiful voice." He swallows hard. "I didn't know that was the song. I'm sorry. Your little sister chose it to sing at the Children's Day Sunday service. She said it reminded her of you and the day you saved her from your mama's boyfriend hurting her. When you stuffed her through the hole in the trailer floor to escape, you said something about crawling toward the light coming through the skirting."

"I did." Now I feel guilty for yelling at her for singing it.

"The song reminds me of you." Bear smiles warmly.

"She told me that." We are quiet for a moment. The wind blows through the trees and mingles with the racket of frogs and toads in the little puddles of water near the road. It smells of rain and Bear. I miss him so.

"I think somebody's been accessing my computer files." Bear breaks the silence. "Even my private documents."

"Who?"

"I've got no clue. Be careful what you send me."

"I hadn't planned on sending anything." I shouldn't have uttered that. It sounded mean like something Meghan would say to me. He nods knowingly, reserved.

"I guess it wouldn't have to be personal. Maybe anything, even a *hello*. Some might construe what I'm doing right now as conspiring with the enemy."

"Me? I'm the enemy?" I laugh. He turns his head, looks back and forth between my eyes hesitantly. I mull over his suggestion. "Because you kicked me off the team?"

"I wish you wouldn't say it like that. I had no say in your dismissal. It was a board decision that I fought. You were not progressing as well as the other girls. I told them to give you a chance. I knew you would come around."

"Not progressing?" I roll my eyes. "Who told you that?"

"All the contender's pre-race stats got leaked online. I saw your times. A company hired by Boucher-Ankrom Global Marketing keeps them, confidentially, for the entire Redneck Run. It's to check the performance of all the competing team contenders versus the potential to sell them as a product line for the event. It's a perk of running the event.  However, since we have competitors entered, we aren't allowed access. Someone did, though."

I turn to Bear. He's studying my face a little too hard. "Are you suggesting *I* leaked them to Bakersfield? If so, no. And my total times are low because I spend my practice times for the Resort at Two Bridge Falls promoting the race instead of getting points to place for the run."

"Promoting the race?"

"Yeah, clubs, sporting organizations, scout groups, newspapers—you know, boosting the fan base for his company. You name it; I've done it, performed like a tamed lion that does tricks for the circus."

"I thought you were afraid of crowds."

"I am terrified. But I want to run. Bakersfield hates me. Anything I can do to make him like me so I can run, I'll do it. Maybe he'll see something in me you, your mama, and your team didn't. Maybe I'll shine." He starts to say something. I stop him with a hand in the air. "But if you saw the times, aren't you worried because your team of runners don't even come close to the times of the pros?"

"Our girls *are* professional runners."

"No," I chuckle. "I know that Carrie, Janie, Michelle, and Meghan run every day, but they certainly don't qualify as professional career athletes. They've been culled from this *county*, not the world. I don't know Meghan's stats, but she's slow. It's going to be a slaughter at the run."

"Not so. All four have gotten lightning fast in the last few months. Meghan's stats are off the roof. She's on fire. Her times are equal or better than anything I've seen posted about Bakersfield's team. I saw what was leaked."

"Really," I say flatly. "And you trust who leaked the information didn't fake the stats?"

"Yes, so much so, Bakersfield's requested to allow all four of his runners not take the route in sequence, but to compete as four separate entities, so they have a chance to win against us. The fastest will finish with the baton."

"You can't be serious." I smile, thinking he's kidding.

"Why do you doubt me?" Bear grunts. "His attorneys say it is the only fair thing to do since we run the event *and* have competitors. Mila agrees. Her firm came highly recommended. I trust her. I trust her company."

"I think it's funny you don't trust me, but you trust a company you barely know." I see no doubt in his mind that Mila Boucher is telling the truth. "I thought I couldn't get any lower than the day you kicked me off the team. *Boom*, I'm down to another all-time low."

"I didn't—"

"Yes, you did. You've taken something that is fun and that unified our community and made it a race between two businesses, a cold-hearted battle of death. You hurt me, Bear. I don't want to be treated like a comfy old hand-me-down only worn when company isn't around. You want the pretty blonde riding your arm."

"It wasn't like that."

I stretch out my arms, look to the door. "Why were you here tonight? It had nothing to do with the text message or Kaylee locking herself in the bathroom. You just wanted *me* to tell *you* about Bakersfield's team."

He grinds his teeth together. "You shouldn't have shown everybody that mouse video in the weight room. It wasn't that funny."

"Ah, the mouse video. Is that what got you all riled up?"

"You're mean sometimes, Brandy, at my expense. Did you ever think how it made me feel when we'd go in during the morning, and you made a quick left to cut up with the cleaning staff?" He stares at me, drops his head. "Screw it. It was all a big mess. We both let each other down. If I asked you to give me another chance, would it make a difference? Your pops told me he doubted it, but I could give it a try."

"You asked Pops?" I look up at Bear. "Oh, God, he didn't tell you that old saying that *if you love something, you need to set it free and if it comes back, it's yours. If it doesn't, it never was or will be*, did he? It usually comes with the story about that old orange tomcat that used to belong to old Willy who lives up the other side of the mountain. He said Willy found out he was feeding it inside and told Pops to put it outside, so it came home. He was stealing it. Pops put it out. The cat chose to stay at Pops."

"That was the story he told me."

"I hate when he compares me with that cat."

"Is that a yes or no?"

"I don't know, Bear. I'm sorry about the mouse video. I get now that I went too far with my pranks." I am. My heart makes a happy thump-thump-thump like it just got breathed back to life with the first chest compressions of CPR. Still, I hesitate. I don't want to go back to sitting in the Crazy Kettle alone waiting for him again. I'm still hurt because he turned his back on me and kicked me off the team. I rise to go inside.

"There is a chance then?" he asks my back.

I turn slightly. "Maybe. I don't know. I'm not going back to the old way. I'm not sitting alone at home every night, not getting stood up constantly. I want somebody to have my back, not stab it when I turn. Period. And I'm damn sure not going to even consider it if Meghan and her gang are in the picture. But so that you know, I asked old Willy about that particular cat one time when I stopped by his house, and he said he didn't know anything about that orange cat or talking to Pops."

## Chapter 64—Deception

I come in two hours and thirty minutes early to Resort at Two Bridge Falls on Friday as directed, even a half hour earlier than Jim Bakersfield requested. I have my coded security pass, and I slide in the back door sourly like a prisoner on a weekend work release program returning after a couple of days freedom to her dark jail cell. It is quiet in the back hallway.

Two days a week for two weeks—that's all I have to come here for a total of six hours each day until the event is over. The entire time I'm here, I think about how Pops keeps puffing out his chest all full of pride and telling everybody he raised a good one, that one and he's talking about me winning that race. Now, my family will show up to see me run and I'm not even on the roster. I've been too embarrassed to divulge the truth. The only prize at the end of this long tunnel is humiliation. It's a waste of time. Amelia Vega was right. I should have paid for an agent to represent me. I didn't know there were so many damn sharks out in this sea.

The lights in the hallways are still early hour dimmed. To get to the offices, I have to cut through the upper section of a small auditorium that is behind glass where spectators can pause and watch what is going on in the fitness center set aside for indoor soccer and volleyball. It is also used as a meeting and conference area.

As I shoot through the open doorway, staring at the screen of my phone, I hear voices. I slow, then come to a halt. It is a strange time, at six o'clock in the morning, for a conference. I'm not sure if I should back up and walk out or breeze through quietly and quickly. The back is shadowed. Nobody would probably see me pass. However, I don't want to interrupt a meeting. Motionless, I waver there, thinking the meeting group is finishing up as I hear footsteps walking toward the podium.

"—if I may say something before we end." A deep voice eases up the dull brown carpeted stairwell. "Bakersfield, you and I are the only event supporters barring Boucher Consulting. I don't like cutting it this close. This is a big investment. If we don't win with these money odds, this loss will destroy my stockholders' trust. It'll destroy me. What kind of insurance do I have this will work?"

"Jim, if I may?" That's Mila Boucher's voice trickling up the steps now. I freeze. What's she doing here? I peek through my hiding place and see Mila Boucher stand up from the front row. "I'd like to address Mister Allison's concerns." I don't see Amelia Vega or anyone from Boar Mountain Resort. My detective kicks in automatically. I press the video on my phone and start to record as I peer around the corner. I see the back of Jim Bakersfield's head bob near a small podium. He steps to one side to allow Mila to get to the small mic.

"I want to reassure you, Gary, that we have laid the ground so that there is no way any other organization in this event will win. Every circumstance has been studied and researched in every way possible. The odds are astronomical." Her voice is cool and calm, almost hypnotizing. "Let's say there *is* some unforeseen circumstance like one of the archers can't be here because of a flight delay. It would be farfetched, and I'm even stretching it a bit saying that it may influence the outcome. But only marginally. We will still win. Period. Arcola Sporting Goods, ARCO United States Banking, and Boar Mountain Resort are the top three contenders. I know for a fact that their stats are nowhere near our own. I'm telling you, there is no way in hell any of the other teams are going to win. We want Boucher-Ankrom Global Marketing and Consulting to be the number one sponsor next year using your companies as shareholders. If they had been a contender, I wouldn't be standing here now, would I? I would be with them." There is quiet laughter. "No. We don't just want a piece of this pie. We want it all. And we want you to be a part of the deal. I've already lined up multi-year deals after we win this event. We'll grow and evolve into a major event, eventually phasing out the politically incorrect and surely, dwindling Redneck Run part of the event and make it a full-fledged marathon. People wanting to see multisport competitions with sequential endurance races are dwindling. We will make it a running event as big as the New York Marathon and other major running events. I guarantee it."

"We're taking the redneck out of Redneck Run," Jim leans into the mic and pipes up. "You won't be sorry—"

I back out of the room. I have no clue how to process this information, the deception. I've simply got no clue. It doesn't matter. While I'm standing out on the field and warming up later, one of the trainers walks up to me and hands me an envelope. I stare at the envelope, then peel back the flap. I pluck the paper, folded and tucked inside. It is letterhead from Two Bridge Falls resort. I open it wide and read: *We regret to inform you that you no longer qualify to be a representative of the elite Two Bridge Resort Professional Running Team. Unfortunately, our selection committee did not choose you for further consideration as you were not able to achieve our basic qualifying standard of performance. Your name has been withdrawn from the team roster. You may leave your security coded identification, training clothing, and shoes at the front desk today. Thanks for trying out for the team! We wish you well in your future.* I'm crushed. I'm cut from the team. It is a blow to my ego. I stare at the paper, tuck it into my bag, and leave.

# Chapter 65—The Night Bear's Light Went Out

"What do you think you're doing?"

I'm taking a break, hands on knees at the bottom of Mine Hollow Road, panting and sweat rolling into my eyes and stinging like teeny wasp bites. No sleep last night. Twenty-six texts to Bear and no reply. Here he is at the bottom of the road yelling at me with a funny smirk hiding beneath his almost-pursed lips.

"I'm running like I always do."

"No, I think you're lazy and unless you want to see this—" He reaches into the breast pocket of his button up shirt and tugs out a picture. It is a runner magazine picture of Meghan jogging along the cover. "Get your butt in gear!"

"Don't yell at me!" I am confused and irritated. What is he doing here? "You're not my coach," I grunt. He doesn't know I'm not going to see Meghan at all. Horrors. I don't want to tell him I got cut from the team.

"Well, you need one. Okay, how about this. Do you want to see the backside of whoever this woman is in front of you?" He draws out a magazine under his arm and holds up a picture of the A-Team members who called me Little Mosquito. "If not, you better get your butt in gear and GET RUNNING NOW!"

I stagger backward. Bear never yell-yells at

me even when we fight. "You're kidding me."

"Do I look like I'm kidding you? Up the mountain and back down twice."

"You're nuts."

"I'm pushing you harder for the race." He points up the mountain. "We'll chit-chat later."

"God, you're mean." I mean-eyes him. But I do what he says. I need to run. I run to run away from my problems.

"You don't know, baby; you have no clue. Meet me at your restaurant in an hour."

"You're sweaty." Bear pokes me with the tip of his finger when I stop just short of the step he's sitting on.

"You used to like sweaty," I tease him. I'm rubbing the sweat with the crook of my arm from my forehead.

"Still do."

I take him in, smile. He smiles back. "What's going on?" I prod, plopping down next to him. I'm squinting against the sweat burn in my eyes. "You caught me off-guard at the bottom of the mountain," I say. He stands up, walks to his truck, reaches inside the window. He brings out a towel and tosses it to me. "Shouldn't you be in meetings or something?" He sits back down while I scrub the sweat from my face and arms with the towel.

"You winning the race is more important."

"You realize I don't run for you."

"Don't care."

"Did you get into moonshine?" I laugh, avoiding the truth I'm not running for anyone.

"I just had an epiphany moment last night." He leans back on his elbows, squints sideways at me against the early morning sun. "I'm lying in bed. I feel alone. I mean alone-alone. I toss and turn for hours and realize I've been doing this for months. Then I also realize I'm reaching over and patting your side of the bed. You're not there. I imagined I could put someone else there to take up that void. I thought about this line of women that could replace you. I only feel—" He lingers, rubs his chin thoughtfully. "—nothing. I look up at the little fake candle-thingies in my bedroom window I put up for me, you, and Kaylee. I see that. My heart aches." He looks away from me. "Sometimes you think you're holding up the world. But, as you're standing there with your arms in the air, take a look around, you realize it already came crashing down around you, and you're standing there holding nothing but air."

He just described my life perfectly. "Ye*ssss*." I close my eyes, draw out the word, let it linger in the air so he knows I understand.

"I realized I was doing just that. I don't know when it started to fall. Because I felt like at some point, you were standing there with me, and when a piece came crashing down, you would lean over, pick it up and gently place it back on." He sighs. "You're like this little light. Whenever you're around me, it's like you bring the good out in me. If things were bad at work, you'd come over, and this incredible feeling would rush over me. The bad feeling would go away. I've read the stuff people write about what you say to them about letting their light shine, show how good they are inside like they say in the bible. I remembered that last night. I sat up in bed. Right when I figured that out, the bulb on one candle went out. *My* candle." He swallows hard. "The bulb died. I'd seen it flicker a few times in the last few weeks. That alone freaked me out. A couple of times I wiggled it in the socket, and that seemed to work. I thought maybe the little sensor wasn't working. I was too busy tossing and turning, trying to sleep, knowing if I got up, what little edge of drowsy I'd been in would slip away. I should have stopped at the dollar store, bought a new bulb or a new candle lamp. I didn't. It just didn't seem like a priority." He rolls his head over to look at me. "That's it. The light is out. I don't want it to go out. I realize I shouldn't have let things go—not just with the candle."

I start to cry. I don't ever let people see me cry. I like to hold it in until I feel like exploding. Not so now. I cry, then I start to sob while Bear puts his arm around me. "Hold me tighter, Bear," I whisper. And he does. Softly. Sweetly. With kisses on top of my head.

## Chapter 66—The Kiss

"Did you get my texts? We need to talk about Mila." Fresh from the shower, I sit back down with Bear on the porch with coffees.

"Whatever happened between Mila and me is in the past. You heard about it—*us*?" Bear leans back grudgingly. "Let's not discuss Boar Mountain. Let's you and me work on making you the best runner."

"*H—heard* about you and Mila?" I stutter. I'm thrown. "What about you and—and Mila?" A thousand horrible, miserable thoughts rudely barge through my head ending in Mila and Bear thrashing about in bed—legs flying, bodies rolling, groans mingling, smiles sharing. "You slept with her? Are you dating her?"

He's reluctant, cheeks glowing pink. "We kissed." He lifts a hand, holding me off. "I mean, she kissed me. It caught me off-guard. I was rattled. I kissed her back. I don't know why I did it. At the moment it happened, I was so unnerved. I didn't expect it and I just thought that it was—" Bear chokes, coughs. "—the polite thing to do?"

"We broke up. You've got a right to kiss other women."

"It was *before* we broke up, a week before you left the engagement ring at the Crazy Kettle. Staff in the parking lot saw us kissing. I figured they told you and that's why you broke it off."

I mull this news over in my head. "I did get some hints, but about Meghan. You liked Mila?"

"Meghan?" he sniffs a laugh. "No, definitely not. Not my type. I thought she was my friend. She's not. I should have kept my distance with her. She's like a sweet cup of coffee until you realize the sweet taste is poison." He shifts uncomfortably. "But no, I didn't like Mila. I only saw her as a business partner. I honestly think she's put a curse on this place. Since she's been here, we've had nothing but bad things happen, one after another." He laughs feebly. "I'm sorry about the kiss. I know you want to know *why* I did it, but I don't know. I guess we'd just lost a lot of marketing when Hartley didn't win last year in the race. We banked on that. It was a pretty big loss, and work has been centered around making up for the loss. It was a big blow for Mom, and she's distraught over it. We can't afford another loss. That's why we hired Mila. She makes million-dollar decisions every day for huge companies across the globe."

"That's what I needed to talk to you about—"

"Please. Will you hear me out first? Then we can put this behind us. I feel like I have to tell you this so you'll understand why I did what I did, why I was never around and why—it seems I let everything go to hell between us. Then we can maybe try to patch it up?"

I've waited this long. Still, I work my phone

out of my back pocket of my jean shorts. I know Bear's not going to believe me. "Yeah, go ahead."

"It is written in the rules that every team can have a wildcard," Bear leans forward and puts his coffee on the little table between the chairs. "You know what that is?"

"Well—"

"Mila set this up as part of a marketing strategy. See, at the beginning of the year when she first got here, she found that none of the girls—Carrie, Janie, or the twins would qualify to race in the run. They weren't that good."

"What about me?"

"I don't know." Bear does his nervous scruffing of his hair. "I didn't do the numbers so don't be mad. You were way behind the others."

"Really," I say cynically, hold back.

"This is why I couldn't discuss these issues with you, Brandy. You get mad and storm out."

"Okay, I won't." I bite my lip. Mila must have altered the timings to make me appear so slow that I would hinder the chance of winning. "I'll keep an open mind."

"Mila had it planned from the start that three of the Boar Mountain team members would run a short stretch this year. We'll have a pro runner do the fourth and last stretch. It's a strategy. We've got to do it because the other sponsoring agencies are putting in well-established, professional runners—they've got the money to sponsor them that we don't. We're asking a lot of this wildcard. He's got to make up for the three women. I didn't want to tell you, but Noah Hartley is our wildcard."

"The same Noah Hartley I outran by twenty minutes last year?"

"He's gotten more trail experience under his belt. Mila showed us his stats. I knew you'd be upset. But we had no choice. Also, the contract had a stipulation brought up by the sponsors. They refused to be a part of the event if we didn't do it. Whatever team wins will choose the location of the event next year."

"You mean, the Fire Mountain Redneck Run wouldn't be here anymore if somebody else won?"

"Yes. But we won't let that happen. It is the number one revenue for New Alliance and the biggest marketing and building block we've got for Boar Mountain Resort. If our team loses, the whole town will feel the impact, the blow. If our team loses, Mom will probably lose the resort. We are standing on the threshold of bankruptcy right now. That's why we had to pull our money from the church funding and invest it in Boucher-Ankrom Global Marketing. All of it. Everything."

"You know it is Boucher-Ankrom Global Marketing *and Consulting?*" I eye Bear cautiously. "Did you also know Mila works with Jim Bakersfield from the Resort at Two Bridge

Falls too?"

"What do you mean? No, she works for us."

"Well, Bear, do you know what moonlighting means?" I ask him. "Your Mila may be making million-dollar decisions, but she'd probably be more than happy to take your fifty or hundred thousand dollars as a loss to take a half-million plus investments from another company to make sure it wins. Do you get what I'm saying? How do you think she makes so much money?"

"She wouldn't do that to us. It's illegal."

"To work for two separate companies? I doubt it. Maybe she's doing it for Bakersfield under the table. Because your Mila works for Resort at Two Bridge Falls too, I can almost guess that's why she got the contracts changed. I saw her there. I got to the resort early. They were having a meeting. I passed through the back, heard everything." Bear stares at me guardedly. "You know, you said just a minute ago that everything started to go to hell when Mila Boucher started working for you? I think it is because she has been sabotaging every chance you have of winning the event." I hand my phone to him. "Take a look. I think she's been faking the stats, making it look like your runners are faster than they are. Your Dream Team sucks. It is like a middle school soccer team before kids start dropping off two days into conditioning. I think you and your mom just might be screwed."

## Chapter 67—Confessions

"Where did you hide the hammer?"

I put myself into this mess, Marcus Freeman dragging John-John Emory, the former night manager at Quail Hollow Express Gas, across the gravel lot outside The Coffin bar.

"He's gonna kill me!" John-John Emory's eyes are bulging. He's short and frumpy wearing navy blue khakis and a dirty gray t-shirt. It's dark out. There isn't a parking lot lamp, only the glow of a half-moon and my low beam truck lights making us little more than dancing shadows on the ground damp from a misty rain. "I don't know what you're talking about!"

"I think you do." I sound indifferent. "I would suggest you answer his question. You know where the hammer is hidden that killed his sister." However, in my defense, Emory murdered a guy in cold blood and helped destroy evidence in three other murders, not to mention he ratted out Katelyn and hid the weapon that killed her. I listened to a confession taped on a mini DV camcorder given to me by Allie Blankenship who came out of hiding long enough to walk into Mister Smiley's at noon, confronting me at the register.

"Leave my parents alone," she'd screamed that at me right in front of Denver Thomas, age 67, who was bagging groceries for an elderly woman. I recognized her immediately—fist-wide eyes, white-blonde hair and thin-as-a-willow legs. He took a step back at her shout. She nearly knocked him over, then, getting to me. "Quit calling them. Quit showing up in front of their house. They don't got nothing to do with this." She proceeded to plop an old leather duffel bag on the checkout counter. It continued down the running belt toward Denver who looked a bit terrified she might be coming after it again in a minute. I stopped the belt and stared, open-mouthed. She leaned on the counter, ended up with her face inches from mine. "I'm warning you; they're going to kill you if they know you got it. But you need to get to John-John Emory. He's got the hammer. He hid the one they used to murder Katelyn."

"Who are *they*?" I ask slowly.

*They* are half the police force and workers in Quail Hollow because even if they didn't murder a victim, they were hiding information about it. Mister Smiley is a notary. In stunned silence, he listened to Allie Blankenship's story, then authenticated her statement in writing at the freezer section of Smiley's Grocery. He placed the document in his safe.

Seventeen-year-old Shelly Holcomb had on-again, off-again relationships with both Artie Lambert and John-John Emory. Artie was mostly a guy-pal she'd known since high school who was just along for the ride. She'd met John-

John the summer of 2000 when she was hanging around outside the Quail Hollow Express Gas after working her shift at Sunrise Camping Resort. On Saturday nights, she'd sit outside trying to talk what she called *old* guys into buying her a couple six packs of cheap beer to share with her friends. Emory would give her beer and cigarettes, and Shelly gave him blowjobs. It was a win-win situation for both. In 2002, Shelly got a job at the gas station part-time and just filched the beer and cigarettes from the store. Allie wrote out her statement like this:

*The night Danny Brown walked into Quail Hollow Express Gas, it was a Saturday night. Katelyn and Shelly had just gotten off work and we were heading out to get some beer from John-John Emory at the gas station. When we got to the gas station, John-John was closing up, mopping the floor. Katelyn went to use the phone to call her mom and tell her she was at my house. She did this all the time so her mom didn't know we were out partying. We were all fooling around pretending to steal candy bars, and me and Katelyn popped open a couple of cans of beer and started drinking. We saw someone walking outside the gas station. John-John told us to go to the back of the store to the breakroom so nobody saw us drinking. Shelly stayed out front.*

*I remember peering out the little square window just when we snuck into the back and pushing my finger over my lips to shush Katelyn because she was already drunk and wouldn't stop laughing. This man in cowboy boots just walked in there and said he knew about Walt Fee killing that woman and two girls last year. He said he knew John-John helped take the bodies down to the creek and make it look like they'd wrecked. He'd taken the car to the top of the hill with the bodies inside and without seatbelts and let it go right down the hill into a tree. He said he knew they had to do it twice because the first time, it missed and just stopped at the gravel lot. He knew cops covered it up—after they arrived, the cops kept moving the bodies around because the scene didn't look like a real wreck. Danny Brown was living in a tent at the homeless camp there. That's how he saw it. He hid behind a tree.*

*Me and Katelyn stood there at the window and watched John-John take a pistol out from under the counter and shoot Danny Brown in the head. There was blood spattering everywhere—on the candy bar rack, the freezers, everywhere. He put the gun in the guy's hand to make it look like it was suicide and called the cops. All us girls were screaming and crying. John-John came back and threw the door open and told us to get out of there before the cops came. He'd kill us if we ever told anybody he killed the man. It was self-defense. He thought he was holding a gun. If we said anything about those two girls getting murdered and the cops covering it up, we'd be killed too. We took off in Shelly's yellow car.*

*Katelyn was acting strange the next week. She kept telling me she was going to quit work, maybe go back to school early. I told Shelly I was scared she'd tell her mom and dad. Two weeks later, Shelly told me one of her friends was having a party at his house and asked if Katelyn and me wanted to go. Katelyn didn't want to go at first, but Roddy said we could get off early. I talked her into it, said we all needed to get real drunk and forget about the shooting. We tried to call her house to tell her brother not to pick her up. The phone was busy, so Shelly said she could just take Katelyn home and she could change and catch her brother before he left. But when we got there, he'd already left to pick her up. We waited for her brother, but he didn't come back. Katelyn wanted to go find him. Shelly said we could go see if he was waiting for her at the campground, but she wanted to stop somewhere on the way. It was Walt Fee's house. Me and Katelyn didn't know that's where we were going. Me and Shelly went inside. Katelyn waited in the car because she was mad at Shelly for stopping. John-John had tarps laid down in the hallway. I'd asked him what he was doing with them. He said he was painting the walls. We were only in there five minutes when Katelyn walked inside, yelling in the door we had to go because she had to find her brother. It was like all of a sudden, Katelyn realized where she was and something wasn't right and she made this funny sound. I saw Walter Fee drag her to the hallway and hit her with a big hammer to the back of her head. I thought he was going to kill me too so I did whatever he said and I knew he had guns so I didn't run. He rolled her up in tarps and put her in the trunk of Shelly's car and John-John stayed to clean up. We drove down to where the shelter was at Stone Cold Creek and Froggy Lake. He started to get her out, and she moaned. I heard her. I was with him. Walter smothered her with his shirt until she stopped breathing. He made me feel for her pulse. I figured he was going to kill me next and I didn't want to die. I took a chance he might shoot me in the back and just ran off. I knew he was going to kill me too. That's why I've been hiding. I put a cross up where she died later. The tape, I took with a mini DV camcorder, is what I gave Brandy Devereauxs. Shelly and me set it up in the store, and I talked to John-John. We were scared that if John-John got caught, the cops would say we had something to do with the murder. He said Walter Fee was the one who killed Margie Pitzer, her daughter, and her daughter's friend a year earlier. That night he killed them, Dana told her mom Walter had been having sex with her since she was thirteen, and he was threatening to kill Dana if she told anybody. Margie started calling him, screaming at him. She went crazy mad saying she was going to call his wife and the cops and tell everyone he was a pedophile. Sarah Thompson was spending the night with Dana Pitzer. Walter Fee came in their garage door and killed Margie with a knife and a hammer, then tied up the girls and killed them too.*

"The hammer got thrown away!" That's what John-John Emory is telling Marcus and me right now. Liar.

"Aw, John-John, don't be an idiot. You stayed to clean up the mess. You have the hammer." I mutter while Marcus back-walks him up to the side of a car and brings his fist up to punch him again. Marcus looks over at me, sighs hard. "What do you think? Let it rip?"

"Yeah, sure. Leave the sack of shit for dead. We'll put a little Post-It Note on his chest with: *I murdered Margie Pitzer.* Then we'll let the police figure out the rest."

"It wasn't a hammer!" John-John hisses. "God, please, it was a mallet. Like the kind you pound meat with. That guy I shot was blackmailing me, gonna kill me!"

I reach out, stop Marcus' fist with a hand on his arm. My eyes are on John-John. "A meat tenderizer? What color?"

"It was silver on the end. Walter grabbed it from the kitchen drawer. I know what it was."

"Cripes. I have a picture of the marks on your sister's head. The wound had the little pyramid-shape of the tenderizers on a meat mallet."

"It's in Stone Cold Creek." He's kicking baby-style into the air. "I tossed it there!"

Three hours later, I'm standing in Stone Cold

Creek with a flashlight, absurd expectations, and an annoying cynic watching me while he sits on his rear on the bank with his arms resting on his knees. "You're never going to find the mallet here," Marcus advises me. "This is absurd. It could be nowhere or anywhere ten miles downstream. The man who told you this is probably, as we speak, digging it out of his kitchen drawer, tossing it in his septic tank."

I am knee deep and walking against a rising current. "If I don't, I'm going to be sitting at home thinking I should have at least checked. Maybe it has been sitting right under our noses." The mosquitoes are biting. One particularly annoying gnat is buzzing in my ear. "This is what you hired me to do. It has been a lot easier than getting run off the road, screamed at by cops, and watching you beat the hell out of some dude."

"The *dude* was a murderer. You got him saying that stuff on your phone, right?"

"Yes, but we have to prove guilt beyond a reasonable doubt." I stand up. "I've got to build a case, Marcus. Like now I know why Artie Lambert ran me off the road. Shelly must have called him when I questioned her that same day. Allie said those two dated. I can tie it together and show a set of circumstances occurring—he was probably trying to kill me or scare me so I couldn't or wouldn't talk."

"You've got a witness and a confession to the

murder. What more do you want?"

"I'm going up against an entire police force, Freeman, that knowingly withheld evidence and mishandled evidence. They probably knew where the evidence was and didn't get it. I would think they will go to great lengths to stop us, so they don't go to jail," I grunt, looking up. "Who do you think the courts are going to believe? The freaking cops from Quail Hollow, who at this very moment are probably tossing out anything in their personnel files that make them look bad, or someone my pops even calls a gumshoe detective *and* her cohort, the hoodlum people still believe killed his sister?"

"*Hoodlum*," he chuckles. "Where did you come up with that description of me?"

"I don't know," I sigh. "Old detective movies, I guess."

"Don't tell me that's also where you come up with your techniques for solving a crime."

"Go to hell." I glare at him.

Twelve minutes later, car lights flash along the old road. I see Marcus crane his neck toward them in the light of the moon. It isn't the first car passing. Each time one does work its way past, we look up. This time it slows then stops. And red and blue lights flash above us on the bank. "Shit. Marcus, you need to get out of here. *Run*. Just run. If I'm not home in two hours, call my Pops. Do you hear me?"

## Chapter 68—Detained

"Where is Marcus Freeman?"

Jack Keeling's weaselly whine gives me chills. I can distinguish he's a bad guy just by the griping bleat of his voice. He embodies every shameless cartoon wolf sneaking up on an innocent cartoon lamb sleeping peacefully. I'm just waiting for the powerful and ominous pipe organ music to play when a villainous character arrives on the scene.

"I don't know," I tell him. He looks coldly at me. He could kill me in this little room in the Quail Hollow Police Department right now. Nobody would know. He could strangle me in a blink of an eye, wrap his stubby little fingers around my neck, and with just the right pressure cut off my breaths. They'd shove me in a body bag, toss me in Stone Cold Creek. Then turn on their police car lights and load me back into the bag — the perfect crime.

I can't believe they haven't murdered me in the last twenty hours I've been here. I'm assuming they don't know what I know or they are buying time to figure out what I know. I look around the room — four pale white walls. One has a two-way glass window halfway up. I see myself staring at it. I know there are people on the other side. "Am I under arrest? Because nobody's read me my rights," I say. I got tackled coming up the little hill. I've got skinned knees from being dragged to the ground by one cop while another stood overtop me with a pistol aimed out into the darkness looking for my counterpart. My heart was pounding so hard. I am sure it drowned out his footsteps running away. But one of us had to run. I had the identifiable truck and no murder in my past.

"Where is Marcus Freeman?"

"I don't know. Am I under arrest? Nobody's read me my rights."

"What do you know about this Katelyn Freeman? Did you steal the truck from the Sandstone Falls Village Transportation Department and did you plan on using it to break into homes?"

"I'm not answering any questions. I want an attorney."

"Then you can stay in here as long as it takes until you decide to talk because we have reasonable grounds to detain you for being an accessory to break-ins at not only Boar Mountain Resort, but also eight homes around the county, and stealing a Sandstone Falls Village maintenance crew vehicle. Maybe even helping to cover evidence in the murder of Katelyn Freeman." He pauses, tries a new tactic. He attempts to get me to say someone saw Marcus getting out of the truck outside the Blankenship house to steal from a neighbor. He tells me they've got my fingerprints on a doorknob. They say at Boar Mountain, there is security video of me sneaking into the building. There's a knock on the door. A head pokes in. "We need you out here a minute, sir."

"Give me another hour." Jack Keeling sits there and drinks bottled water in front of me. I'm so thirsty, I could suck the sweat off a lemon just to get sated.

"—we won't release her." There's a second voice behind the back of the cop poking his head inside the door. "This is our jurisdiction."

The door closes. I look to the two-way glass mirror. It's a strange feeling knowing you're being watched in a police station. It may be reflective on this side, but I know it is transparent on the other. The head pokes in again. "Dee Reynolds is out here. He wants to talk. He says he won't take *no* for an answer."

*Dee Reynolds.* I see Jack Keeling blanch outwardly. He says a long line of curse words, smacks his hand on the table. He leans in, jabs a finger at me. "I got your ass." He pokes a finger to the security camera above. "You're going to jail. This isn't over."

My Aunt Jillian is somewhat of a card hustler. Every one of my aunts who play with her on the rickety table on Pops enclosed back porch on Sundays after church knows she can do a quick sleight of hand and somehow, she's got the magic card that wins the game. Somebody always counts the cards before.

Somebody counts the cards after. But when Aunt Jillian leaves, there's always hushed deliberations about how she comes up with the perfect hand from poker to Go Fish. I asked her once how she did it and if she could show me the trick. Aunt Jillian told me: *I don't cheat. Everyone thinks I do. I'm just not afraid to take risks like those old hens who spend half the game checking under the table thinking I'm stealing their eggs. When I know I might lose everything, I take a chance.* She smiled and shrugged. *Besides, if you noticed, I always sit with my back to the kitchen door where there aren't windows. You'd think after forty years, they'd figure out I could see their hands mirrored in the glass.* Wink-wink.

I suppose I look at it like Jack Keeling and his boys are like my aunties. I am like Aunt Jillian. I'm all in for taking chances especially when I think I don't have a choice. But I also have a few tricks up my sleeve, and that is hearing the voice of Dee Reynolds and knowing there's a two-sided mirror where they've been watching me all night and now, all morning. I do not want to end up dead in a ditch. I don't doubt that I will if these men have any clue what I know. I wait until Jack Keeling leaves. I can barely hear a heated battle ensuing outside the not-so-airtight room. I stand, walk up to the glass window, and stare at myself, knowing who is on the other side.

"Hey!" I wave my arms all around trying to

get the attention of anybody out there. "Hey!" I look up to the security camera and then back to the window. "Get out your pen and paper, ladies," I say. "Turn on your video cameras. What I say *will* be used in the court of law. I'm going to tell you who murdered Katelyn Freeman. I'm going to tell you who killed Dana and Margaret Pitzer, Sarah Thompson—and you're going to crap your pants when I do, Jack Keeling. You're going to crap your pants right now!" And I started naming names.

I'm maybe three minutes into the discourse when the door bashes open. I cower, arms held up over my head because it sounds like a shotgun going off.

"Shut up!" It is Dee Reynolds reaching out one hand and grabbing hold of my skinny upper arm. He latches on tightly, dragging me across the room, so my hip hits a chair and I keel to the right. "I'll take care of her," He growls mad-wolf. "She won't be talking to anyone." *I'm going to die.* That's all I can think when he half-drags, half-escorts me to his cruiser in the parking lot and shoves me in the back seat. *He's going to take me out to Stone Cold Creek and shoot me dead.*

"My Pops will search for me if you shoot me and dump my body," I tell him when he hits the gas, and we take off.

"If *I* shoot you, he'll never find you. Never."

## Chapter 69—Big Girl Timeout

"I've seen the McCallisters do some dumbass things, but this one takes the cake," Officer Reynolds says that to Bear, Pops, and Marcus when he pulls up Pops' gravel-dirt drive. He slams the door behind him. "There are five men with firearms in that station. She's dancing around like she's doing the Macarena across the floor, naming every one of the men holding those guns as being a part of some conspiracy. She might as well wrap a North Korean flag around her, paint a bullseye on her back, and run in front of crazy Willy's house."

Dee Reynolds doesn't let me out. I'm nothing more than a six-year-old left on the school bus while the driver leans out of the door to discuss some wrong I've committed like putting gum on the seat. He didn't say a word driving from Quail Hollow to Fire Mountain. Officer Reynolds only grumbled, shook his head, telling dispatch to hold his radio traffic because he was *on a run*. Pops comes up with a sour purse to his lips. "Looks like you're in a big girl timeout for a day or two," he says. I can hear Bear and Marcus guffawing like two drunk men at a comedy club and Pops just delivered the punch line at the pivotal point of a really bad joke. *How many Brandies does it take to screw in a lightbulb? Sixty—one to hold the bulb and fifty-nine to turn the house—*

## Chapter 70—Hiding Out

Amelia Vega stood outside of the doorway that leads to the running track at Boar Mountain Resort. She held an old stopwatch she'd dug out of the lost and found box at the front desk. Amelia matched the timing of her four runners in perfect synchronization to a technician Mila Boucher hired to monitor and record the results. These, she wrote down on the back of a spiral-bound notepad. When the times came to her as they usually appeared in her e-mail box as an attachment, she opened them wide and compared hers to those Mila Boucher provided.

"They were not even close to my tallies. When I timed myself doing my early morning run, *I* got better results than Janie Mills. But the girl has been trolling around the buffet room an awful lot. Every time I pass, she has a plate plopped in front of her full of carbs. I entrusted the nutrition guidelines with the trainers and dieticians Mila hired. When I mentioned to Janie that I thought she seemed to be eating a lot, she told me Mila suggested she needed to gain some weight for endurance. Janie's stats were incredible when Mila's team placed them on paper; I wasn't going to question something that was working. But they were false. Noah Hartley never even showed for times. Two weeks to the race and we're screwed."

She is now sitting in Bear's kitchen across from Bear and me. Pops and Dee Reynolds concluded Bear's house was as close to an impregnable fortress I was going to find. He said his high-tech home security fence, gate and alarm system are probably rated for a zombie apocalypse. I talked to him and two Federal officers for four hours this morning with Pops by my side, disclosing copies of the information I'd collected.

Pops says I need to trust a law enforcement agency and if it had to be anyone, he'd put his eggs in Dee Reynolds's basket. If for no other reason, he saved my ass at the Quail Hollow Police Station dragging me out of there on the pretense they would be under suspicion if I somehow got hurt or fled. Pops said Officer Reynolds was a crappy baseball player in high school, but if he got tagged out and the umpire missed the call, he was honest about it. Officer Reynolds also said while he sorted this out for a couple of days with the Feds, I should not be anywhere near anyone in Quail Hollow associated with the murders. Bear offered Marcus a room until things smoothed over. Surprisingly, he took it as did Bear's mama who Bear conceived was too stressed out to go home to an empty house and would go back to work.

"This whole thing is a travesty," Amelia moans. "What else have they scammed us with?" I see her peering curiously into the room at Marcus in the same way a timid Victorian woman might steal into a sideshow and peep at the merman with two penises. *What's his story?* she whispered earlier when he was in the bathroom. I told her he'd been framed for the murder of his sister, had gone to jail for it. He was a good guy barring he was a bit salty about life for all of it. She chewed on this for maybe six seconds and said: *I have a kitty cat like that. I got him from the pound. He bites.* I had no clue she had a cat she saved from the shelter.

"Did you ever find who stole money from the safes?" I ask. "Maybe it's Mila Boucher."

Amelia picks up her phone like she's going to call someone. "I didn't think of that. Mila suggested it was you. She hinted you had access to Bear's computer with the codes."

"I don't get on to Bear's computer. I kept running away from Marcus out there because I thought he was stalking me. That's why he was down there, trying to find me so I'd look into his sister's death."

"You should have come to me." Bear sighs. "I could have done something."

I look at him over the tops of my eyes. "You were out of town." I'm surprised he doesn't look at his mama. The two usually lock eyes when I say something like that—bestie second-graders clasping hands in unification on the playground when one of their classroom nemeses walks by. Instead, Bear gazes at me intently. "You're right. Mila wasn't just good at throwing our business under the bus for her benefit. She is very convincing. Brandy, I thought you were coming on those trips. She told me at the last minute, you freaked out. She sandwiched me between Meghan and her on the flights. I texted you. You didn't text back. Mila was always grabbing up my phone to place new contacts on it for me. I'm slow typing them in with my big fingers. She's impatient. She must have blocked you off my phone. Then, though, I guess I felt you let me down a little. On the way back, Mila told me just to keep our trips a secret from now on so we didn't embarrass you."

"And you listened."

"Shoulda, coulda, woulda. Stop bickering, you two. You both made mistakes." Amelia waves both our words away with her hand. "Say bygones. Learn from it and move on or end up single like me. Besides, you won't be able to fly out anywhere soon. We're going to be taking the bus if this blows up in our faces." Bear catches my eye and smiles. "Bygones," we both say at once and laugh.

I'm not sure how to take Amelia right now. She usually reminds me of one of Pops' stray cats he feeds on the front porch with recycled plastic fast food restaurant bowls lined up side by side. The strays are meaner than wet panthers with claws flying, mouths hissing, and teeth bared if you try to pick them up or step on their tail or otherwise insult their desire to be wild, and yet be fed three meals a day of Happy Whiskers Cat Food. Amelia Vega sits across the table from me with the TV blaring in the living room while Marcus cheers on some baseball game. She looks more like one of those tomcats coming down off the anesthesia after Pops brings him back from the spay and neuter clinic to get fixed.

"I've contacted our attorneys, met with them. They are as thunderstruck as I am. What if they dissolve the contracts and have spent all the investment money? Mila Boucher had access to everything until we locked it down this afternoon. We can *lose* everything. What is going to happen to our credibility? This is going to end us." Amelia keeps shaking her head, ranting. "The thought never occurred to me Boucher's company was corrupt. I checked into them. They had impressive reviews. I should be at work sorting this out."

Reviews? Everybody knows you can't trust reviews. They are unreliable. Companies write up hundreds of fake 5-star rave reviews all the time, banking on employees to use fictitious names and e-mails. Competitors write up 1-star dishonest reviews.

"You have something to say?"

"Huh?" I yawn. She's wearing a sleek black-striped business suit. "No. I'm wondering what you'd look like in a pair of jeans and a t-shirt."

"Your world is falling apart around you, and that's all you can think about?" she asks me. She looks at Bear for reinforcement. It's a classic Amelia move.

"*My* world isn't falling apart," I tell her flatly. "Mila Boucher's and Jim Bakersfield's world might be crumbling around them, but they cut me from their team. Better for me. I don't have to face Bakersfield and get bullied by him anymore. Maybe your world is collapsing because you didn't do your homework. Me, I just got a bunch of dumb cops wanting to lynch me because they conspired to cover up some murders for a brother officer. That's nothing new for my family or me. People in general routinely lie to serve their interests. I'm riding high. All's I ever wanted to do is be a chef and run. I've got a restaurant. I can walk out the door anytime I want and run in the woods. I don't need a stupid marathon to make me feel whole. I don't like the runners who are like those cops and so dead-set on winning they'll break the rules to get to the finish line."

"You got cut?" Bear looks genuinely concerned. "Why didn't you tell me?"

"I don't know. You treated me like crap, why add more fodder for you to feed on?"

"I'm sorry." Bear takes me in, starts to rise as I do. "What about us?"

"Bear, I love you." I don't care if his mama is

listening. Pops found someone that will love him for his stupid stray cats, and that he's dragging a five-year-old along for the ride, *and* he's got skunk-stinky socks *and*—me. Maybe not flaws or defects, but all the stuff that makes him *him*. He loves Miss Lila regardless of her shortcomings like thinking she's a psychologist and can solve everyone's problems by adding some chamomile to their tea. If he can do it, I can too.

"But?"

"That's it. Don't treat me like crap anymore. Don't hang around Meghan. That's how I feel. It would tick me off if we let Mila Boucher win."

"God, I love you too. Is this the part that your Pops says is when the cat comes back?"

"I told you that story wasn't true."

Marcus comes into the room, reaches out with my phone in his hand. "You left your phone by the TV. Somebody keeps texting you." I stand, take the phone, and look at the texts. "There's a ton of texts from MAMA popping up on your phone." She probably wants to bum some cash for cigarettes, beer, or pot. I used to drive her home every Friday night because she'd drink too much. Not a normal mama-daughter relationship. I poke in: *What u want?*

*Come see mama. I need a ride.*

*I can't.* I won't. I don't want to.

*Where you at?* She doesn't reply.

## Chapter 71—60:40

"I got a call from Dee Reynolds." Amelia comes through the open bathroom door while I'm brushing my teeth. She closes it behind her. It's raining outside. Even in Bear's fortified cabin, I can hear the patter on the tin roof. "I thought you'd want to know."

"Yeah?"

"He said the FBI came in and gathered up almost the entire lot of the Quail Hollow individuals who were involved in the murders." Amelia fixes the curtain on the shower although nothing is wrong with it. "He said two were still at large along with three who worked at the maintenance fifteen years ago and live out of state. They are going to reopen the case of Walter Fee's second wife found drowned in the bathtub around the time of the murders."

"We're safe then?"

"He didn't say. You've got toothpaste on your chin." She picks up a washcloth and simulates wiping her mouth before she hands it to me while I put the toothbrush back on the sink. "He said it is best we stay here until we know for sure." Amelia stands still while I wipe at my lips. "What a horrible thing that poor man has gone through." She's referring to Marcus because she's flailing her hands over her head to display his wild hair. I watched her talking to him in the living room. She had seemed almost distraught at times. I nod. "I suppose you know that, though, that's why you helped him. You must know how he feels."

Boom! There I have it. "Just because I come from Fire Mountain doesn't mean—"

"No, Brandy," she interjects softly, one hand waving at me. "The way the young women treated you, the way Jim Bakersfield treated you, the way—I treated you. I was so invested in Mila Boucher; I failed to see her deceptions."

"I didn't see them either." I wonder why she thinks I saw through it any more than she did?

"Nor did Bear. I hope you believe him." She sighs pensively. I don't fall for it all the way. I latch on to what she's offering for the moment. At least my mama's moods are just a few and decipherable—happy, sad, mean. I've seen Amelia Vega's many, many sides, especially the charming. They change quickly like a chameleon's everchanging color evolves to match its environment. "He says to me: *Mom, I don't want to do this anymore. I can't. It's killing me. It's killing us.*" She looks into the mirror, pretends to poke at a wrinkle on her cheek. "And I know he's not talking about him and me. He's talking about *you* and *him*. We were on this flight five months ago." She turns again and faces me. "He works his way back from his seat three rows up, and he leans over Michelle who is sitting next to me. He has a picture in his fingers, and he holds it out over her head. It's a picture of you sitting up against the wall in one of the rec rooms and being silly. It's rounded, you know, like it's been in his wallet." Amelia holds up both hands, pushes forefingers and thumbs together to form a square. "One corner is pinched ragged from him tugging it out so much. He says *I'm sitting on this plane staring at a picture in my wallet and I realized I'm loving an image of my girl because that's all I got now. I'd jump off right now to be with the real thing if I didn't think it'd kill everybody on here. Because I'm dead inside without her, you realize that? You get that, Mom? I'm not like you. I'm not like her or that airhead sister of hers.*" She pauses and gets a slight curl to her lips. "He pointed to Michelle when he said it. Then he told me: *I don't want to be married to my job. I want to be with her. I'm not doing this anymore. I'm done.*"

I shift. I'm not sure how to digest this while I'm chewing, chewing, chewing on her words. It is quiet barring a roll of thunder far away. Is this Bear's mom I'm talking to or an alien in her body? She seems to sense this and shakes her head. "I tell him that please, please, please I need him until the Redneck Run is over," she goes on, "just like I told him when he confronted me in my office and I begged him to stick with the resort until we get the new improvements on the restrooms. Then take a break, fly her to Italy. Then it was that spring extravaganza for the baseball teams and there's the golf course plans and—it goes on. Each time, Beau says to me: *Mom, I'm done. You promised.* And I plead with him, knowing he's a good son, knowing he won't turn his back on me. Then all of a sudden, Brandy, you were gone. I realize he went with you. Not in body. In soul. He's like a zombie walking around yelling at everybody and being his father. He hates me. I think he's dead inside. But a little part of me knows that maybe there's still a little bit of life in there because he still has that damn picture in his wallet and he still pulls it out twenty times a day. He thinks I don't know it. I do."

"But Meghan, I know—"

"She was the sorry replacement I tried to throw at him, to fill that void. Don't believe what they say." She pulls on her work face right about the time the rain pours harder, a crackle of thunder bursts through the night sky. "What would it take to get you to come back to him? What's your price?" Amelia sighs.

"You're trying to—pay me to like your son? Isn't that kind of like prostitution?"

"Well, it did indeed sound like that. I apologize. I—"

"Sixty-forty," I belch out. "I get him sixty percent; the resort gets him forty. I suspect you'd want ten percent somewhere in there, so you'll have to take it out of that forty. You have to treat me with respect. Period. And Meghan has to go after the event. Gone—"

## Chapter 72—Perfect

Bear holds me close tonight for the first time. We listen to rain on the roof. His embrace is so gentle like he knows I might be wrestling with old feelings, the scared ones. Still, I am wrapped like a Teddy bear in his huge bear hug. I stay up for two and a half hours (eyes begging to close, me forcing them back open) blissfully falling into his cuddle and experiencing for the first time, the wonderful, wonderful bounce of belly, a jump of heart, and a new sense of feeling completely and utterly protected.

It didn't start like this. He'd gone to bed. I stayed up and watched TV with Marcus. I didn't know where we stood. He didn't offer up a bedroom so when I went upstairs, I stopped and knocked on Bear's door. Bear was awake, maybe reading. I heard him shuffle on the bed, beckoning me inside. I came through the door not sure if I should close it behind me. He's sitting on the side of the bed only wearing flannel pajama pants, no shirt just his muscled arms by his side. It catches me off-guard; he's a bit shy about being shirtless. He still feels fat inside. I see it in his eyes while he timidly looks up at me. He's visibly uncertain, searching my eyes for a reaction. I find that an incredible turn on that he cares so much about how I feel that he's humbled at my presence.

"I wasn't sure what room to take," I whisper.

"I was hoping you'd stay here with me." He's got a grin on his face, nods to the bed. I prance like a frisky kitten across the room and pounce on him so hard, I knock him back on the bed. I sit up and straddle his belly. He comes up to meet me, so I'm kneeling on either side of him. Bear cups my jaw in his hands gives me a long, passionate kiss leaving chills sprinkling tickles along my arms. He smells beautifully of strong aftershave and mint toothpaste and *Bear*. God, I've missed his scent, missed him, missed his kisses that half the time miss my lips because I never stop moving. I shiver, kiss him back, roll my hands through his hair. It smells like expensive man shampoo. I drink him in like a tall glass of lemonade on a hot August day. I don't tell him on a whim I stopped at the mall off the highway one day on my way back from Resort at Two Bridge Falls and pretended to test the scents of aftershaves and shampoos at the high-end counter of the store. I couldn't find his scent. I went home feeling empty.

"What?" he asks in a hoarse voice, kissing my neck. Then he's kissing my lips like crazy. I pull back long enough to answer. "I don't know. You like to play. I like to play." I let him kiss me—earlobes, shoulders, arms. "Can we pretend I'm stronger so I can hold you down?"

He flops back, dragging me with him. I stretch my arms out, clasp fingers to his and drag them upward with me. I'm small. He's big.

His arms are only bent while our bellies press together. "Don't move, or else," I tell him in a gruff voice, but he's got this silly lop-sided grin like he's going to bellow out a laugh.

"Or else, what?" He's trying out a timorous voice to play my game. It's not working. He's on the verge of busting out laughing.

"What?"

"What are you going to do to me if I don't?" he prompts.

"I don't know." I sit up with my elbows on his chest. The hair tickles my arms. I scratch each elbow, one at a time. Each time I lean on the other, Bear grunts with the pressure. "I didn't think you'd ask." I contemplate. "How about I pull the hair on your legs."

"Oh, no! Woman, don't do that." He is being silly and bursts out laughing. "Those bony elbows digging into my chest might be a start."

"My elbows aren't bony," I contest, digging each in a little. I start laughing with him, flop down on his chest. We lay there quietly. He plays with my hair, rolling it in his fingers.

"My belly's jumping. You feel it?" I ask him.

"Um, maybe. My heart's pounding. You feel it?" Oh, I do. And mine too. Together they pound, off-key and like two dueling sets of drums. I started kissing him again. We end up rolling across the bed, tangled in the blankets and each other and lying like we are right now close as I've never felt before.

## Chapter 73—Protector

The drop of a single pebble to the surface of a small pool of water causes the water to surge outward and away from it. Even the tiniest ripple expands, and the waves impact everything around it—the wee minnows disturbed by this occurrence swimming in its wake make a startled swim forward, wary it might be a bigger fish coming to eat them. A heron steps forward, seeing his next meal in those little minnows darting about and disrupts the sand on the shore. The repercussions caused by that one single action spreads—the ripple effect.

I am the one who threw the pebble into the water, teeny as it was. It was me, Preacher Murphy's little flicker of light, who was not what everyone thought I was. I am the one who was, all along, slowly chipping away at the community. It hovered there just out of reach as I fell into a blissful sleep to the sound of the thunderstorm, the flickering of the lights when the downpour hit harder. It was as if being basked in sudden silence in the middle of the night brought it all to light.

Mama texted me back. I heard the *ting*. I saw a message was from her. I shouldn't have looked at it. I did. She said: *If I die right now, it's your fault.* It's like a trigger, her mean words. Aunt Jenny has told me a million times my mama is manipulative and will toss all her garbage on other people's lawns to make their yard look as bad as hers. And she wasn't talking about her dingy little mobile home at Fire Mountain View Trailer Park. That's when I started thinking there's a lot of things that are my fault. I was the pebble. I wasn't sharing my light with anybody; I was puffing them out. The sad part was, I spent too much time thinking of me. I never did a thing about the preacher's misfortunes. I could have made it stop, the Holy Trinity Church in town wouldn't be empty this Sunday for lack of a congregation and preacher. The Boar Mountain Resort wouldn't be dangling over the edge of a cliff by a string along with everything the business helps to keep working in the town. I wouldn't be imprisoned at Bear's house while Mama is probably hitching a ride with a serial killer or walking stoned and lop-sided down the middle of the four-laner to get home while a semi-truck creeps up on her in the dark. It overcame me with the crash of thunder, the silence when the electric goes out like it does, it seems, with every storm through our mountains while a line gets downed by a falling tree.

"The electric is out. You okay?" That's Bear asking in a sleepy voice. "It's probably a tree on the line. The generator should kick on in a while if hornets didn't nest in there again." Bear does have a backup generator, a huge whole house standby monstrosity that kicked on last winter during an especially long and bitter three days of wet winter snow and then an inch or two of ice atop without electricity. It stayed steady until the power company got the trees off the line. It tends, however, to be a low priority on his list of things to do—checking the battery, putting it on auto mode.

Bear doesn't want to admit it, but he's superstitious about things. He never opens an umbrella inside, always steps around a ladder and never goes beneath it. His back is to the window. He's facing me. I'm facing the window. I see the electric candles not flickering and worry he's going to freak out they went out too. I grunt a muddy *yeah* and tell him it's not like we're going to freeze to death if it doesn't. I tell him not to move; it's just perfect, he and I all snuggled up. He falls for it. He can sleep in silence. I don't. I'm not surprised when the generator doesn't come on, and the only sound is Bear's snores.

I peel his arm off me and gently slide his leg off my hip, slip off the bed, so the one who was trying his damnedest tonight to show his mama I am his TOP priority doesn't lose faith because the twinkle lights that probably have battery backup and represent a part of our relationship are completely out. I tiptoe to the window, wiggle the little bulbs and shake them gently. I sigh. No batteries. I stand there wide awake for the longest time. I'm thinking it overcomes me, embraces me in its dark grasp until I can see nothing but Mama over and over slipping into the serial killer's car.

"Mama, I have to hurry before anybody realizes I left." I'm standing outside the nearly vacant Crazy Kettle in my track shorts, my old high-top running shoes Bear still kept by the back door, and one of his white t-shirts crumpled up and hanging by a thread to the side of the laundry basket in the utility room. "It's only a matter of time before they go back on and somebody wakes up and assesses the situation, then realizes I'm not there."

The hem of the shirt is scrunched up into a ponytail held tight by a hair tie then tucked up underneath to hold the excess shirt up around my waist. It is all I could grab to sneak out of the back door at one-forty-five in the morning. I thought I heard Amelia moving around in the bathroom. Mama texted me again. *Please, baby, mama's drunk. The lights is out. There's some man in the parking lot and he wants to give me a ride. Don't make your mama do this.* I didn't want to get up. I simply wanted to take my little cold feet (because Bear likes the air-conditioner on subarctic) and press them up to his shins to warm them. I always tell him it's my right and he's okay with that. Instead, I'd pushed my truck three-quarters of the way down the driveway in the pouring rain and then let it settle by the road before starting the engine.

I noticed the electric is off all of the way down the side of the mountain. It's black all the way to the Crazy Kettle where she is waiting. I've only got my low beam lights, and I'm waving my mama from the side of some guy's old truck. It's his and two others on the far side that are left. One belongs to Billy Winkle, the bartender. He usually sticks around and makes sure the lot is empty. I can't see her man of the evening, only her. The rain is pouring, gusts of wind picking up the droplets and tossing them like pebbles through the shine of headlights. She's leaning against him, fawning all over him.

"I'm comin', baby girl." She pushes away lazily, still lingers in the dark. "That's my girl over there. Brandy. See her? Ain't she pretty?"

"Well, hey, Brandy. Just keeping your mama busy until you got here." At first, I give the guy a flippant wave of a hand. I've been picking up Mama since I was sixteen. It's not the first time that whatever man she's straying towards at that particular time drunk-sees me and starts making passes, thinking the apple doesn't fall far from the tree. They are wrong. I carry a baseball bat in my truck just to prove it. I've used it twice. I mean, I've brought it out and wiggled it in my hand. That's as far a fight I've ever been in. Marcus was right the first time we met on the road to the resort. I'm not a fighter.

(Well, except for the random battle in a gas station over a video against two geeks I know aren't going to hit a woman back.) I'm more a hollow-threatener or a run-like-heller. Still, I know how it works. I don't move more than a foot from the driver's side with the door open. It's under the seat and right by the door. It's heavy. Kenny made it for me. He drilled a hole from the hitting end and through the barrel and filled it with melted copper pennies. It packs a powerful punch.

"I appreciate that," I tell him, my voice almost overwhelmed by a semi-truck rolling along the highway. "Now I'll take her home."

"I'm not here for her."

That's when I get the sinking feeling in my chest. It's like Kenny drilled a hole in my brain just like he did to the bat and the heavy stuff is flowing down to my belly. I stand there rigid.

"Do I know you?"

"You sat outside my house. You should. White house in Glen Allen Ridge."

"You know my Brandy?"

"I do. I don't think we've formally met. I'm Walter Fee." I grasp I will be following in the steps of at least four other women before me. I'm wobbly with terror.

Mama's stoned. I know her different levels of smashed. At the lower end of the scale, she wiggle-walks and snorts when she's just a bit sloppy drunk. She usually gets a little slappy right around twelve beers or five or six shots of hard alcohol. My cheeks and little butt remember that well. That's about midway. When she's high, she gets super-giddy, comes down hard with sad. When you mix the two, that's like the upper echelons. She's happy, sad, angry. That for me was Mama waking me up to play out on the swing set at two in the morning, crying at the bottom of the slide on to my three-year-old shoulder because she suddenly thought she was ugly and also decided it was a stupid thing for a mama to do at two in the morning. Then, she'd latch on to my scrawny arm and drag me into the house for no other reason than I was staring at her knowing what was coming and knowing not to say anything at all or I would get a whooping *I'd never forget*. Why am I here, you might wonder, considering what she's done to me? She's my mama.

Right now, I can see she's midway out of giddy and heading to sad. She's got no clue that the guy who is shoving her down and away with one hand didn't pick her up in the bar and offer her free drinks because she was the hottest woman he'd ever met.

"What you doin'?" Mama's words slush out of her mouth, slurred and distorted. She kind of crumbles in half when he pushes her down and boots her with his foot. "You dumbass stinky, old skank." Walter Fee laughs forcefully. "You ugly. What you think I'd be doing with you?"

She falls to her knees, keels left. I'm watching her, not the man with what appears to be a metal pipe in his hand through my eyes blinking against car light and rain. He leans over and grabs up Mama's arm. He raises it high and lets it come down. I hear Mama squeal, a scared goat kind of bleat, bleat, bleat. It rattles me. Mama.

"Mama!" I huff the words while she squeals a cry. It's not a bluff. I hear the sound of flesh and bone meld with the clank of metal.

"Shut up!" Walter Fee brings up his weapon, whacks her again. "I'll kill her. Then I'm gonna bang, bang, bang the shit out of you!" But she won't stop crying. I hear her grunting for me something like *baby, help me, baby help me.* Blood is dribbling from her forehead, streaming down her right eye. I'm not a fighter. I'm a middle-finger-flicker. I'm a runner. Mama hit me so many times, I couldn't count the bruises on my head, legs, and arms. I never hit back, only warded off blows with my forearms.

Walter Fee strides forward while I fling my hands in the air futilely holding him at bay. I see what he holds in his hand now. It is a thin, metal water pipe. It is long enough, he hits me between neck and shoulder while I stand there unable to run because Mama's lying in a heap three strides away. I can't even run. Now I'm not even a runner. I'm still not a fighter. I'm just a *stander* that's turning into a faller when he lets his water pipe bounce off my extended arm flailing in the air before he turns back to Mama screaming behind me. "Shut the hell up!"

I fall on my hands and knees. I suppose of all those things that I forgot while I'm feeling the water splash from my fingers to my face is that I am also something else. I remember Kaylee crying in my arms the night Mama's boyfriend chased us down in her trailer to the bathroom. I clawed my way through the rotted particle boards of the floor and shoved my little sister out the bottom. *Go to the light,* I told her. I stood there and took Mama's boyfriend's blows, praying to God Kaylee was escaping. Not because I thought I was going to die, but because I knew he would kill her. So, I may not be a fighter, but I am *a protector.*

The pain in my jaw and just below my eye is searing. For a moment, I'm blinded. When he raises his weapon again and tells Mama: "You're the bait-whore who was stupid enough to let me put you on a hook and toss you in to catch my fish." I knee-run, slopping my way to the truck four clumsy steps away. I slap wet fingers into the open door of my truck, grapple with the bat. I use the side to pull myself to my feet. I hear Walter Fee make this cackle-laugh, but his head is still turned to mama while he brings up his weapon for one final blow. Then I take six steps. I pull that baseball bat back pro-player style, and I swing it hard and fast. "Leave my mama alone," I scream. "Leave her alone!" It hits him hard in the head just above his right ear and makes a crunchy *pphlat* sound, not once, but three times while I haul my arms back, swing away. I don't stop. I can't stop. I'm suddenly swinging that bat over and over while he falls to his knees and then keels to the right. I hit Walter Fee over and over like he hit those girls—

"Whoa, there—Brandy—whoa." I hear the voice, feel a hand on my arm. I blink, look up in the rain. "It's Billy Winkle." Billy, the bartender. "He's down, sweetie. Easy now, he's not getting up for a while. The cops are coming. I called the cops—"

## Chapter 74—Race Day for Everybody but Me

I've got a big banner outside the restaurant on the day of the race—*Brandywine Restaurant and Tavern. At the Foot of Fire Mountain—Home of the Fire Mountain Redneck Run.* The town is filled to the brim with people. It rained during the night, but the forecast doesn't call for more rain until the evening. The sun is shining. It's seventy-four degrees. Cars are lined up and down the highway looking for places to park along the sloppy edges of the roadside. It's been two days of celebrating and festivities. I've missed most of it outside. Because inside my restaurant, it has been an onslaught of customers.

I am baking and frying, stirring and passing out menus. Pops said it is baptism by fire. I opened on Thursday to a full house lining up at the door. My entire family is taking shifts helping me cook and serve until the event is over. Amelia sent down three of her restaurant staff for me to borrow. I stayed up the last two nights making packed lunches for people, so they don't have to wait two hours to find a table. Uncle Craig scoured the mountain for twelve picnic tables he's set outside. Once in a while, I stop to look at my little hands. I can't believe they are capable of hurting someone as big and bad as Walter Fee. My fingers are scratched. I broke the bat. Billy, the bartender at the Crazy Kettle, heard Mama's screams and my yells and came out and wrestled the bat from my hands. He told the cops I was saying over and over: *You ain't gonna take the shine out of any girl's lights no more!*

He won't. He's in the hospital, then straight to jail. Bob and Jack Keeling and Artie Lambert have all been apprehended. And mama's okay. She's got a broken arm. At least that's what Joyce Acres told everybody on the six o'clock news after I kept up my end of the deal and gave her my story. That was a week and a half ago. Today, Preacher Murphy is sitting on a wooden bar stool in the kitchen. My chatter has come back to haunt me. He's got his hands clasped like he's praying, but he's not. Beneath, there is a newspaper with this splashed on the front page.

*Will the Light Still Shine for the Redneck Run? When Amelia Vega, owner of the Boar Mountain Resort and Conference Center, was approached by the consulting firm Boucher-Ankrom Global Marketing and Consulting, she was both delighted and flattered this world-renowned consulting agency was interested in working with her on the event. Boucher-Ankrom Global Marketing is known for its work with stellar billion-dollar corporations like Amherst Pharmaceuticals and Godard Data Storage. Little did she know what she had stepped into and then, it was too late.*

*Within only a matter of months, the entire venue for the competition had changed along with rules Vega said were outlandish. "Then we lost our best runner, Brandy Devereauxs, due to Boucher's deceptions," Vega told us. "Devereauxs has always been a shining light to those of us in our community and to the resort, an inspiration to us all. I recognize now she also brought inspiration to people around the world. That was when I began to recognize something was going incredibly wrong. . . then it spiraled out of control like a top spinning off a table." Or a light puffed out for the Redneck Run. Now Vega and her son are left holding an unlit candle in the darkness caused by the firm while attorneys sort out the mess and aftershocks of the scandal. "If we lose this Redneck Run," Vega laments, "we lose it all." The question is, will the light still shine for the Redneck Run if Devereauxs isn't there to win or lose or simply be there to inspire us all?*

"Crud, Preacher Murphy, I'm not even running," I groan at him. "Why would they print *that*? There wasn't one thing in there about me solving that murder. That's why I talked to Bill Gaynor and Joyce Acres."

"Because it's the story of the day and billions of dollars are tied to this Boucher Consulting company. As my wife put it: *it's all about the drama.*" He's giving me the kind of sad smile you give people when you know they are carrying a lot of baggage, but don't want to talk about it. "I thought you'd want to hear it from me and not wonder why everybody's looking at you funny today. I told you that you're a little light. Maybe you can take a break and mill around a while, talk to your fans."

"Fans." I snicker. I know Gabe sent him over to make sure I'm not going to *explode into a billion pieces of crazy hillbilly*, as he put it. Gabe and Ben, on the other hand, are picking up Bobby Reese and some buddies from the rehab center to watch the competition. Then they, along with Sandra, are picking up a late evening shift helping me in the restaurant.

The preacher has talked to me about everything from boxing up all the stuff in his house to perhaps becoming an assistant pastor at some huge church in Cleveland. I think I'm helping him more than he's helping me. "—but they let us stay this final week so the kids could go to the festival one last time."

"Do you have to go?" I ask him, stirring a pot of chicken noodles. I've borrowed two students from Fairview State College, my favorite former professor, Dean Popovich, recommended to help me in the kitchen. They do as I say just like I heeded the words of the chefs who took me under their wings. They are bustling about around me.

"Yes. Unless you got some of that good luck shine left in you," he teases me, reaches out and gives me a nudge on the arm. "Change is good, right?"

"Are you asking me or telling me—?"

Just then, Bear rounds the corner of the kitchen. He gives Preacher Murphy an awkward wave. I'm not sure how things went down with the loss of funding for the church. Nobody has said anything to me.

"What are you doing here?" I look up from a plate I'm preparing. He's harried. He looks at Preacher Murphy. His eyes drop to the newspaper beneath his palms.

"Are you mad about the article?" I ask him. "I thought the focus was going to be on Katelyn Freeman's story."

"It's a *good* thing," he interrupts. "It is." He smiles. "Mom knew. They interviewed her, so it isn't a surprise to her. It's started all sorts of crazy, but Mom loves the drama." He deep-sighs. "Jim Bakersfield has decided to stay in the race." Bear scruffs his hair. I divulged to him last night that it was a turn-on for me. He smiles knowingly. I grin back. "He's having *his* attorneys hold off *our* attorneys until afterward. He's laying blame on Boucher-Ankrom, denying any collusion. We can't stop him. He probably hasn't read the newspaper. It's to our advantage as far as public opinion." He comes up beside me, gives a quick peck on the lips. "I'm here because of the sixty-forty. Isn't that the deal you made with Mom?" He points to my head. "That chef hat is cute."

"Yes, I made that deal. She's not haggling?"

"I guess not. *I* don't have a say in this?"

"No. And the hat is called a *toque blanche*. It is supposed to display a sense of cleanliness in the kitchen." I touch the white hat on my head. "I prefer a skull cap, but Pops insisted." I point to the net hats in a box by the sink. "Put one of those on and make yourself useful. If I've got you sixty, then you're going to be in here a lot until I can afford to hire staff." He plucks one from the box, walks over, and kisses the top of my head.

"Your Pops is proud of you." Preacher Murphy starts to rise like he's going to leave.

"Remind me of that when the next bank loan payment comes due." I add some garnish to the plate, move it around until it is just right. "After tossing in all my Mister Smiley work money and the five-hundred Marcus paid me, I had just enough to pay off the expenses to start this week. I've got to make enough to cover the payment."

"Yeah, tell me about it." Bear takes the knife I'm holding with my hand, wields it like a Samurai. "I might be putting in an application for a job here."

"Maybe me too." Preacher Murphy sniffs a laugh.

"Whoa there, Samurai Benihana," I say, slowing the knife with my hand on Bear's wrist, taking it from him. "Let's keep it lowkey until I move you up to a skullcap, okay buddy? No knives." He laughs. "What's that mean, you'll be getting a job here?" I don't have time for antics, point to the white plates I need to fill. "Hand me those."

"It means, we will lose it all, dear." *Dear.* I turn. Amelia Vega is standing just inside the doors. She says it much like the growl-purrs of the feral cats Pops feeds just as he puts out the food on his porch railing. They hate him for being human. They love him because he's holding the food. "Noah Hartley didn't show. His agent called this morning after seeing the flood of front-page newspapers with the story. He didn't want to be a part of a scandal. We had to drag Rush Gordon and eight of his friends out of a bar last night at four in the morning dead drunk."

"Rush Gordon." I roll his name around my head. "You know, he's the one who talked me into going to Bakersfield's resort when you kicked me off the team."

"Rush?" Amelia says. "*Our* Rush?"

"Have you ever thought Mila Boucher might be giving him a high payoff to slow things down on his part in the Redneck Run?" I hold my fists up, driving-ATV-style. "For a couple thousand and some future sponsorships, there are a few folks who would pretend their ATV was breaking down on a course. It's not his typical fare, this type of race. He doesn't lose points on any standing by losing in it." I let them chew on this and eye Amelia. "What are you doing here? Don't you have an event to run?" I ask, gently laying the meal on the plates.

Martha Hershberger swoops past, picks up the plates I am handing her. She has decided to be the go-between me and Kenny, who is acting as a host and keeping track of the waiting line. I think it is so that she can flirt with him. Aunt Jenny caught them making out in the bathroom earlier. "I would expect Rush Gordon is another one of Mila's picks. If you're banking on him to win that ATV run, you're going to be sorely disappointed."

## Chapter 75—Royally Screwed

Amelia watches Martha turn on her heels and head back out, sees me reach up to snatch another order. "We are—how do you put it, Brandy? *Royally screwed.* Mila Boucher was the leading committee member who chose the contenders in the race leading me to believe—" Amelia winces, "—Rush is probably on Bakersfield's side. She was falsifying your stats and finding ways to make us believe you were *not* performing your job well while the four other girls on the team *were* performing beyond imaginable, so there were no possibilities we would win."

I guess I've waited a long time to say it, never did. "I'm sorry for you, Amelia, no matter how badly you treated me. But I've got a restaurant to run."

"I don't think you understand," Amelia rubs her forehead with her hand. "It isn't going to do you any good to have a restaurant in a ghost town. That's what New Alliance will be if we lose the race which is in the top revenue producing events in the state. The event also helps sustain our resort. It keeps our hometown running with the money it brings in to the businesses. If we lose, we lose it all. This is another Mila Boucher ruse I was persuaded to do. She told me we were an easy shoo-in. Even if we win the battle over that company's fraud, if Bakersfield isn't held accountable, he will get the event. One by one, businesses will close."

"Like Holy Trinity." I hard-stare her.

"Yes. Like Holy Trinity."

"Run the race for us," Bear says point-blank. "There are a lot of people looking for you to run. There're signs everywhere. They don't know you *aren't* running. Bakersfield's touting that you're running the race for his resort, so he gets his advertising bucks." Bear gets this cheeky gaze. He's making a mint with your protein bars."

"*My*—protein bars?"

"They are good. I had one." Preacher Murphy is still hovering. Everyone looks up at him. "I did. You didn't know about them? The Official Redneck Run Nutrition Bar—Brandywine Grand Nutrition Bars. It tastes like dark chocolate brownies with dried cherries."

"It's called Bear's Delight." Bear grunts. "*My* protein bars. She made them special for me when I was having horrible cravings for cake in the middle of the night."

"I gave the recipe to Bakersfield's driver off-handedly. I didn't think they'd steal it."

"He's getting a lot of pressure," Bear tells us. "There have been articles and articles about you. Your story sells, Brandy. It's *their* story too. These people are looking for this hometown girl to run. What they are getting are outsiders, people from out of the country who, at the end of the day, go home to Nigeria or South America or wherever they came from that isn't the United States nor are they the girl next door. You've written back hundreds upon hundreds of people with special notes to each. Who wants to root for strangers or some guy who is just running the marathon circuit when this girl, who is like a big sister writing home from camp, is out there to cheer on? The folks who come to this event, they can't identify with these other runners. They don't *want* to identify with them. There's a little kid in a wheelchair that asked about you—Zach, I think? He's out there already lined up on the route with a bunch of other kids from some youth group. You met him at an event. He's got a sign."

"He's from the Care Together Youth Foundation?"

"His entire club is here."

I chew on his words. "Bear, I—I would let them down, let the town down. Those women running for Bakersfield have Red Rovered me on the track fifty times. They form a wall, impenetrable, unpassable, indestructible. This is all they do, run. Day and night, they've got nothing else to do. They have the support of their country, wherever it is. I am a girl from the mountains." I whisper, trying to focus on the next order. "I run trails—I don't have a snowball's chance in hell especially if three other contenders on the team are rigging the event so you lose."

"You're such a big, whiny baby. I've been telling Pops that for years. Now I've got proof." That's Kenny's reproachful snarl. He pops in the door with papers in his fist and pretends to play trombone for sound effects. Martha is on his heels, passing him to hand out another order. She stops long enough to take in the drama. *"Whaa Whaa Whaaaa.* You're an embarrassment to your roots, Brandy Sad Sour Candy. You're a redneck, frigging act like one. And I played Red Rover with you when we were in first grade." Kenny pokes an accusing finger at me. "You always cheated. You'd drop your head and set your aim right at Zane Unger and me and take off at a sprint. Everybody'd be watching while we latched on hard. Then boom! You'd shift your gate, still looking at us, and break through kids twice your size. Use that crafty, devious little mind of yours to cook up something sneaky and underhanded. Beat them at their own game." He plops some papers on the counter. "These are from a bunch of bratty kids who won't leave me alone in the parking lot. Grow some balls."

I stop for a moment and pick up the papers. It's a drawing. It's a mosquito with a flag as a cape running. *My Superhero. By Elizabeth Thomas. The Mighty Mosquito named Brandy Devero. Run!* I stare at it.

"Are you going to run or not?" Kenny spats at me.

"How do we get Kenny and Martha on the list so they can race?" I wheel around to address Amelia. She whips her head toward me. "What?" She is rigid, unsure.

"What?" Kenny is shaking his head adamantly. "Oh, no. I've got no ATV and—just, no way. I'm not doing it." Martha has this huge grin on her face looking back and forth between Kenny and me.

"You can borrow Pops' ATV," I offer.

"*Borrow*? With you, that means to steal, then beg sorries *after* you've either broke it or lost it. No. No way. Nope." Kenny shakes his head adamantly. "Uncle Lee wouldn't talk to me for three weeks because I dinged up Old Yeller last year. I'm not signed up anyway, right?" He snaps his gaze to Amelia who blinks at him.

"All the members of your team from last year are on our lineup." Amelia looks at Bear. "There's no event rule we can't shift someone from the lineup last minute."

"I'll do it." Martha shrugs.

"There isn't any way we can trust Rush or anyone Mila chose," I toss out. "We don't have a choice. We'll borrow Pops' ATV, Old Yeller. We'll go get Bobby Reese from the nursing home."

"He had knee surgery two months ago," Amelia utters.

"He is better than someone who is going to sabotage the race," Martha agrees with me. "She has a point. My grandpa's old too, but with age, comes wisdom and a lot more experience. I bet he'd do it. Bobby's got spunk."

Everybody's staring at Kenny. He looks like a treed raccoon with hounds baying three branches below.

"What would convince you to ride," Amelia asks. I see her fumbling in her purse like she's going to pull out a wad of hundred-dollar bills and offer it up to him.

"What?"

"I'll pay you. Offer something up."

Kenny's looking across the room, a faraway gaze in his eyes. I bet he imagines stack after stack of soft porn Backwoods Babes magazines piled floor to ceiling. He's probably ready to retire on the stack of money she'll give him. "I think Preacher Murphy needs his church back."

There's silence in the room. Of all the things I thought he'd ask Santa Vega, Holy Trinity wasn't even remotely close to one of them. All eyes whip over to Preacher Murphy except Kenny's and Amelia's. "You can do that, right?" Kenny asks Amelia, his eyes not veering from hers. "You can make that right?"

"If you win, I'll make that right."

"Then you'll do it?" I ask Kenny. "We'll go get Old Yeller." Kenny narrows his gaze. "I've got witnesses, right?" He looks at each person in the kitchen one by one. "It's Brandy who always got me in trouble with Pops. He always laughed at me and said there wasn't no way." He wags a hand in the air, lets it drop to me. "I got proof now. And when Uncle Lee says there ain't no way a grown beagle can get bullied by a pint-sized kitten, you tell him that little kitten can—"

"—mosquito." Everyone's head turns to the kitchen door and the wheelchair settled there. "Mighty Mosquito." It's Zach rolling into the kitchen, pointing a finger at me. "She's not a kitten. She's a mosquito. So, fly, mosquito. That's your superpower. Fly—"

## Chapter 76—Pops Says to Shine

"Pops is going to know we stole Old Yeller. You're gonna pass him," I disclosed that to Kenny an hour ago when we snuck up to Pops' barn and pulled the plastic tarp protecting his PRIZED ATV from dust.

"Why are you bringing this up now?" Kenny's jaws work hard. "I promised I'd run it."

"Why'd you bet the church?" I asked him. "Are you getting in good with your churchy-girl?"

"I guess. Well, maybe. Mama misses Preacher Murphy. He's been doing the services up the mountain at the Fire Mountain Church. She got a taste of a real preacher, and she can't get enough of it. She talks, talks, talks about him and how he puts the word of God into the real world, so she understands. She started going to Wednesday Bible study too. She cried when they closed it." He shrugs. "And it just kind of came out of my mouth."

Ah, the truth. I laugh out loud, this long pebbles-on-tin-roof laugh I haven't felt bubble up from my belly in a long time. Kenny picks up the laugh, his sounding like a boy hawk in spring cackling at the girls. I pat Pops' coveted ATV. It's warm beneath the canvas. I can almost smell the sweat and blood Pops and Uncle Craig put into the ATV—Pops is always more than delighted to hold up his hand to display the long, pink scar on his palm he got while putting on a slipper clutch in the same way a soldier proudly displays his battle wounds. The tires alone are worth more than the truck I drove up here to steal it. The engine is modified for racing, Pops' pride and joy next to Kaylee and me and now Miss Lila too. It is illegal in forty-two states. "I'll be going so fast that he won't be able to stop me." That's what Kenny had said. Inwardly, we both knew better. If Pops sees Kenny pass in Old Yeller, he's going to walk right out on the trail and drag him off it. "Not if he's got his shotgun," I teased him. Kenny had looked at me wildly. I saw the second thoughts rolling around in his head. "We don't have a choice, Kenny." He knew the truth. I knew the truth.

So did Pops. He caught the gist of things through the family grapevine which was Aunt Jenny texting Uncle Craig who called Pops who then brought us to a skidding halt at the end of Fire Mountain Road with his truck coming straight at us. "We're dead. We're dead." Kenny was white-knuckle driving anyway. He turned and looked at me with the dust flying and his arm rolling up the window desperately. "We're—"

"—dead," I finished for him. "Should we lock the doors?" I whispered. Pops had knuckled the passenger side window. He pops off his ballcap, rubs red hair with his hand, and puts it back on. Crap. That's not good. He was tetchy. His eyes were narrowed, dark. "Get out." I felt six again and caught lighting a match in the barn to see if I could do it. Neither Kenny nor I moved. "Do you think he'll give us a whooping?" Kenny asked. I nearly punched him in the arm because he was sneaking a nervous laugh.

"Don't laugh at him," I grunted. "Kenny, are you nuts?"

"GET OUT!" Pops booms. I'd slid out slow-motion. Pops had pointed to his truck. "Get your ass into my truck. You hear me?"

"Yes, sir." I follow his finger. "But I—" I'm going to run.

"But you should have *asked first*—"

"Yes, sir."

"And we'll discuss this later, but Kenny's got to get to the lineup in fourteen minutes. They are waiting for him. You've got to get into your position before he gets there."


"Why are you looking so glum?" Pops asked me after I got into the truck and slid on my old worn-in running shoes. I was fine until I was lacing my shoe and saw a stack of newspapers on the floor, the top one with the frontpage exposed and the mugshots of seven people arrested for the murders and coverup of Katelyn Freeman, Dana and Margaret Pitzer, and Sarah Thompson.

Pops' eyes follow mine to the floor. "Your Aunt Jenny bought those at the dollar store. They got your picture in there talking to the cops after the arrest." He eyes me carefully. "Don't think about that now. Focus on running." I nudge the paper with the toe of my shoe. "Why are there so many bad people in the world, Pops?"

"There ain't now. There is more good than bad."

I rub my face uneasily with my hand. "Walter Fee and his buddies at the police station were just plain bad. Officer Reynolds told me this whole thing started because all those men helped Walter Fee cover up the murders of Margaret Pitzer and the two girls. Then they helped Walter Fee cover up Katelyn's murder when he killed her for overhearing what Danny Brown confessed he saw. Not one of them was a good enough person to tell the truth. That's a lot of people for this place."

"They made the mistake of helping him in the first place, Brandy. Then they couldn't back out. Dee Reynolds is good. You know, he helped Bradley Devereauxs get a job working in the office at the police station? Preacher Murphy talked to Dee about the family needing to get money the right way and not like their mama did with drugs. Dee made it happen." Pops rubs the gristle on his cheeks. "We don't have a lot of time. Here's what I need to tell you. Missus

Vega is not putting those four girls in *at all*. Not Michelle or Meghan. Not Janie or Carrie. She's pulling them off the lineup."

"What?" Holy crap. "That's crazy talk. She can have four, Pops. The Vegas need all the chances they can get even if the runners go slow, so they don't win. What if I fall or get tripped or go the wrong way?" I sit up. "Bakersfield is having four of his runners race at the same time to give him four chances. It'd be me against all them. They are fast. They won't let me pass them."

"But those girls on the Boar Mountain team can also do something stupid and get the entire team disqualified. They could trip someone from another team to get thrown out to disqualify Boar Mountain." He makes the turn, heads toward the side of Fire Mountain where the runners are set up. He pauses, takes off his ballcap, flops it back on. "I'm not trying to convince you. It's done. Missus Vega ain't changing her mind. I believe you can win. You did it all by your lonesome last year. The only thing stopping you is—"

"—my big ears," I finish for him and tug on my earlobe and smile up at him.

"Huh? You ain't got big ears. Where'd you hear that? I was going to say the only thing stopping you is them big ones running from the other teams."

"You *always* tell me nothing's stopping me

but my ears."

He chuckles, takes off his hat again and gently slaps my bare leg. "I was kidding you, baby girl. There ain't nothing stopping you." He drives on, then pats his steering wheel. "By the way, Bear said to count candles along the way."

"What?"

"I don't know. Your boy said you got scared around lots of people, so he's got candles set up to remind you to shine." *Your boy*. That's Pops' way of telling me he's accepting Bear back into our pack again. I smile.

"Shine."

"Let your light shine. Then nothing's gonna stop you."

## Chapter 77—Mud Wrestling

There isn't anything stopping me except three women from the Boar Mountain Dream Team who, at this point, have no clue I'm taking their place. And a fourth who is screaming at Bear and a security guard right before they are to escort her off the runner area. They can't have five entered in the event or on the course at the same time.

"What? Why?" Janie Mills isn't happy at all. She is taking the thick black ponytail on top of her head and twirling it around furiously. Her already pink cheeks are ten times pinker, and she's bouncing up and down on angry tippy-toes. "I hate you!" Her yells are almost lost in the boisterous chatter of the crowd. "That's bullshit! Give me your phone. Meghan's gonna hear about this!"

I feel like the crowd is staring at me, defining me, smothering me. I think I'm going to throw up. I look at them, they wave. I wave back, feel my heart pumping. Eyes on me, me, me. It's overwhelming. I hate crowds. That's why I end up sitting on the faded yellow curb next to a mucky ditch and just inside the course checkpoint area for the runners, partially obscured by a long line of tables.

I've donned the team uniform shirt, a brash red and black muscle t-shirt with FIRE

MOUNTAIN SHADOWS embroidered on the back. I refused to wear the SparkMax Light Professional Running Shoes. I've donned my old jean shorts. I mean, what kind of redneck would I be representing if I wore the two-hundred-dollar Belgium Core Sports IU spandex shorts? I've got my hair shoved atop my head with a hair tie Kaylee tugged off her ponytail. Pinned on my back, I've got a race tag/timing number. There's a chip inside, and spectators can track the athletes mobile and live on a map.

It's controlled chaos. Hundreds of spectators crowd into the parking lot from downtown streets packed full of tourists. They form a multi-color caterpillar-like procession along the shoreline of Fire Mountain Creek and surging upward along the roadway where it rises and follows the uphill climb of the mountain. It rolls along old logging paths gently graveled for the event. Spectators are kept at bay by yards of yellow police tape. They keel over the tape, leaning in to catch a view of the passing of the baton from ATV racers to runners. I am settled at the far end of the stopping point for the ATVs where the riders will dismount and run the expanse of twenty feet to the runners and hand off a small baton. There is a chip inside the baton. I have to get it before Janie runs amok, stretches out her hand to grasp it.

I hear Pops calling out from behind the yellow police tape. He is holding his phone to his ear like he's talking to someone. He's nodding. He makes this slow-motion walk forward with his legs marching high. A lady moves out of the way before he steps on her, gives him a furrowed-brow glare. I think most people around him believe my Pops is going crazy. He's pantomiming the race results as he sees them falling into place while miming the words to me. I hold out my arms to my sides. I mouth: *WHAT?*

"He's saying someone named Gabby is finished. He's slow but did well. Are you deaf?"

I twist my head over, so intent on Pops, I didn't see the woman coming up beside me. Abby. I cringe. "Bobby," I correct her. "It's Bobby who is our archer." Why did she break from the bunch, come over to me? My attention is caught again. Pops is waving his arms wildly like he's drowning before he pats his rear.

"Your swimmer drowned," Abby translates. "He's saying we kick your team's ass."

He paddles his hands a little harder. I bob my head up and down, ignoring her. He gives me a big wolf-like grin and thumbs up. If I were a sheep, I would run. I'm not. That's Pops' smile of approval. I'm assuming she hasn't drowned. Still, I heard ATVs coming down the far side of the mountain. I feel my belly spring up wildly—alarmed, anxious, worried. If Martha is only now starting the swim across the creek, then our team is behind, way behind. I keep telling myself what Bear told me before he left. *I'll love you whether you're first or last or somewhere between.* But will he? Will *I* love myself any more or less?

I focus on the muddy hillside where Kenny will park, then run to me. I'm hidden from Janie Mills' view. Up until ten minutes ago, she didn't know I'm going to take the baton Kenny is going to pass to me. She had no clue Rush isn't racing just like nobody else knew Tyrone Hill wasn't shooting bow and Benny Rogers isn't swimming across the creek. Because it could blow the entire race if any one of the Boar Mountain contenders are taking a payoff from Bakersfield and decide to slow it down farther. None of them can be trusted. One by one, Bear is pulling them off the course before I get there. But if I lose that baton, if I don't have it in my hand, all is lost.

I groan, see Abby's shadow pooling at my feet. I want to walk off. I don't. "What are you doing here, Mighty Mosquito?" She's white-tooth grinning at me, a coyote's bared-back muzzle. I think she's cut from the pack who are stretching across the parking lot and wondering if she can take down this tiny prey on her own and without help. I rise, wish I could turn and go backward. I can't. I'm cornered between the tables and the slimy mud of the ditch, still draining water from last night's rain.

"Abby," I address Bakersfield's Uppity A-Team runner with as much vigor as if I'd taken a big swig of spoiled milk. "I'm running. Same as you."

She reaches out and points to my back and the number pinned there. "Um, for another team. The tattle-tale is a traitor now?"

"I never told anyone it was you who hit me with the locker if that's what you are implying about being a tattletale. I'm not a traitor. I got cut."

"I meant going to the newspapers about our sponsors. You told on them. You bite the hand that feeds you, isn't that what you Americans say?" She folds her skinny, long arms across her chest. "And why would you think it was me or any of the girls who hurt you, huh? It was not. You drag us into your mess."

"I wasn't getting *fed*, Abby. Unlike you who is getting a buttload of money. It's not *my* mess, now, is it?" I spat at her. She is eyeing me cautiously. "That said, I'm not running for Bakersfield. But *you* are. Another thing we Americans like to say is *Birds of a feather flock together*. You understand what that means to people who see *you* are still running for a cheater like Bakersfield?"

"I like money. I have a contract. But I wouldn't be as worried about us." She gives me a chuck of her chin over my head. I follow. To my right, I see a deathly pale man skinny from bald head to spindly ankles. He looks like someone fileted the bones right off his body.

"That bald-headed Q-Tip is running for Nester-Jones Marketing Group, see?" she tells me with a sly smile. "He runs so many marathons, they call him Miles." I feel my heart stop. "He didn't want to run this, you know? He could hurt his ankles. He runs roads. He's qualified for every marathon he's tried out for. Wins them all too."

"Then why's he running this one?"

"I think he's bored with winning everything on flat land." Her eyes shift over my shoulder. "I think you have more trouble than Miles. It seems to follow you, Mighty Mosquito, wherever you go." She snickers haughtily.

I snap my head toward the place her eyes are alighting because she takes two steps back with a slight smile to her lips. Sure enough, I see Janie whipping her body around and digging her heels into the ground, her head dropping forward, a bull charging toward a flapping red matador cape. I am that cape. Bear is standing still with his hands outstretched, whirling around like he's looking for someone to help. He can't cross the police tape for fear of disqualifying the team. The security guard, with his orange vest, has stepped away momentarily for crowd control. He's busy walking the inner line, hands aggressively shoving the air and addressing onlookers stepping across the line to move back. Janie must have picked that exact moment to buck. The crowd is surging. Someone calls out, points a finger at her curiously ducking beneath the tape and sprinting toward me.

"Oh," I gasp. Janie gets about three steps from me and snaps up her right knee, launching her body forward as if she is trying to football-tackle me. It's slow motion. Still, I stand steady gawking stupidly at her.

Bam! She hits me like she's giving me a huge bear hug, arms outstretched and sliding around my shoulders. I'm probably twenty pounds lighter than she is and six inches shorter, packing nothing but skin and bones and a stupid gape to my lips. That said, I try to step back and my feet fumble along the curb where I had been sitting. I lift one heel and feel myself keeling toward the muddy ditch.

"Crap!" I scream with arms flailing wildly, then career straight back with a slight keel to the left. We both come crumbling to the ground in the muddy trench, the contents making a high splash from our weight. Janie's fists are pummeling me. I'm fending her knuckles off with my right forearm and the fingers of my left hand scrambling to latch on to her ponytail to snap her head back. I really think she is trying to bite me.

We slide left, then slip right, tossing and tussling to the roaring challenges of a hundred spectators who have broken through the caution tape, poured into a circle to cheer us on as if this mud bog wrestling was part of the event. I would have made Bobby Reese proud. I rose up to the occasion of his olden days mud wrestling dreams as I grip Janie's shirt in a vain attempt to slide to the right when a security guard stretches out his arms to grapple with her slippery, wet shoulders. Much to the crowd's delight, he falls on his rear in a spray of muck, wallowing like an upside-down box turtle with his feet kicking in the air. By the time he gets an unsteady footing, I have a hold of her collar. It takes two more security personnel called to the scene to peel us off each other. And yet, I still manage to also skin the shirt clean off Janie's upper body to expose her sports bra beneath.

While this was going on, Bakersfield's A-Team faded down the course along with the man Abby called Miles. I'm swiping my arms to get the mud off, dismayed and disheartened. I look up where Bear had been earlier. He's standing on the outskirts, bunched in with the crowd. He's looking at me. I know he sees my face drop. I'm looking at him. Bear, he doesn't look worried at all, just amused. He's still hanging on to a laugh like he thought the entire battle with Janie was a part of some big plan I had to entertain the crowd. I roll my eyes, take a bow. He acts like he's trying to hold back the laughter and a grin spreads across his face. It's like our eyes meet, linger for the longest time, his brown eyes to my pink-yellow. He brings up a finger, then waves his hand over top it.

*What*? I mouth. He does it again, and I shake my head. He laughs and acts like he's wiping it away with a cloth. *I love you.* That's what he mouths then. His hands come up, forefingers and thumbs meeting to form a heart. *You're my light.* I start to return the heart-shaped symbol, hear bellowing. I don't turn until I see Bear's wide eyes. I follow them. Kenny's coming to a skidding halt on his feet next to me. "How'd you get here so quickly?"

"I'm fast, Dandy Brandy," he yells at me. "Don't be stupid. Run!" I start off, hear him call out again. "Bear said don't forget to count the candles!"

## Chapter 78—Red Rover, Bitches

*Running.* It's been so much a part of me since I was four years old. I don't realize until I'm six miles into the course and I'm passing contenders right and left, forging through them, what got me running. I have time to think. Orange flags are lining the path to point us through our journey, almost a thousand, along with orange route markings with arrows when there are turns and twists. There are two-hundred and forty volunteers from different areas who direct the runners and make sure someone doesn't turn those arrows around, sabotage the course. And real-time security cameras are monitoring the trail that Amelia must have paid a fortune to run because a company is monitoring it for the entire race. It's tough, the route, but simple to follow. It gives me time to think about running. I've always known that I run to put all my doubts and fears behind me. I run to get as far away from Mama and all her baggage as I can.

"Brandy Devereauxs! Runner One-Four-Seven." I call out as I pass Checkpoint 1. I don't have to announce my name and number like I'm entering the stage of a beauty pageant. But last year there was some question that I cheated. I didn't. I don't want to have fingers point at me again. "Brandy!" I hear someone scream my name. I look up at strangers staring at me, boring a hole through my soul, I think. I cringe outwardly, almost lose my pace. I know I cower from the crowds. I force a fake smile, forge on. I hear them cheering their favorites. I hear my name chanted. I force myself to look up again. This time, I see Kaylee and Miss Lila holding up a sign. LET IT SHINE, BRANDY, FOR FIRE MOUNTAIN! Kaylee's holding up a little flameless, battery-operated vigil candle like we use for the Christmas Eve candlelight service instead of the real-flame congregation candles with drip protectors. Judy McMillan caught her hair on fire six years ago at the service bending down to pick up her purse she'd dropped off her lap. Real candles were traded out for the safer battery-operated candles. I wave. There are fourteen candles held in hands coming up as I pass. I see Miss Lila point to the far side. "Don't think of the crowd. Count the candles!" I count eight as the road climbs.

Sweat is forming on my brow. I'm not winded. I'm not tired. I wave away a drink, pause long enough to make sure one of the female runners standing on the side is alright. Her knee is bleeding from a fall. She waves me on.

It was at Checkpoint 2 that I got to drudge up the old, stale memories. It is here that I pass Carrie Edwards. She's just standing there looking at me. I think she is going to chase me down like Janie. She doesn't. She's standing with Pops and looking mentally beaten down.

Pops makes a quick display of a candle he plucks from the breast pocket of his t-shirt, holds it up in the same way he raises his empty beer bottle to express his happiness when his team wins a game on TV. He gives me a big smile and waves me on even as I slow near the tape.

"I talked to her, go! I'll see you up—" His voice is drowned out by crowds cheering. I shiver. Crowds. Nine candles on the left. Twenty-two on the right before the throng peters out. Carrie waves sullenly at me before she turns and sits down just outside the tape. Pops is full of old stories that teach lessons. I think if Jesus were passing through in nowaday times, he'd ask him to write the Book of Lee and add it to the New Testament.

I'm sure Pops told Carrie the tale about the ancient blind miner who would carry his lantern each morning and night along the dark and winding trails of Fire Mountain. He was heading toward the mines as he had for so many years before he lost his eyesight to an explosion. As he went, miners heading the same route would follow along with the dangerous cliff edges and through the narrow stone passages to work the mine. The other miners would make fun of him, telling him he was blind and could not see the coal inside to work, nor could he see the light from his lantern spread out on the trail. They asked: *Why bother?* The blind miner answered that he carried his lantern along the trail each night and day to shine the light so the other miners could see. I'm assuming the moral to that story is to look past her views and let me run—I'm faster. For me, it was usually to shut the cupboard door when I finished pulling the cereal box from the shelves, so Pops didn't bang his head on it in the morning before his first cup of coffee opened his eyes wide enough to see it.

*Running.* It is here I think of Pops. For a few minutes, I'm partially alone, passing runners already slowing. I see a candle shoved into the ground, count eleven I pass. I was four when Mama left me at his house for a weeklong drunk binge. Two weeks later, she realized I was gone and came and got me so she could collect her food stamps. She dragged me back to her mobile home with empty food shelves and the electric turned off. When she took me, I remember Pops standing at the doorway of his home, one hand resting on the doorframe and a coffee in his other hand. He'd begged my mama to let me stay. He offered her his truck, three-hundred and ten dollars in his bank account (which was all he had), and a hundred bucks a week from his paycheck. He had tears in his eyes while she screamed at me dragging me down the path to her boyfriend's truck. She needed my presence to get her public assistance, that which she'd trade for pot and beer. I'd pressed my face to the passenger side window and pushed my tiny hand to the glass. Pops had held up his palm in the air as if we could touch. Then all I saw were my tears and my nose smudge on the window.

"Brandy Devereauxs! Runner One-Four-Seven." Checkpoint 5. It's mile twelve. I'm focusing on the candles, not the crowd. I wave at those holding them, catching my eye. I remember some of them from groups I'd visited. It's like looking out at an old friend. It doesn't seem like the same bunch of people who judge-gawked at me when mama drunk-walked into my choir concert.

I'm not winded. I run these mountains daily and have done so forever. I can't say that for eighteen runners I've passed who are winded, red-cheeked, and slowing. I doubt they've traveled much through the woods, much less along a West Virginia mountain. I know most of them came from comfy, soft beds in warm suburban homes and hadn't been left alone in a playpen with nothing but a bottle of water and a generic box of stale cereal for two days while their mama slept away drunk in jail.

I'd say they are subdivision street runners who aren't running from their past. They want to plop another medal on the corner of a picture frame with an image within of them looking skinny and victorious crossing a finish line.

They are track runners who circle and circle and possibly, as a high adventure, jog through a few well-manicured park trails once in a while so people can *ooh* and *ahh* at them. But they've got fourteen miles to go—grueling uphill climbs that work the front upper thighs like the devil himself is latching onto the muscles and dragging them to hell, exhausting almost-straight-down downhill falls that work the back of the thighs and calves until they cramp up along the spine. They've got tree trunks to jump, briars to power through, and boulders to climb. I'm not even close to gaining on the hardcore runners. I pace myself. I'd been running twenty miles a day on these mountains, up and down, up and down.

*Running.* The same evening that Mama came to get me from Pops', she got drunk with a couple of boys down the street. I wouldn't stop crying and was ruining her party, so she slapped me silly, plopped me in my old playpen, and told me she'd kill me if I got out. I waited until she fell to sleep on the couch, climbed from my prison of the playpen, and traversed the passed-out bodies on the living room floor. Then I pushed through the front door, ran out into the dark dirt street, and on to the main road. I ran. And I ran as fast as my skinny, little legs would take me. I had no clue where I was going, only that Pops lived *somewhere* and I knew he'd find me. I ran. I ran.

I ran until I couldn't run anymore and it was dark. Someone saw me and called the cops. The cops filed reports and sent me home. Not to Pops' house. Away I ran again until they put me in a foster home. Then I ran away from it. Pops told me later, it took him five months, but he asked them to give him a chance. If I didn't run away from him, maybe I could stay? And I did. But I still ran, but not away from Pops. Never. Not once even when he'd get mad at me.

I am alone on the trail. I hear my breaths, feel my heart pumping. I pass three competitors who are leaning hard into the highest climb of the mountain. It's like they are running standing still. Two more are walking. I ask them if they are okay. They nod. About ten minutes later, I pass four who have stopped at a remote medical checkpoint. It is when I look up from the tent that I see Bakersfield's A-Team. I force myself to set a pace. I quickly catch up. They are quietly running. It is strange. They are like ghosts. "Are you having fun?" I call out. One turns slightly. She is sweating profusely like the three others. Their backs are slumped as I have never seen them slump before.

"Go away, Mosquito. You'll never win." That is Abby.

"Let me through. I want to pass." I'm back to Red Rover. I try left. They form a wall. I try right. They form a wall.

"You need to get out of my way."

"No." Even on the trail, they form a barrier to stop me, won't let me pass.

"Brandy Devereauxs! Runner One-Four-Seven." Checkpoint 7 is straight up Fire Mountain. I'm eighteen miles in, eight to go. Home. My home. But on the far side that Pops doesn't own. "Let me pass!" I shout.

"Nope."

I can't do this. I can't go this slow. I've got to catch the lead runners. I tuck my chin, remember what Kenny said. I kick my right leg up, aim right. I see the girl on the left turn. For the first time, I see her nod to the right. She's taking my lead. Hell, that's why they always know where I'm going to try to pass.

"Red Rover, Red Rover, bitches," I stare to the right. "I'm coming over."

## Chapter 79—Jelly Legs

Bam! I lunge forward to the left, swivel sideways and feel my body slip between the gargantuan woman to my right and a ragged pine tree to my left. My back skims across the flaky, hard bark. I feel free while I see the vacant trail before me.

My victory is short-lived. I feel the women quickening their steps, knowing good and well no one can keep up such a fast pace on the mountain. I feel a sudden urgency. Nothing is stopping them from passing. I quicken my stride where I love to test myself, on the margin of the trail and straight up a killer incline. My heart pumps double-time while I set my sights for the top of the mountain. My legs pump hard, a dead run that I can't keep up for eight miles. I've got to drive onward. I must.

I do. It isn't difficult for me to catch the lead runner a mile and a half later because Miles isn't running. I almost run over him coming around a bend in the trail. He's wobbling, can hardly stand. His legs are bending and bowing, two bowls full of Jell-O beneath him. He's hit the wall. *Keep going* my mind tells me softly. I don't see the spectators here. I don't see runners. I only see a dirt trail that goes on and on and on. *Somebody else will come along.* But I know the only ones who are coming along are four wannabe-Olympic runners hell-bent on winning.

"I—I've hit—jelly legs," he says, falling to hands and knees. "I'm okay. Only two more miles." He is muddled, reminds me of Mama with a half-drunk bottle of rum. *Go, go, go!* I hear myself. *Run to the next checkpoint and tell them. It's only just around the bend. They can see he hasn't moved from the chip on his tag.* I can't. I can't leave him.

"No." I stop, turn, and walk back to him. "There are six and a half more miles. I'm going to help you to the checkpoint." He can't rise. I have to bend over and lug him up. Yep, he's as wonky and unsteady as drunk Mama clinging to me, arm slung over my shoulder while we stagger sweat-sloppy and stumble along the trail.

"For a skinny guy, you weigh a lot," I silly-gripe to him. His legs still don't work. He takes two or three steps, then almost falls forward. I wonder if he can die from this?

"Jelly legs. I had the flu a week ago. I shouldn't have run."

"Just focus on walking," I say and try to sound patient. I'm not, even though I'm smiling. I'm worried. I'm not sure if people can die from jelly legs. He's dehydrated, maybe anorexic, maybe starving himself to death. I'm worried because I hear the pad of feet behind us.

"I was sick, did I tell you that? I feel like I'm

going to die. I want to finish—"

"You're not going to die." I am half-dragging him along the trail. I can hardly do this. He's not heavy, but not weightless either. "I got to get you to the checkpoint. They can get you an ambulance."

He isn't talking, just folding over my shoulder. I can't carry him; it is a drag-walk. I hear the footsteps pounding harder, know the A-Team is coming up behind me. It's a relief. Help is coming. I pause for a moment, ready for one of them to slide an arm under Miles for support.

"God, I'm glad you guys are here—" I pour out, comforted by the knowledge I'm not alone with this man who can't walk, who is edging on irrational while he mutters nonsense to me. It is short-lived. I watch, both shocked and dismayed. The four women pass, two on either side as if we are mere shadows in their eyes and nothing more. They say nothing, do nothing. I watch the backs of their uniforms as they pass.

"Hey! Some help here!" I call out. They act like they don't even see me. I watch them disappear into the copse of trees and around a bend. It is quiet.

"Well, that was rude." Miles wobbles. I give him a shove up on my shoulder again.

"Yeah, it was."

## Chapter 80—All Riled Up

Pops asked me one winter day what makes me run so fast. He'd raced me from the bottom of Fire Mountain in his old truck to the top. He was driving on a solid sheet of ice mixed with sleety snow and ankle-deep ruts of mud. Me, I was slip-sliding along the crusty, snow-covered edge with a layer of gravel beneath. Pops had skidded and scrambled, sometimes sideways up the old road while I ate most of the muck his tires spit out at me when he had to make a veer. When his tires failed to catch on one particularly icy spot, he kicked the accelerator. The tires had spun and spewed out a cloud of tiny rock and salt pellets the township had tossed on to the road. It was a hundred tiny, angry smacks on my chilly cheeks.

I looked up with a saucy stare, caught Pops' image in his driver's side rearview mirror. He was belly-laughing at me with tears in his eyes. "Eat my dust!" he'd called out. Oh, it made me go from irritated to livid in less than three seconds. I'd gnashed my teeth together, dug in my heels, and took off up that road. I'd gotten so mad at him that I was drying off from my shower even before he got his truck parked in his barn. *Dang, girl. You was as fast as the wind. What makes a girl like you go so fast?*

*So, what makes me go so fast, Pops?* I'd growled at him while I scrubbed the towel across my wet hair, infuriated my cheeks still stung. *Anger. Revenge. You got me all riled up, that's what.* He said to tuck that feeling in my pocket, remember it when I wanted to achieve something big. Because whatever it was, it worked.

The A-Team's got me all riled up. I had to drag Miles nearly a quarter mile to the next checkpoint where the forest opens up for just a half mile. This is the most punishing part of my journey. I'm already completely drained and hardly smile at the spectators spending more time taking pictures of us than helping me get him to the nearest volunteers rushing forward to relieve me of my burden. Onlookers have parked their cars up and down the old service roads. They are sitting on their hoods, standing along the road. All's I can think is that my shoulders ache. I forgot to count the candles when I dragged Mile's butt to the outstretched arms of two EMS.

"Brandy Devereauxs! Runner One-Four-Seven," I mumble this time. I turn and slip out of the tent area knowing I can't catch Bakersfield's A-Team.

"You can't do this. You're not a fighter. You're like four feet tall and not feisty enough."

I recognize the voice, snap my head up. "Marcus?" He's standing there trying to look snotty. "You might as well stop and chit-chat trivial fluff over cookies and milk again." He looks at me. "You'll never beat them. Never. That's what they said when they passed."

"What are you doing here?"

"Bear got worried you hadn't shown up. He said to tell you if he missed you, that ring you left at the bar's been in the cardboard box at your Pops' house this whole time. If you still want it, it's now sitting in his glovebox."

I laugh, but it still makes me feel a chill up my spine. I can't help it. He's holding up a candle in his left hand. Pops must have told him the story of the race up the mountain. Geez, my pops likes to tell people stuff. He's right. I work the image of Abby into my head poking a finger at me and making me feel small and vulnerable—*Mighty Mosquito.* I conjure up the image of Meghan Reynolds and her little pack of mean girls making fun of me—*Dollar Store Dolly.* And Mama being a drunk and stupid mama again enticing me into Walter Fee's trap.

I catch the A-Team almost too easily three miles later. Well, three of the A-Team. The fourth, Abby, has broken from her pack. I know it immediately. She's ready for the win, has the baton clutched in her fingers. She's the chosen one taking the last leg, three and a half miles. I knew it would be her. The other three, they are just holding block for her. They will all get compensated well from Bakersfield for winning the event, placing it in his greedy hands next year and probably the next. But unlike them, I won't get paid for it in dollars. I need to win my end of the race to support my team, to keep my town from turning into just another old ghost town.

It drives me right through the whole lot of them. I burst right through the middle of them, shattering their wall. "Oh, I'm sorry. I forgot to warn you. Red Rover, Red Rover—" I pause, change the game song up a bit. "The Mighty Mosquito just stung your sorry asses," I call out and extend my middle finger in the air at them. I run these trails every day and have for way over twenty years. They are breathing like they've hit high altitude. Not me.

The ring. It can't help but sneak into my head. Yes, I want the ring. Yes, I miss him. Focus. I've got to focus. I see Abby's back ahead of me. I know she hears me coming. My feet are pounding the mud-dirt trail beneath the trees. I know most don't think I can make it. I know everybody watched me get tossed from one sponsor to the next, flung like an old, unwanted doll from one yard sale to the next until I ended up in the pile as I did with all the other unwanted dolls on the Island of Misfit Toys. But here I am stride for stride with Abby.

"I am surprised you made it this far," she hisses. She's not breathing hard. I am. I had to double pace her to catch up. "You're out of breath."

"You could have stopped to help the runner."

"It's a race." She rolls her eyes, looks down at me. "When you run a race, you know the price you might pay. You've got to be in it to win it. At all cost."

"That's not what it's all about. It's about stuff like good sportsmanship, Abby."

"It's all about the money, the sponsors, and winning, stupid girl." That's when she leans to her left, shoving her shoulder into me. It is subtle, the shift of her feet, almost as if she had started to trip, then began to right herself but fell into me. I spin out of control, ram my shoulder and hip into a tree, and smash into it. I skid to a halt three feet away. I don't even take a breath, rise again and narrow my eyes at the woman almost fading away.

"You'll never win, Mighty Mosquito," Abby says when I catch her again.

"What makes you think that?" I ask her, waving my hand between us. "I've overtaken you three times on this race already."

"You're not a fighter. Look. You don't fight back."

"Maybe. When it's just me, but if I've got something to protect like my town, you're wrong," I say. "I guess you didn't hear about a certain serial killer and me and a Louisville Slugger."

"I'm done with the chatter. Who cares about Mighty Mosquito? Nobody. Who cares about this ugly little town? Nobody." She darts off not realizing that I'm right on her rear. I am beginning to see people along the trail as it widens not far from the main road to the resort.

"Go Fire Mountain Shadows!" I hear people calling out my name. I look. Many are strangers. Some are not. I see Preacher Murphy and Gabby and their kids. I see the Ladies Society of Grand Falls that I'd visited and others who I'd met along the way. And an entire section of orange t-shirts that say Care Together Youth Foundation with kids holding fake candles and little cardboard drawings saying: THANKS FOR HELPING US SHINE, BRANDY. Some are holding candles high, and my heart soars.

I've got my second wind. I shoot off, catch Abby, then pass. "That's what it's about!" I call out, jabbing my finger at the kids. "See? You may see roaring crowds and money. I see a thousand tiny candles ignited from one little light to make one big shine." For ten minutes, she tries to keep my full-out running pace. Then I shoot out on to the asphalt roadway and the last one-half mile. The crowd is incredible, cars and people and I'm dizzy with running, dizzy with the onlookers and the roaring crowd. I'm hauling ass. Then the finish line is in front of me. There. Only feet ahead. I blast through it—

## Chapter 81—The Place It Always Starts and Ends

It's Friday night. I'm sitting on a torn vinyl stool at the Crazy Kettle Bar in New Alliance, West Virginia waging worthless bets with the bartender, Billy Winkle. It seems to always start and end here at this old rundown bar just off the buckled-asphalt highway in the middle of nowhere—

"He's late. I'll bet two free dinners at your restaurant he doesn't show," Billy offers up while he swipes that same mungy-smelling washrag along the counter he did last summer.

"I'll bet one more ginger ale that he will." I wave my hand to fend away the stale scent of the rag. Billy rolls his eyes. My belly is jumpy.

"Then why are you shaking like a leaf?" He asks me. I groan. Billy sniffs a laugh, turns and plops a newspaper down in front of me. "You got the front page again. You know, you're probably the first MacCabe that's ever made the front page without robbing a grocery store to get it."

"Go to hell, Billy." I turn my head to the paper. My face is on the front.

"I'm just saying. You'd think this hillbilly craphole would have more stuff going on than some event that only happens once a year."

"I solved a murder," I grumble. "Why doesn't

anybody know that?"

"Because Amelia Vega does your marketing." He pokes a finger on the page. I've already read it. It went something like this when they interviewed her. She said—"Brandy Devereauxs told me this after the race—*I know what was missing all the time. It was being a part of a team. I wasn't a part of a team with Boar Mountain and Resort at Two Bridge Falls. It was me against the other runners. Last year, we had a team no matter how rich or poor, good or bad, win or lose. We were in this together. That's the way it used to be and the way it should be.*" Amelia Vega went on— "I realized she's right. We are all a team here in these mountains, Fire Mountain and Boar Mountain tied together with New Alliance between the two. We come from different backgrounds, we're different ages and colors and religions—all those things that make us diverse and like that big old pot of homemade vegetable soup with carrots and potatoes and onions Brandy says makes up those who live on Fire Mountain and Boar Mountain. But we're not a team until we support each other. So, Boar Mountain will once again support Holy Trinity with Preacher Murphy as the pastor. We're going back to the way things were with the Redneck Run before all the huge investors. There won't be any pulling of money or support just because it isn't making a profit. Because the bottom line all comes down to the way team members are there for each other. Sometimes we lose sight of what is important. No more."

That's in the Sunday paper. It's to the side. The huge picture on display is what Bear keeps showing everybody, me running right past the cameras and the news reporters to get to his truck parked next to the finish line checkpoint and digging into his glove box for the engagement ring I'd left right here in the bar. Then, it's me jumping into his arms with everybody swinging candles all around us. They kept asking me how I'd won by such a margin. I told them I didn't win it. My *team* won it. It's the town that embraced us, nurtured us. We're like a family. We need each other. In good times and bad times, we support each other—

A guy comes in, sits down next to me. He's lugging a cardboard box in his hand. "What's a pretty girl like you doing in a bar like this?" I shake my head. He's huge and still has that wild hair. Instead of a scowl, he's got this little grin on his face.

"So, Marcus, does this mean he's not coming?" I look down at the box. All the time, he's got that goofy grin now that he's been pardoned of the murder and is going to get a huge sum of money for being wrongfully accused and sent to jail. He's also made himself comfy amongst Bear's pack of geeky friends playing Hero Diaries of a Rogue. Marcus is somewhat of a celebrity in the group. From what I understand, there is a vintage computer game of the same name and he was one of the original beta testers for the series back in 2000. It has made him quite the VIP in the group. He didn't have to fight his way into the clan. I did. And *I* have to bring the snacks each time to enter.

"No, he's been out in the parking lot with your pops—"

"Pops is trying to drag him in? He doesn't have his shotgun does he?"

Marcus laughs, thinks this is funny. "No, Kaylee dropped the butterfly box, and it took a few to catch what we could. "There's one left to release. I wanted you to be there when I did it." He holds up his hand. I realize he's got that butterfly standing on his fingertips. "I don't think he wants to let go."

"I think he needs to." I look up at Marcus. "I think we both need to let go of our pasts. It just seems to always start and end here at this old rundown bar just off the buckled-asphalt highway in the middle of nowhere—" I repeat what I'd been thinking earlier.

"You ready?" I look up. Pops is standing at the door all dressed up in a suit and a tie and not the one he's owned since I was four when he had to walk into the courtroom to adopt me. "Spread your wings, baby girl. It's time for you to fly. He's waiting, and he's one nervous Nelly out there." I stand up, gather the white dress around me. "And I've been waiting a long time to walk you down the aisle."

I walk to the door, hook arms with Pops. Just as I do, Marcus sweeps around me, and that little butterfly lets loose from his fingers. It flaps its wings, hovers just a moment, then catches the breeze and flies toward the skies. Everybody claps like that was supposed to happen, a part of the wedding. Kaylee drops the rose petals she's supposed to be spreading between me and Preacher Murphy and she squeals with delight.

Maybe it was. I feel the eyes of the entire town on me because I think that everybody in a fifty-mile radius has shown up for our wedding. I'm going to be cooking after for ten hours if they stay to eat. I start to get that jumpy, terrified, closed-in feeling. "Look up," Pops whispers to me to the sound of Bobby Reese playing the wedding march on his fiddle. Next to him, Kaylee falls in and she nods her head up and down. Quickly, Bobby changes from the wedding march to *This Little Light of Mine* and for the first time, while my little sister belts out the song, it doesn't make me feel bad. I look up and see Bear all handsome in his suit and softly singing along with her, waiting for me, waiting to put that wedding band on my finger and me to put a band on his. He's looking at me. His eyes are big like he's staring at the most beautiful bride he's ever seen. I forget the crowd. *I love you,* he stops singing long enough and mouths. And, God, I love him too. It started in this old bar in these old mountains, our love. But I think it isn't going to end here. It's going to keep going as long as Fire Mountain keeps standing, we'll be here together.